$\mathcal{Un}$TRESPASSED

HARD BROKE SERIES, BOOK THREE

ENGLISH MICHAELS

Untrespassed
© 2019 English Michaels

Visit the author's website at www.englishmichaels.com

First Edition
ISBN: 978-1-7321229-4-9

Cover design by Sarah Hansen, Okay Creations *okaycreations.com*
Editing and Proofreading Twin Tweaks Editing *twintweaksediting.com*
Formatting by Champagne Book Design *champagnebookdesign.com*

Rash daredevils with a score to settle. Swaggering jet jocks with no regard for rules or safety. Unchecked egos battling for superiority. This is the picture Hollywood paints of the military fighter pilot—but what really happens behind the closed doors of an Air Force fighter squadron?

English Michaels knows.

All seventeen-year-old Charlotte wanted was a raspberry slushie and a plan for getting the hell out of Iowa.

Resolve and hard work granted her wish, and now Charlotte "Miles" Christman is an Air Force pilot, savoring self-reliance and relishing the chaotic camaraderie of fighter squadron life. The constraints of her childhood shaped a person with an unquenchable thirst for independence. Her passion for flying and craving for freedom leaves no room for intimacy—a complication Miles studiously avoids—until one cataclysmic morning alters the course of her life for good.

Flight Lieutenant Oliver Bloodworth, on an RAF exchange tour, is elated to be assigned stateside near his best mates—cousins Vivianne and Jacob, a Scorpion squadron pilot. Nothing's more important to Oliver than family. He hopes for a love to nurture and a family of his own someday, but the prospect appears distant—until he makes a random stop at Kwik Shopper.

A chance encounter over a raspberry slushie causes their paths to converge, but the timing couldn't be worse. Miles is at a crossroads, forced to consider the cost of her treasured self-sufficiency. Patiently, Oliver navigates Miles's carefully constructed defenses as she examines the choices that brought her to this watershed moment. His steadiness and careful protection as Miles weathers the storm contrasts sharply with the powerful way he loves her in the dark. Far from limiting the freedom Miles desires, his devotion is giving her wings—and she's falling fast.

Change is afoot, but consequences seem inevitable. In the face of so many obstacles, is love always enough?

A NOTE TO THE READER

The concept of flight is a romantic one; the military pilot, in particular, holds strong appeal for many women, especially romance enthusiasts. I am only one example of a young woman who was secretly taken with the raw magnetism and power of a handsome man in a flight suit striding toward his jet, helmet in hand, ready to casually stare death in the eye.

Reality invaded my overly dramatic fantasy life when I fell in love and married a kind-hearted, ridiculously sexy, utterly flawed, devastatingly handsome Air Force pilot. While our love match has enjoyed the qualities of many long-lived marriages—the marvelous and the mundane—his military career over the first decade of our lives together also afforded me a front row seat to the fascinating world of the fighter pilot.

In July, a little over a year before we married, I took a seat in a stiflingly hot Air Force base auditorium, dressed in a black taffeta cocktail dress and fidgeting like the twenty-year-old I was. That afternoon, I watched my boyfriend stride across the stage to receive his Air Force wings, signifying his successful completion of Undergraduate Pilot Training. It was a sentinel moment in his life, as it is for every military pilot. Printed on the last page of the cheap paper program was a poem I'd never seen but would come to know by heart.

John Gillespie Magee was a young pilot in the Royal Canadian Air Force who died in the service of his country in 1941. Mere months before his passing, at the tender age of nineteen, he penned this sonnet and beautifully captured the allure and romance of flight.

"High Flight"

By

John Gillespie Magee

"Oh! I have slipped the surly bonds of Earth
And danced the skies on laughter-silvered wings;
Sunward I've climbed and joined the tumbling mirth
of sun-split clouds,—and done a hundred things
You have not dreamed of—wheeled and soared and swung
High in the sunlit silence. Hov'ring there,
I've chased the shouting wind along and flung
My eager craft through footless halls of air....

Up, up the long, delirious, burning blue
I've topped the wind-swept heights with easy grace.
Where never lark, or even eagle flew—
And, while with silent, lifting mind I've trod
The high untrespassed sanctity of space,
—Put out my hand, and touched the face of God."

GLOSSARY

The world of the military pilot has a language all its own, as confusing as a foreign tongue to the uninitiated. This glossary is offered to assist those unfamiliar in navigating the technicalities, jargon, and buffoonery. A few medical terms are included for additional clarification. The first occurrence of each term within the text of the book is bolded.

99 Percenters—Law-abiding motorcycle clubs; references a comment by the American Motorcyclist Association that 99% of motorcyclists were law-abiding citizens, implying the last one percent were outlaws.

A-10 Warthog—The Fairchild Republic A-10 Thunderbolt II. More commonly, "the Warthog" or just "the Hawg." The only USAF aircraft designed specifically for the Close Air Support mission: supporting troops on the ground in contact with the enemy. Designed around the lessons of Vietnam and the threat of massed Soviet tanks in Europe. Maneuverable, survivable, and lethal. Pilots refer to themselves as "Hawg drivers."

ADC—Area Defense Counsel; the Air Force's staff of defense attorneys. Typically in short supply, spread thin and overburdened.

ADVON—Advanced Echelon; a relatively small team of military personnel sent out in advance of the rest of the squadron to do the setup/prep work for the main group.

AIM-9—Also Sidewinders; short-range air-to-air missile with infrared guidance; a heat-seeking missile or a "heater."

Bean Counter—Marginally derogatory term for non-pilot Air Force personnel; office or headquarters staff.

BFM—Basic Fighter Maneuvers; the essential building blocks of air combat maneuvering. When a single aircraft is engaged in aerial combat with another single aircraft, BFM is the set of maneuvers and techniques used to move from a neutral to an attacking position relative to one's opponent. Developed in World War I and formalized by German ace Oswald Boelcke.

Big Blue Team—A mildly derisive term for the Air Force; generally used by members in a sarcastic or tongue-in-cheek comment about the service. "The Big Blue Team, in its infinite wisdom…"

Blues—A common reference to the Air Force's daily uniform. Flight suits or ABU's (Airman's Battle Uniform—camos) are considered utility uniforms and inappropriate for many venues. Pilots generally view being compelled to squeeze into their often ill-fitting blues as a particularly loathsome form of punishment.

BOQ—Bachelor Officer Quarters. A holdover from a bygone era. The "Q" would be a small efficiency apartment in a dormitory-style building on base, often with a shared kitchen. Unless required to live there, most single officers elect to live off base in apartments or rentals.

Call Sign/Tactical—A fighter pilot's semi-official nickname. Generally bestowed by other members of the squadron based on some egregious or hilarious buffoonery. Glorified in the movies with names like Viper and Maverick, but, most often, far less flattering. Pilots generally address one another exclusively by their tactical, and it goes with one to the grave.

Commissary—Grocery store on military bases for exclusive use by active duty and retired personnel and their dependents. It resembles a civilian grocery store with excellent prices and no sales tax but with several oddities like one-way shopping, better parking for those with a higher rank, and crowds of retirees on the first of the month who empty the shelves with surprising efficiency.

Crew Rest—In the military or FAA, specific regulations governing flight time, time on duty, and required rest between periods of duty. Crew rest is a pilot's mandated rest prior to a flying assignment.

Cross Country—A non-local aircraft sortie; departing from one base and landing at another. In the Air Force, this is normally flown over the weekend when aircraft are not needed for local training. Ostensibly for training, but more often a travelling road show. The ultimate good deal. "Take four airplanes, three friends, and a government gas card, and we'll see you Monday!"

Crud—Fighter pilot game invented by the Royal Canadian Air Force and typically played on a pool table (side pockets blocked) in the O'Club or squadron bar using two balls and no cues. The shooter uses the cue ball to ricochet the object ball into a corner pocket while the defender may visually block—but not touch—either ball. Shots may be made only from the ends of the table, and the object ball must remain in constant motion, resulting in fast-paced play. Physical contact is at the discretion of the referee, and player skill is greatly enhanced by alcohol consumption.

FEB—Flying Evaluation Board. A formal hearing before a board of senior, rated officers to determine if an Air Force officer may continue on flying status. The board must determine if there is a documented failure to perform to standards.

Flight Line—Open airport ramp area for aircraft parking or staging.

FNG—Fucking New Guy. A term of endearment.

G-forces—Also G's or pulling G's. One G is the force gravity exerts on the body. Acceleration away from the earth increases the G-forces; the sensation of being forced down into the seat at the bottom of a big hill on a roller coaster is approximately 3-4 G's of short duration. Fighter pilots routinely sustain 4-6 G's; sustained G's of 7-9 are not unusual.

Guard (radio)—In this context, a dedicated emergency radio frequency. Pilots, civil and military, maintain a continuous listening watch on this frequency. In outdated parlance, they "guard the channel," thus the term.

Hard Broke—An aircraft with a maintenance issue is referred to as "broke" provided it's expected to be repaired in time to launch with only minor delays. With a longer or even indeterminate delay of return to status by maintenance, the aircraft is said to be "hard broke."

JAG—Judge Advocate General. Military prosecuting attorneys.
Knock-it-off—Fighter pilot radio call to terminate a maneuver, engagement, or training exercise.

LIFT—Lead in Fighter Training. Formerly, an Air Force transition course for pilots moving to their first fighter assignment. Students fly the T-38, an aircraft they are already familiar with, while learning new fighter skills. Old dog, new tricks. Now designated IFF, Instruction to Fighter Fundamentals.

Line of Sight Tasking—Time-honored technique of assigning work: The boss has an unsavory chore to delegate, so he peers out his office door and assigns it to the first LPA member he sees. Universal bad deal.

LPA—Lieutenants Protection Association. A mythical association of young officers in a squadron having one another's back, protecting themselves from the OFA—Old Farts Association, aka everyone else. In reality, the LPA usually represents the lieutenants as a group when they are assigned unsavory non-flying tasks: snack bar maintenance, party planning, going-away skits, etc. A long-standing tradition in fighter squadrons.

Manual Reversion—In the A-10, a rudimentary system connecting some of the flight controls to the stick via cables. This gives the pilot basic control of the airplane in flight in the absence of hydraulics. A key survivability feature designed into the A-10 to get the pilot back over friendly territory before an ejection may be required.

OAP—In the United Kingdom, an Old Age Pensioner; a widely accepted term referring to older, retired persons, whether or not they receive a pension.

OFA—Old Farts Association; see LPA for further explanation.

Officers' Club—Also O'Club, The Club; in the past, the Officers' Open Mess. A members-only restaurant and lounge on base that is restricted to officers, their families, and accompanied guests. While membership is theoretically optional, not joining is an instant career killer. Site of most formal military functions. At a flying base, it usually includes a casual bar where the standards of decorum are somewhat more "relaxed."

Ops Officer—Second in command to the squadron commander. Focus is strictly on day-to-day operations like scheduling and training. Flight commanders report to the operations officer. "The OpsO."

OTS—Officer Training School. One of the three primary commissioning sources for new Air Force Officers along with the US Air Force Academy and college ROTC (Reserve Officer Training Corp) Due to the length of the course, graduates are teasingly referred to as "ninety-day wonders."

Perch—In this context, a position for beginning a BFM exercise. The attacker is positioned above and behind the defender, figuratively "on a perch" with both an energy and positional advantage.

Remote—A tour of duty, usually one year, unaccompanied by dependents (family).

Schoolhouse—Generic term for the organizations that qualify new or returning pilots in a specific aircraft type. For the A-10, the Schoolhouse is at Davis-Monthan Air Force Base in Tucson.

Shack—A direct hit on the target when bombing or shooting; also used to indicate enthusiastic approval or agreement in general conversation.

SOF—Supervisor of flying. A qualified pilot and supervisor on duty (usually in the control tower) as a resource to airborne aircraft. Makes decisions regarding weather, coordinates with outside agencies, and assists with checklists and technical support in the event of an aircraft emergency.

Stick—The control stick in an aircraft as differentiated from a traditional control yoke or wheel. In a fighter aircraft, the pilot flies with right hand on the stick and left hand on the throttles. Both stick and throttles are festooned with multi-function buttons and switches to control aircraft and weapon systems. Also, in context, a naturally gifted pilot.

TDY—Temporary duty—personnel temporarily performing duty away from their home base.

UPT—Undergraduate Pilot Training. Air Force flight school. A rigorous course, approximately one year long, culminating in students being awarded Air Force Pilot Wings.

Valsalva Maneuver—Also an Anti-G Straining Maneuver. A pilot's primary means of combatting the effects of G-forces. Pilots tense muscles in the abdomen, thighs, and calves, then forcefully exhale against a partially closed airway.

Weapons Officer—An officer in each squadron who has attended an intensive, aircraft-specific course at Nellis Air Force Base, literally a doctorate in flying fighters. The singular expert in the squadron on all weapons, tactics, and employment. Often referred to as "Patch Wearers" or "Target Arms" owing to the distinctive bull's-eye patch they wear.

Wing King—The Wing Commander. Typically an O-6 (Colonel) but often an O-7 (one-star Brigadier General), depending on the size and complexity of the base. Commander of all functions on a base.

Chapter ONE

"I Love This Bar"

Miles

Fuck waiting until Friday night. After a week like this one, Thursday was party night; we'd just continue the unwind tomorrow at the **Officers' Club** after flying was done. A car horn sounding in the driveway sent me jogging out of my bedroom where I'd changed quickly into my faithful skintight Levi's, a Huey Lewis tee, and the ever-present Chuck Taylors. I grabbed my purse from the kitchen table where I'd tossed it and started for the door. Skidding to a stop, I circled back to the bedroom and chugged the last half glass of Pinot left on my dresser. No sense in letting perfectly good Meiomi go to waste. Besides, buzz time on a work night was at a premium. I locked the door and hurried down the three steps of my condo to where Rock awaited, more or less patiently, his Porsche Boxster idling away at a low rumble.

Rock raised one eyebrow at me. "No need to get all dressed up on my account, Miles."

Smart-ass.

"It's the Hogwash, Hayes, not the fucking Plaza. And I don't give a shit what anybody thinks about how I look; I'm out to have a good time, not impress the boys." The Hogwash Saloon was a favored after-work watering hole for the Scorpions and many others stationed at Davis-Monthan Air Force Base here in Tucson. The beer selection was above average, and there were enough happy-hour appetizers on the five-buck list to keep those who weren't serious about drinking fed and content.

That group did not include me.

Hayes "Rock" Hudson frowned at my use of his given name and then leaned forward to study my face. "Have you already been hitting the Pinot?" He shook his head. "Damn, Miles. We just left the squadron an hour ago; tell me you ate something. You sure as shit didn't use the time to do anything to your hair." He indicated my hastily concocted updo. In reality, the term "updo" might have been a little charitable to describe what I'd accomplished in three minutes with a big plastic alligator clip and my trusty Aqua Net.

"I ate a tortilla, thank you for asking, and it's none of your fucking business what I do with my time *or* my hair, Rock." He was annoying me already, and my admission that I'd eaten nothing but a tortilla was bound to add fuel to the fire. Food was a means to an end in my book. Good thing, because I was seriously lacking skills in the culinary department. Truthfully, I was incompetent in all the "womanly arts"—cooking, cleaning, decorating. Hell, you could add laundry, hairstyling, and makeup application to that list and probably entertaining. Sewing was out of the damn question. But Rock did offer a ride before I'd needed to ask.

"But thanks for the ride; I'll drive next time." My mind scrambled to fill the conversational void; we both knew I wouldn't be driving next time. I never drove because I didn't like leaving my Mustang in the bar parking lot overnight.

Paying for a one-way cab ride was the price of admission when you enjoyed a night out, and I'd never dream of getting behind the wheel after drinking. But I made a habit of avoiding designated driver status at all costs.

"So who's coming out tonight?" I flipped the mirror down and studied the mass of unruly dark red curls I'd twisted into a topknot. Rock was right; it was frightening. Screw it. I slicked my lips with ChapStick. "Hung said he's riding with Boo and Torch," I informed him. Radley "Boo" Harper and Jackson "Torch" Thomas were two of my best friends and fellow **LPA** members. Walker "Hung" Jackson was the B Flight commander and my boss.

"Sounds like all the ingredients of a party to me." Rock's grin was engaging. "Coach and Deliverance said they might swing by too, and I don't know where Bashful is." Coach was the Scorpion **operations officer** and a colonel, which officially made him **OFA**, but he was cool all the same.

It wasn't much of a drive at all to the Hogwash Saloon on East 22nd, even from my condo in the Foothills. The establishment fulfilled the trifecta of requirements for a pilot bar: cheap, convenient...and cheap. Rock parked the Boxster at the furthest point from the front door, so I chastised him as we walked around the dilapidated concrete block building.

"You can say whatever you'd like, Miles, but I know you'd do the same thing with the 'Stang if you ever drove." He shot me a smirk. "Which you don't."

I tried to think of a quick comeback, but they seemed in short supply, so I settled for opening the door for him with a flourish. "I already said thank you, Rock."

He grabbed the door handle from me and guided me through the entrance with a hand on my shoulder. "I always open the door for a lady, Miles." It was my turn to raise my eyebrows. "Yes, Lieutenant Christman, even you."

Rock was one of the nicest guys I'd ever met in the Air Force, seriously hot—not that I gave a damn—and a true gentleman. But in that moment, his perfect manners were pissing me right the fuck off. No wonder at all that I was alone and likely to stay that way.

"Dudes!" Torch and Boo called to us as we entered the darkened bar, taking a moment for our eyes to adjust to the low light. They were situated around the pool table near the rear of the room, engaged in a heated game of **Crud**. I approached the bar as Rock joined the other guys after greeting them with that manly handshaking/back-slapping thing guys always seemed to favor. I bellied up to the bar, greeting the older bearded bartender with a warm smile.

"Hey, Arlo. How's it going tonight?" He poured two icy pitchers of draft beer before I could ask and handed them across the bar.

"It's karaoke night, Charlotte. Or did you already know that?" Nobody called me Charlotte. Well, nobody but Arlo—and my brother.

"I didn't know that, but it's not a bad thing." I grabbed the glass he offered and poured myself a beer, stopping for a long drink. "Hey, Arlo, how about a shot to get this train out of the station, huh?" I shot him my most fetching smile.

"And what did you have in mind, my dear?" His tone was barely tolerant, and that damn sure rubbed me the wrong way.

"Anything would be fine. Stoli? Maybe Patrón? Gentleman's choice."

He poured me a less than generous tequila shot. "School night this evening, Miles?"

Now he was really irritating me. I turned away from my friends at the pool table and tossed off the shot, returning the small glass to Arlo. "It's technically a school night, yes, but I'm not on the schedule to fly. Plenty of time to get my eight hours of beauty sleep, so don't you worry." I patted his cheek with affection I wasn't feeling, picked up both pitchers, and headed for the pool table.

Rock summoned me without averting his eyes from the fast-moving game in progress. "Get your ass over here, Miles. I'm playing 2-V-1…hurry up." I poured a couple of beers for Rock and me and then joined him in the Crud match.

"S'up, Miles?" Boo slapped my back as he jogged around the corner of the table. "We beat you here tonight by almost half a beer. I think that's a first."

Torch grunted his agreement.

"I took some extra time with my hair, in case you dirtbags didn't notice." I patted my hair and stuck my tongue out at Rock.

"Looks good, dude." Torch didn't even look my direction as he took his shot.

Hung emerged from the bathroom, still in his flight suit, and settled on a barstool at the edge of the room.

"Hey there, Miles…Rock. Bashful sends regrets. He said he'll catch up with everybody tomorrow night at the Club." He took a glass from the three Arlo deposited at the bar's edge for our use and helped himself to the pitcher. "No need to wait until the game is over; let's get right down to it. What's everybody think of the **FNG**?"

Earlier this afternoon, at the large outdoor pavilion, the Scorpion change of command ceremony installed one Lieutenant Colonel Nathan Morgan as the new commander of the 82nd Tactical Flying Squadron. The ceremony was filled to the top with all the usual official pageantry—appearances by the **Wing King**, other general officers, oaths, and a thick frosting of pomp and circumstance. There was the usual comic relief of pilots trying to march and a huge reception with all the best food the squadron members and their spouses could roll out.

Hung stretched his long legs in front of him and grinned as he watched the match in progress. Torch and Boo were kicking our asses. "Deliverance called the pilots marching in from the squadron a 'clusterfuck on parade.' He accused me of sleeping through **OTS**." True, the marching skills he learned there could have used work, but I didn't think we looked half bad.

Deliverance, the Scorpion **weapons officer**, appeared from the other side of the bar, beer in hand. "I've seen junior high school bands march better." His pronouncement was delivered with a big smile and his signature drawl. Davis Foster hailed from Savannah, Georgia, so his accent and southern roots scored him his **call sign**. "I don't judge y'all, Hung. I feel sorry for you; not everyone is an alumnus of the finest military institution in the world."

Torch groaned and grinned at Deliverance. "Don't start with that Citadel crap, D. It wasn't *that* terrible; nobody was watching us anyway. The Cobras fucked up our flyby. Big time. Number three was way outta position, but that's what we get for not doing it ourselves."

Hung refilled my glass after I handed it to him as I jogged around the table. "It's tradition for the host squadron to do their own flybys, but Coach wanted us all together to welcome the new guy."

I walked away as the game ended, pouting a little. "Well, I think he's an asshole. That speech at beer call last Friday sounded like the scolding a bad kid would get from his daddy. He doesn't know us. Pappy was a real fighter pilot, not some brown-noser the brass sent to housebreak us. We don't even know if he can fly and shoot."

Deliverance pulled up a barstool next to Hung, his expression serious. "I think that's the point you're missing, Miles; maybe a lot of the Scorpions are missing the point. Rifle is dead, and the follow-on investigation made the Scorpions look like a ship of fools. Morgan was sent on a specific mission, and I think we'd better get our heads out of our asses."

Hung shot him a grim look and a nod. "The investigation board's findings weren't out of line, sad to say. Change is afoot, and it's long overdue. It still hurts, losing Rifle."

Joseph O'Connor, call sign Rifle, died in an aircraft accident at the beginning of the summer. It was a damn shame to be sure; he was a great guy. The powers that be indirectly implicated our former squadron commander, Pappy, saying lax discipline and procedures were the root cause. I didn't have time for the bullshit Deliverance and Hung were spewing. Pappy was on the short list of people who treated me like a fighter pilot, not a *girl* fighter pilot, and he deserved respect. He'd gotten a raw deal.

I marched over to the bar and ordered kamikaze shots for the group, downing mine and ordering a replacement before returning to where the guys sat. I deposited the tray on the small bar table in front of Rock and Boo. "It's a load of crap, and you all know it. Pappy was a real live fighter pilot, and he got hung out to dry. Nothing more than a sacrificial lamb for the politically correct brass." Boo and Deliverance declined their shots outright, but Hung took a tentative sip.

The karaoke DJ completed his setup and the music began. I polished off my third kamikaze in five minutes and regarded the group gathered around the table. "You guys are a bunch of pussies. Let's see how you do in supporting your wingman, gentlemen. I'm going to start with 'Honky Tonk Women,' and you can pick between 'Paradise by the Dashboard Light' and 'Bohemian Rhapsody.'" I ignored the eye-rolls, poured my third beer, and went to talk to the DJ.

Rock, about two hours later

Hung shook his head in the direction of the stage and took a long slug of his soda. "Boo, are you about ready to get out of here? I need to go in early and look at grade books. I can grab a cab if you'd rather hang out."

"No, I'm ready, and I'm good to drive. Swapped to water a couple of hours ago." He pointed with his elbow at the diet drink. "That stuff is gonna kill you, Hung; you gotta get off that chemical dehydration wagon, man." Boo treated his body like a temple. Most of the time. "Hey, Torch, you coming with?"

Torch and I studied the stage where Miles commanded the attention of the entire bar. Present company excluded, it totaled seven including Arlo. Her rendition of "Like a Virgin" was drawing plenty of attention from two older gentlemen seated at the bar, both seriously inebriated. But even they were not as inebriated as our would-be Madonna. She stumbled through what I was sure she thought was a sexy little dance, singing off-key.

The bartender approached Deliverance. "Is she flying tomorrow morning, Captain?" Arlo was a retired crew chief who'd served during the Vietnam War. He and his wife had a special tie to their customers stationed at Davis-Monthan Air Force Base, offering discounts and hosting occasional fundraisers. He was respected in the local military community and took pains to return the favor.

"Nope, Arlo. She's not on the schedule tomorrow so you can rest easy." Deliverance sighed and looked at his shoes. "Who's on duty? I can do it if it's my turn."

A heavy silence hung over the group, and then I spoke. "I'm up." I stood and stretched my arms high overhead. "I'm good to babysit our girl, but can you call me a cab, Arlo? I've had enough to leave the car here overnight. I'll run this direction in the morning and pick it up before work if that's okay."

Arlo nodded and reached for his phone.

We all stood and reached for our wallets to settle up. Hung spoke for the entire group.

"This is getting pretty fucking old."

"Wakey, wakey, Charlotte." I shook Miles firmly, only partially rousing her from the deep sleep she'd settled into on the short cab ride to her condo.

The cab driver was obviously pissed. "She'd better not puke on the upholstery, buddy. Pay up, and get your girlfriend out of my cab. I just got the carpets shampooed last week."

I nodded, tired. "Got it. But don't worry; she never pukes." As we pulled into the complex, I handed him a ten and a five with instructions to keep the change and looped Miles's arm around my neck. She slumped almost to the ground as we exited the cab, so I picked her up and lugged her up the front steps. A hundred and twenty pounds wasn't so bad—unless it was dead weight. Good thing I'd found her door key on the ride home.

She was out cold, so I unlaced the Chucks and wiggled her out of the Levi's with significant effort. Only after laying her on the bed did she rouse enough to let me know she was going to make a liar of me. I got the garbage can to the bedside in the nick of time, glad I'd forgotten to take the clip thingy out of her hair.

The girl could test the limits of friendship, and Hung was right. It was getting pretty fucking old.

Chapter TWO

"Go Rest High on That Mountain"

Miles

The knock on my door was more insistent the third time. "Charlotte, Daddy really wants you to come down. Open the door. Seriously now, Bugs." My brother's voice was uncharacteristically firm.

I sighed mightily. I was all cried out and couldn't stand the thought of my granny or her twin sisters, Aunt Berta and Aunt Myrta, clasping me into their overly perfumed bosoms one more time. They smelled like old face powder and night cream. But Bertie was right, and I knew it. I would have to go down and join the reception. The tragedy of my mama's passing brought the entire town out, everyone bearing casseroles and wearing their Sunday best, as long as that Sunday best was black, gray, or navy.

If there was anything a small town excelled at, it was grieving. My Aunt Berta said it wasn't intended as anything but a kindness, but it made me so tired. It was impossible for me to see the kindness. The requirement to bleed in full view of the entire town felt cruel. No matter the circumstances of a death, the family was surrounded almost from the earliest moments, and heavy sadness accompanied neighbors, friends, and acquaintances as they trickled endlessly in and out of the house. They arrived at all hours for the first several days; some staying for minutes, some for hours or even longer. Most told stories detailing the exemplary character of the deceased, but that alone could be challenging, depending on who had passed. In the case of my mother, no one was called upon to stretch the truth or to dig too deeply for an anecdote. Mama was beloved in our little town, charitable and generous. She was a good neighbor and a church-going lady. For my part, even at the tender age of ten, I already knew what was expected. I would rise as early as if it were a school day and dress nicely, carefully considering my choice. The dress couldn't be frivolous—that would reflect poorly on my family and my rearing. Children normally accompanied their parents as they dropped off food. Under different circumstances, it would have been a treat to see my friends, but they were as uncomfortable as I was. There was no malice in any of it; the traditions were nearly as old as our little farming community itself. They were all here to continue the ritual that began when Daddy walked with Bertie and me out of the hospital and into the parking lot four nights ago. Everyone was doing what convention said was beneficial, but at my core, I knew it was heartless, depriving the grief-stricken of the opportunity to suffer and allow their wounds to ache in private.

Bertie didn't like for me to call him that, and I was the only one who did. He said it sounded like a girl's name, and I should call him Robert like everyone else. But when I was little, I couldn't say Robert, so Bertie it was. We were a happy family then; I'd shown up unexpectedly, well after Daddy and Mama thought their little family was complete with only one child. Bertie was almost eight years older than I was, so they could be forgiven for thinking there would be no more babies. My big brother was my constant companion from my earliest memory; I'd idolized him from the moment I toddled across the room to fall into his arms as he laughed and tousled my curly, red hair. The years had been kind to him; I always thought he won the genetic lottery in our family. Now he was tall and handsome and looked so much like Daddy.

I'd never seen my daddy cry until today. We'd dressed quietly at home and remained silent on the ride to the church. A tidal wave of relatives and old friends of Mama's greeted us with teary eyes and hankies at the ready, but Daddy steered us clear as we made our way into the church's foyer. He held my hand when it was time to go up to the coffin and look at Mama. I didn't know why we had to do that; it made Daddy and Bertie and me cry. It wasn't Mama anyway, I was pretty sure. The old man who owned the funeral home must have put a life-sized doll in there and painted it up to look like her. Daddy's tears as we stood at the side of the coffin ripped into me. The prospect of a house filled with weeping mourners was too dreadful to consider, so I'd escaped to my room as soon as we returned home.

My thoughts were rudely interrupted by Aunt Myrta's raspy, old lady voice. "Charlotte Louise. Open the door so I can see to you, child. Your father needs you downstairs; you need to greet everyone who came to pay respects to your mother."

I looked forlornly at the patent leather Mary Janes Granny had picked out for Mama's funeral. They were so stupid and babyish; not anything a ten—almost eleven-year-old—would wear. A look into the oval mirror on my little vanity table made me scowl; Aunt Myrta would be irritated with my puffy, red eyes. But I couldn't stop the crying jags any more than I could hold back the sea. She'd given me a firm talk about being more considerate of Daddy and our visitors by controlling my tears. The whole thing made me angry; I just wanted to yell all the swears Johnny Parnell taught me behind the gym last year. I could never have imagined back then that Mama would die; the worst fear I entertained was that one of those dirty words would slip out accidentally, and I'd get my mouth washed out with gritty Lava soap. Again. Even a memory like that one seemed to keep Mama closer, so I tried briefly to hold on. It was wasted effort, though, and I knew it. It wouldn't help anyway, so I stood and slid the Mary Janes back on, smoothing the skirt of my ugly black dress. Granny had picked that out, too. The dresses Mama picked out were always pretty—and they were never black.

I shuffled toward the door, despondent. None of it mattered anyway; Mama was gone, and I had a feeling nothing would be okay ever again.

It was the coldest of January days and snow blanketed the fields and yards in our little northern Iowa town. But the downstairs of our house was full and so hot I couldn't breathe. The old oak dining room table and matching sideboard handed down on Mama's side groaned under the weight of platters of fried chicken, mashed potatoes, and every kind of pie known to man. I wondered how long we'd have company in our house; that was certainly the reason all this food had been brought to our door.

I wanted nothing more than for everyone to go home and leave Bertie, Daddy, and me alone.

Daddy's hand was on my shoulder, and he pulled me close as he talked to three old church ladies I didn't recognize. It had been a long time since I'd eaten, and I hated the cinnamon toast Aunt Berta made this morning. I eyed the sideboard; maybe there was some mac and cheese or baked ziti. The women discussed me as if I wasn't even there. As if I couldn't hear all the things they said about Bertie and me... "Sad little orphans...only their father to look after them...poor lambs, all alone." One of the old ladies touched my face with her cold hand.

"Now you're the lady of the house, Charlotte. It'll be your responsibility to take care of the menfolk, you understand? A woman is the soul of her home."

I looked up to see Daddy staring out the window. He didn't even hear what was being said, so I answered the way I'd been taught.

"Yes, ma'am. Thank you for coming."

She beamed at me while somehow showing pity. "Such a lovely young lady. Your mother would be proud of you, Charlotte; see to it you don't let her down."

I wandered into the kitchen in search of quiet and pasta. There was indeed a casserole dish filled with steaming home-made mac and cheese, so I dug directly into the dish with a spoon found on the counter and wolfed down several spoonfuls. The kitchen was especially stifling, and the crisp, snowy land-scape outside Mama's favorite kitchen window suddenly looked inviting. I took one more large spoonful of cheesy goodness and stepped onto the covered porch, the icy, early evening air biting at my face.

This was my mama's favorite spot in the whole farmhouse. The old glider still held her sewing basket and the patchwork quilt she'd pieced while pregnant with Robert. She loved to tell the story of how she and Daddy were too poor as newlyweds, and farmers to boot, to buy a proper layette for their firstborn. She'd learned to sew out of necessity and discovered an acciden-tal passion. She made a habit of sitting on the porch to hem my dresses, mend ripped jeans, and replace missing buttons as the sun went down. Daddy would return from his long day of work on the farm and come onto her porch to give her a kiss on the cheek and help her carry her mending indoors. As the years pro-gressed, Daddy's farm became more successful, and Mama could easily have afforded to send her mending out, but their evening routine continued, uninterrupted.

I stared across our property, the fields nearly indistinguishable from the farm roads that divided them because of the snow. Gradually, I became aware that I'd left the kitchen door ajar. Aunt Berta's lumbering footsteps moved across the kitchen, and Aunt Myrta's voice followed.

"He won't recover, Berta—I can tell. He blames himself." Water from the tap filled the sink, and the sounds of the sisters washing dishes followed.

"Of course he blames himself, Myrta. The fool. She never drove that car and didn't like to drive; her eyes never was any good, and it's no surprise she didn't see the truck. She was always the nervous type, Louise was. He should have taken her around to the preacher's house himself; she's dead as good as if he'd done it himself."

Aunt Myrta sighed and the dishwater splashed. "I never liked him when he was young. Never thought he was good enough for Louise anyway, but it ain't Christian to weigh his shoulders with that burden."

There was silence in the kitchen, and I listened from the porch, careful not to breathe so my aunties wouldn't hear. "She's dead all the same, Myrta. And those children are as good as orphans; I can see it in his eyes, can't you?"

Bertie sat on the side of my little bed under the eaves of our farmhouse, rubbing my back. I didn't know how he knew where I was. I had sneaked through the house after overhearing my aunties talking in the kitchen. Fortunately, the stairs were at the back of the house opposite the front room where guests still feasted on fried chicken, mashed potatoes, and sweet potato pie. Stealing a glance into the crowded room, I wondered how they all chatted and smiled as if Mama weren't gone. And as if Daddy didn't stand at the window, staring out over the winter scene with unseeing eyes.

Bertie's voice was low and soothing—so much like Mama's. "Don't you worry, Bugs. Daddy and I are gonna take good care of you—as good as Mama did. I promise. I miss her so much already, but it'll be okay. It's just you and me and Daddy now, but we'll be enough if we all stick together. You'll see."

I had my doubts about that, and they turned out to be justified. But the trouble didn't come from where I thought it would.

Chapter THREE

"Call Me Irresponsible"

Miles

"I can't believe you're such a stick-in-the-mud, Boo. Rock and Torch already bailed on me, but I thought I could count on you."

Boo sighed. "I would like nothing better than to heft a few cold ones with Snake and Badger. And I think Snoopy still owes me money from the last time they were through town. But I need every minute of shut-eye tonight, Miles. I know you don't see the value of eight solid hours, but it's nonnegotiable if you're trying to stay in shape. And I am. Anyway, I'm an old man."

I groaned at his weak-ass excuse. "You're a year older than I am, Boo, but whatever." I rolled my eyes and turned the Mustang off Golf Links Road. "Gotta run, asshole. I'm almost to the Club; see you in the morning." It would seem untoward to the uninitiated, but insults and name-calling were what passed for affection in pilot circles; Boo, Rock, and Torch were my best friends. This was our first assignment following **UPT**, and we were having the time of our lives flying the **A-10 Warthog**. Being a lieutenant in a flying squadron was an interesting mix of work and play. There was still a great deal to learn in the flying arena, and the amount of studying required was frequently intense, but there was always a party just around the corner. Tonight was no exception, and I was disappointed none of them had agreed to meet me at the Club.

Four of our mutual friends from **LIFT** were at Davis-Monthan **cross country**. We'd spent three eventful months in the backwater town of Alamogordo, New Mexico, at Holloman Air Force Base learning the fundamentals of flying fighter aircraft. The town itself was quiet, but there were plenty of good times at White Sands, a national monument nearby known for a dramatic landscape of improbably white gypsum sand dunes. Weekends often found our group camping there, sledding down the enormous white dunes and slaking our thirst with kegs of beer we'd buried in the sand. Our friends found out late this afternoon they had two broken jets, and that meant an additional night in town. As far as I was concerned, it also meant good cause for a reunion of our gang from Holloman, but I'd been unable to convince any of the usual suspects to join me on a school night. They'd each demurred; Boo needed to catch up on his sleep, and Rock and Torch were both approaching check rides and needed some extra study time. No matter. These guys were plenty of fun all on their own.

I dropped my phone onto the seat, returning the gate guard's smart salute. I had the first go tomorrow with Deliverance, an early flight. The base search and rescue exercise kicked off bright and early, but I reasoned there was plenty of time to push it up and still get home for a solid night of sleep and recovery.

I sighed. *I could use a drink.* It had been a long couple of months since Colonel Pain-in-the-Ass hung out his shingle as squadron commander. There were moments of brilliance, sure, but taming a group of fighter pilots was a fool's errand. I was convinced it would eventually dull our competitive edge and turn us into a laughingstock in the A-10 community. There had been a couple of pretty decent parties, and the float trip on the Salt River near Phoenix was a good weekend outing with plenty of booze and sunshine and buffoonery. But he was insisting on more professional military discipline and tightening the thumbscrews on record-keeping and quarterly requirements. That was **bean counter** bullshit that shouldn't have been a priority when dealing with a group of pilots. To make matters worse, the flight commanders, as well as our weapons officer, Deliverance, were drinking the Kool-Aid. It was depressing to see this group of formerly free spirits giving up the fight.

I wouldn't be so readily domesticated. I'd watched from a young age as the world tried to force me into a mold, to demand I become what they expected. Daddy wanted me out of harm's way, safe from anything that could snatch me away. He couldn't bear any further loss after Mama, as Bertie and I had discussed many times. But I saw the writing on the wall early and plotted a path away from his watchful eye. The Air Force Academy in Colorado Springs, Colorado, was the brass ring at the end of my teenage years, so I fixed my eyes firmly on the prize. It was ridiculously competitive, requiring stellar grades, extracurriculars, and a Congressional appointment, but it was my best shot at a pilot training slot, so I threw myself wholeheartedly into the process.

My middle and high school years were destined to be an exercise in keeping Daddy together, body and soul, as he slowly lost the battle with grief over Mama's death. I ultimately found that Myrta and Berta were right: he blamed himself for not driving her to the quilting bee at Sister Bailey's. But he was tired after a long day of repairing the big tractor and prodded her to drive herself the short distance to town. Her vision was terrible, worse at night, and she pulled directly in front of an oncoming semi truck. She literally never knew what hit her. He never emerged from the haze of depression after her passing except to obsess over my every move, going to extremes to protect me from anything he deemed dangerous. I wasn't allowed to drive a car until my eighteenth birthday. Even then, it was only my contention that I'd require a car to get to the airport and fly home from college that persuaded Daddy to take me to the DMV for my driver's test. I wasn't allowed to spend the night with girlfriends, go to camp, or attend concerts. My curfew was ten p.m. on the rare occasions I was allowed to go to ball games or school events with friends. I once overheard my friends' parents talking in hushed tones at church and found out even *they* pitied me.

The Air Force Academy campus was wild, stark, and severely beautiful. I was thrilled to be away from Daddy's smothering and on my own. Almost all my classmates found the structure and discipline restrictive, but I thrived under the new regimen, demanding and exacting. I threw myself into every challenge I could find—the most difficult classes and physical challenges—reveling in the newfound ability to make every choice for myself. In the summer following my sophomore year, I finally experienced the exhilaration I'd craved during the Soaring program. Flying experiences in an unpowered glider provided a foundation for the path that would eventually culminate in receiving my pilot wings. The unbridled freedom I felt as I soared through the quiet blue sky told me everything I needed to know about my future.

I was meant to fly. And never again would anyone take my independence from me. Like Henley, I would be the captain of my own soul.

Colonel Nathan Morgan wanted to extract a piece of that hard-won freedom from the Scorpions, I knew. He was sent to bridle the essence of what made us warriors, but I tried not to blame him personally. It was what the privileged bureaucrats and politicians in Washington, starched and pressed within an inch of their lives, thought was required. I shook my head at the irony. How could entitled old men with soft hands sit in mahogany offices and pass judgment on those who stood ready to fight and give the last full measure of devotion?

It didn't matter because I didn't live my life with eyes fixed on the standard of the idiots in Washington. I'd lost too much of myself to someone else and been fortunate to see the other side. And I was never going back.

I sauntered into the casual bar at the rear of the O'Club, calling out greetings to the foursome crowded around a small table in the corner. Badger, Snoopy, Snake, and DaisyJane flew the F-16 Falcon, a slick, sexy little sports car of an airplane, the polar opposite of the hulking Warthog. The F-16 was an object of good-natured derision in the A-10 community since it had only one engine and was notoriously fragile and broken. Like now.

Snake stood as I approached and gave me a big hug before handing me a frosty mug of draft beer. "About time you got here, Miles. Were you getting your hair done?"

"Yeah. You've got room to talk there, Snake. What's this I hear about your powder puff derby getting grounded this afternoon? One of you gals break a nail? Or did one of your birds get its period?" I grinned big at the guys.

"Awww. Fuck off, Miles." DaisyJane pulled me in for a hug, his huge hands squeezing my shoulders. "Missed you, girl. How's Rock? And the rest of the guys?"

I settled onto a barstool Snoopy pulled up. "We're doing good, man, all of us. Great to see all of you; sorry I'm the only one joining you. They all had pathetic excuses."

Badger signaled the bartender for an additional pitcher of beer. "It's no problem, Miles; we didn't really expect to see any of you guys. Torch texted me earlier that he's got a check ride day after tomorrow. If I had one, I'd be hunkered down too." He gestured to the man seated to his left. "I think Snoopy's the most disappointed."

Snoopy shot me a wide grin. "I was hoping to see Boo; bastard owes me money. I kicked his ass in the Crud tournament last time we were cross country, but I'll catch him next time. Anyway, one of our jets is **hard broke**, and they're bringing a part from Holloman, so we're not flying until late tomorrow or early Tuesday. You guys are flying tomorrow, right?"

I nodded, sipping the beer.

"We won't keep you up too long; you'll need to head home pretty early to make **crew rest**."

I raised my glass in a toast. "It's not every day my old buddies from LIFT drop in, so let the record reflect that the only one of the old gang who didn't pussy out tonight is the one who actually has one."

DaisyJane raised a glass, along with everyone else, and gave me another big bear hug.

"This is you, right?" Snoopy leaned toward me, his face a mask of concern. "Come on, Miles. I'll get you upstairs."

I sighed and struggled a moment to focus. "Nope. Not necessary, but thanks for the ride, dude."

"I swapped over to Coke Zero after two beers, and that was a couple of hours ago." He unbuckled and opened his door.

I groaned at the wave of nausea that threatened to overtake me. "You need to cut the cord on those diet drinks, Snoop. Boo says it's gonna kill all of us."

He opened my door and reached for my hand. "You gonna be okay, Miles? I can help you upstairs if you need me to; I can stay…"

I wobbled to my feet with a feeble grin. "You want in my

drawers, dawg. I get it. No dice, Snoopy. But you're the man, seriously. Thanks for the ride. Lock the keys in it, and leave it in front of the **BOQ**; I have an extra set, and I'll grab it tomorrow." This was far from the first time I'd had to make arrangements to pick up the 'Stang offsite; an extra set of keys was a must. I gave him a quick hug and waved goodbye. "It was great to see you guys. Really."

He leaned on the hood of my car, arms folded, until I let myself into my condo. Despite the price I knew I'd be paying in the morning, it sure was good to see old friends. The problem was, I had no idea how steep the price was.

Chapter FOUR

"This Is It"

Miles

W ell. This was gonna be a shitshow.

Last night with my old friends from LIFT was worth the price of admission, but it would cost me dearly today in terms of physical pain. **BFM** rides involved tight turns, rapid climb and decent, and acrobatic maneuvers—all of these exerted **G-force** on the pilot's body. That, in turn, required the pilot to take measures like wearing a G-suit and performing the **Valsalva maneuver** to remain conscious. It was surprisingly demanding, and we returned from training rides tired and soaked with sweat.

As it was, I was already sweating profusely and suffering from a well-deserved headache. Too bad today's ride was with Deliverance, widely acknowledged as the best **stick** in the squadron, some said the best at Davis-Monthan. There was scuttlebutt among those who'd flown with Happy Morgan that he was giving Deliverance a run for his money in that department, but I had my doubts. There was even a hot rumor Happy had taken

D's money, beating him soundly in the informal shooting and bombing contests every fighter squadron the world over engaged in at the range.

Deliverance wouldn't take it easy on me. One of his many roles as the Scorpion weapons officer was to educate us on the employment and capabilities of our weapons systems. Additionally, today kicked off the SAREX, an annual exercise meant to sharpen search and rescue skills, an essential role of the A-10 in combat. I'd hoped to play a more visible role in the exercise, but Happy put the kibosh on that, as he so often did. He was pissy about some LPA fun that went down at the Club a few weeks ago, and his memory was apparently long. Instead of giving me the more advanced checkout I'd hoped for, Happy was getting it. Jacob Travis, aka Bashful, who was the C Flight commander, would be flying on Happy's wing.

Whatever.

I stopped briefly in the ladies' room to splash my face with cool water and swallow four more ibuprofen tablets. If I could get one more bottle of water down, the healing would begin. I knew down deep that, while I was certainly not intoxicated, I was also not fully suited for the demands that flying would place on my body this morning. But I was well familiar with the cycle, and my body was adept at bouncing back quickly. Would a late morning go have been too much to ask for today? After all, it wasn't every day you had the chance to see old buddies.

"Morning, Miles." Deliverance was irritatingly handsome and chipper, especially for 0600. He had that clean-cut, square jaw, perfectly mannered Neanderthal thing working, and like so many things, it pissed me off. He would be too polite to say anything, but I looked like something the cat hunted down, chewed to pieces, threw up, then dragged in.

Our briefing proceeded uneventfully, and I was soon strapping into the seat of my Warthog, one more bottle of water consumed and feeling more like myself. As a particularly small woman, I often marveled at how people questioned my ability to fly the large aircraft. As if I had to bench press the jet rather than fly it. People could be so ridiculous sometimes. I tried not to take the inquiries as an insult, but it echoed a lifetime of Daddy's hypervigilance and controlling behavior. As a woman, I lacked nothing needed to excel as a fighter pilot. If my feet could reach and hold the brakes—and they could—I was tall enough. I longed to be taken seriously as a skilled pilot, not a female masquerading as one.

The first hint of trouble was the G warm-up maneuver; upon achieving the desired G-force, I was greeted with a mild closure of my peripheral vision. I was more peeved than concerned at this turn of events. Reaching over to double-check the connection on my G-suit, I determined to refocus and use more energy with the Valsalva. At the ripe old age of twenty-four the years were obviously catching up with me.

Shit. Everything hurt. *Everything.* The following turn was six G's and narrowed my field of vision to the size of the view through a soda straw—almost a complete blackout. The mission hadn't even started, but admitting I wasn't fit to fly was out of the question. I could hack it.

Deliverance's voice came through the radio, requesting I set up on the **perch** first, positioned as the "attacker," above and behind him. This gave me both the positional and energy advantage at the outset.

"Lead's ready." Deliverance's tone telegraphed easy confidence.

"Two's ready." In the aftermath of a large night, I needed to show him I could still bring it. Days like today happened to every fighter pilot.

Didn't they?

Deliverance was in his element; I wondered if he was ever less than adequately prepared. His drawl interrupted my thoughts.

"Fight's on…"

I dove toward the inside of his turn, trading altitude for airspeed. But as I started to pull lead, D abruptly turned directly into my flight path. The angles and closure rates changed, forcing me to ease my turn and slide across D's six o'clock.

Deliverance rolled the opposite direction with no hesitation, repositioning his jet rapidly above and behind me. That fucking drawl, "Fox Two," indicated he'd won the fight by "killing" me with a simulated **AIM-9** shot.

"Deliverance, **knock-it-off**."

"Two, knock-it-off." And the engagement ended.

Deliverance was endlessly patient. Only one of the many attributes he possessed that made him a superior weapons officer and human being. Motherfucker.

The second engagement was identical to the first, frustrating me to no end. Deliverance was unruffled and encouraged me to relax and try again. "Let's do this again; you're not flying to your capabilities at all. You feeling okay, Miles?"

"Twoop," came my terse reply. I was determined not to repeat my mistake and be embarrassed again.

"Lead's ready."

"Two's ready."

"Fight's on."

I dove hard from my position on the perch, striving for max airspeed and positioning my nose well in front of Deliverance's turn. He repeated the same high G turn directly toward me again, but I was absolutely determined not to overshoot. I pulled on the stick with both hands, rolling into even more bank and watched the G indicator move to 7.33, the A-10's upper limit.

Dammit.

The increased back angle left me belly up to Deliverance's jet, and I lost sight of him. Not that it mattered, the increased G's had squeezed out what was left of my vision. It was a complete blackout, the result of a terrible night's sleep and a badly bruised ego. I should have called, "Two's lost sight, knock-it-off," but my wounded pride made me press on, stupidly risking everything. It was arrogant and foolish, an unconscious willingness to endanger my life, as well as my friend's, all in pursuit of my ego's salvation.

My tactics were so wrong—so far outside the bounds of what we trained for and what Deliverance expected—that it took him an extra split second to process my calamitous blunder. It was a split second we didn't have. Too late for either of us to maneuver out of harm's way or even make a radio call to warn the other. We were out of options. The sound was deafening, and my body jolted mightily in the seat harness as the two mammoth jets collided.

I instinctively rolled level and initiated a gradual climb. The **G-forces** eased somewhat, allowing my vision to recover, but I almost wished it hadn't. Warning lights and every imaginable caution light illuminated the panel by my right knee. No good news to be found there. Nausea that rolled over me like an ocean wave almost prevented rational thought, but I forced myself to look down. I was desperate for any evidence at all that D had somehow miraculously escaped harm; but instead, what I saw confirmed my worst fear.

Black smoke rose menacingly from the desert floor off to my left, and I nearly lost the battle with nausea, fighting back vomit that clogged my throat. Almost simultaneously, the control stick stiffened in my hand, and I noted both of the hydraulic reservoir caution lights were among those glowing on the panel. The hydraulics were toast.

Hopelessness held me momentarily in its chokehold. Then, from the edge of my periphery, I caught a glimpse of an orange, white, and olive drab emergency parachute swinging in the sky below me. There was no way to know his condition, but

Deliverance had gotten out. I selected the emergency frequency on my radio, stomach still churning.

"Mayday, Mayday, Mayday. Deliverance Two on **Guard**. Deliverance lead is down—positive chute. I say again, Deliverance lead is down—positive chute."

Fighting hard with panic, I reached for the flight control panel with little thought and selected **manual reversion**, a rudimentary system connecting some of the A-10's flight controls to the stick via cables. It was an emergency system, purpose-built for circumstances like mine.

There was only a split second of dead air between my pronouncement and the sound of Colonel Morgan's clipped baritone through my radio: "All aircraft on the Goldwater Ranges, Sandy on Guard. Knock-it-off, knock-it-off, knock-it-off."

Happy and Bashful were nearby; my shoulders relaxed incrementally at the realization. The rescue exercise I'd been grousing about only an hour ago now dealt me a flash of hope. Happy's next transmission was directed at me.

"Deliverance Two, Sandy on Scorpion Victor, how copy?"

I swallowed hard, trying to tamp down the panic and focus. "Deliverance Two, loud and clear, boss."

"Say location."

"Over the hills just east of Ajo. Deliverance is down." My voice broke slightly despite my best effort, but Happy was all business and sounded for all the world like it was just another day at the office. "Miles, hold high and dry. Keep D in sight. Help is on the way."

I felt, rather than saw, Bashful rejoin on my wing before his familiar voice reached me through the squadron frequency. "S'up Miles?" Silence from me. "You've got a lot of damage, there. I'm gonna recommend that we head for the controlled bailout area and give this baby back to the taxpayers." He referred to the designated area each base had nearby for a safe, controlled ejection from an unlandable aircraft. It was absolutely the most conservative approach and entirely reasonable under the circumstances, but anger and fear combined in my gut and boiled over.

"Oh, hell no, Bashful. Hell, fucking no. Even for me, this has been a record-setting day of fuck-ups, and I'm sure as shit not gonna cost the Scorpions another jet before lunch." The radio silence was deafening; then he spoke, resolute and firm.

"Look, Miles…" His voice gentled. "Charlotte."

Something in my chest cracked. No one called me Charlotte. Charlotte was the girl who'd struggled to be taken seriously. Unsuccessfully waged a power struggle with her grieving father. Held every fear and every insecurity captive while she battled for independence. It was no coincidence few people knew my given name; that girl and her vulnerabilities had languished in the shadows for years.

Bashful's tone was calm as he tried to reason with me. "You know a controlled ejection is the best call; landing your jet in this condition is a great way to get dead." He hesitated only a moment, but I heard his harsh breathing. "The Scorpions are gonna kick my ass if something happens to you, Charlotte Christman. You're important to all of us…to me."

Fuck. Me.

He'd broken the unspoken rule between me and everyone I'd flown with. Don't mess with my walls. The barriers carefully erected over the years to protect me had served me well, and I considered them impenetrable. Humor, sarcasm, bravado, swagger, partying. They all served the purpose, shielding me from people who surrounded me every day. People who cared and had my best interests at heart. I had to hold myself removed from the possibility that my soft underbelly of imperfection and vulnerability could be discovered, exploited. But the simple act of calling the woman, Charlotte, by her name broke the fragile, flawed agreement I'd forged and cracked the wall right down the center. The epiphany was like a blinding flash of light illuminating my nakedness.

There was so much work to do.

I barely recognized my voice, softer but surer than it had been in a very long time. "I have to do this, Bash; I need to try. I've been angry for a long time. Had so much to prove. Things will be different, but I need your help. Grab the checklist and call the **SOF** and help me get this broken jet on the ground."

I was struck by the realization that I had such good friends in my corner, always drawing out the best in me. Letting me see their affection and loyalty. If I wanted to move into uncharted territory—to allow Charlotte to emerge, learn, succeed, and fail—these were the people who would stand at my back. Untrespassed ground wasn't so formidable if you weren't alone.

"Hey, Jacob?" I choked a little on the words. "No matter what, thanks for everything. You've always been one of my favorites."

Chapter FIVE

"Minute by Minute"

Miles

B ash contacted the SOF with the plan we'd worked out; I'd declared an emergency and requested a single frequency approach to assure Bash, the SOF, the tower, and the fire department would all listen and communicate together on my radio frequency.

Taking another deep breath, I blew it out and called the controller. "Deliverance Two, emergency aircraft, 5,000 feet."

His voice was steady and reassuring.

Nothing to see here.

"Deliverance Two, D-M. Radar contact, ten south of Davis-Monthan, plan runway three-zero. Say your request, ma'am."

"Deliverance Two, request vectors for an extended visual, three-zero, at least twenty miles."

"Roger, Deliverance Two. Fly heading one-two-zero. Advise ready to turn base. The fire department is on frequency and standing by. You are number one to the runway."

Flying the jet in manual reversion was a skill I'd had little time to practice, at least until today, I thought sardonically. During initial A-10 training, there was one opportunity to try it, but, of course, landings were not attempted. Landing was difficult, to say the least, and had only rarely been attempted. The nuances of hydraulically powered flight disappeared in manual reversion, rendering the 30,000-pound aircraft's controls sluggish. Even small deviations in pitch or power exacerbated control difficulties. It all looked impossible from my viewpoint, but I recalled the ancient joke Mama told me as a little girl.

How do you eat an elephant?

One bite at a time.

The plan was to fly a long, straight approach, giving me plenty of time to extend the landing gear and slow to the very rapid 190-knot approach speed. Additionally, I'd have a bit of extra time to get a feel for the handling characteristics. Bashful would remain close by, chasing me all the way to the runway, offering input without distraction. One bite at a time.

The loss of hydraulics meant no landing flaps—an emergency extension of the landing gear—limited emergency braking after touchdown, and no nose wheel steering. That represented a terrific loss of control, and if I was honest with myself, I had to wonder if I'd even make it that far. My emergency landing would close the base's only runway, and I had enough fuel for one attempt.

Only one.

If I were unsuccessful, I would immediately resort to plan B—flying to the controlled ejection area and punching out, as Bashful initially suggested. The lack of fuel by that point would leave me no choice.

"Deliverance Two, ready for base turn." I was about twenty miles from the runway.

Please, God, just leave the door open for a second chance; I promise I won't let you down.

The controller called with instructions to turn final and advise him when I had the field in sight.

I blew out another breath. "Deliverance Two. Field in sight."

Once again, the controller's voice was calm, confident. "Deliverance Two. You are cleared for the approach; cleared to land. Good luck, ma'am."

I'd probably landed the Warthog hundreds of times before today, but this one would be forever burned in my memory, assuming I lived to tell the tale. A quick glance confirmed Bash still on my wing, so I gave him the visual signal I'd be lowering the gear. He cheated his position a bit outboard; neither of us was sure how my aircraft would react. The emergency gear extension procedure went off seemingly without incident, and three welcome green lights on my control panel indicated three safe landing gear in place and ready for me to attempt landing.

One bite at a time, Miles.

Starting the descent, I battled the stick, which felt heavy in my hand; control was difficult. My learning curve needed to be lightning-quick; I couldn't afford any big mistakes. The procedures called for a shallow, power-on approach, and I searched for balance, experimenting with power settings.

One shot.

Bashful's voice was calm and as conversational as if nothing was at stake. "You've got this, Miles. Small corrections. Focus on the pitch and accept some airspeed deviations to avoid the big power changes."

My jet continued the seemingly endless final approach, careening and pitching along the descent. It must have been terrifying for what I assumed were the many observers.

Deliverance's smiling face flashed momentarily through my consciousness, followed by the gut-wrenching scene of the smoking hole I'd seen in the desert only minutes ago.

No time for that shit, Miles. Eat the fucking elephant. Focus completely on this landing; it's exactly what D would tell you to do.

Only a minute or so until touchdown. Bashful hung right with me, calmly calling parameters as I approached a mile. One more scan of the instruments as I crossed the runway's threshold, Bash's voice in my ear. Composed. Reassuring.

Thirty seconds.

Twenty.

A little too high. Pull the power back. Only small corrections now…very small. Pitch back just a bit, power on and…

BAM…oof.

The jet landed with remarkable force, temporarily stealing my ability to breathe, as if I'd been punched hard in the stomach. I glanced quickly at my speed, which was way too fast. I had only five brake applications and a little over two miles to stop. Steering with my feet, I applied the brakes as smoothly as possible, doing everything in my power to avoid a skid.

So far, so good, Miles. Eat the elephant.

God, still so fucking fast.

Bash was in my periphery, a scant twenty feet off the ground and right on my wing as I tore through two plus miles of D-M's runway far too rapidly. With the fourth application of the brakes and the runway's end now clearly in sight, I began to relax slightly. The speed bled off at last.

My Hawg creaked, badly wounded but not broken, and rolled to a stop.

The parade of emergency vehicles and fire trucks converged from the opposite end of the runway, rushing in my direction. The whine of two big General Electric engines reached my ears just as I saw Bash's jet pull up, casting a brief shadow over my cockpit. On the squadron frequency, he sent a parting shot.

"Shit hot, Charlotte."

Back on the tower frequency, his fighter pilot voice was back, low and cool as a cucumber. "D-M tower, Sandy Two request tower-to-tower to Tucson International, emergency fuel."

I braced my hands on the canopy, taking several deep breaths to calm my racing heart and churning stomach. A nagging ache in my right shoulder under the seat harness prevented me from stretching any further, but I barely noticed. One thought crowded my mind.

Deliverance.

Two big fire trucks and an ambulance stopped near the rear of the aircraft, and I released the canopy. It opened slowly, and the sound of pounding footsteps became louder as I carefully pulled my helmet from my head.

"Ma'am...don't move, ma'am." I felt and heard someone scrambling up the side of the jet, and then the head of a young firefighter popped into the cockpit, his face etched with concern. I moved to unstrap my harness, but he stopped me with a hand on my wrist.

"Please don't move, ma'am." He was a big boy, and he meant business.

"I don't think I'm hurt." I found his name tag on the breast pocket of his bunker gear. "Sergeant Joseph...I'm not hurt." I reached for the harness again but winced when a sharp pain sliced through my right shoulder.

"Lieutenant Christman. Don't move again." The concern was quickly turning to pissed-off firefighter, so I sat quietly, letting him unstrap me. "The jet doesn't seem to be in any danger of catching fire, but we've got guys with hoses on standby as a pre-caution." He studied me for a second or two. "Does anything hurt besides the shoulder?" I shook my head; everything else seemed intact.

He turned and shouted to someone out of my line of sight. "I'm going to try to bring her down; everything seems okay except one shoulder." He turned back to me. "Can you stand, Lieutenant?"

He stood on the ladder on the aircraft exterior, supporting me under the uninjured arm, and I gingerly stood. So far, so good.

Moving at the speed of molasses, I climbed out of the cockpit and down the ten or so feet to the ground. Unexpectedly, my legs seemed suddenly unable to support my one hundred twenty pounds as they'd been doing for years, but Sergeant Joseph caught me around the waist as we walked toward the waiting ambulance. There was a great deal of talk, all the professionals exchanging information and discussing next steps as I was helped into the ambulance and compelled to lie back on a stretcher. I answered the questions but couldn't peel my eyes from the trusty aircraft that had just delivered me safely to terra firma, odds notwithstanding.

Sergeant Joseph leaned into the truck, eyes still filled with concern. "I hope the shoulder's alright, ma'am. But you're damn lucky to get out with no more damage than that, if you don't mind me saying so." That earned him the first smile I'd cracked this morning. "And you must be a helluva pilot to get that bird back on the ground with both of you in one piece, ma'am."

I reached out with my good arm, awkwardly shaking his hand. "I don't know about that, Sergeant Joseph, and it looks like only one of us is in one piece—but thanks anyway." He lifted his chin with a grin and slammed the rear doors to the truck. He slapped the side of the truck twice, and we were off to the clinic.

The nurse attending me for the short ride was friendly but quiet. She took vital signs and carefully checked me from head to toe, asking a few cursory questions about how I felt. Pulling into the single ambulance bay that served the old emergency room, I was surprised to see a small assembly of medical personnel, all clad in familiar green scrubs, clustered outside the receiving doors.

I shot the nurse a wan smile. "You guys expecting a celebrity?"

She stood, one reassuring hand on mine as the ambulance doors swung open. My stretcher was pulled toward the door.

"Today, Lieutenant Christman, you're the celebrity."

I sighed.

I studied the clock on the wall of the tiny cubicle. It seemed impossible that it was only 1125—not even lunchtime. It had been quite an eventful day, even for a Monday.

The medical staff completed their work: a standard battery of tests including a thorough physical exam, a couple of X-rays, and lab work including alcohol and drug testing. I knew the results would be unremarkable except my right shoulder. I was nevertheless relieved when the flight surgeon informed me the shoulder pain was likely nothing more than a badly bruised tendon; the X-rays didn't show anything more serious. The news was welcome, but I was consumed with worry about Deliverance and his condition. My repeated requests for information or a phone to call someone—anyone—were gently rebuffed.

I was at once exhausted and anxious. When testing was complete, the nurse returned with crackers and ginger ale. She explained that a variety of physical symptoms were likely to appear in the aftermath of an event like this one. Nausea had been a near constant, and I was freezing cold. I was swathed in warm blankets, and she promised to return when someone could share news about Deliverance.

It seemed to have been hours since she'd left, but the clock proved me wrong. I'd been strictly instructed not to attempt to stand the first time without assistance and was weighing the consequences of ignoring that directive when the door opened a few inches.

A wild mane of hair, blond but bordering on white, framed an inquisitive face with pretty blue eyes. Its owner wore shapeless hospital scrubs, but I noted they were of the unattractive blue rather than ugly green variety.

She tapped on the door, eyes adjusting to the dim light in the little room. "Miles? Is that you?"

I sat up and leaned in for a better look. She looked vaguely familiar, but my thoughts were too scrambled to identify her. "Yes, I'm Miles, but I'm afraid I don't…"

She smiled and approached the stretcher, hand extended. "I'm Samanthe Barber, Miles; we've met at a couple of Scorpion parties, but I'd be shocked if you remembered me. Especially today; you must be absolutely fried."

I nodded absently. *Oh yeah, totally fried.*

Samanthe moved through the door, lugging an over-sized tote, which seemed to be working overtime to contain what she'd stuffed in it. She turned on a light under the work counter, then opened the cabinets and thoroughly inspected the contents, grunting either approval or disapproval of what she saw there. She was obviously not on active duty—the hair situation alone was well out of regulation—but she certainly made herself right at home in the hospital room. She turned to me with a warm smile as she washed her hands with the pink antibacterial soap used by the nurses and doctors.

"Helluva day, right?" She didn't wait for my reply but finished washing and rummaged through her bag, producing a big, colorful quilt, which she spread over me. "I'll bet you're freezing your ass off. It's always so cold in these rooms, and I thought a warm, homey quilt would be a nice change from a stack of sheets. Anyway, I forgot to finish introducing myself. I'm a registered nurse and work in the emergency department downtown with Camille and Luckie."

Uh-oh.

Camille Sullivan was the charge nurse in the emergency department at a big hospital downtown; she and Happy Morgan were dating hot and heavy. Luckie Page was another one of the ED nurses and Camille's best friend. Deliverance and Luckie's relationship was the worst-kept Scorpion secret in history. Both of this woman's friends were tearing up the sheets with two men who had every reason to hate me.

She pulled up a chair and sat close to my stretcher. "Most importantly, I'm bringing you news about Davis: he's alive and in surgery, but he's going to be okay. Camille met the helicopter that brought him in and took care of him until he was taken to the OR. He has a badly broken leg they're in the process of repairing and about a million abrasions and bruises, but the important thing is that he's expected to make a full recovery, Miles." Her eyes zeroed in on mine. "Full recovery, okay? Camille sent me here with specific instructions to make sure you understand Davis is going to be just fine."

I stared dumbly at her, unable to form a response; then a huge, choking sob bubbled up from nowhere. With no warning at all, I was utterly undone and wailing. Samanthe stood and held her arms open, wrapping me up and stroking my hair. "Let it all out, Miles…you must have been so frightened and anxious." Her fingers combed gently through my hair, now dirty and matted from the helmet and sweat. Her other hand rubbed my back, and she hummed soothingly, rocking me in her arms.

I don't know how long it was before the well began to run dry; it felt like forever, but Samanthe seemed at ease with my tears. When I finally quieted, she reached for the bag again and produced two tissues.

"Now, blow." She smiled sweetly and rolled her eyes. "I know you're going to think I'm a head case for bringing tissues to a hospital, but you need to remember I work in one. Use that sandpaper more than once—on your face or your ass—and you'll need a skin graft. Trust me on this."

I blew my nose hastily, drying my eyes on the sheets that still wrapped me. "I'm sorry, Samanthe. You must think I'm off my rocker. Bawling my eyes out in front of a virtual stranger; I'm so sorry."

She shook her head emphatically. "Don't start up with that shit, girl. I'm here for a number of good reasons, and we've already checked off the first thing on the list. First big ugly cry? Check. It's done and out of the way. I need to get the other ugly thing out of the way, as long as we're doing the hard stuff." I must have looked alarmed, but she waved her hand dismissively. "Nothing serious at all. Also, you may as well know that most of my friends call me Sam. Entirely against my will, but you should feel free to do it too. Samanthe is a mouthful." She handed me an additional tissue before walking across the room, reaching into the cabinet for a washcloth, and wetting it with cool water. She wrung it out and then pressed it to my face, carefully wiping my swollen eyes.

"Here's the plan, Miles—I'm taking you back to your house, and we'll…"

I interrupted her. "That's so thoughtful of you, Samanthe…"

A raised eyebrow.

"I mean Sam, but it's unnecessary; I'll be just fine, I promise. The shoulder is the only thing, and it's practically nothing."

She held her hand up, effectively stopping my chatter. "It's all been decided. I spoke to the charge nurse and got discharge instructions and prescriptions; Camille's been on the phone with the flight surgeon. Nathan cleared the decks for that, and they cooked this up." She flipped on the overhead light and helped me off the stretcher. "It's a solid plan, and you don't need to be alone tonight. Besides, as you'll soon learn, I'm delightful company. And that leads me to the second reason I'm here." She waggled her eyebrows dramatically. "I have spring rolls, pho, and orange chicken from Miss Saigon."

I narrowed my eyes. "Jasmine rice?"

"Of course, jasmine rice," she scoffed. "Do I look like a fucking amateur?"

Sam the mystery nurse seemed like solid people, I had to give her that. I managed a little smile. "Okay, I'm sold. I'll get dressed."

Chapter SIX

"You've Got a Friend in Me"

Miles

I resisted when Sam first extended the offer to take me home, but the clearer heads that prevailed got things right. Unbeknownst to me, the clinic required that someone stay overnight while I was taking the medications prescribed for pain and sleep. The flight surgeon was pleased my companion would be an RN, but it was uncomfortable to have a complete stranger assigned to my care and feeding. Still, I could see now that staying alone wouldn't have worked. I was unsteady on my feet, and the shoulder pain was worse than I admitted. Sam pulled into a pharmacy drive-thru to pick up medications the flight surgeon had called in, and then we made straight for my condo. She noted he'd ordered a few pain pills and a mild sedative; she had instructions to let me rest throughout the remainder of the day and tonight. The stronger medications, while welcome, were a sharp reminder that I wouldn't see the inside of an airplane cockpit anytime soon. It was something I decided to obsess about, but later.

Samanthe made a couple of trips to her car after helping me up the stairs and settling me in the warm bath she'd poured. I never took baths, but she'd insisted. Right again. The hot water loosened the knotted muscles in my back and shoulders, and my eyelids began to sag in spite of the nagging shoulder pain. I heard the deadbolt on the front door latch followed by a rap on the bathroom door.

"Room service for the naked and injured," she called out cheerfully, sashaying in with comic effect. "I'm gonna treat you so many ways, girl…you're bound to like one of them." She was funny, and I liked that. She washed and conditioned my hair before helping me scrub the parts my complaining shoulder wouldn't let me reach. "I know this is aching, Miles, and I'll get you all set up with a pain pill as soon as we get some food in that empty belly. I don't allow puking on my watch." She helped me stand and rinsed me head to toe with warm water poured from a pitcher she'd found in a kitchen cabinet. Soon I was dressed in soft pajamas and settled on the sofa.

Sam bustled around my little kitchen like she lived there, reheating the food and bringing me a steaming bowl of pho. The delicious smell and warmth in my belly soothed some of the jagged edges of the day away and quieted my jangling nerves. I'd never found myself in a situation like this one, requiring nurturing and attention. Since Mama died, and following the years-long power struggle with Daddy, I'd resisted anyone who tried to care for me like this. If I deserved independence, it followed that I had to be self-reliant. Yet today I found myself in an unforeseen scenario and nearly completely dependent on someone I didn't know. Someone who seemed perfectly comfortable looking after me with zero expectation. I hadn't seen a twist like this coming, and it would require examination. But for now, pho.

After disappearing for a couple of minutes, Sam reappeared in bunny slippers and a long, threadbare sleep shirt, and joined me on the sofa with two plates of orange chicken. I tasted the food she handed me and groaned with pleasure. "The jasmine rice smells like flowers and tastes like heaven." I accepted the pain pill she offered after a couple bites of food. "You didn't have to do all this, Sam, but thanks. My shoulder hurts like a bitch, and I'll admit I'm glad to not be alone tonight."

She snapped her fingers, obviously remembering something, and jumped up from the couch. Returning after a quick trip to the freezer, she arranged a flat ice pack wrapped in a thin cloth over my shoulder, then secured it with some sort of stretchy sleeve. "We'll ice this for about twenty minutes every couple of hours tonight, but don't worry, I'll take care of it." She talked around a mouthful of chicken and rice and kicked back on my sofa as if we'd known one another forever. "Between that and the Percocet, you'll be able to sleep, but you're going to feel like you lost a bar fight with John Cena for the next few days. I'm just warning you. After forty-eight hours, we'll switch to over-the-counter NSAIDs." I frowned and cocked my head, unwilling to stop shoveling food long enough to ask a question. "Ibuprofen. Nothing that will impair your ability to take care of yourself or drive. I'll be here until then."

A near stranger sent—at least indirectly—by people who should be very angry with me. And she was here to take care of me and stay overnight in my house. It boggled the mind, but Sam kept talking.

"I just took a call from Luckie, by the way." My stomach roiled. "She left the PACU, the recovery room where Davis was, about half an hour ago. He's very sleepy, which is expected after surgery. But he was awake enough to talk for a few minutes, and the first thing he asked about was you, Miles." My eyes filled, but Sam waved me off. "Don't start the waterworks; I'll comfort you, but not until I finish my chicken. He wanted to know if you were hurt, and he was amazed at the thing you did. The manual diversion thingy…whatever. He was impressed, and from what Luckie said, the whole squadron's buzzing about it. You must be some kind of hotshot pilot to pull of something like that." She grinned. "Also, Luckie said Dr. Taft was very happy with how the repair went and said Davis will recover fast. The guy's a complete douche—Taft, not Davis—but he's a fucking genius in surgery."

I set my bowl aside, body sated and beginning to buzz a bit from the medication. I couldn't recall having ever taken anything stronger than over-the-counter pain relievers, probably more of my misguided efforts toward self-sufficiency.

The Free and Sovereign State of Charlotte. How's that working out for you, Miles?

My mind and heart felt full and completely overwhelmed. Words were swimming aimless laps in my head, and thoughts were increasingly difficult to arrange. Sam seemed to sense my unbalanced state and plopped my feet in her lap, pushing both thumbs into an arch and kneading.

"Here's the thing, Miles. This is a marathon, not a sprint. I don't know the ins and outs of what happened, but I'm not a girl to pull punches. I know you fucked it up, and I know you're feeling confused and scared and guilty. It's normal. If you didn't feel that way, I'd know something was really seriously wrong with you. I don't know all the people you work with very well either, but I've met them a few times socially. They seem like good people, but here's what I do know: two women I know very well and love like sisters have great respect for your people. And that alone tells me you won't be doing whatever you have to do alone."

She was reading my addled mind and sorting the pieces out better than I could do for myself. The room felt warm, her skilled hands were massaging my feet, and my belly was full of warm soup and chicken…

"You won't remember all of this, Miles, but just remember you won't have to do it alone. You can get to the other side of hell—if you have to—as long as you have your people. I've seen it many times." She moved our plates and closed the heavy drapes, blocking out the afternoon sun.

"Close your eyes and rest, Miles. I've got everything under control. Sleep."

And I did.

The remainder of the day and night passed like some kind of fever dream. There were snippets of Sam waking me for a few bites of crackers or soup along with medication. She iced my throbbing shoulder, and then rubbed my feet until I fell asleep again. All of this was interspersed with nightmares. The accident in slow motion, then me kneeling over Deliverance's lifeless body, frozen with inaction. I woke sobbing more than once in the dark with Sam's arms about me, rubbing my back. The night seemed endless, looping back on itself like that movie about the day that never ends. Just when I couldn't fight the pain and exhaustion any longer, Sam would appear and soothe it back to the margins of my consciousness.

I woke just before dawn and stretched carefully, groaning; Sam was absolutely right about the post bar-fight feeling. I must have slept off the medication because the fuzzy, buzzy feeling was gone. Inexplicably, I was also in my own bed, although I didn't remember a nighttime change of venue. I tiptoed into the living area to find Samanthe sprawled on the sofa, sleeping soundly and wrapped in the quilt she'd brought in her gigantic bag of tricks.

Ugh. So thirsty.

The cottonmouth rivaled the world's worst hangover, so I took a page out of Luckie's book and made for the fridge, grabbing the OJ and swilling several large swallows directly from the big container. Luckie swore by the restorative powers of vitamin C.

"Better take it easy on that juice, patient of mine." Sam's voice was hoarse from sleep, but she smiled up from her nest on the couch. "I take it you're feeling better?" She stood and kicked off the bunny slippers, stretching her body before dropping into stretching exercises that looked like she was readying for something more strenuous. "Be careful, now; it'll be easy to overdo and end up feeling worse tomorrow. I want you to get outside and take a ten-minute walk this morning, but nothing more. And two short naps, along with icing the shoulder."

I sent her a Benny Hill style salute. "Yes, ma'am, ma'am. I'll be fine today, Sam; you really don't have to stay."

She shook her head even as she stripped off the ancient Power Ranger sleep shirt and pulled on running shorts, shoes and a snug running bra. I guessed nurses weren't skittish about nudity. "I know I don't have to stay, but we're just getting this girlfriend sleepover off the ground. Our to-do list isn't done yet. I'll grab a quick shower when I get back, and then we'll get breakfast on the way to the hospital."

The shock must have shown all over my face, and a huge lump formed in my throat. I tried to swallow it away; I knew the answer but asked the question anyway. "Which hospital? Why?"

She tied her shoes and opened the door. "TMC. Luckie texted me this morning; Davis is asking for you, and she wondered if you were able to come for a short visit. I said yes, of course; we'll be outta here by eight or so. Get yourself ready for public consumption, and wear something loose and comfortable. I'll be back in an hour."

With that, she was gone, and I was left standing in the kitchen with my heart pounding out of my chest. I was at once desperate and scared shitless to see Deliverance. But something inside me knew I wouldn't believe he was really alright until I'd seen him with my own eyes. I poured another glass of juice and returned to the bedroom to begin damage control on my face.

Chapter SEVEN

"More to Us Than That"

Miles

I felt like puking right on my shoes.

Samanthe and I stood outside the fourth-floor room on the orthopedic level where Deliverance had been for the past twenty-four hours or so. She must have sensed my state of mind because she placed a comforting hand on my back. "You'll feel better once you've had a chance to see him and talk. Let's do it, Miles."

She pushed the door open, and my stomach dropped into my shoes. The big man took up every inch of the hospital bed, and his leg was suspended in some complicated contraption. Every visible inch of him was covered with bandages, bruises, and scrapes; I was sick with the knowledge that I was the singular cause of all this pain and brokenness. His face was relaxed in sleep, his complexion much more pale than usual. He roused when the door opened, breaking into a wide smile when he saw me standing in the doorway, frozen in my tracks.

Luckie spoke first, standing up from her chair next to the bed.

"Hey, Miles. It's so good to see you; I wasn't sure you'd feel up to getting out today, but Davis hoped you'd come." She was wearing blue scrubs like the ones Sam had worn when she came to the clinic yesterday, but they were much more wrinkled. There was a smile in her tired eyes, and she turned to look at Davis. One hand smoothed the sheet over him then reached down to feel the toes where they emerged from the cast. "Look, Tarzan. You must have won the lottery; you have two beautiful visitors. I'll bet they've even bathed for the occasion, unlike your personal nurse."

Deliverance's laugh was weaker than I was used to hearing from him, but just as infectious. He held out one arm to me, beckoning, and adjusted his big frame slightly in the bed. "I need a hug, Miles. I know it's not how we usually roll, but I'd say this is a special circumstance." I approached him tentatively, fighting the lump blocking my throat, and bent to embrace him gingerly. Another one of those damned unexpected sobs tore from me as he wrapped his huge arms around me and whispered in my ear. "We're gonna get through this together, Miles. I've got your back; we'll figure it out a day at a time. In the end, we'll both be stronger than we were yesterday morning when we walked to the **flight line** together."

"Good Lord, Lucinda. You look like death warmed over; do you ever bathe?" Sam's tone was light and teasing, and she held out one hand to her friend. "Get your ass up, and let's run you through the shower down in the nurses' lounge. Or a car wash or something. I'll go across the road and get bagels for all of us. You don't mind watching Luckie's patient for a few minutes, do you, Miles?" She smiled at me, and Luckie grabbed a bag from the corner.

She bent and kissed Deliverance quickly. "I'll be back before the doctor rounds; you guys take some time to catch up." She shot me a brilliant smile that didn't hold even a trace of animosity.

They waved goodbye and were gone, leaving me alone with the evidence of the most unforgivable mistake I'd ever made. Had I been the one lying in the bed, I didn't know if I could forgive the person at fault. How could I ask Davis for that much grace?

I was still mute and breathing hard. My stomach churned dangerously, and I couldn't meet his eyes. He waited only a minute for me to compose myself, then spoke. "Come sit by the bed, Miles; pull the chair close, so I don't have to turn."

I pulled up the chair and eased myself into it, groaning softly.

"So I see I'm not the only one who feels like I got hit by a truck?" His voice was tinged with a bit of laughter. He conducted a search in the knot of sheets and pillows, finally producing and pushing a button attached to the box on the IV pole. "I've got a leg up on you, I'm afraid." He shot a comical look at his left leg, trussed up like a Thanksgiving turkey, and laughed. "See, Miles, if you don't half-ass your way through this—if you really do it up right—you get the happy juice on demand." He waved the button with a wink. "It's the good shit."

I relaxed slightly. He was obviously going out of his way to make me comfortable. He must not have been pleased with the results, so the song and dance continued.

"The food leaves something to be desired, but I've got a hot nurse at my beck and call. And she'll be even hotter once she's had a shower. I told her…"

I leaned forward, touching his hand, and interrupted. "God, Davis. I'm just so sorry. So fucking sorry." My voice could barely choke out the words, but I plowed ahead. "I don't even know where to start; I should be in that bed instead of you. You're such a good guy—the best—and everybody loves you. Hell, even I love you. Every Scorpion from now until eternity is going to hate my stupid ass for trying to kill the best pilot…the best weapons officer we've ever had. I fucking hate myself, and I can't even tell you how much. I've been so stubborn and so irresponsible…"

The tears were running down my face and picking up speed as I blathered on. With obvious effort, Deliverance shifted himself toward me, grabbing both of my hands. His face was twisted in pain. "Stop it, Miles. Just stop. It kills me to see you like this; come back over here." He held his arms wide.

I bent a little awkwardly toward him, and he caught me in his arms again. But this time he pulled me to his chest and patted my back with his big hand, shushing. I was immediately swept back in time to my little bed under the farmhouse eaves where Bertie had rubbed my back after Mama died, shushing and soothing the pain away. How long had it been since someone had comforted me and taken care of me in a crisis? Now two people in as many days attended me when I was at loose ends. Samanthe, virtually a stranger, appeared at one of the very worst moments of my life and took the reins as if we'd been lifelong best friends, expertly anticipating everything my body and soul needed when it was all coming apart at the seams. Now Deliverance, the guy everyone liked—practically revered—who had every reason to hate me? He was trying to bind up my wounds and stave off the bleeding, all from a hospital bed I'd put him in.

"Enough with the self-flagellation. It's gonna sound trite, Miles, but I'm saying it all the same: we all make mistakes. Some are bigger than others, and sometimes it's impossible to see the devastation they'll cause until it's too late. But they all have one thing in common: you can't undo what's done. You can only do damage control and learn the lessons from what you fucked up." I tried to push away from his chest, but he held tight. "Not done, Charlotte. Now you listen to me good. This is going to be a long road, but we're going to walk it together. Those lessons we're meant to learn? They're not just for you. There are some in there for me, too."

I finally extricated myself, noting with embarrassment that the front of his hospital gown was soaked with my tears. I wiped my face with both hands and stared into my lap. "I don't know what comes next, D. There's so much to figure out and fix, and that's if it can even be fixed." I shot a worried glance at his leg, but he relaxed back into the pillows and gave me a little grin.

"Now, I thought you knew me better than that, Miles. You don't think for a minute I'm gonna let a fractured femur get the best of me, do you? It'll take a little time, but my prognosis is good. I'll be back on flying status in no time, and you can take that to the bank."

I blew out a breath. "Is that just your ego talking or have you really gotten good news from the doctor?"

"Better than that, I'd say." He laughed. "Bibi's already been here, and she has the game plan all mapped out. She knows my surgeon, and they had a powwow before she came calling last night. I'm going to be her special cupcake." Bibi Ditka was not only a well-respected pediatric PT, but she also happened to be Coach's wife. All the circumstances surrounding this accident were incestuous as hell, I thought ruefully.

I snorted at his description. "You're special, all right. But I thought Bibi only worked with children."

"She does. Can you think of a bigger kid than me? I'm her pet project until I'm back in the saddle—her words, not mine."

I relaxed a little; his ability to fly again really was one of the main sources of the anxiety breeding in my head. "I'm glad to hear it, seriously, but there are so many things…" My voice died out, strangled from the many forms worry took when I considered the repercussions of a Class I accident that was entirely my fault.

His expression was serious but kind. "There are a million things to lie awake about after something like this happens, and you have to know I'll be losing sleep over some of it. Probably Happy will be burning the midnight oil, too. And Coach. When there's a big fuckup, Miles, it's rarely the fault of one individual. I get that you don't buy that, but it's the truth. I need you to know I'm not absolving you. I'm not telling you anything you don't know when I say you should've called 'lost sight.'"

I nodded, eyes brimming again. It was a moment I'd relived in my head over and over in the last day. I'd give anything to go back and make the right decision.

"I know you've wished for a mulligan on that one a thousand times, but you can't undo what happened." He leaned forward and fixed me with a laser beam stare. "So here's what you have to focus on right now: why did you make the decision you did? What brought you to the place to disregard what you knew was right, what you've trained for years to do? Other decisions in the past paved the road. The assignment now is to find out what's at the root of those choices."

God, he was right, and there was nothing in the world I wanted to do less than look inside. I swallowed hard and tried to think of something to say, but he wasn't finished.

"Your assignment is a fuckuvalot harder than mine. And it's difficult for me to say this, Miles, because I really like you, but I'm gonna shoot straight. No bullshit. I can see the pain you're in, but listen to me. If you can't do the work of being honest with yourself and finding out the answer to those questions, you don't have any business ever climbing back into the cockpit of a jet."

I could see it cost him to deliver the harsh truth; it wasn't in Deliverance's nature to be cruel or inflexible. The task he'd set out looked like an insurmountable mountain too dangerous to climb. Being honest with myself would be terrifying, but I took a long look at the man in the hospital bed. If there was a way to thank him for what he'd done today, for the graciousness and forgiveness he'd extended—if there was any way to honor him for that—it would be to do what he'd asked of me.

Everything inside settled into place, like a puzzle finally solved. Instead of ignoring reality, I would choose to run willingly toward truth.

"Thank you, Davis." A measure of peace blossomed inside me for the first time in years. "I'm going to accept your challenge and try to make you proud of me. Someday."

He sighed and shook his head with a little smile. "The first step will be the hardest, Miles. And hearing you say you're willing to try makes me proud already."

Chapter EIGHT

"Don't Fence Me In"

Miles

I'd been locked in my room since returning from school a couple of hours earlier. It was almost dinnertime now, but two hours of angry crying and practice arguments with the mirror yielded no results in terms of a new strategy. Trying to reason with him was a study in circular logic I could never break. His head remained firmly in one sphere, ruled entirely by fear and paranoia. Each day, he seemed to drift further from the reach of reason. I wiped my eyes and blew my nose one last time before bounding down the stairs to the kitchen where Daddy sat at the table. He heard my footsteps and began the response to my demands before I'd even rounded the corner.

"Charlotte, we've gone over this a thousand times. I know you don't understand, but I'm the adult in this household, and it's my responsibility to make sure nothing terrible happens to you. Your mother, Bugs—I never thought..." His voice trembled, then caught as it always did when he invoked her name; he rarely completed a thought where she was concerned. "It's just not safe, and I won't take any chances with you. At your age, you believe nothing bad can happen. You think you're immortal, but someone could drown or get lost in the woods or..." Daddy was exasperated with me, but not as much as I was with him.

"You act like you're the only one who lost her!" I shouted the accusation, immediately realizing the spiteful tone that delivered it was too cruel, even under these circumstances. "Bertie did—I did, Daddy. We all lost Mama, but it doesn't mean you should keep me under house arrest. You can't lock me up just to prevent something from happening; bad things happen all the time, and there's nothing we can do to stop them." These days my frustration increasingly bubbled over into anger, but it didn't further the cause. It hurt Daddy, but it didn't change his mind.

Nothing ever changed.

I tried to calm down and use my reasonable tone. "Daddy, please. All the girls are going; Frannie is my very best friend since third grade. You know her and her parents; we've all been going to church together since Frannie and I were little. Her mom is going to stay all night, and I promise to call every hour if you want." Frannie's family owned an old cabin at the lake, and we'd been planning a weekend sleepover for months to celebrate her seventeenth birthday. Fran, Josie, Denise, and I worked out the menu, made mixtapes, and had endless discussions about which movies we'd watch through the night. Her mom even planned to set up an all-you-can-eat ice cream sundae bar in the kitchen and keep it replenished throughout the night.

But even as the plans developed, I'd harbored a suspicious fear about Daddy ruining something else for me. It seemed to be what he did better than anything. I'd moved beyond disappointment and was passing angry on my way to furious.

"I'm the only girl in the whole junior class who doesn't have her driver's license and can't even sleep over at a friend's house." I'd raised my voice to Daddy, something I never did, but frustration was at a boiling point.

Bertie and I had seen the problems bubbling below the surface almost as soon as Mama passed away. In the days after the funeral, things gradually returned to normal in our little town, as they are wont to do, even after a startling tragedy. People stopped dropping by to visit, and the food deliveries slowed to a trickle before they stopped as well. Pastor and Sister Bailey came by the following two Sundays after church for a brief visit but stayed only long enough to offer a prayer and encouragement. After the first week, my third-grade teacher called Daddy to inquire after my well-being. I hid in the hallway bath with the door partially open to eavesdrop on the dressing down she received simply for checking on me. I was only ten years old, but I knew that day—and on many days that followed—that Daddy wasn't handling Mama's passing as he should. Had I been older, I might have known to ask the pastor or another adult I trusted for help, but I didn't know any way to help except to be a good girl. A better girl. I tried to convince him with exemplary behavior that he could trust me, but it was unsuccessful. The older I grew and the more freedom that became available, the more frustrated I became at watching it slip through my hands.

I talked to Bertie about my problems with Daddy until I was blue in the face, but he'd had no luck convincing him to loosen his grip either. Bertie was twenty-four now and lived in an apartment in town, only a few miles from the farm. He had been a sophomore at Iowa State on a full academic scholarship when Mama died, but in the few days following the funeral, he decided to take a semester off and to help on the farm until Daddy could get a handle on life without his beloved wife. He made all the appropriate phone calls to the registrar and one quick trip to Ames to pack up the meager contents of his dorm room and return home.

Upon his return, he dove right into a life of farm chores and cooking for me. I loved having him back home after only a little over a year away, but even as a young girl, I could easily see the burning desire he had to return to college. I was a third grader struggling with fractions and geography and Venn diagrams. I couldn't relate to my brother's thirst for knowledge, but it was something I came to understand later in life.

Neither of us was surprised when the day never came for Bertie to return to college. Daddy didn't tell him not to go, but when a new semester approached or Bertie mentioned reapplying, Daddy would sink deeper into the depression he constantly battled. He'd spend several days in his bedroom, declining food and ignoring the crops and cattle. On a farm, crops might abide a certain amount of neglect, but animals would not. My brother and I took a divide-and-conquer approach; he managed the farm chores alone, and I dedicated myself to cheering up Daddy. My efforts usually took the shape of trying to make his favorite foods—a task for which I was singularly unsuited—and spending evenings in his room on the lumpy sofa opposite his bed watching the movies he loved, old westerns and war films. Eventually, both Bertie and I would wordlessly admit defeat, and he'd mention casually to Daddy that he'd decided against a return to school. This pattern played out, with no discernible variables, three or four times over the first few years following Mama's death before Bertie abandoned his college dream altogether.

It was then that I saw the change in my brother. The fire in him flickered and died out. With little fanfare, he took a job in town as the assistant manager of the local hardware store, Franklin Brothers. He moved his few belongings into a walk-up flat above the buffet restaurant three blocks away; it was a dismal space with only the barest essentials. Bertie drove his pickup to the farm seven days a week at five a.m., cooked breakfast for the three of us, then helped Daddy with the chores until lunch while I was at school. He would return to his little flat after lunch, shower and dress, then work from one until eight at Franklin's Monday through Friday and every other Saturday. He went to church but was never otherwise engaged in socializing with other young adults. No parties or dating, and so much quieter than he'd been when I was younger. Like Daddy's existence and mine, his was an empty shell of what it was when Mama was alive.

I fought the inevitable with Daddy, using every weapon available. "I'll run away. You can't make me stay here." My eyes flashed as I challenged him like I'd never done before. The room fell deathly silent, and fear transformed his features. He had gone too far this time; my attempts at autonomy were laughably minimal compared to those of my peers. They drove, dated, traveled to ball games and concerts, and even sneaked beer from their parents' refrigerators on occasion. I was too terrified of the consequences to join them; the threat of Daddy's major depressive episodes was enough to keep me on the straight and narrow. But Frannie's birthday party was a different matter. He coughed a little as he drew in a deep breath, and I pressed on.

"I'm not a little girl, you know; I should be allowed to make decisions for myself sometimes." Surely there was no way he could argue the point. I left silence to cloak the room and waited for his response.

His voice was barely audible and shook with the fear I'd already seen. "I can't lose you, Bugs. Don't you see that? I'm not hanging on any better than I was the day the cops came to the door. And you look just like her, honey. The hair…your eyes. I just…" His voice was gone, eyes blindly fixed on something past me. I tried to swallow the lump in my throat and willed myself not to give in again.

"Daddy." Bertie's voice came from the back doorway, and we both turned. I looked with new eyes and saw not Bertie, but Robert. He was tall with dark eyes and wavy dark hair, just like

Daddy's had been when Mama died. His own hair was snowy white now. Robert was broad and trim in all the right places, terribly handsome, and kinder than anyone I'd ever known. He should be having fun, going out to parties. He should be dating girls, I thought. He should be finding someone to love like Daddy loved Mama.

Robert ambled slowly into the kitchen where we stood and stuffed his hands into the pockets of his well-worn jeans. "Daddy, you can't just keep her locked up here with you forever; she's a young woman. And she'll be leaving soon. Leaving for college." He spoke the last bit with more purpose.

Daddy's eyes darted between Robert and me several times before he spoke. "Yes. College. It won't be too long now, will it?" He stood stock-still, not speaking and looking at his boots. Robert and I stared at one another, trying to decide the next move. Daddy walked toward the hallway door, never looking up. "I'll be up in my room if you kids need me."

As he shuffled out, I shot a panicked look at my brother.

Good God, not again.

But instead of following Daddy, as he'd always done, he walked toward me, arms outstretched. My whole body fell against his chest, inhaling the scent of soap and aftershave. I heard pitiful sobs, and it took a few seconds for the realization to dawn that it was me. I cried until the front of Robert's tee shirt was soaked through. When the tears abated, he lifted my face up and looked at me with his big brown eyes.

"Go to Frannie's birthday party, Bugs. You go and have a good time; don't worry about Daddy and don't ask him again. I'll handle it." He hugged me tight and kissed my head. "You've got a whole life to live, and goddammit, you're gonna live it."

I never knew what Robert said to Daddy, but I did go to the lake cabin and had more fun than I'd ever had in my young, sheltered life. Things were never again the same between Daddy and me. He grew increasingly withdrawn and, although I continued to live at the farmhouse, I relied on Robert more and more. My heart ached for all Daddy suffered, but I longed for the chance to live my own life. That day, I got my shot. And I owed it all to Robert.

Chapter NINE

"Take a Chance on Me"

Miles

They wanted to see me.

I knew it would happen, and frankly, they'd been more lenient than I'd expected, considering I'd trashed thirty-eight million bucks of Warthogs in one fell swoop only one short week ago. I'd passed the week in my condo, mostly in silence and deep thought after Sam left early on Day Three. She hugged me warmly, wished me well, then grabbed my phone and programmed her number into it.

"You will call me if you need anything. Anything at all, you understand? We have accomplished what is never done; we have skipped the awkward 'getting to know you' phase of friendship. We are all dug in now, Miles, and I fully expect to hear from you. Not just when you need something, but when things get better. Normal. We're going to go out shopping and get sushi and buy shit we don't need. And we'll go to the movies. I like caper flicks, but I can tolerate rom-coms if we smuggle in wine. Got it?"

This was uncharted territory for me and pretty exciting. I

didn't have many female friends.

Okay, none.

But Sam gave me something I didn't expect to need: acceptance when I felt unacceptable. It was a shot in the arm that helped me face what this Monday morning was serving up.

Coach phoned Sunday afternoon, ostensibly to see how I was feeling. He was friendly and talkative, giving me updates on Deliverance and asking about my shoulder. Sending Bibi's regards. Then he lowered the boom. "You need to come to the squadron in the morning, Miles. Happy and I will be meeting with you to ask some questions and outline next steps. We'll begin at 0800, okay?"

I knew it was coming, but there was no preparing for this meeting; I would never be ready to face the music with Happy and Coach. They would be so disappointed, so pissed off, and I had no ready explanations. I had put them both in a tenuous position, and the week I'd spent in the sanctuary of my home had likely been hell for them. To make matters worse, I didn't know where to start along the road Deliverance had prescribed. If I knew which direction to turn, I could at least tell the two of them I was doing something.

I drove through the front gate of the base, unconsciously returning the salute of the gate guard, and turned my car toward the squadron building. Pulling the Mustang into an empty space, I clocked Bashful leaning against the tailgate of his pickup, arms folded as he watched me park. I locked the doors and walked toward where he stood.

He met me halfway and wrapped me in a big bear hug. "I didn't visit you, and that was shitty of me. I feel kinda bad about it, to be honest." He shot me a guilty grin. "Truth is, I was afraid it might get emotional, and a guy like me with all this testosterone? I can't handle that shit." His levity was welcome; I was in need of a distraction to help me settle down before my meeting with

Happy and Coach.

Bashful patted me on the back and bent to grab his helmet bag. "Let's get inside, Miles. Word is you've got a big meeting this morning. You don't want to be late."

I groaned and started toward the door. No sense in postponing the inevitable.

I avoided the snack bar where most of the Scorpions were likely congregating this morning, filling coffee mugs and readying for flying sorties and various other tasks. I couldn't bear the thought of all the emotional conversations welcoming me back. I would need every ounce of fortitude I could muster to face Happy and Coach. Glancing at my watch, I saw time was up. I rapped softly on the door while staring blankly at the small brass plaque that read "Colonel Nathan Morgan, Commander 82nd TFS."

Coach opened the door and extended his hand, shaking mine warmly. "It's good to see you up and around, Miles. It's been a shit week, but the fact that you're in one piece is a bit of good news we're all grateful for." I nodded, again fighting for composure; it seemed ridiculous that he would waste compassion on me. Turning my attention toward the other side of the office, I took in the tall, dark man standing behind the big metal desk. His face was serious but not angry, and he leaned forward with both hands flat on the desktop.

My voice sounded very small in the heavy quiet blanketing the room. "Lieutenant Christman reporting as ordered, sir." I walked up to his desk, straightening, and gave a sharp salute. I could only imagine what thoughts crowded his mind as he studied me. I knew he'd pegged me as trouble almost from the beginning; this wasn't the first time I'd stood in his office waiting for the commander's wrath to rain down on me. This time, though?

This time made the other occasions pale by comparison. I made a decision the first day at the beer call where he was introduced that I didn't fucking like him. He was brought in to fix what Pappy had purportedly broken, and he was all the things I didn't like or want in a commander. He was a straight arrow and a rule follower; and most importantly, *he wasn't Pappy*. I pretended differently, but I was hostile and petulant toward him. Bitterly indignant that he would step into Pappy's shoes as if there were any possibility he could fill them.

In that split second, standing in front of Happy's desk, a thought tickled at the back of my consciousness for the first time. Why the loyalty to Pappy? What was it about him that earned my regard and set me at odds with his replacement? The answer came almost as quickly as the question had, and it hit like a lightning bolt.

Pappy fed my craving for independence. He didn't tell me what to do, and he didn't question my autonomy—he literally let me fly. That was all I'd ever wanted since the day Mama died. I'd resented Daddy for clipping my wings to protect himself from losing me. In the aftermath, I gravitated toward anyone and anything that fed my hunger for free agency.

Yeah, Pappy gave me the carte blanche I desperately craved—hell, he gave it to all the pilots—but at what cost? He gave us plenty of rope to hang ourselves, and we'd damned well done it. We were the Wild West of flying squadrons: no holds barred, anything goes, and every man for himself. But the result? We'd lost Joey, a good guy and a good pilot who became a victim of lax discipline. Deliverance could have been the second casualty, and his blood would have been on my hands.

"Lieutenant Christman? Miles…" Happy's voice was louder than usual and mildly irritated; I realized he'd probably addressed me more than once.

"Sorry, sir. I was lost in thought for a second. It's been

happening quite a bit this week."

Not getting off on a great foot here.

"I'd imagine so; there's been plenty of thoughtful quiet in my office as well. Please sit down." His tone softened. "Coach speaks for both of us, as well as all the Scorpions; we are very thankful you weren't seriously injured. In situations like these, we have to count our blessings where they come. I also understand from Lucinda and Bibi that Deliverance is expected to make a full recovery."

I sat on the edge of the chair across from him; Coach had pulled up a seat alongside mine. "Yes, sir. I saw him while he was still in the hospital, and we've spoken on the phone a few times. I can't tell you how glad I am that he'll be okay, but that only scratches the surface of all the things I'm feeling about the accident."

He sat back, nodding and thoughtful. "Yes, I'm sure there are a number of issues at play in your mind. Today's meeting is primarily to address how the Air Force will handle this matter, and what the ongoing plan and consequences may be regarding your future."

It all sounded like the death knell to my flying career, and that was no less than I'd expected in the few moments of honest reflection I'd allowed myself about flying. It felt like the height of conceit to expend any worry about my own future when I'd so selfishly jeopardized the life of my friend.

"Yes, sir. I understand."

Happy took a deep breath. "The accident investigation will be ongoing for some time yet, but we don't wait for final results before taking measures to correct presumed causes. You are not required to do so, but are there details surrounding last Monday's events that you'd like to share with us?"

He studied me quietly, waiting. I hadn't anticipated the request, having spent other disciplinary visits to Happy's office standing silently at attention. He didn't want to hear from me on those occasions, but today was different.

"I think about it all the time." I couldn't help looking down, finding my hands clasped so tightly together the knuckles were white. "I don't really think about much else. When I visited Davis in the hospital, he talked about root causes. He challenged me to do some thorough navel-gazing and figure out why I made the choice I did. Not to call 'lost sight.'" I swallowed hard and looked up to find Happy listening intently. "I'm not good at seeing and judging myself honestly, but now that's cost me more than I ever dreamed it could. So I've decided to try as hard as I can to do what Deliverance asked of me."

"Introspection is a learned skill, Miles." Coach leaned forward, elbows to knees, and trained a serious look on me. "It's not something you can do effectively without instruction and support, but I applaud your efforts. Go on."

"I only have some pieces of the puzzle so far, so I can't see the whole picture yet. One of the disappointing things I've recognized is that I've been careless and irresponsible with my lifestyle. I don't always get enough rest, and I've been cavalier about alcohol and partying too much."

Happy's voice carried a sharp edge when he spoke. "The drug and alcohol tests came back negative; are you telling me I should suspect otherwise, Lieutenant?"

"No, sir." It was humiliating to admit the truth. "I wasn't under the influence of alcohol last Monday, but I'd been at the Club the night before and stayed out later than I should have. I wasn't well rested."

"And did you drive home, Miles?"

"No, sir." I wanted to be emphatic on that point. "My behavior has been unacceptable many times, but I've never once driven after drinking." His body relaxed noticeably at that.

It was challenging to knit together the things that had been marinating in my head for the past week; all I saw in myself was fault. Shortcomings. None of it would make sense the way I expressed it, but they'd asked me to try.

"My father was overly protective of me after Mama died, and it left me with a strong appetite—almost an unnatural craving—for independence. I'm afraid of what it's looked like to my friends. To the two of you and other authority figures I had in college or UPT. I have to figure it out, but I have no idea where to start."

Happy and Coach exchanged a knowing look, and Happy raised an eyebrow. "You thinking what I'm thinking, Chuck?"

"The Tuesday Game?"

I didn't understand the question or what Coach's answer referenced, but the exchange was obviously not meant to include me. They nodded at one another, thoughtful.

After the moment passed, Happy stood and folded his arms in front of himself. He was somber, but I still couldn't detect the outrage I'd expected. He seemed to have a tight rein on his emotions; when he spoke, the words were carefully measured.

"General O'Cherry sat the squadron down last week; flying resumes today. There have been safety meetings and briefings, and the general was here Friday morning to address the squadron. Had you not been injured, you would have joined us, but I also had concerns about your state of mind. Whether or not you'd be suffering from a form of survivor's guilt, for lack of a better term. I think what you said helps me draw a finer point on that issue. There's something Coach will tell you about when I'm done that I'd like you to strongly consider as you go on this quest for root causes. Deliverance is a fine man and a superior pilot and weapons officer, but I'm learning he's also wise. His advice to you is right on target, as far as I'm concerned."

He paced behind his desk, and I clenched my hands into sweaty fists as I waited to hear the consequences. "Miles, there's almost no way to overstate how serious your situation is. You have cost the taxpayers millions due to your actions and inaction at a critical moment. The ability to think critically and act accordingly is literally what we are paid to do. But even that pales in comparison to the fact that this squadron was perilously close to losing two of its own. I sense you understand the gravity surrounding the possibility of losing Davis Foster. But I think you fail to realize it would be equally tragic for all of us if we'd lost you."

I blinked and looked down again, absorbing his words.

"You are grounded until further notice, pending the results of the accident investigation board. We are discussing how your time can be best utilized while you're not flying, but there's a certain amount of work here in the squadron that will occupy you for the time being. I strongly expect, no matter whether you spend your work days here or in another squadron, that you will remain fully engaged with the Scorpions. Your actions surrounding the accident will be scrutinized, and you'll be reprimanded or disciplined accordingly. But no matter what happens, Lieutenant, you are one of us. Don't forget that." He settled in his chair, lifting his chin toward Coach.

And that's when things got interesting.

Chapter TEN

"A Change Would Do You Good"

Miles

Happy settled back into his chair. He grabbed his coffee mug and took a long drink before coughing and staring down into the cup, brow tightly knit. I gathered he'd finished with what he had to say, at least for now. There would be more to add when the accident investigation board handed down its findings, but that would probably be a few months from now. Coach turned his chair to more directly face mine and stared out the window as if thinking about where to begin.

"Happy already addressed the official action he's decided upon in the immediate aftermath of this Class I, but I want to add something to your plate. I think it may be helpful in your journey toward self-awareness, Miles. There's a story, and it's a long one. Do you two want coffee?"

Happy's face screwed into a distasteful grimace. "Is that what we're calling this?" He brandished his coffee cup, which I noted bore an image of a cartoon Warthog. It read: Go Ugly Early.

"Tastes like motor oil and sludge. We've gotta up our game in that department. And I'll pass."

I shook my head, anxious to hear Coach's mysterious suggestion.

"Alright then. About ten years ago, Bibi and I came to Tucson while I was at the **Schoolhouse** for initial training. The **TDY** here was about four months before we headed off to Alaska, but it was an eventful four months. On the day in question, I was sent over to Wing HQ on an errand for the self-important prick who was our **OpsO**; I was on the schedule to fly and wanted to grab lunch before my sortie. What happened over the next half hour was remarkable mostly because of the person I met; his behavior was counterintuitive to anything I would've expected in the story I'm going to relate. This was true even though I was surrounded—then and now—by people I considered the cream of the crop. I'd never met anyone exactly like Keeper Bond.

Coach, about ten years ago

I was going to starve to death, and it was my own damned fault. I was on the schedule for the 1400 go, but Hannibal insisted I had plenty of time to swing by Wing HQ on my way to grab a sandwich. The Wing King's secretary had a packet he needed *yesterday* about the Fall Festival we were hosting for the military dependents and civilian children in the surrounding area. It was all community goodwill stuff aimed at strengthening our relationship with the city, and I certainly had no problem with that. But I had a big problem playing lackey for the OpsO. He was an asshole who enjoyed throwing his rank around. Anyone in the squadron was at risk of being victimized by **line of sight tasking**.

I parked and jogged into the building, scanning the directory for the correct office. A secretary guarded the inner sanctum where the general spent his days doing God-knows-what, but she had what I needed. I grabbed the big manila folder labeled "Hannibal," wished her a good day, and hit the door running. The result was predictable: I got in a goddamn hurry backing out of the HQ parking lot, didn't clear my mirrors like I should have, and managed to back my pickup over the biggest fucking Harley you've ever seen. There was a terrific racket, and I jumped out to make sure no one was hurt, although I was fairly certain it was only parked in my blind spot.

I was correct, at least on that point, but there was a shitload of crumpled chrome under my old truck. It suddenly occurred to me that I wasn't anxious to meet the owner of the bike. He would likely be a burly, bearded dude with a bandana tied around his bald head and an anger management problem. I stared at the hunk of metal under my bumper, hands on hips, and sorted through my options. It was a fairly quick exercise since there was only one, and I berated myself for falling victim to an obviously ridiculous stereotype. I started toward the front door, planning to go back indoors and begin the search for the bike's owner so I could confess.

I was brought up short as the character my head had conjured up walked out the front door of HQ with his arm around the Wing King's secretary. He was huge—taller than my buddy Toga who was six feet, two inches—and all tattooed muscle. I recognized immediately that my life was over. He would come over, examine the ball of crushed metal under my bumper and pound me into a greasy spot on the asphalt. I swallowed and held my hand up in a half wave, hoping he'd be merciful and kill me quick. He walked right over to where I stood frozen in place.

Slowly, he leaned over and took in the sorry mess that had been his pride and joy ten minutes before. After looking for a second, he straightened and shook his head sadly, then turned to the woman, saying, "That's a shame, isn't it, Emmay? It was a real fine bike." He sighed and took another look, shrugging. "But there's nothing to be done about it. At least no one was hurt."

I was still bracing for a punch, but he turned to me and stuck out his hand. He shook my hand all friendly and polite and said, "Morning, friend. It looks like you're not having a real good start to your day, and I sure am sorry about that. My name is Axel Bond, and this lovely creature is my woman, Emmay."

Emmay grabbed my hand and pumped it energetically while I stood, shocked and completely mute. She started to talk, words coming out of her mouth like machine gun fire. "You just say it like the two initials—M.A. My real name's Mary Adrianna, but Axel says it's too much to say when he wants to talk sweet to me." Then she clammed up all at once and blushed bright pink. He was looking at her the whole time like she'd just hung up the fucking moon in the sky. I hadn't picked up any of that vibe when I grabbed the packet not five minutes before, so I just nodded my head again and didn't say a word.

That's when the big guy picked up the conversation again. "You'll have to excuse Emmay, friend; sometimes she babbles on a bit. Call me Keeper if you're inclined; that's what my friends call me." Still not a word about his motorcycle wadded up under my truck.

I figured I'd better say something soon, so I finally found my voice. "I sure am sorry about this, Mr. Keeper."

His grin split his face wide open as if he was glad to be enjoying a conversation with me. "Nope, Captain. It's just Keeper."

"Ah, well, okay...Keeper. I'm real sorry about this, and I don't have any excuse at all. It's my fault, and I should've been more careful. I'll make this right—I promise that." I fished around in my flight suit pockets and came up with a pen and scrap of paper. Pulling out my wallet, I started copying insurance and contact information, using the hood of my truck as a writing surface. Instead of questioning me as I expected he would, Keeper leaned against the fender, a little closer than I felt comfortable with. I wasn't overly familiar with the concept of personal space, but he was in mine, that was for sure. He folded his arms, which were decorated from the knuckles with a myriad of colorful tattoos that reached up his arms and disappeared under his sleeveless cut. They emerged at the neck of his black tee shirt, but it was hard to see because of the gloriousness of the beard.

His appearance really was all about the beard, and I'd have been willing to believe both men and women would agree on that point. It was every color of the spectrum between silver and gray and white as snow, and it fell down almost to the top of his belly, nearly covering the embroidery on the breast pocket of his cut that said, "Keeper." The beard looked soft and clean, unlike most I'd seen. Military pilots weren't permitted to have beards; it interfered with the oxygen mask's seal. Of course, you covet most strongly the thing you're forbidden to have. For me, that was a beard. It was probably a good thing they were off-limits; it'd be too embarrassing to want one and find out I couldn't grow a decent one after all.

While I busied myself annotating details of my insurance, Keeper alternately watched me and stared off into the distance, taking the opportunity to explain in some detail the philosophies that defined his life. "I've found a great deal of satisfaction—peace really—in letting go of material things as a touchstone to my contentment. It's not the things themselves, Captain, but the way they keep us from being present in the lives of others." I stole a glance at him, unsure of whether or not I was expected to stop my task to take in what he was saying. It didn't seem so though; he spoke to the horizon. Now it was Emmay's turn to gaze adoringly at him.

"This unfortunate event here today," he gestured to the remains of the dearly departed under my truck, "you see, is different for both of us. For me, it's a test of my spirit. A chance to see if I really believe what I say. An opportunity to strengthen my resolve, to nurture character development. My goal is to lead a simple, mindful life; this is a checkup to see if I'm doing that to the fullest."

I had no idea how to respond, so I just handed him the paper I'd finished. I was about to thank him or say goodbye before calling a tow to drag the bike from under my truck when Emmay spoke up, chattering so fast it was hard to keep up.

"Axel did his undergrad in world religions at UC Berkeley and got his master's from Columbia in counseling psychology. I'm so proud of all the good work he does, and now you can see why. He just opened a practice as an LPC."

I shot a questioning look at Keeper, now plainly lost as to what we were even doing.

"Licensed Professional Counselor, friend." He said it mildly, having picked up on my bewilderment. He'd have needed to be blind to miss it; I was barely hanging on.

"Anyway, I'm awful proud. There's nothing more important we can do than help other souls on the journey, and my Axel's made it his life's work. What could be better than that?" She didn't wait for an answer but continued without so much as a breath. "You'll come to dinner at our home because it's a gift to meet a new friend. Does Thursday work for you?"

Coach smiled as he finished his story. "So that's how Bibi and I met two of our oldest friends, Keeper and Emmay Bond. When it came time to shop for my next assignment, the long friendship with Keeper and Emmay played into our decision to prioritize Tucson. They still live in an old adobe near Sabino Canyon, off East Catalina. Keeper built a thriving counseling practice and has helped countless folks over the years; hurting and confused people dealing with grief, addiction, life-controlling issues, you name it. He still practices part-time. Cut back because he wanted more time to play golf. And to ride with his club, of course. Emmay's retired from her secretarial gig; she's a yoga teacher now."

Happy had kicked back in his desk chair as the story progressed; now he was wearing a big smile. "Goddamn, I love that story, Coach. I would've given my eyeteeth to see your face when Keeper came out of HQ. Come to think of it, I'd love to see what he looks like playing golf." He guffawed at the mental image.

I felt as confused as Coach must have been in the story. The guy sounded like a genuine character, but I wasn't getting it. "So, you'd like me to see your friend for counseling?"

Coach shook his head. "Not exactly, Miles. I mean, that's a possibility, if you decide you could benefit from formal counseling at some point, but I had something else in mind. What I heard you saying before was that you have several parts of your puzzle—the answer to Deliverance's root cause question. Keeper is skilled at distilling complex problems into simple answers. In other words, he's great at drilling down and finding an issue's root cause. Of course, I haven't spoken to him about this, and I'll have to check it out with Keeper before I offer it up officially."

"And what exactly is on offer? If not private counseling, then what?" I was still unsure.

He smiled and leaned forward, elbows on knees. "On Tuesdays, Emmay and Keeper host a gathering of past counseling and yoga clients as well as friends. The feel is part shindig and part serious fucking business. It's a gloves-off, no bullshit get-together to discuss what's on the front burner in everyone's life."

Interesting.

"It's also a card game."

"Pardon me?"

"A card game. Uno, actually, and everyone plays. Sometimes it's an hour, sometimes it goes until after midnight. Just depends on what comes up. There will be between six and twelve people—never more—but that doesn't include Keeper and Emmay. Also, you bring dip. Everyone does. And chips or veggies according to what's appropriate. I think the Uno is a bit of a distraction; it keeps things more casual, so the focus isn't on any one person."

I'd never heard of anything so loony in my entire life, but here we were.

"It's called The Tuesday Game. I'll check in with Keeper and get back to you later today. He'll probably want to meet you for coffee or breakfast and talk it out."

"Fine. Tell him I'm in if he'll have me. I suck at cards, but I'm up for anything that might help me get from point A to point B."

Happy smiled. "Attagirl, Miles. Nothing ventured...you know. Keeper's a good guy; I've met him."

I had one more question. "Hey, Coach. Why Keeper? You said it was on his cut, so it must be his club nickname; but what kind of call sign is Keeper?"

Coach stood and gathered his things to leave. "The Travelers—that's Keeper's club—they're a clean, upstanding bunch, **99 percenters**. Nothing shady or illegal, and most of them are in caretaking professions, like healthcare and law enforcement. A couple of the doctors Bibi knows are Travelers. Axel's role in the club is similar to the one he has at work, and he considers his work his life's calling. He's the gatekeeper, finding people who are hurting and connecting them with those who help and heal."

He opened the door to let himself out, and the noise in the hall let the real world leak back in. "I've known Keeper a long time, though, and I think there's a different reason." He smiled and gave me a little taste of the hope I'd been missing all week. "I think he's the keeper of the secrets—and I also think he has a lot of the answers."

Chapter ELEVEN

"We Are Family"

Oliver

L ife was pretty damned sweet right now, I thought with a smile. It required a nigh Herculean effort on the part of Jacob and myself, but we'd managed to gather a little remnant of our happy family in one city, at least for a while. It happened to be hotter than the surface of the sun, and I'd learned my British constitution heartily disapproved of daily temperatures over a hundred degrees. Small price to pay for pulling off this minor miracle, however.

My earliest memories involved not only my mum and dad but Jacob. He and I were partners in crime from the time we learned to toddle about, two little boys born four days apart to sisters who were best friends. They were as close as Jacob and I came to be and faced the same obstacle we eventually did. They were best friends separated by an ocean. Our fathers met because of their status as brothers-in-law but formed a lasting bond of friendship that eventually resulted in a business partnership. They owned a collection of boutique-quality hotels scattered throughout the English countryside and Wales. The reputation of the lodging was stellar, and it became a desirable destination among the moneyed set. Business flourished and grew to include a burgeoning assortment of unique luxury properties in Bucks County, Pennsylvania, and along the Maine shore from York to Yarmouth.

While building the family business, Benjamin and Annalise Travis added to their family as well, although I was too young to understand the details at the time, of course. They'd longed for another child but found themselves unable to conceive a second. Undeterred, they pursued adoption. After many months of anxious waiting, they welcomed two-year-old Vivianne Serafina Travis, namesake of her aunt Sera, my mother. She was the star of the show from the minute she arrived; there was simply no word to describe the pint-sized toddler but riveting. Her eyes were piercing and emerald green, her skin milky despite Asian ethnicity, and her silky hair as black as night.

She was a hellcat; Jacob and I were smitten. She was like the cartoon Tasmanian Devil, a whirling dervish of endless mischief and energy. Annalise and Benji were dismayed to learn she could climb like a monkey, and they were forced to booby-trap her nursery with a device that alarmed when she sneaked out of the room at night. That measure was employed after Benji discovered her on top of the cooker in the kitchen at midnight. She learned to climb trees, hit a baseball, and ride a two-wheeled bicycle before we started school and was a frequent flier in the local emergency room as a result of her adventurous spirit. The three of us were only two years apart and completely inseparable. The problem was the aforementioned ocean. I lived with my mum and dad in Oxfordshire while Jake and Vivvie grew up in the verdant hills of rural Connecticut. We were fortunate, though; our families were close and well-off. Their priority was family; and that meant Jacob, Vivianne, and I were British Airways

Executive Club members before we started kindergarten.

We traded off summers and school holiday weeks at one another's homes throughout childhood, constantly bargaining with our parents for more time together. The teenage years were busy ones, however, and crowded with sports and social obligations; the higher educational period even more so. We waited impatiently for the cousin visits, but time was increasingly difficult to carve out. After graduation came new careers—the military for Jacob and me, nursing for Vivvie. We bemoaned the inability to spend more time together, but our status as young professionals made time off scarce. We agreed to be patient and take advantage when the occasion presented itself to live closer to one another.

Jacob and I cooked up the plan to co-locate our threesome after I'd begun my service to the Royal Air Force and Jake was at his first operational assignment, a **remote** in Korea. Viv had grown restless in her job after seven years as an RN and was ripe for a change of venue. Many phone calls and emails ensued as we all investigated the possibilities. An RAF exchange tour with the U.S. Air Force became available at Davis-Monthan AFB in Tucson, Arizona, the schoolhouse for the A-10, and it appeared our plan finally had legs.

I was the last of the trio to arrive in Tucson. I relocated in the spring and was whisked away to training without delay, so it was midsummer before I finally returned to settle in Tucson. Jacob had sussed a superior home west of the city for me to let—a large, classically styled southwestern house built around an expansive pool. It would have been far too expensive, save the advantageous exchange rate—and the fact he'd decided we should live together. When his lease was up in early October, he would move in, and we'd kit out our hacienda to be the premier bachelor sanctuary in the city. Vivvie declined our offer to take the third of five bedrooms, citing our status as "icky boys," and continued remodeling her home near the hospital. She'd opted to purchase rather than let, but Jacob informed me it had more to do with her close female friendships than with the two of us.

The remainder of the summer passed without an opportunity for me to attend one of the infamous Scorpion squadron parties, but today all that changed. It had been a season of tumult and tragedy for Jake and his friends, culminating in a terrible midair collision of two of their jets near Ajo only about a month before. Everyone was grateful that both pilots survived and would, in fact, be in attendance at today's monthly party. It was also rumored that the full complement of Vivvie's friends, all nurses in the emergency department where she worked, would be there. Jacob saw this as a prime dating pool and was urging me to go for a dip.

I wasn't at all sure that was a good idea. I enjoyed companionship of the female persuasion but never felt the passion some men displayed for "the hunt." Never had a few dates grown into something I felt a singular urge to pursue. It might not be the pinnacle of judgment to set about dating Vivianne's friends when I felt little drive. I enjoyed lavishing time and affection on those close to me—Mum and Dad, of course, Vivianne and Jacob and Aunt Anna and Uncle Benji. At no time did any of the ladies I'd dated casually spark something inside that tempted me to invite them into our little circle. The family teased me mercilessly about my alleged "playboy ways," but the opposite was true. I dated only occasionally, preferring the companionship of my mates and family. That said, there were times there was no substitute for the company of a soft, sweet-smelling woman.

I parked my Range Rover at the park's edge next to a behemoth pickup truck—what was the Yank obsession with those things?—and grabbed the bouquet I'd brought for Viv. Beginning the trek across the park, I noticed an attractive couple with two large coolers in tow as well as a terribly grumpy bulldog and a smashing long-haired cat. The pussy was not permitted to walk but was instead carried, first by the lovely blond woman and then by her much-taller companion. I wondered if they were a part of the squadron festivities.

From well across the green expanse of lawn, various members of the Scorpion collective lounged in the late-day sun, wilting in the intolerable heat. A homemade banner hanging in the tree notified the public this was the "Scorpions' End-of-Summer Party," but I failed to note any evidence of summer's demise. I briefly pondered the possibility of a large-scale ice maker for the swimming pool at my new home. Sporting equipment, baseball bats, and mitts—as well as American and English footballs—lay abandoned on the ground, and the gaggle sucked down gassy, overly cooled American beer to steel themselves against the onslaught of heat.

As I approached, I heard a huge man with his leg in a cast give voice to my thoughts: "Y'all, this heat is gonna fuckin' kill me, I swear. I'm from the South, but this is just bullshit." The dialect was different, but the sentiment was mine exactly. Vivianne's screech pierced the air a split second before she hit me at full speed like a featherweight linebacker from my blind side. Her arms and legs wrapped around me like an octopus, and I staggered to regain my balance as she covered my face with enthusiastic kisses.

"Missed you, cousin of mine…I've hardly seen you since you got back from training. That's a poor fucking effort after all the trouble you went to moving here." She climbed down and surveyed the slightly crushed bouquet of roses and daisies, batting her big, green eyes. "Those for me?"

"Vivianne. The mouth on you, love. Of course, they're for you." I held them out, plucking off one destroyed rosebud. "You know you're my only girl."

She grinned and took the flowers. "Why don't we see if we can't do something to remedy that, Oliver?" She cut her eyes to indicate the assortment of ladies scattered under one of the larger trees, variously fanning and slathering themselves with sunscreen. It was remarkable, I mused, this ability of women to look beautiful despite the heat.

I spotted Jacob before he saw me, so I called out to him. "So, then, any left for your cousin from across the pond, Jacob?"

He turned his head, mouth still full of whatever he'd been eating, and waved enthusiastically.

Jacob jogged over, pulling me in for a hug. "Glad you could make it, man. You're going to fit in like…well, like a Brit at an American picnic. I'm glad the Scorpions finally get to meet you." Just as he finished speaking, the handsome couple I'd noticed before approached. Vivvie grabbed my hand and led me toward them, waving and smiling.

"You guys, I want you to meet my cousin, Oliver."

As the man approached, he shook my extended hand with a friendly smile. "Is this Oliver, as in the range controller?"

He knew me? I returned the smile. "The same, mate. Who do I have the pleasure…"

Jacob laughed heartily. "Oliver, meet our commander, Nathan 'Happy' Morgan. You've actually met him once before when you busted his chops on the range at my request."

Well, now, this was just embarrassing. I was complicit in Jacob's foolishness at the expense of his commander. I felt a bit of flush creeping. "My apologies, sir. Must've thought me mad as a bag of ferrets, calling you five at three."

Nathan laughed and motioned to a chair between his and Bashful's. "The thought crossed my mind, but I understand, what with being the FNG and all. Do you enjoy American barbecue, Oliver?"

I tucked into the big plate of barbecue, beans, and pasta salad, washing away some of the heat with a cold beer. Vivianne and Jacob were my favorite variety of company, and we talked over one another, laughing and joking. A good-looking bloke who seemed to have an affinity for my cousin was introduced as Walker Jackson, call sign "Hung." It was difficult to get a bead on the dynamic between the two of them. There was an obvious attraction there, but something else was afoot. I decided not to explore further, for now. Anyone interested in Vivianne would receive a thorough vetting from me—and from Jacob, I was sure.

I surveyed the assemblage. They ate and chatted happily along, seemingly comfortable in the company of one another. Several of Viv's friends sat slightly to one side, under the biggest shade tree, but they were anything but removed from the group at large. Several of the men and women from the squadron wandered over, laughing and talking with them as well. There was nothing to indicate the big man I'd overheard talking earlier was the primary casualty of the aircraft accident last month, save the extensive cast contraption on his leg. People drifted in and out of his orbit, chatting with him and exchanging pleasantries. I knew few details, only what Jacob had shared. But something nearby caught my eye, eclipsing my interest in the personal dynamics at play. A beautiful woman sat next to the injured man, and everything about her called to me.

The petite redhead sparkled and crackled, demanding my attention, despite her position, tucked away at the group's edge. She sipped a canned soda and smiled at the antics of the big guy and his companions. I tried to play it cool, but there was no looking away. I considered their body language, wondering if they were a couple, but her regard for him didn't seem to bend that direction. As if to give a timely answer to my unspoken question, a stunningly beautiful woman with an ebony complexion and big brown eyes approached from behind and leaned between them, nuzzling the man's cheek and brushing a kiss there. She also spoke briefly to the redhead before handing a heaping plate of barbecue to the man.

All the partygoers and their activity faded as I studied her. Riveting blue eyes flitted around her circle, warm and full of fun, and she reached up occasionally to brush away wild, ruddy curls the breeze blew into her face. But something in her manner betrayed restlessness. Her hands twisted nervously in her lap from time to time, and a nearly full plate of delicious food sat, untouched, on the ground nearby. Three, then four times, her gaze wandered away from the group, and she stared into the distance, evidently deep in thought. As she refocused the fourth time, her eyes caught and held mine. I felt as if I'd grabbed a live wire with both hands and held tight as it whipped and pummeled me helplessly about.

She was stunning. Sweet and a little mysterious. She gazed right at me for a second, then two. She looked away and the beautiful blue eyes clouded again.

Jacob's hand rested on my shoulder. "Whatcha lookin' at, cousin?" His eyes followed mine to where they rested on the bewitching redhead. "Ah. That's Miles, Ollie; she's a looker, right? She's a good friend of Deliverance's." He indicated the injured man with an outstretched hand. "This whole ordeal has been pretty tough on her." He looked away for a second, his features revealing regret. "Miles has always been a bit of a wild child, but this may be what tames her." He sighed and looked back at me. "I hope it just takes the edge off without breaking her. She's one of a kind."

She noticed us talking and quickly looked away. Jacob clapped me on the back, oblivious to what was transpiring between the redhead and myself. "That woman's a true work in progress. Best keep your distance—at least for now."

I didn't mention it to Jacob, of course, but I was intrigued. And I had no intention of keeping my distance.

Chapter TWELVE

"Force of Nature"

Miles

"**I**'m meeting someone." I scanned the crowded dining room of the Denny's while I spoke to the young hostess with her bouncy ponytail and overdone blue eye shadow. Truth be told, any blue eye shadow was too much at 0600. I was no beauty expert, but even I knew that. Keeper phoned last night before Coach could even call me back with his answer. He was concerned that an early morning meeting would be inconvenient, but that wasn't the case. When Coach and I spoke later, he told me to expect regular work in the squadron for the time being, from 0700 until 1630 or so. It was a relief I'd be able to work at the squadron, even if I was grounded for the time being. I'd texted Happy requesting an hour of leniency for breakfast with Keeper and offering to work through lunch if he needed me. My primary responsibilities would probably be answering the phone and handling various administrative tasks; I hoped to use what would ordinarily be tedious work to show Happy how much I appreciated his offer of a second chance.

Now I searched the room for someone matching the description of one Axel Bond. The story Coach told was vivid, and I believed I had a full-color image of who I was looking for. Coach laughed when I asked how I'd find the man I'd never met, and now I knew why.

A tall, bulky man stood in front of a booth in the rear of the room, one colorfully tattooed arm waving at me. His beard was at least as magnificent as Coach had described, reaching the top of a slightly rounded belly and white as snow. I'd never seen its rival—the beard, not the belly. There was no indication of his motorcycling affiliation, I noted. He was dressed as many middle-aged Tucson residents were—well-worn jeans, a white tee shirt, and a long, soft suede vest. Despite the relatively subdued appearance, he wouldn't have disappeared into any crowd. First, of course, there was the beard, but even more notable was the booming belly laugh that broke from him as I approached. He'd engaged the young couple in the next booth in a short conversation that was interrupted by his warm laughter. They had nothing in common on the surface of it, but they were so deep in conversation I realized they must have been friends.

As I approached, I was surprised to hear him bid goodbye to the couple in the booth. "My dining companion has arrived, so I'll wish you both a good day. It was awful nice to meet the both of you. My Emmay says it's always a gift to meet a new friend." Then he turned and held his big arms open as if we'd known one another forever, sending me an engaging smile, and directed the booming voice my direction. "Well, you must be Miles, friend. I didn't think you'd be too hard to spot; there still aren't too many beautiful gingers who are pilots." His eyes twinkled, and the thought briefly crossed my mind that he must be tapped every year to play Santa. He'd make one hell of a great St. Nick in the right getup. He stepped toward me. "But I did worry about you finding a wallflower like little ol' me." The laughter burst forth again, and he held out his hand, motioning me into the booth.

I relaxed, feeling immediately at ease, and it was impossible to pinpoint why. In the middle of a circumstance worse than any since my mama died, I sensed he was trustworthy. For one thing, it was unusual for a complete stranger to drop everything and meet someone with an offer of help. Coach's long friendship would obviously have an impact, but this man didn't know me or owe me anything. I recalled what Coach said about Keeper's and Emmay's words at their initial meeting, "…being present in the lives of others. There's nothing more important we can do than help other souls on the journey."

The waitress came by to pour coffee and found herself engaged in lively conversation; Keeper complimented her smile, then thanked her once we'd ordered breakfast. He asked after my physical health, and I updated him on the basics, at once grateful and guilty that my report was so much better than Deliverance's. I wondered if all my friends and all of the squadron saw inequity in the way the accident had affected Davis and me. Surely they knew, as I so clearly did, that I deserved to be the one suffering both physically and mentally. Coach must have filled Keeper in on the details of my circumstance, at least partially. He certainly had the knowledge and background to understand what the Scorpions had on their plate with me. I wondered if there would be the usual awkward pauses and hesitation as Keeper and I danced around the elephant in the room.

I needn't have worried.

Keeper took a sip of his coffee after doctoring it thoroughly with cream and sugar, then sat back and shot me another relaxed smile. "Miles, are you familiar with Edna St. Vincent Millay?" Wasting no time, he answered his own question. "American poet, playwright, Pulitzer Prize winner. My favorite quote of hers is something to the effect of, 'It's not that life is one damn thing after another; it's the same damn thing over and over.' That's a loose translation, but I've found it to be very true. Things in your life, as I understand it from Chuck, have come to a zenith of sorts. I sense you're finding yourself in need of some clarification."

Fucking pegged that.

I tried not to stare mutely; there had been far too much of that recently. "Yes, Mr. Bond, I'd say you summed up my situation pretty much perfectly, all before I told you a thing."

He reached one over-sized hand across the table and patted mine. "I'm real glad to hear that, Miles, but you're gonna have to call me Keeper. I'd use that tired old saw about Mr. Bond being my father, but there's no proof of who my father was, so I can't employ that particular saying." He grinned again. "Let's agree, despite the situation, to refuse to feel uncomfortable. I want you to be at ease, and that's one of the reasons I wanted to meet before I invited you to the group. I hope you'll join The Tuesday Game after I tell you a bit about what it is and the purpose, as I see it."

I nodded, leaning in. "I know we're all supposed to be aware of what drives us, but I've come to a disappointing realization over the past few days. I haven't paid much attention to cause and effect, as far as my motivations and where they came from." I felt a little sick admitting it. "It's only now, when my actions have cost my friends—one of them in particular—so much, that I'm trying to study why I do what I do. But I'm a pilot, not a psychologist. Or a therapist. And I don't know if there's anything I can do to change things for the better." I stopped, focusing on his coffee cup. He didn't speak, giving me space to collect my thoughts.

"I mean…what if there's nothing I can do? I guess I'm afraid it's too late to change." The idea made my throat ache as tears welled; I was getting tired as shit of dealing with these unanticipated emotions.

Keeper's rumbly laugh rang out as our breakfast arrived. "Too late? No. No…I don't think so, my friend." The laughter stopped, and he smiled more gently, reaching again across the table to pat my hand. "How old are you, Miles? Twenty-four? Twenty-five?"

I stared at the table. "Twenty-four. I know it sounds stupid to say it's too late to change. I know it's never too late, but that's all academic, isn't it? It feels hopeless because I don't know how to take the first step. Don't even know which direction to move."

We sat quietly for a moment sipping coffee, and I took another minute to collect myself before speaking again. "So, what's The Tuesday Game? Where did this all come from?"

"Yes, okay." He nodded and smiled as if remembering. "It was pretty organic, and if I'm truthful, I didn't even see what it was until the train was out of the station. My practice was pretty new back then, but I got busy fast. I had a lot of friends on the Air Force base because of Emmay. And you already know she invites near-perfect strangers to our house; it's always been that way, and we both enjoy having people around. So as not to blur professional boundaries, I drew the line at clients who were currently receiving counseling services. But Emmay somehow managed to stay in touch with folks as they moved on from the practice. There were never enough nights of the week; so we started having groups of people show up on the same night, and sometimes we'd play cards. The talking happened without any encouragement from me, but I think people sense when they're in a safe place—where they can be themselves. We've had every issue imaginable trotted out in our family room."

"But I have to ask—why Uno?"

He laughed. "That would be Lillian. She was a friend of Emmay's from work who was terrified of flying. Her daughter had moved to Australia with her new husband a few months before, and the word came back they were expecting. Lillian had a kitty cat over lunch with Emmay one day; she was hell-bent to see her girl and that new baby but found herself on the very horns of a dilemma. She wound up at one of the first few Tuesday

Games, and I'd had a mind to introduce something to depressurize the evenings—to redirect things. Diversion is generally really effective, so I thought of cards. We went through about every card game I could come up with—bridge, hearts, spades, poker, war, rummy—the woman couldn't even play crazy eights. We finally hit on Uno and found an old deck in the drawer of the coffee table; it's easy enough to play without too much thought. But it still serves the purpose."

"I have to say, I've never heard of anything like it before, and I don't think I've played Uno since I was a kid. I appreciate the invite. I'm in unfamiliar territory, so any help is welcome. Even if it takes the form of a card game."

He busied himself tucking into the enormous breakfast. "Eat up, girl. Big day today; you've got to go to work. And I have a tee time. Next week, you're coming to your first Tuesday Game, and we're gonna get this show on the road. The first step is the hardest one." He shoveled a huge portion of hash browns into his mouth.

"Yeah, stepping into your house for the first time will be on my mind all week. It's a big leap for me."

He'd barely finished the bite in his mouth before the signature laugh burst forth. "Oh no, the first game isn't the leap of faith, Miles. Meeting me this morning was."

Chapter THIRTEEN

"Smooth Criminal"

Oliver

One day each week, I attacked paperwork in my tiny office on the base in town. It was a welcome change from solitary days spent in the range tower, although the work suited my personality quite well. Still, I relished the busyness of the base as a contrast to the regular routine; Jacob and I also made a habit of meeting for lunch when our schedules permitted. Usually, I could manage to stave off scurvy by squeezing in a **commissary** run to pick up fresh fruits and vegetables, a valuable augmentation to my less-than-stellar bachelor diet. There wouldn't be time for that today as I had a terrific stack of paper, mail, and emails to attend. I'd have no patience for shopping by day's end, I was sure. The most expedient solution I could muster to the dinner predicament was canned soup. Unappealing, but it would do in a pinch.

Easing the Range Rover into the parking lot of the Kwik Shopper on Golf Links Road, I slowed, carefully avoiding potholes big enough to swallow a horse. I berated myself for allowing the rations at home to sink to this level. The base commissary would be a superior solution, both in price and selection, but an unacceptable amount of time would be wasted in the queue. The **OAPs** favored payday for their monthly shopping; this meant crowds of elderly ladies socializing at the deli counter and clucking at me for proceeding the wrong direction in the aisle. Who'd ever heard of a market with one-way shopping? Only in the Yank Air Force, I thought with a smile. The entire prospect was distasteful, so I would content myself with whatever the Kwik Shopper had on offer.

Piss poor planning and only myself to blame.

I opened the door, frowning. Many of the small food markets in the States were clean and well lit, but this one didn't fit that description. The door glass had been partially shattered and then reinforced with duct tape, and it listed precariously to one side when opened. A middle-aged woman behind the register, curiously attired in pajama pants and flip-flops, spared me a brief glance before returning rapt attention to the scandal sheet she was reading. Unsurprisingly, I was her only customer; I made a mental note to assure today was my first *and* final visit to the Kwik Shopper.

I walked the aisles, scanning two of the long shelves for soup, but turned up only snack chips, biscuits, and a plethora of candy bars. Sighing, I rounded the final corner and moved toward the refrigerated cabinet in the rear of the dreary establishment. Today was off to a very poor start indeed.

But I wasn't the sole customer. Partially obscured by a truly colossal stack of soft-drink boxes, a petite redhead studied the contents of the cooler filled with energy drinks. Her hair was burnished copper, coiled into a big knot just above her neck, and I surmised there must be quite a bit of it, judging by the size of the chignon. Her elegant neck comprised almost all the milky skin her attire revealed, a true pity. She wore a flight suit, a notoriously shapeless garment that had the singular distinction of showcasing the bottom of its wearer surprisingly well. Her bottom was quite obviously a work of art, even covered in Nomex. I wanted to see the face that went with the hair, translucent skin, and luscious curves; so I wandered closer to the case, carefully maintaining a nonchalant air.

Her movements telegraphed she'd registered my presence, but she didn't verbally acknowledge me. I pretended to examine the contents of the drink case, but curiosity won out in a moment of weakness, and I looked.

It was the woman from the picnic.

There was no mistaking the bright blue eyes moving to meet mine or the prompt recognition passing over her face. We both started to speak at once.

"I believe we…"

"Weren't you at the…"

We both stopped, laughing, and I extended my hand. "Oliver Bloodworth, at your service." I offered what I hoped was a relaxed, charming smile. She was quite stunning. She placed her small hand in mine without squeezing or pumping it industriously; it seemed as if we were holding hands rather than enduring an introduction ritual in the most pedestrian of places. My heart instantly picked up the pace, interested.

"Hello, Oliver. I saw you at the picnic; I'm Miles, or rather Charlotte Christman. I heard Deliverance say you're a relative of Vivvie's—and Bash's."

I gently squeezed the hand I still held before releasing it and laughed. "You'd think all three of us blooming mad for the greeting Vivianne gave me otherwise, now wouldn't you? Vivvie and Jacob are my cousins and a large part of the reason I'm here in the States." I indicated the RAF uniform I wore.

Charlotte abandoned her search in the drink case, allowing the door to close. "Your uniform is similar to our **blues**, but I can see the differences now that we're up close."

She gestured between the two of us, accidentally brushing my chest as she did, and a slight blush bloomed on her pretty cheeks. She wore no makeup that I could discern, but that full, pink mouth didn't require embellishment. And her eyes...they were as bright as the Caribbean Sea on a sunny day. I tried not to gaze at her like a lover might; it would surely make her uncomfortable and turn her into a possible flight risk. I needed to keep her engaged until I could find a suitable way to ask about ringing her up.

"I don't at all mind the service dress, but I understand most pilots despise wearing them."

She favored me with a dazzling smile. "It's punishment, sometimes almost literally." The smile faded at once, and she shook her head a bit ruefully, glancing at her feet. "But the biggest reason is the contrast to the comfort of the bag." She indicated her flight suit. "Once you've washed one several times, it feels almost like pajamas."

Her cheeks pinkened charmingly once again, likely from nothing more than the roundabout mention of bedclothing. Surely she wasn't that shy? I hurried along in case she was flustered.

"So then, Charlotte. What brings you to this fine establishment so early in the morning? I hope you didn't have designs on finding something fresh or delicious for breakfast. After examining the options, I believe they're out of both. Perhaps permanently."

"No, no...I was debating an energy drink or bar for a pick-me-up later on, but I'm afraid my baser nature may win out." She folded her arms and looked past me toward the bank of drink machines on the outer wall. "I'm a sucker for a good slushie, preferably lime or raspberry." She shrugged. "But then, aren't we all?"

"Keep-fit enthusiast, eh?" I grinned. "What's not to love? What they lack in flavor they make up for in sugar and artificial coloring."

She rewarded me with a brief eye-roll and mock disapproval. "Blasphemy. I don't like what I'm hearing, Oliver. You have no grasp on the great pleasures available at the Kwik Shopper. I'd almost forgotten how a slushie can brighten the prospect of a long workday, but speaking to you this morning has brought me some clarity. I guess I should thank you for that." She stepped across the aisle to the machine, selected a cup and domed lid, and filled it with an icy concoction in an otherworldly shade of blue. She waved the cup in my direction.

"And what flavor might that be, Charlotte? Food is simply not blue, you know."

"Raspberry, of course." She almost smiled at my commentary. "Everyone knows raspberry is blue. It would be red, but there's already enough confusion with cherry and strawberry; raspberry had the good sense not to pile on and make the problem worse. Ergo: beautiful, pool-water blue. And you don't know what you're missing, Oliver Bloodworth." And with that, she turned on her heel and strode toward the front of the store.

The bell sounded, indicating the door had opened, so I stole a quick glance to reassure myself she hadn't managed to pay and leave so quickly. In fact, a third hapless shopper had joined Charlotte and me, so I had only a few seconds to choose a subpar food item and follow her to acquire her number. I studied the drink case briefly, selected a couple of the energy drinks she'd rejected, and decided to solve my dinner issue in some other way. The Kwik Shopper did not hold the answer to my quandary. Or perhaps any answers at all. I turned toward the front of the store, then stopped abruptly, quietly backing myself against a nearby shelf.

The door had evidently opened moments before to admit

a middle-aged man who now stood at the register. He was of medium height, I guessed about five foot nine, almost skeletally thin, and had greasy, dark hair curling past his collar to shoulder length. Most importantly, he'd trained a handgun on the register attendant who had finally found something more intriguing than the tabloid to occupy her attention.

The attendant held her hands in the air, crying loudly and babbling in response to the burglar's demands. Their conversation was garbled, and I couldn't make out what was said from the rear of the store. A quick study of the small space revealed no obvious mirrors that would betray my presence to the burglar, but I noted there were cameras that recorded what was happening. The man's tone was panicked and becoming more so as he yelled at the woman, and his hands shook uncontrollably when he brandished the weapon. Charlotte stood a few feet behind him, as still as if frozen, holding her drink slightly aloft. She silently watched every move he made but didn't flinch or appear at all frightened, even when the man waved his weapon her direction. The blue eyes, so full of laughter moments ago, were now sharp and attentive, analyzing him when his attention focused on the cashier.

As quietly as I was able, I rounded the endcap of the aisle and crouched, moving toward the front of the store. Creeping slowly along, I also palmed my mobile and switched it to mute. Dialing 911, I set it carefully on the top shelf next to me. I waited until the thief's voice indicated his back was toward me, then peered out from behind the crowded shelving.

He was screaming at Charlotte now, quaking and irrational, but her face remained impassive. She didn't respond and held her hands partially aloft, that distasteful drink still in her grasp. She obviously knew I was there but gave no indication to the burglar; and the register attendant seemed, mercifully, to have forgotten about me. She was terribly distraught, and I thought it fortunate she hadn't noticed I was hiding behind the shelf. She would surely panic and scream, thereby wasting my singular advantage—surprise. I was hopeful the open line to the authorities would connect, and whatever information they could make out would aid them in getting to us more promptly. Studying the scene for a short couple of seconds, I formulated a rudimentary plan, hardly foolproof but better than nothing. Glancing out again, I made several small gestures to indicate what I intended to do, hoping Charlotte could see. Mum had insisted on tae kwon do when I was a boy. If it came in handy today, that would be a mercy indeed. Years had passed since I'd been a regular practitioner, but I stayed fit; perhaps it would be enough with this agitated and obviously unbalanced man.

As he continued his rant, still directed at Charlotte, I took two, then three silent steps into the open. With absolutely no warning, Charlotte's relative calm facade crumbled. She was instantly undone, consumed with hacking, choking sobs. The loud, unexpected racket elicited the desired effect, startling the thief. He straightened, confused and shocked. The hand holding his weapon sagged almost imperceptibly, but it was enough. Stepping close, she flicked her wrist hard with no hesitation, tossing the entire slushie forcefully into his face. He spit and choked, enraged, but it was no use; she'd created the ideal opening. I took a couple of big steps forward and brought my knee up. Visualizing the grace and force of my sensei

all those years ago, I rotated on my heel almost 180 degrees and turned the shin over, aligning it parallel with the ground as nearly as I was able. Using the length of my body as a counterbalance and aiming beyond his body, I kicked with all my might. The lower part of my shin contacted the side of his head near the ear with a mighty *thwack*, and he fell to one knee, groaning and dropping the gun. He scrabbled in slow motion, reaching, but Charlotte was lightning-fast and plucked it neatly from the puddle of bright blue slushie, training it on him.

Her voice was cold. "Don't move, motherfucker." She turned her gaze back to me, those delightful eyes dancing once again. "Nice move, Chuck Norris."

I'd regained my balance by now and took a step forward, pushing the would-be thief the rest of the way to the ground and kneeling with my weight on his back. I pulled his hands behind him, unsure of the next proper move in the absence of handcuffs like the police had on television. The attendant behind the counter was frantically dialing her mobile but took a break to toss me a couple of large plastic zip ties. I trussed his wrists behind his back and examined my work before turning my attention to the register attendant.

"Are you alright, miss?" She appeared shaken but unharmed, ignoring me and swearing under her breath.

The man struggled beneath me as the puddle reached his face, sputtering and spitting out the raspberry drink, which I guessed couldn't have tasted any worse for its trip across the filthy vinyl floor, but Charlotte pulled a pouty lip. "Awww. My delicious slushie...another tragic victim of crime."

The police arrived in moments, ably taking control of the scene and relieving Charlotte of the gun she still held. Our statements were taken expeditiously, and the thwarted burglar, still dripping, was loaded into the cruiser. As the last officer cleared out, the cashier looked up at us, apathy fully restored, and offered, "You can take the drinks for free. No snacks." She searched the floor and retrieved the tabloid rag she'd dropped, settling back into her seat.

I took a new cup from the stack and filled it with the vile blue slushie, then handed it to Charlotte. "And to think, I thought blue was a color alone, not a flavor as well." She accepted the cup with a smile and sipped from the long straw.

I opened the door for her as we shared a laugh. I walked her to her car, and she leaned against the fender, polishing the shiny navy blue paint with the sleeve of her flight suit. We were both quiet for a minute; the adrenaline fizzing through my blood had quieted while the police did their work.

"I have to be honest, Charlotte." My eyes met her fathomless azure ones, and the noise of the nearby motorway faded into the distance. "I was searching for a way to ask you to dinner the moment we met in the back of that store. Then when you brushed me off for that appalling drink..." She looked down to her boot-shod feet, shaking her head and laughing under her breath. "I realized I needed something extraordinary to give me an opening."

She raised her head again, still smiling. "Give me your phone, Oliver." When I wordlessly handed it to her, she tapped her number into it. "I think we can consider the first date a success. Why don't you give me a call sometime so we can see about making the second one a little more tedious?"

Chapter FOURTEEN

"Poker Face"

Miles

I'd parked the Mustang in front of the little adobe house off East Catalina at least ten minutes ago. I'd gotten out of the car, locked it, walked around it and then a little way up the street where I'd stared into the empty darkness for a few minutes. Then back to the car, which I unlocked. And started. I sat, methodically contemplating my options again. Deciding there were none, I got out yet again.

I locked the car, then unlocked it and retrieved the items I'd been instructed to bring. I hadn't thought to ask about what to wear, but Keeper didn't seem the type to stand on ceremony. Hopefully, my everyday uniform of jeans, a tee, and Chucks would be appropriate. I'd even selected my sixties vintage All Star Original Blue Trainers for a rare spin out of the house. I bought them on eBay several years ago, and they were a real find and one of the most prized pairs in my extensive collection. Of course, that wouldn't matter to the card players. They didn't know me, and I didn't know them. When I'd accepted Coach's invitation to meet Keeper, I never thought my nerves would be so frayed. I lectured myself on the short trip to the front door.

You're just visiting a damn card game, Miles. What could possibly go wrong? Stop being a little bitch and eat the fucking elephant.

Approaching, I could hear discussion and laughter in the house and quickly swallowed back a big case of nerves and nausea. Not allowing myself to hesitate, I rapped on the door right away. Immediately, there was a tap of heels on a tile floor and a shriek. "No, I've got it, Axel. I've got it." The door was flung open, revealing a tiny middle-aged lady with a head full of wild brunette curls that looked as if they'd never done her bidding. Large brown eyes were nearly hidden with enormous horn-rimmed glasses, and her bright pink lipstick was everywhere but on her lips. She beamed at me and grabbed my hand, shaking it warmly. "I'm Emmay. Now you say it like the two initials—M.A. My mother named me Mary Adrianna for the Blessed Virgin and my paternal great-grandmother, Adrianna, but it's too much, right?"

I'd never heard anyone rattle off so many words at once. *So many.* She was firing faster than the GAU-8 on a Warthog. She continued before I could answer her rhetorical question.

"And you must be Miles; you're just lovely. Simply lovely. Axel and I are so happy you've chosen to join us. So happy, Miles, truly."

I was taken aback by the effervescent welcome, although I didn't know why. I'd met Keeper; why would I suppose Emmay would fail to amaze?

I thrust a plastic Safeway sack awkwardly into the space between us. "Keeper said I should bring dip so I brought dip here it is." I spoke all of it like it was one sentence, as if I'd forgotten how to be part of polite society.

Emmay smiled warmly at me, then peered into the bag. "Wow, Miles, that's just so…what is it? My niece told me…"She frowned, thinking, then brightened."It's the bomb dot com;

everyone loves French onion dip. Now you come on in and meet everybody."

She clasped my hand and pulled me through the door. Keeper was standing in the living room with a couple of guests, but he stepped forward to shake my hand. "I see you've met Emmay." He smiled warmly and gestured to the room at large. "Everybody meet Miles; she's a friend of Chuck and Bibi's." He pulled me a little closer, resting a hand on my shoulder in a friendly gesture that unspooled some of my anxiety. "Miles, I'd like you to meet Meg. This is Harry and his partner, Glen; that's Covington, and Lori Beth's in the kitchen."

A disembodied voice called from the direction of what I assumed was the kitchen. "Hi there, Miles. I'm slaving over dip, but I'll be right in."

Meg was a pretty girl in her late twenties, with big eyes and an easy smile; she addressed the room. "Where's Sue? We did a spin class on Thursday, and she said she'd be here."

Lori Beth responded from stage left. "She's coming; she's gonna be late because—you guys, get this—Mommy Dearest showed at her apartment this morning. Completely unannounced. Again."

A loud groan went up from the entire room, and then Emmay spoke. "That…lady needs to stay in Alabama; another unexpected visit from her is the last thing Sue needs right now. I think she's dealt with that woman enough."

At that moment, Lori Beth emerged from the kitchen and grinned at everyone while holding a platter aloft. "Ladies and gentlemen, dip is served." She made a show of presenting the dish for everyone's inspection, and I realized I'd seriously underestimated the appetizer game at this gathering. The plate held some variety of a cheese ball nested in a presentation of various crackers and a few vegetables. It was oblong and shaped like a football, covered in dozens of tiny, sliced pepperonis, all perfectly layered. The laces on the football were formed out of little pieces of string cheese, and a plastic goalpost was set up at the end of the platter.

Keeper reached out, snagging a cracker, and scooped a generous bite from the edge, sampling the perfect presentation. He popped it into his mouth, smiling at Lori Beth. "That's some good stuff, LB, but let me ask you a question." He grabbed an additional bite, apparently savoring the flavor before he addressed her again. "It's delicious, but didn't we just have a conversation a couple of weeks back about your ability to conquer that pesky perfectionist streak? Are we wading into quicksand here?"

Lori Beth laughed and sat the tray on the coffee table. "Didn't you note my lack of concern when you took the first bite of my perfect little football, Keeper? That should tell you what you need to know; I'm still a striver in the culinary department, but I'm winning the battle on perfectionism." She smiled and grabbed a big corn chip from the platter. "See? I'll even help destroy it myself." She dug deep, snagging a couple of pepperonis in the process and wolfed it down before grabbing the plate. "Come on, let's get this show on the road. Sue will be along after a while, and we can catch up on her mommy issues." She found a seat on the long, overstuffed sofa and patted the seat next to her. "Sit with me, Miles; I'll show you the deep mysteries of Uno."

She grabbed the double deck of Uno cards and began shuffling like a Vegas pro; the remaining members of the group filed into the kitchen and emerged with trays of artfully arranged veggies, several dips, and enough appetizers to feed twice our number. I turned to Lori Beth. "Should I…"

Emmay brought up the rear of the group, emerging from the kitchen with a pretty azure pottery bowl and plate. "I plated your chips and dip, Miles, hope you don't mind." It looked a helluva lot better on her pottery than in the Safeway bag, and I made a note to check with Bibi about how to up my culinary game for Tuesdays. "Umm, thanks, Emmay. I didn't know about…"

Didn't know what, Miles? How to bring a nice plate of food when strangers invite you over?

Glen reached for the plate just as Emmay set it on the coffee table and popped two of the chips in his mouth, groaning with pleasure. "Damn. I love Ruffles; there's just nothing better. I'll eat them 'til my ass is the size of a barn if someone doesn't stop me."

Harry reached over, patting his hand. "Glen did this after work, so get it while it's hot." He pointed to a bright, hand-painted platter with artfully arranged cheese, and something I couldn't identify but guessed was intended for dipping. "It's individual flash-fried goat cheeses with julienned radish, accompanied by homemade zucchini, beet, and sweet potato chips."

Glen waved a bandaged thumb at the group. "Damn near cut off my thumb with the mandolin this afternoon, and they still can't touch Ruffles in the flavor department. Thanks for bringing these Miles; you and I are gonna get along just fine." He flashed me a funny grin before wolfing down the chips. When he reached for them a third time, Harry playfully slapped his hand away.

Emmay passed around small plates, and everyone began loading up on the snacks. I relaxed as the group chatted and Lori Beth dealt the cards. Keeper took a big mouthful of goat cheese on a sweet potato chip and picked up his cards.

Showtime.

I must have done a poor job of concealing my terror because he reached across the coffee table and grabbed my hand. The pale blue eyes crinkled as he smiled sympathetically. "The biggest journey starts with a single card game, Miles. It's a big job, not an impossible one. And you have help." The room had quieted, and I looked up into a sea of strange faces. Where I'd expected to see pity, there was kindness. Understanding. And something else—they were determined, resolute.

I'd already pegged Glen as the class clown. He liked to make people laugh, and the open, boyish way he'd presented himself made what he said a bit startling. The fun boy was gone, and in his place sat a serious man. "Miles, we have a lot of fun together, but everyone in this room has slogged through some heavy shit to get to where we are." He looked across the room at Harry with affection in his eyes. "When Harry and I came out to our families and told them we were in love and planning to marry, they disowned us—all of them. Harry's mother told him she wished he'd never been born."

Harry leaned forward, elbows to his knees. "This group has been a big part of getting us through the pain of losing our families at the very moment we were beginning our lives together. I don't know what you're in the middle of, but everybody has a story. We want to help, if we can; it's just that simple."

Everybody has a story. Their own elephant to eat.

I swallowed hard. "I don't know what to say, you guys. I'm not even sure I deserve your help, but I need to find the answers to some questions that have me stumped. If I have to endure some uncomfortable situations to get there, I'll do it. Be patient with me, please—I can't even cook."

With that, everyone laughed, the ice was broken. We'd just begun the first hand when the sound of the front door opening brought the play to a halt. A woman's soft voice called from the stoop. "Covington, darlin'. Are you here? Can you come give me a hand?" Covington, a handsome middle-aged man with dark hair and silvered temples, was immediately on his feet and jogging toward the foyer. A few minutes passed, and we finished the hand, visiting casually until the kitchen door opened again. Covington held the door for a tall, pretty black woman with coal-colored eyes and curly black lashes. She carried a black iron skillet and sat it on a corner of the side table with a thick potholder beneath it. She turned to me and extended a hand.

"Hi there, honey. I'm Sue, and I'm sure sorry I'm late. Covington says you're Miles."

I stood to greet her and shook her hand. "And what is this in the skillet? I just confessed to everyone right before you arrived that I have no kitchen skills."

She laughed and opened the package of graham crackers she carried. "This is s'more dip, y'all; it tastes just like Girl Scout camping back in the day."

Emmay grabbed a cracker and swiped it through the skillet filled with melty, toasted marshmallows and the rich chocolate chips underneath. She rolled her eyes as she tasted it. "Oh, Sue, stop it. This is too good." She pointed her gaze at me. "Sue is a Southern girl, and she knows how to cook from way back. Her mother taught her." She shot a look at Sue. "Why don't you have a seat so Lori Beth can deal you in; we need a Mama update."

Chapter FIFTEEN

"Queen of Hearts"

Miles

S ue sat down between Emmay and Covington. She picked up her cards, studying them briefly, then fell back into the sofa and sighed. "Y'all. I did good. I think you would've been proud of me."

Keeper shot her an encouraging smile and threw down a card on the discard pile, drawing. "We're proud of you no matter what, but what's important is that you're standing up for yourself now. Facing your issues head-on. The question for you is: how are you feeling after seeing your mother?"

Play proceeded casually, and Sue spelled out the complexities of her path to this point. Her mother was a manipulative, inflexible woman who set standards impossible for her to attain. She'd flown out to Tucson specifically to coerce Sue into marrying the emotionally abusive man her mother had picked out for her. The situation had been a source of terrible stress for Sue over the past two years as she'd capitulated to her mother's demands to maintain their uneasy peace. Today was the showdown the entire Tuesday Game crew knew was coming.

The color was high in her cheeks as she relayed the conversation. "So, I finally said, 'Mama, I love you, and I always will. But I'm a grown woman; I'm going to make my own choices and take responsibility for myself. You are no longer welcome to visit me without calling first. You are no longer welcome to meddle in my personal life or tell me what to do. And you will no longer manipulate me.' I'd practiced it in the mirror, just like you said, Keeper. I kept practicing until I could get all the way through without crying."

Keeper didn't interrupt her but smiled encouragingly, nodding. Covington touched her hand. "Go on, Sue. What happened next?"

"Well. I thought she might agree with me or at least just leave, but no such luck." Sue took a long drink of her soda, looking down to study her hand before laying down a Draw Four card; she looked sympathetically at Emmay. "Sorry about that. Anyway, Mama got this mean look on her face—it's the one she uses when things aren't going her way. Then she said, 'And how exactly do you expect to enforce your demands, little girl?'"

Glen snorted derisively. "What a bitch." His eyes flew to Sue. "Sorry, Sue; I didn't mean for that to come out on the outside."

Sue just snorted a little. "Don't you worry, Glen; it was probably her being such a bitch that gave me the courage to lay out what I said next. I took a deep breath, just like Emmay taught us in yoga class, and found my center. Then I looked right into her eyes and said, 'Mama, if you can't abide my conditions, you won't see or speak to me anymore. I'm an adult, and my boundaries aren't negotiable.' And, y'all, she turned around without saying a word and walked right out my front door."

It was quiet, save the noise Glen made stuffing another handful of Ruffles in his mouth. Harry shot him the stink-eye, but I could tell he was fighting off a smirk.

Keeper leaned back in his chair, balancing on the two back legs, and stroked his long beard thoughtfully. The group was relaxed, amazingly at ease with the silence. Then he addressed Sue with his low, unruffled baritone. "Have you had time to sort through how your head and heart are doing, Susan?"

She looked up with a small, sad smile. "You know, I think I'm gonna be just fine, Keeper. I've had all of you beside me, almost every week for the last couple of months, telling me that I could stop trying to make my mama happy—that I was a grown woman who could make my own decisions." She beamed as she looked around the room, and Lori Beth reached across to grab her hand.

"And we were right, weren't we, Susie Q?"

Sue broke into a bright smile and squeezed Lori Beth's hand. "You were right." Then she looked down briefly, her expression more somber. I was the only one who heard her softly murmur, "Uno." I grinned.

Chaos reigned for a few minutes while the group expressed enthusiastic admiration for Sue's handling of the difficult meeting with her mom. It occurred to me she might be facing the possibility of never seeing her mother again, an eventuality I couldn't fathom, had mine been alive. But she had solid guidance and backup.

Keeper was one of the few still seated; most rose to hug Sue and commend her courage in confronting her mother. He waited until the racket abated and everyone took their seats after refilling their plates with the remaining selection of dips and appetizers. Despite the presence of a few with kitchen skills and some real talent, the Ruffles were gone and the store-brand French onion dip ran low. Then Keeper spoke.

"We were proud of you, no matter what, Susan. But you were brave today, just for yourself. Congratulations." His expression conveyed the satisfaction of her success and his pride in it.

"Winner, bitches!" Sue slapped her last card on the coffee table and pumped both fists in the air.

It was after ten p.m., and I needed to leave soon to be rested for work tomorrow. Sue won two more hands and basked in the support offered from every side. Having lost my own mother, I felt the loss she was facing. Harry briefly addressed a phone call from one of his brothers representing a potential olive branch; some ideas were exchanged, and Harry seemed to mull the possibilities.

There was a lull in the conversation, and Emmay turned to me just as she played her card. "Miles, there's no requirement for you to share tonight; it's only your first night. But would you like to tell us all something about yourself or the road you've traveled on your way here?"

I was frankly amazed—and so thankful—no one had asked before now. When the anxiety-laden version of me envisioned tonight, I'd been standing on a chair, baring my soul to a roomful of strangers. Armed with a cursory knowledge of The Tuesday Game, I felt the reassurance of good people around me who had faced their demons and eventually fought their battles. The room was a safer place than I'd anticipated. I looked past Emmay, focusing on the stuccoed wall behind her.

"My mother died when I was ten, but that probably isn't really the root of my struggles. So many people have lost a parent, even at a young age. It's not unique...having no mom." I drew a card and stared at my hand. "It was more about what happened to Daddy after that."

Keeper smiled at his boots, sitting back after he'd drawn his own card. "It's still early, Miles; you don't have to put your cards on the table."

"Thanks for trying to give me a break, Keeper. I appreciate it, and I'd love to chicken out here and clam up," I took a deep breath and looked around the circle, "but I don't have the luxury of time or of going easy on myself. I'm here because my daddy coped with my mama's death by trying to shelter me from the slightest risk, anything at all, really. He said he couldn't bear to lose me too, although there was no reasonable cause for him to think he would. Mama's death was an accident, and I was a healthy little girl. As I grew and became a teenager, he never allowed the independence I saw my friends enjoying, and I resented him for that." I looked down at my hands; the room remained quiet as I considered what to say.

"And I guess I still do. Resent him, I mean." I almost choked on the admission. "It's pretty shitty hearing those words come out of my mouth; he's my only living parent. He lost his wife, for God's sake; why would his own flesh and blood hold his behavior against him under a circumstance like that?"

It was becoming difficult to speak around the big lump in my throat, but play had mercifully progressed to me, offering a welcome diversion. I drew and discarded, trying to beat back the deep disappointment I felt in myself. Keeper leaned forward again.

"I'm going to stop you there, Miles; your first night with us should feel more like eating too much dip and playing cards. Nobody here wants you to feel like you're in the hot seat. This isn't therapy—at least not in the conventional sense. But I do have two things for you to chew on." I cleared my throat and tried to steel myself for the harsh truth or painful advice that was surely coming next.

His eyes were kind and reassuring. "No child is responsible for the mistakes of their parent, and we all stumble as we deal with the ones we love. The resentment you've carried with you isn't insurmountable. The question is how you choose to handle it going forward." He gathered the cards left from the hand that had just ended. "I'm not the one who can tell you how to build a bridge over that chasm; you have to figure it for yourself." He shuffled the cards several times over and then glanced up again as he dealt the next hand. "Oh, and I think you and Meg need to get a cup of coffee this week."

Meg played a red card as the game began and laughed, pointing at Keeper with her remaining cards. "Great minds, Keeper; those were my thoughts exactly." She pulled out her phone and passed it to me. "Put your info in there, Miles, and I'll text you tomorrow. Are you a breakfast kind of girl?"

Play continued, but Emmay declared this the final hand. I still couldn't believe I'd spoken aloud; the issue I'd so carefully avoided for the past decade was out in the open. Keeper—hell, the entire group—appeared nonplussed at my confession about the anger I held toward Daddy, a widower mired in an endless cycle of hopelessness and grief. No blame or disapproval, just simple encouragement to look for a way past the animosity.

The directive for a coffee date with Meg was a bit odd, but everyone except me seemed to see it as a foregone conclusion. I'd even noticed Glen and Covington nodding their agreement when Keeper mentioned it.

Lori Beth and Glen led the brief cleanup effort, quickly scooping leftover dip and veggies into plastic storage bags and then washing and drying bowls and containers. Covington and Meg folded extra chairs, and Harry quickly ran the vacuum over an area rug.

Keeper approached me at the sink, leaning against the wall as I finished drying a platter. "I know it probably seems strange that I suggested you spend some time with Meg, but I think you'll understand it better after you've had time to break bread—or maybe bagels, as the case may be." I was starting to see the wisdom of trusting his instincts.

Chapter SIXTEEN

"Drinks After Work"

Oliver

"Hey, Ollie," Jacob hailed me with a wave from his stool at the bar. It was midweek and we'd made arrangements to meet at the Hogwash for a couple of beers and a burger. It had been over two weeks since our schedules permitted time to catch up, and I welcomed the opportunity, greeting my cousin warmly.

"Good to see you, mate." I pulled my stool alongside his and shook Arlo's hand over the bar.

"Oliver, welcome back, son. What's your poison this evening?"

I ordered a draft IPA to accompany a burger Jacob assured me was a superior choice.

"It's past time for us to have a pint and a chat, Jake." I accepted the frosted glass from Arlo; I guessed I'd never become accustomed to the way Americans overcooled their beer, craft or otherwise. "I haven't had a chance to hear the details about the midair a couple of months ago. I was in the range tower and heard the Mayday come up on Guard." It wasn't the first time I'd heard emergencies in progress, but it gave me a start all the same. Since it occurred in airspace my cousin and best mate occupied almost every day, there was potential for great personal loss. "I understand from the rumor mill that you were on the squadron commander's wing at the time."

A shadow passed across Jacob's face, and he nodded ruefully. "I was giving Happy his Sandy checkout, and it's a damned good thing. We were nearby and able to put eyes on Deliverance fast; Happy directed the rescue effort, and I brought the broken bird home on my wing."

Harrowing.

"Word is, the jet was landed in manual reversion." That bit was gossip alone, and there was no proof apparent out on the flight line. I guessed the wrecked aircraft remains were promptly hauled away for accident investigation purposes. Landing an A-10 in manual reversion was the aviation equivalent to walking on water. Damage from the midair would pose a number of challenges. Add the difficulty of manhandling the behemoth with reduced control capabilities and things got very dicey.

Jake nodded as he sipped his beer. "Yep. It took some years off my life, that's for damned sure."

I was mulling the scenario, wondering why the hell Jacob hadn't insisted on a controlled ejection when the cook appeared in the kitchen doorway bearing two plates with mouthwatering burgers and a mountain of chips. Tucking in without delay, I groaned. "It was worth sending you colonists packing to improve the food game. This is the best meal I've had all week."

Conversation lagged temporarily as we tore through our dinner. I wouldn't ask Jacob more about the accident; it was truly enough to know he was safe. But it was a sobering reminder that my cousin's career choice placed him in jeopardy, not only during wartime, but each time he flew.

Time to steer the conversation in a more cheerful direction;

I knew Jacob was a friend of Charlotte's. I had every intention of taking her out to explore the fascination I felt and the unmistakable attraction between us. It would be duplicitous not to tell my cousin about my intent. "Right. I've been hoping for an opening to inquire about someone I noticed at the picnic, Jake."

He favored me with a sly grin. "Yeah, I thought so. Vivvie told me you insisted you weren't interested in meeting anyone right now, but she was sure someone would catch your eye. Those girl-friends of hers from work are prime real estate, that's for damned sure." His eyes glazed noticeably as he mentioned Vivianne's co-workers, and then he mumbled something under his breath and shook his head.

I studied him, amused, as I took the malt vinegar Arlo brought for my chips. "Didn't quite catch that, mate—what are you on about?"

Jacob rolled his eyes and gave me an embarrassed little smile. "I may or may not have it pretty bad for one of Viv's friends. Guess I'd better hope it's not the same one you're going to ask about."

"Yes. About that." I turned on the barstool to more fully face him only to notice the saloon door swing open. A chorus of voices calling their greetings accompanied the arrival of what must have been two full carloads of Scorpions.

"Bash—s'up?" Torch and Rock reached us first, pulling bar-stools up with no preamble. Hung, Marilyn, and three other pi-lots from another squadron were right behind them, also joining our party. There was a brief discussion about the need for food, and a consensus was quickly reached. Hung ordered pitchers of beer along with five dozen hot wings.

Rock rolled his eyes as Hung completed the order and Arlo disappeared into the kitchen. "Good thing Boo isn't here to hear that order. If he knew we were about to polish off five dozen wings and a yet unknown volume of beer, he'd have us all doing push-ups in the parking lot."

Marilyn laughed as he took a pitcher from the bar and began to fill the pint glasses Arlo had left. "I don't ever remember Boo taking issue with beer drinking—ours or his—and the wings are pure protein. A veritable gold mine of nutritional goodness." The group joined Marilyn's laughter as the pitchers were drained and glasses distributed.

"A deep-fried gold mine covered in blue cheese dressing, more like it," Rock guffawed. "But I ain't afraid. I'll run it off tomorrow—tonight, we feast!"

There was a general bellow of agreement, and I realized I'd missed the window of opportunity to discuss my interest in Charlotte with my cousin. We'd have more than enough time to talk once we moved in together, I reasoned. The move was on the docket for this week if our schedules permitted, next week at the latest. It was good to see Jacob so happy, surrounded by friends and doing work he loved. My work was more solitary, but it suited me. I was as content as he, and we both enjoyed unusually satisfying family ties—made all the more so by our relocations. Being near family again reinforced what I'd always known subconsciously: that family was so important I couldn't picture the future without a family of my own.

The solitary empty corner in my life could only be filled by a romantic relationship. The bar was high, and I'd never met a woman who interested me enough to explore something further. Not until I encountered the slushie-swilling Charlotte Christman. She had nerves of steel, but she blushed easily. She was enigmatic, and I was intrigued. I needed to know more.

I'd need to speak with Jacob sooner rather than later.

Chapter
SEVENTEEN

"Solitaire"

Miles

I was considerably more relaxed awaiting Meg's arrival than I had been a few days ago at The Tuesday Game. She was only a few years older than I, probably late twenties, I guessed. She was very approachable, and I was curious to unravel the mystery of why the entire Tuesday Game crew knew it was a good idea for us to meet together.

I'd arrived a half hour earlier than we'd agreed to meet, hoping to spend some quiet time having breakfast and focusing on Keeper's advice. Coach was right: introspection was a learned art and one I'd not mastered. I'd spent a lifetime to this point avoiding self-examination. Although there was an obvious benefit I'd missed, it wasn't exactly common in the pilot community, this habit of soul-searching. As a species, we lived by the seat of our pants and sailed through life without a great deal of deep thought that didn't involve systems or weapons or tactics. Searching for the reason I made a choice that almost cost my friend his life…well, it was hard work, and it went against my grain, to say the least.

The two things Keeper offered didn't initially settle well. First was the idea that I wasn't responsible for repairing my daddy's broken heart and the mistakes his grief visited on me. It made objective sense, but my heart was stubbornly conflicted. Second, the notion that all the resentment I'd lugged around like baggage was potentially subject to resolution? I'd never considered it. Daddy and I were mostly estranged, and that rendered me a functional orphan. If there was a way to build the bridge Keeper had mentioned, I wanted to look at the possibilities.

"When was the last time you saw Daddy, Bugs?" Robert had asked last time we spoke on the phone, but I couldn't even recall.

I was pondering the question when my phone buzzed from the depths of my huge purse. Rummaging through the gum wrappers and old receipts, I thought wryly that a good purging was likely in order. Finding it on the fourth ring, I noted an unfamiliar local number but answered anyway. The deep voice was soft and adorned with a cultured British accent that launched my heart rate into the stratosphere.

"Hiya, Charlotte. It's Oliver." He chuckled low. "Oliver Bloodworth from the armed robbery."

My mouth was instantly dry as dust, like a damned middle schooler talking to a boy. "Yes. Of course, I remember you, Oliver."

"Bloody hard to forget, if you ask me. Jacob's been taking the piss out of me over it every day since; Vivianne, as well. And I'm afraid her repartee and practical jokes exceed her brother's in both skill and imagination."

With his charm turned to high beam, it was the work of a moment to put me at ease. "Bash is pretty quick to keep everyone in line. I'm afraid I don't know Vivianne as well, but Bash says they're peas in a pod, what with being twins and all."

Oliver snorted. "That old saw. Are they still trying to pass themselves off as identical? That shtick dates back to primary school, you know, and they convinced one of the teachers quite thoroughly."

"Someone still falls for it now and then." I grinned at the thought. "Mr. Barnum said there's one born every minute."

The silence stretched a split second too long. My heart pounded in response before he spoke again. "So, Charlotte. Our first date was smashing—not sure we can top it."

My tummy flipped over. Stupid, traitorous body. Self-assured women, all fortified with independence, didn't behave like little girls waiting for their first kiss.

"But it's past time for a second one—perhaps Saturday if you're free during the day. There's a ski lift on Mount Lemmon to the top of the mountain. The views are brilliant, and I thought we could have a late lunch at the restaurant at the base of the mountain."

"I'd like that, Oliver." My voice sounded breathy, almost girl-ish, and completely foreign to my ears. I tried to inject some confidence into my inflection. "Sounds like fun."

"If it's fun, we've already outpaced the first date, haven't we?" The deep British clip shot straight to my center. I hadn't had a physical reaction to a man, never mind a voice on the phone, in years. Maybe ever, upon reflection. "May I pick you up at home? I know that's a bit unusual for a first date these days, but our circumstances are quite different from most."

"I'd…well, yes. That would be nice." Engage full stammer mode. "I'll give you my address if you…"

"Would you mind texting me the details?" he interrupted gently. "I'm all tied up at the moment."

I gave some incomprehensible response in the affirmative, and he graciously ignored my awkwardness. It must have required effort because my discomfort needed its own zip code. A life that was gaining momentum; hopefully the phone call would be over soon. I'd need to look into getting my shit firmly together before Saturday rolled around.

"Thank you, Charlotte. Don't forget to bring a sweater; it can be fifteen or twenty degrees cooler at the top of the mountain, I'm told. I'll ring off now, but I'll be looking forward to your company." I stared dumbly at my coffee cup, ineffective at responding, but he continued. "Until then, love."

"Yes. Bye." He disconnected. Is this the same gal who landed a fighter jet in manual reversion only weeks ago?

Nice job, Miles. Super smooth. Where's the ice water in your veins now?

My heart still pattered rapidly in my chest, and a persistent throb beat along in time between my legs. I worked with a veritable all-you-can-eat buffet of male deliciousness every day, but they were like a collection of annoying brothers. Objectively mouth-watering and oozing testosterone, but utterly off the menu. This was something different entirely. What timing. I was dealing with the biggest fuckup of my life as well as a tall drink of English lusciousness who made my mouth water. Among other things.

I wondered idly what I'd wear on the date and promptly realized that was a question I'd never before asked myself. Because Charlotte Louise Christman had zero fucks to give about her appearance and other peoples' opinions.

Well, Bugs. You're well and truly screwed now.

Sighing, I lifted my hand in a half wave to attract Meg's attention as she looked around the room.

"...the flight attendant said he'd never seen anyone as small as I am throw up that much. And that was the last time I flew." Meg was laughing so hard by the time she finished her story that a few tears were rolling down her cheeks. I'd been in stitches almost from the time she arrived. "I'm not afraid of flying, Miles. I just feel terrible that a perfect stranger could have the bad fortune of landing in a seat next to me, thinking they're in for a normal flight. Can you imagine?"

"You're a laugh riot, Meg, but I wouldn't be anxious to board a plane under those circumstances either. " I took a few bites of my breakfast plate, still nearly full since I'd been afraid I'd spew it all over Meg if one of her anecdotes caught me with a full mouth.

She smiled warmly, spreading a piece of toast with strawberry preserves. "I'll bet you wonder why everyone at Keeper's wanted us to have coffee this week; there's no way that escaped your notice."

"Yeah, I'm curious. I didn't lay all my cards on the table, but it was enough to land you here." I smiled and relaxed into my chair. "So spill it; why did you get the nod to be my mystery date?"

Meg's smile didn't fade, but she clasped her hands on the table and leaned toward me. "I come from a very wealthy family, and I'm not just bragging. It's material to the story. It's old East Coast money and plenty of it. When I was seventeen years old, I was kidnapped in broad daylight at the corner of Broadway and Tower in New Haven, Connecticut."

I gasped and slapped a hand over my mouth. "Oh shit, Meg. I'm so sorry. I had no idea, or I wouldn't have been so flippant, I swear. I didn't know."

She was shaking her head, a small smile still softening her features. "Of course you didn't. Ancient history, Miles. Don't worry. I'm just giving you the lay of the land. It was a classic snatch-from-the-sidewalk-into-a-windowless-van thing, just like on television. They pulled a bag over my head, drove for so long I couldn't stay awake anymore, and I woke up in a dark room I later learned was a basement. They didn't hurt me, they fed me fast food, and—as I suspected they would—demanded a pile of ransom money from my family. Ten million, which my dad promptly paid. The FBI set up a sting at the drop-off, and the bastards were caught." She pursed her lips. "Except for the two dirtbags the agents shot. The Feds were top-notch. I was returned to my family less than three days after the abduction—filthy dirty, but without a mark on me."

She let the quiet hang between us as she nibbled on her toast, watching my face. "You're trying to do the math on why we're talking about this, but you don't have all the pieces of the puzzle yet."

I nodded slowly. "I'm still shocked, Meg. You caught me off guard, but go on."

"Okay." She leaned back and crossed her legs, continuing the story. "So my family did all the right things, the things you do when money is no object." She ticked them off on her fingers. "They had me checked out physically by a couple of different doctors, then started individual and family therapy. Dad took a leave of absence from work, my big brother left college for a semester to stay home, and they huddled around me, giving any support they could. Mom slept in my room at night until I threw her out. I felt fine, and they believed I was out of the woods—no lasting damage done. I thought so, too.

"Then the anxiety episodes jumped up out of nowhere and kicked my ass. They were out of control and terrified all of us. I ended up in the emergency room having a trillion tests done the first couple of times, and then my psychiatrist was called in and untangled the knot. Anxiety episodes weren't unexpected under the circumstances, so my parents breathed a sigh of relief and upped the visits with my psychiatrist to daily. We all knew I was suffering from the terror associated with being taken. Obvious, right?"

I nodded dumbly. "Sure, obvious."

She shook her head. "Nope. We all looked the wrong way,

but I'll spare you the weeks of frustration and dead ends we all tripped over on the way to the finish line."

My face betrayed the confusion swimming in my head. Surely Keeper couldn't think this girl's kidnapping bore similarities to my experiences.

"See, Miles, it wasn't the kidnapping per se. In other words, the issue wasn't the men who took me; they were never the heavy hitters in my dreams. The FBI was very capable in dealing with them, and that was somehow enough to settle the matter in my subconscious. But it effectively mined and exposed a long-standing issue I'd not handled. Didn't even know it was a problem."

She accepted a coffee refill from the young woman making rounds with a pot. I ordered another latte and turned again to face Meg. "So what did you find?" This had to be the thread tying us together.

She nodded, doctoring her cup with a healthy dose of sugar and cream. "Growing up wealthy has plenty of perks, but there's a downside, too. My parents and grandparents ran in circles with the cream of New England society. My parents—my mother in particular—were very concerned about appearances. From the time I could remember, we had to be perfectly turned out for every occasion. A great deal of money and effort went into the image of the 'elegant, affluent family.'" She finger-quoted that for emphasis. "I never owned a pair of jeans until I left home because Mother said they were common. I wasn't allowed to play sports unless she approved, which is how I wound up in the croquet club." She laughed. "And that was only after the debacle when mother made me try sailing—don't forget about the motion sickness we discussed earlier."

I snorted and shook my head. I'd only known the girl a few days, and even I knew sailing was a spectacular mismatch.

"Mother controlled every aspect of my life down to what I wore every day, who my friends were, and what classes I took in school. She watched and commented on what I ate, making sure I knew how unacceptable extra pounds would be—damned miracle I didn't wind up with an eating disorder." She rolled her eyes. "And it was all in the name of maintaining appearances and social standing.

"I saw the writing on the wall as my seventeenth birthday approached; she'd continue to control everything unless I took drastic measures. So I did. On the evening of my birthday, at dinner with Mother and Daddy, I staged the big showdown. It was my personal declaration of independence; I told her I'd make my own choices and do my own thing from then on."

I smiled and looked away for a moment, remembering Robert's pleading of my case in the kitchen of the farmhouse. He'd declared my independence for me. "I had a similar watershed moment, but it was my brother who did the honors."

"Well, mine was a flaming train wreck. Mother raged on and on about how ungrateful and stubborn I was, cajoling and making threats. Dad finally stepped in and talked her down. Life got better from there; I was thrilled to be free to do things and make choices—like clothing and free-time activities—all things my friends had been doing for years. I jettisoned a friendship Mother had insisted I cultivate with a girl who bullied me unmercifully. Things were looking up for the first time I could remember."

She shot me a look, eyebrow arched. "You see where this is going, right? Four months after my birthday, I went shopping with a couple of girlfriends downtown. They were trying on clothes, and I went outside to take a call. I wandered around a corner, into an alley to get away from the traffic noise, and…"

"Oh my God." My hand flew to my mouth. "They grabbed you right after you'd begun to reclaim your life."

"I was absolutely terrified, but let's fast forward to keep things on track. After several weeks of therapy with my boundlessly patient psychiatrist, we figured out the reason for the episodes. It

wasn't the obvious. It was the sudden loss of my hard-won freedom. I'm no psychologist, but apparently, the kidnapping represented a return to a life where I had no say. The anger I had
directed at Mother over the 'years in captivity'—as my friends
called it—had settled into low-grade hostility. I couldn't act out,
so it just simmered inside me. I didn't talk to her about it, even
after she settled down. She was apoplectic and consumed with
guilt when I was taken; she needed as much therapy as I did.
Three days is a long time when you don't know if your daughter's
dead or alive."

Robert always said it didn't do to give in to pity because there
was always someone who had things worse than you did. Meg
was a timely reminder that Robert was absolutely right. Even
with all she'd faced, she was looking at it from the other side—
and using her pain and hard-earned lessons to help me.

I chewed on my lip, soaking it all in. We were as different as
could be, and the animosity I was facing came from a different
source than Meg's. Still…

"So, Meg. I know you can't offer guarantees, but I hope you'll
show your hand anyway. What was your next move?"

Chapter EIGHTEEN

"Two of a Kind, Workin' on a Full House"

Oliver

"**M**other. Fucker.**"** Jacob and Rock struggled under the weight of a giant bureau. They wrestled it through the door with great difficulty, finally setting it down on the saltillo-tiled entryway. Rock wiped his perspiring brow with the tee shirt he'd long since discarded and thrown over the door. "Bash, I lift. A lot, in fact. But I didn't know they made furniture out of concrete. What the hell's this thing made of anyway?"

Jake smirked at him. "So you lift a lot, do you? It's just good old-fashioned oak, Rock. Don't be a pussy."

I gave one corner of the big cabinet a lift, groaning as I set it down. "No dresser weighs this much." I opened the second drawer and burst into laughter, nudging Rock. Three of Jacob's medium barbell plates sat atop a stack of tee shirts. Further investigation revealed more of the weights sharing space with underpants and two dumbbells bunking with the jumpers. I cocked my head at him. "What wanker packs for a move like this? Gym equipment with the trousers, Jacob? Really."

He sniffed dismissively at me. "Moving's not my long suit. Sue me."

"Moving's not anybody's long suit, Bash." Happy was sweating as profusely as the rest of us; he nodded at the two large boxes in his arms. "Read the side for me, Oliver." He turned so I could see.

"Bedroom, both of them. I'll give you a hand." I took the top one, and he led the way down the hall.

He glanced over his shoulder at me. "That fiasco at the Kwik Shopper, man. Could've turned into a genuine disaster if you hadn't been so light on your feet. Damned impressive. Miles gave me the blow-by-blow. What was that kick—tae kwon do?"

"Yeah, I got lucky. It's been years, but the lessons must have taken root somewhere in the gray matter. I haven't trained since I was a lad." I set the box down and began rearranging the room, clearing a path through the chaos. Happy pulled the bed frame into place, and we both hefted the box spring onto the frame. "You should've seen Charlotte, Happy. She was ice-cold, clearly intended for a life of deception." I grinned at the memory.

His head snapped around. "Charlotte?" He was just as confounded as everyone else. "She doesn't allow anyone to call her Charlotte. I didn't even know her given name until I was…" He hesitated. "Filling out some paperwork recently."

"It's how she introduced herself to me." I shrugged at his arched brow and continued. "You'd have been amazed, Happy. She read my abominable sign language without betraying me to the burglar, then burst into a fit of hysterical wailing on cue, howling like she'd gone mad." I chuckled remembering the scene; funny now only because she emerged without a scratch. We adjusted the mattress on top of the box springs, and I threw the pillows and quilt from an open box on top of the bed.

Happy laughed. "I'd love to have seen the performance; Miles is one of a kind, no doubt."

Funny. Those were the exact words Jacob had used to describe her. I wasn't the only one who saw something special.

The final pickup truck was unloaded at last, and work was winding down when the doorbell announced the much-anticipated pizza delivery. Jacob grabbed his wallet and jogged for the front door as I handed cold beers from the fridge to the tired, sweaty group. Hung accepted one with a grateful grin and twisted the cap.

"So, Oliver. How do you pass the time out in the range tower? Must be a solitary existence out there." We settled onto an assortment of mismatched barstools and kitchen chairs. The decorating scheme was shaping up to be what could charitably be described as eclectic.

"Yes, I call it the Fortress of Solitude, but the truth is I rather enjoy the quiet. I get my socializing done after work hours, usually with Jacob and Vivianne."

Hung rubbed his forehead with his thumb. "Yes…Vivianne." He mumbled her name under his breath, not speaking to me or anyone else.

Interesting.

"Bit of a geek, I'm afraid. I love to read; so when the work's well and truly done, I love a nice, thick tome on military history."

Rock paused his shelf check of the refrigerator's meager contents and turned to Boo. "It's worse than we thought, Boo. He reads."

Boo nodded somberly. "I expected the news to be bad, but this…" He shook his head with mock sorrow.

Marilyn smiled indulgently at the comedy duo and turned to me. "The LPA never disappoints, even when they're sweaty and smell like a donkey's asshole."

"I know I'm speaking for both of us—Jacob and myself—when I say we're grateful for all the help we can get, even if the smell is dodgy as hell." I clapped Marilyn on the shoulder just as Jacob deposited a stack of pizza boxes on the worktop.

"Dig in, men." Jacob flipped open two boxes and produced a roll of paper towels. "This is what passes for fine china since I've blocked the cabinets with stacks of boxes. Thanks for the hard labor; we really appreciate the help."

"To the new place." Boo lifted his bottle to toast before taking a big bite of sausage and mushroom pizza.

"To the place." Torch lifted his bottle and toasted with Boo. "Bash, that sucks way too much. A spread like this should have a good bachelor pad name, man."

"I suggest the Chicken Ranch. Or the Mustang Ranch." Boo spoke with some difficulty around another mouthful of pizza.

I shook my head. "We don't have any animals on the premises; it's not a proper ranch at all."

Everyone laughed, and Happy spoke up. "Cultural differences, Oliver. Those are both infamous American brothels."

Ahh.

Rock piled on. "Yep. Whorehouses. I like where your head's at, Boo. How about One-Eyed Jacks? That's a classic."

Happy and I regarded one another with a side-eye, and he shook his head. "No idea."

Marilyn piped up from his perch on the lone unoccupied worktop. "*Twin Peaks*, early nineties. Even I wasn't born when that was on; nice reference, Rock."

Rock affected a spooky leer. "Fire. Walk with me."

"Yeah, that was a pretty fucked-up show." Marilyn turned his attention to Jacob. "Your sister may feel some kind of way about your naming your residence after a cathouse."

That made me laugh. "She'd definitely have an opinion about it, and she'd find a way to make us wish we'd decided to live under a bridge instead." Vivvie was sharp as a tack and not adverse to torturing us with practical jokes just as she'd done when we were kids. When I'd caught her sneaking out to meet a boy one night after curfew, I ratted her out to my aunt Annalise who grounded her with extreme prejudice. Viv retaliated by carefully prying the letter keys from my brand-new laptop and rearranging them. A few years earlier, when Jacob teased her into a seething rage over her new braces, she froze his car keys in a block of lime Jell-O. She was not a woman to be trifled with.

"I'm feeling a hard pass on the bordello references, Boo. But keep thinking."

The conversation was easy as the eight of us polished off five pizzas with minimal effort. Moving was always hard work but especially so since everyone had already put in a day's work flying. Fortunately, today had been a day off for me, so I'd gotten a jump on the relocation efforts. Flying tales were exchanged, and bragging rights about the shooting and bombing capabilities argued.

"Better watch it now, boys." Marilyn finished his beer and clapped me on the shoulder. "We've got the ultimate hall monitor in Oliver here. If he decides to talk out of school, it'll ruin all our reputations." He grinned big. "I guess Happy's probably in the clear."

He was right. Happy was world class at the range, and everyone knew it. I nodded my agreement. "I can attest to that; Happy's brilliant, and your Deliverance is as well. I was gobsmacked the only time he flew while I was in the tower. The Scorpions have two of the finest I've ever seen."

"Very kind words, Oliver. Thank you." Happy sent me a half salute.

"And how is Deliverance feeling these days? I hear a bit from Vivianne and understand he's expected to recover fully."

Happy's tone was serious, but he allowed a small smile. "Yes, he'll recover completely in due time, but the road's been a long one. Luckie's a godsend; we're all glad she was on the job taking care of him. She even accompanied him to Savannah back in October when he went down to prep us for Reforger."

Rock stood. "LPA, time to hit the road. I've got the early go. Everybody ready?"

Torch, Boo, and Rock shook hands and said their goodbyes, soon followed by Marilyn and Hung. Happy flattened empty pizza boxes and helped me stuff them into an oversized trash bag. He spoke as we finished loading the bags into a wheeled rubbish bin. "I'll be on my way soon, too; thanks for the workout. This is a hell of a great house for a couple of single guys." Happy extracted car keys from his pocket. "I believe a house-warming party is in order, gentlemen."

I smirked. "I can't stand for a single thing about this city to be a degree warmer than it already is, but a party is a superior idea. I'd fancy involving the pool."

"Let me know the particulars when you work it out, and we can get all the Stingers out to christen your hacienda properly."

Jacob and I lolled in a couple of lounge chairs by the pool, limbs relaxed by the tumblers of scotch sitting on the glass table between us. The moon was nearly full and lit the night sky nicely. After a period of silence, I sat up abruptly, apparently emboldened by the alcohol.

"I should tell you something, mate."

He sat up too, listing a bit. "Wait." He gained his balance and turned to stare at me. "What's up?"

"Look, I know there's no requirement to tell you. You're not her guardian."

He looked directly at me, all effects of the alcohol suddenly evaporated like the morning mist. "Whose guardian? What did you do, Oliver?"

"I didn't do anything, Jacob. Not yet." I sighed. "I have a date with Miles—I mean Charlotte. We're going out…this Saturday."

He rolled his eyes and grabbed the scotch, draining it in one drink, then scrubbed one hand down his face. "I'm not her father, Oliver. You're both adults, and you can make your own decisions. But could there be a worse goddamn time to pull this? She's eyeballs deep in the biggest crisis of her life. "

Now it was my turn at instant sobriety. "What's happened, Jacob? Is she hurt?" The tranquility we'd been enjoying was shattered, and I was almost shouting at my cousin, utterly confused as to what could have happened. "What crisis, for God's sake?"

Jake shook his head at me and stood slowly, folding his arms. He seemed baffled at my response, as if I should have been privy to what had befallen Charlotte. Anger formed a growing knot in my gut as the frustration with my cousin increased.

Suddenly I saw understanding dawn on his face; I stood to meet his eyes as he spoke. "You really don't know, do you, Ollie?"

I shook my head wordlessly, waiting. He put one hand on my shoulder.

"It was Miles…Charlotte. She was on Deliverance's wing when he went down." He squeezed my shoulder even as his gaze dropped to his bare feet, and he mumbled something I couldn't understand.

"What was that, mate? Couldn't hear you." A hush had fallen over the backyard again, and Jacob's response was barely more than a whisper.

"It was her fault, Oliver." He swallowed hard. "She was the cause of the midair. It's a goddamn miracle Deliverance is alive."

Moonbeams lit the pool with an otherworldly glow. Both Jake and I stretched out flat on the loungers, staring at nothing at all. Nearly an hour had passed, and the scotch bottle was now half empty, but no further conversation had passed between my cousin and me. My thoughts were a chaotic tangle, a logjam that left me reeling. So many questions and precious few answers. The only certainty was that my determination to get to know Charlotte was undiminished.

I stared at the moon as I spoke. "I didn't plan it, Jacob, I swear."

His voice was as quiet as it had been before. "So why now? Why her?"

I only hesitated for a moment.

"No choice, mate. She captivated me."

Chapter NINETEEN

"Thank You for Being a Friend"

Miles

It's said that a person will make time for the things most important to them. Using that assumption, it was easy to conclude that men were not at all important to me. The closer truth was that relationships were not at all important, at least not those involving romantic entanglement. I was surrounded almost exclusively by men every day at work; they comprised nearly my entire social circle. We worked and played and even traveled together occasionally. And despite the fact they were nearly all supremely fuckable, our bonds remained effortlessly platonic. There was never a whisper of impropriety because…*no.* They were like brothers. Aside from the lack of exposure to the remainder of the male population, a flying career alone would readily expand to fill all the available space in your life, if given the chance.

Of course, it didn't *have* to be that way. You didn't have to be Dick-fucking-Tracy to figure out what was up when Happy looked at Camille with his big, brown puppy-dog eyes. He was gone, baby, gone. He'd managed to fall in love despite having his hands full with a brand-new flying command and a rebellious lieutenant who couldn't keep her airplane from running into another one.

Shit.

The point is, flying didn't have to be your whole life, but it could be if it was convenient. For me, it was utterly convenient. I was glad for my friends and family who'd found their one and only. They'd settled down to life in captivity, their freedom glibly exchanged for the "ties that bind." Maybe glad was too strong a term…I was skeptical. I wished them happiness but could never visualize myself parting with my independence. It was, after all, my most prized possession.

That line of thinking took me briefly back to the epiphany I'd had in Happy's office weeks ago. Placing my personal autonomy above everything else—making every choice in my world based on maintaining it. What had that choice cost me? I was estranged from my father, had no girlfriends to speak of, and played the role of the rebel without an apparent cause in my squadron. I was practically a mascot, drinking and partying too much and too often. My friends had to pass around the "care and feeding of Miles" with a good-natured eye-roll. How many times had Rock alone dragged me out of a bar before I humiliated myself?

I didn't want to be that girl anymore.

It was at this crossroad in the shitshow that was my life that I'd decided I really, really needed a raspberry slushie from the Kwik Shopper. And the magnificent Oliver dropped into my world, all sky-blue eyes and boyish charm. The accent alone made me want to lick his face. The effect of the wavy, ginger hair and the eyes…it was guileless and youthful. But his long, powerful frame told a different story. He was an entire foot taller than I with long limbs and big hands he could wrap around my waist—if he wanted. When I allowed my mind to focus on those big hands, it made my center tight and hot.

I'd dated on occasion, but I sucked at playing the part of the deferential, cloying female. Evenings generally ended with both of us feeling uncomfortable. The experience was far from pleasant, so I didn't accept dates very often. Acquiescence just wasn't my long suit.

My unsteady, eager reaction to Oliver's call left me off balance. I didn't usually give much thought to the idea of romance, a notion I'd come to mistrust. I was a bit disgusted with myself; it was just a date—nothing interesting ever came of it. Still, there was something about him that seemed different and exciting, and my body's response was indisputable.

It was the curious feeling of excitement surrounding this date that caused me to descend into the first and only wardrobe-related panic of my life. I absolutely did not put extra effort into my appearance. The realization made me wonder idly if this could be yet another manifestation of my infatuation with independence.

No matter the reason, I spent as little time as possible on my hair, wore only minimal makeup, and kept to an unfussy workout that usually consisted of running several times a week until I was an exhausted, sweaty calamity. As for clothing, I owned an enviable collection of Chuck Taylors that occupied nearly every flat surface in my walk-in closet. Aside from that, I had all the uniforms required to fly on the **Big Blue Team**, a waist-high stack of well-worn Levis, and two drawers full of tee shirts. There was a full complement of bathing suits and snow ski attire as well as the odd dress or skirt for the occasions that demanded it, but I didn't stray far from the formula.

Under ordinary circumstances, I'd have insisted that any date be tailored to match my wardrobe. In fact, my signature look, plus a denim jacket—I probably had one somewhere—might have worked just dandy for a ride up Mount Lemmon, but I had the strangest compulsion to up my game. The desire was there, but the closet was uncooperative. My problem required the assistance of a skilled girlfriend.

Without hesitation, I sounded the alarm late Friday afternoon.

"Yoo-hoo," Sam's voice rang cheerfully through the condo after she'd pounded on the door. "Let me in, Miles; I come bearing wine."

I jogged from the bedroom where I'd been staring fruitlessly for ten minutes into my closet. It dawned on me in the past few minutes that some variety in my shopping efforts wouldn't have been a terrible idea. "Hey, Sam. Thanks for coming."

She flung a huge armload of clothes on hangers onto the sofa, set three bulging shopping bags on the floor, and threw both arms around my neck. I was unaccustomed to this kind of affection, but she was so at ease that I felt more so.

"I have a bunch of stuff still in the car, and Grace will be here in the next few minutes; she had to run by her place. She's one of the other nurses who works in the ED with Camille and Luckie and all the rest of us. She wears your shoe size, so she's bringing options." She emphasized the words with her hands. "It's all about having options." Taking in my worried expression, she reached deep into the last shopping bag and produced a bottle of Malbec. "Don't panic; Grace and I have this handled, and we're going shopping at the earliest opportunity to ensure this isn't an ongoing problem. Open the bottle, pour three big glasses, and I'll be right back." She turned on her heel and strode back outside. Her confidence was inspiring—maybe they could actually help. I wasn't terribly adept at many classically feminine pursuits, like shopping and dressing. Also cooking and decorating, and this line of thinking was rapidly throwing a wet blanket on my mood. I went to the kitchen to open the wine. At least that was an area where I didn't lack proficiency.

Sam gyrated enthusiastically to the Spice Girls' "My Strongest Suit," and I stood in my bedroom, clad only in a bra and little cotton panties, sipping wine and singing along. I'd already figured out nurses were strangely comfortable with nudity; at least I knew Sam was after the time she spent with me after the accident. The list expanded when a stunning, petite brunette breezed into the condo dragging three additional shopping bags and took the glass of wine I offered.

"Hi there, Miles. I'm Grace…nice to meet you. I've got the goods, and you've got the wine." She grinned at Sam. "Let's get her nekkid, Sammy."

We'd adjourned to the bedroom and consumed two good bottles of red while they turned me into a Barbie doll. "I didn't know anyone had this many clothes, Sam."

Sam pulled a soft, cream-colored sweater over my head and studied the effect. "This isn't everything we have, Miles, and your closet is full. You probably have as much stuff as either of us do."

"It's just that it's all jeans and tees and tennis shoes." Grace tsk'ed as she pointed at the closet. "You have to have options, but I'll bet Sam already covered that."

"She did, and they're not ordinary tennis shoes, you know—they're Chuck Taylors. Classics." I eyed the long caramel suede boots Grace held out for me to try. "How tall are these things?"

"They're over the knee, and they're hot as fuck." Sam held up two different scarves, comparing them with the sweater. "Try them, Miles. They might be too much for a first date, but I wanna see."

I sat on the bed and slid the boots on. They felt like soft puppy-dog fur against my legs, and I groaned, standing. "These feel amazing, but I'm not sure these are my best bet with a sweater and panties."

Sam let go with a low wolf whistle. "I don't think Oliver would agree if he could see what I see, girl. Holy fucking fuckballs, Gracie. Look at those legs."

Grace studied the effect, mouth agape. "Yeah, we probably need to tone it down; but, seriously, look at that ass. You've been holding out on us, Miles."

I swiveled to look in the full-length mirror on the closet door. My legs did justice to my call sign, and my butt was curvy and firm. "You guys sure?"

"I hope you can trust us on this one; you look amazing." Grace continued to study me as they both flipped through the stack of clothes on the bed, each selecting a few items. I tugged off the sweater, and Sam produced a pair of tan leggings, along with an oversized plaid scarf in shades of red, caramel and tan. Grace added a dark red jersey tunic. I pulled the boots off, hesitant to part with their softness, and began to dress. The pair lounged on the bed, sipping their wine.

"You don't date very much, do you, Miles?" Sam lifted her eyebrows as I puzzled over the scarf, and Grace punched her lightly on the shoulder.

"Samanthe Josephine Barber. I can't believe you said that. Rude." She punctuated the word with a pointed finger and a serious tone in her soft voice.

I finished dressing, and Sam knotted the scarf, adjusting it this way and that. "It's okay, Grace." I smiled at Sam. "After you've had your bath time supervised by another grown woman, familiarity isn't that uncomfortable." I wondered briefly if all girlfriends bantered together this way. "To answer your question, Sam, I *don't* date much. Sacrificing a night out with the guys for uncomfortable time with a stranger? It's been a bad tradeoff more than once. I'd rather sit at home with a bottle of wine and a book."

Sam pursed her lips and shot a side-eye at Grace. "At the risk of getting in even more trouble with this one," she made a show of pointing at Grace, who'd taken over the scarf arranging, "what about sex?"

Grace rolled her eyes. "Still rude."

I just shrugged. "I like sex just fine, but is there a man out there who's any good at it?" I knew the wine had taken a toll when we all collapsed on the bed, laughing. "I mean, it doesn't really measure up to book- or movie-grade passion, in my experience."

"So what kind of experience level are we talking about here?" Grace was sheepish.

"Now who's rude?" Sam laughed at her friend but pulled me to my feet and in front of the mirror. "We haven't talked makeup or hair, but what do you think?"

I couldn't believe the woman who stared at me in the reflection. Long, lean legs and soft curves accentuated but not overly exposed. I'd never turned myself out like this and had no inkling an outfit could lend this degree of confidence or make me feel… different. Pretty.

"You're a knockout, Miles." Grace rested a hand on my shoulder. "It's okay if it feels unusual; you don't usually dress like this, but you should still be yourself. You need to feel comfortable in your skin." She looked over my shoulder into the mirror where my eyes remained fixed on this new version of me. "Does it work for you?"

I nodded slowly. "Yeah. It works. It really works. I might even feel more confident when Oliver shows up."

Sam smirked, and I started to undress. "Yesss. Oliver." She rolled the name leisurely around in her mouth. "I saw him at the picnic; he's Vivvie's cousin. And he's a lot of man, my friend. A lot of man." She wiggled her eyebrows at me. "Let's get back to the former topic, the experience level Gracie mentioned. What are we talking about?"

I sighed and rolled my eyes. "Pretty standard, really. Lost my V card in a freight elevator at the Zoo…"

"Whoa up there, missy." Grace put out both hands in a "stop" motion. "A freight elevator? What zoo, Miles, and what the hell?"

"The United States Air Force Academy, also known as the Zoo. There's not much privacy on offer; so if you want dick, you get it where you can. On that particular night, we stopped the elevator between floors. After a quick trip around the bases, Duane slid into home plate standing up while I held onto a couple of safety handles above my head like my life depended on it."

They stared at me, down to my undies again, and then Sam sputtered with amusement. "Romance, thy name is Duane." After a few minutes, she grinned and jumped up, starting to repack the shopping bags. "Just tell me it got better; surely the quality has improved as time's gone by."

"Beds are softer than freight elevators." I shrugged. "There just haven't been that many over the past few years. I don't sleep with anyone until there have been several dates, at least—and that doesn't happen often. When it does, I guess there's more skill on display—even an orgasm once in a blue moon, if I'm fortunate. But I haven't felt a damn thing that passes for affection."

Grace folded her arms. "You don't look forward to a call? Hope to see them again?"

"Not so far."

Samanthe joined the circle, bags abandoned. "Here's the kicker, though, Miles. Is this different? Do you feel anything for Oliver?"

My belly actually flipped over when she said his name. I blew out a long breath and looked down, scuffing my big toe on the thick carpet. "Yeah. I can't even lie to myself about that, and I'm pretty good at lying to myself." I looked at each of their faces in turn. "He makes me feel like there's a band around my chest; I can't breathe right. My heart pounds in my ears, and I'm afraid he can hear it. Maybe even over the phone. I get a little shaky, and my hands sweat; it's gross."

"What about your pussy?" Sam's voice was matter-of-fact.

"Samanthe!" Grace was horrified now.

"Legit question, Gracie. Does he make you wet, chica?"

I didn't need to think it over. "Hell yes he does. And I don't think that's ever happened before; we've barely even touched."

"It's a good sign, a real good sign." Grace nodded her agreement as Sam continued. "You didn't ask, but let me give you some advice for tomorrow, girl. You're a grown, educated woman. You have your shit together and are great at what you do..."

"Debatable," I mumbled under my breath.

Sam continued, undeterred. "You're used to being in charge and calling the shots, but I want you to relax that death grip you've got on the controls tomorrow. Let yourself enjoy the flow of being with him, and focus on listening to what your head and heart are telling you about him."

Grace's additional input was more softly spoken but no less potent. "Your head, your heart. *And* your body."

Chapter TWENTY

"Gimme Some Truth"

Oliver

Charlotte's condo in the foothills of the Santa Catalina Mountains was a scenic hour's drive from Mount Lemmon, and it was no coincidence I'd chosen this location for our first date. Several days passed between our eventful "meet cute" at the Kwik Shopper and my call to request a date almost a week later. I bided my time, carefully considering the best course of action to approach Charlotte. She wasn't like other women, and the story wasn't told merely in the effect she had on me. Of course, she was stunning with her brilliant smile and hypnotic blue eyes that laughed like we shared a private joke. But a multitude of invisible scripts ran at lightning speed in her head as you spoke to her; and if you weren't incapacitated by her beauty, the undertones of disquiet were unmistakable. I was drawn to her like a moth to a flame, but I didn't know exactly why.

But I intended to find out.

I formulated our first date after a few days' consideration

devoted to cracking this specific nut. She required more attention and care than was customary. That was especially true if I
harbored any hope of drawing her out of the sanctuary where
she sheltered herself against…well, I had no idea what. If I was
honest, I'd have not taken the trouble with another woman. I
never had before. Something remarkable, shimmering just beneath the surface, drew me to her and made it worthwhile. Now
it remained to be seen if I could forge something between us.

I knew what to expect when she answered the door; so I read-
ied myself for the beautiful woman I'd met. She'd be cloaked in
her customary armor of unfussy, gender-neutral attire. She was
on a fool's errand, trying to obscure the incandescent beauty; and
I couldn't work out why she made an effort, but she was far too
clever to attempt it with no cause. I was caught utterly off balance
when she answered the door in a silky tunic, leggings, and—God
help me—soft suede boots that reached over her knees and gave
me thoughts I was embarrassed to admit. The length of my cock
stretched against my zipper before our first words were spoken.

I prided myself on my command of the language and the ability to articulate my thoughts, but the King's English failed me
just now. The opening volley I'd carefully orchestrated over the
past week went like this: "Hello, Charlotte."

This would be followed by an agonizing, cavernous pause.
Utter silence.

Then she smiled cautiously. "Hello again, Oliver. You look
awfully nice."

I stared down dumbly, taking in my dark dungarees and ox-
ford button-down as if I had no idea how I'd dressed myself. I
peered at her again, taking in the growing alarm on her face.

"Will you come in for a moment?" She motioned me in and
then walked toward the open door of what must have been her
bedroom. Her long, slim legs in those boots were a fucking miracle; I begged my dick to ignore the scene unfolding as she crossed

the room. "I just want to snag a jacket; you mentioned it might be chilly. But I need to see what's in the back of my closet. I can't remember the last time I needed something warm."

I stood in the living room, despite her invitation to sit, and wandered, looking at the photographs on the wall near a sliding glass door. The little girl in the photograph had dancing blue eyes and coppery curls that someone had tried to tame with a headband. She couldn't have been more than eight or nine years old and seemed to be enjoying the time of her life, holding on for dear life atop the shoulders of a handsome bloke of sixteen or seventeen. Despite the age difference, it was easy to see they were related; he was the very image of the man in the photo who had a lovely woman, whom I guessed to be in her thirties, held tightly to his side. They laughed at their daughter's antics with the teenager.

Charlotte's voice was quieter than usual behind me. "That was taken the year before Mama died. We all spent a week that summer at my uncle's lake cabin, and I got to swim as much as I wanted every day. Bertie even taught me to do a somersault off the dock." I turned to see the faraway expression on her face. "I spent so much time in the sun that week, I had a tan for the first time ever. Maybe the last time too, now that I think about it. It's no mean feat for a redhead, you know." She grinned at me for just a second before slipping away again.

"The young man holding you—is that Bertie?" I tried to tread lightly as we were obviously in delicate territory.

"Yes. Robert Winston Christman Jr., my big brother. I couldn't—or wouldn't—say 'Robert' when I was little, so it was Bertie back then."

I took a step backward to stand alongside her. "I didn't know you lost your mum, Charlotte; I'm so sorry. You all look so happy here; relaxed and laughing on holiday. It must be a lovely memory for you."

She sighed and looked away, shoulders sagging. "It's a *very* happy memory. One of the last ones I have."

The quiet settled in again briefly before she pasted on another smile and took a big breath, looking back at me. "I risked life and limb but managed to find a jacket in the depths of the closet. I'm all ready to brave the altitude and frozen heights of Mt. Lemmon if you are."

Her eyes shone too brightly, and my chest hurt for the little girl who'd lived nearly the whole of her life without her mum. I couldn't fathom our family without the love and gentle guidance of Serafina Bloodworth. I tamped down the warring sorrow and lust and guided her toward the door with the touch of my fingertips at her waist. "This way, lovely lady. My chariot's at your service."

Most of the drive was predictably filled with small talk about the years at university and our respective careers. I steered clear of family, taking pains not to veer accidentally into territory that would bring the pain back to her blue eyes. She was clever and so funny, entertaining me with stories about Jacob and the antics of the Scorpion squadron, but we avoided anything more serious.

It was easy to see she was practiced at protecting her borders. But I had inadvertently breached the walls with a conversation about a family vacation photograph.

"...so Bash realized drastic measures would be required. He knew the house was perfect for the two of you, but the rent, as they say, was too damned high." Charlotte was deeply involved in the story of how Jacob managed to negotiate the rent on One-Eyed Jacks down into manageable territory.

"Well, don't leave me hanging. I'm riveted. But I'm still trying to figure out why the arrogant wanker never bragged about his superior bargaining skills."

She snickered. "And I'm still trying to figure out how you two named your beautiful home after a whorehouse from a creepy nineties crime drama."

I shrugged and maintained my focus on the road, smirking.

"So he showed up at my condo one Friday afternoon with a fifth of Weed and…"

"Sorry. Weed?"

"Jeremiah Weed." She rolled her eyes in mock disgust. "You embarrass us all when you pretend to embrace ignorance, Oliver. Jeremiah Weed is a ninety-proof blended whiskey distilled in Kentucky. It is *not* tasty. Some have described it as razor blades and kerosene with notes of Drano."

I cut my eyes in her direction. "Sounds delightful."

She waved a hand dismissively. "It's imperative in fighter pilot culture and an insignificant detail in my story. So Bash showed at my door with the Weed and a pizza from Grandma Tony's. You know how it works: you ply a woman with charm and food and alcohol so you can have your way with her." She sent me an evil leer. "And so he did."

I feigned shock, clutching my chest. "The rejection…the pain. All on our first date."

She continued as if I hadn't spoken. "After I was sufficiently full of pizza and whiskey and had departed the moral high ground, he let loose with the plan. He'd found one of those pregnant belly prosthesis things on eBay."

I groaned.

He'd arranged a meeting with your landlord to discuss lower rent, but his confidence was wavering; he knew the odds weren't in his favor. So he brought me along as an insurance policy. He peppered the conversation with references to my hopes to quit my night job and stay home with the baby. Then, when things went south, we pulled out the ace in the hole."

"I'm terrified to ask," I deadpanned.

"I went into labor."

"For the love of God, Charlotte, please tell me your water didn't break."

"Duh. The cardinal rule is not to overplay your hand. I'd watched YouTube videos to get the details just right. The landlord is a middle-aged bachelor, and the plan worked like a charm. He panicked like most people would, scared shitless I'd drop a baby in his living room. You know that only happens on TV," she offered helpfully, in case I ever needed to deliver a baby.

"Anyway, he rushed us to the car, bundling me inside and shouting to Bash about a two-year lease and a ten percent discount. When I howled that I thought the baby was coming, he threw in pool cleaning for six months."

"You're a treacherous woman, Charlotte Christman. I'm frightened to share an enclosed space with you."

She shifted out of storytelling mode and laughed along with me. "All for the greater good, you know. Bash has been a great friend to me." She quieted and stared out the window as the scenery shifted from residential to the scrubby pines and cactus along East Catalina Highway. The starkness of the arid landscape always served to quiet the jumble of thoughts crowding my mind; it was one of the reasons I didn't mind the drive to the range complex for work. The quiet, natural beauty fed my spirit, something I'd always attributed to my introverted tendencies. Stealing a furtive glance toward the passenger seat, I took in Charlotte's thoughtful expression. I'd wondered earlier in the week if the lengthy drive would seem tedious to a woman who struck me as outgoing and sociable. Quite the opposite, the hushed simplicity that calmed me seemed to do the same favor for Charlotte. She turned back to me after several minutes, tucking one slim, booted leg underneath herself.

"I can't imagine that Bashful hasn't told you at least some of the story about the accident several weeks ago." I stole a longer look at her, interested to know where this would lead, but left the talking to her. "It's no secret, really, and I'd be surprised if you didn't know what happened."

"I know that the board of inquiry won't complete and release their findings for some time, perhaps a few months, much the same way the RAF would handle the matter," I began slowly. "But that's not what you're asking, is it?"

She shook her head. I was unprepared for the candid way she approached the issue. I hadn't planned to broach the subject; it didn't seem like a suitable topic for first-date conversation. But her manner was so forthright that I decided instead to follow her lead.

"Jacob did share some of the fundamentals."

She blushed. An actual blush appeared across the fair, smooth expanse of her neck and climbed to color her face prettily.

"You asked him about me?"

I reached across the console without a thought and touched her hand lightly. "You're unbearably charming when you're flustered, Charlotte. The pink on your cheeks is quite becoming."

She pursed her lips, but the blue eyes shone brightly and held my gaze briefly.

"Of course I asked after you. There were so many people at the park that day, and my cousins must've introduced me to nearly everyone. But you drew me, and I hoped there would be occasion for us to meet." We both chuckled a bit at that. "I didn't think weapons and raspberry slushies would be involved, frankly."

"And what did Bash tell you about me?" She suddenly seemed slightly nervous, and her little pink tongue darted out to lick a full bottom lip. It'd been some time since I'd enjoyed the company of a lady, and this one had my full attention. My cock stretched again, swelling rebelliously against his constraints.

Down, boy.

"He told me you were one of a kind; coincidentally, Happy described you using the very same words. I'd have to agree, despite the limited time I've had to enjoy your company." She smiled but didn't reply. "Jake also told me you'd been involved in the aircraft accident and were in the midst of a very difficult time because of it. Since we're being forthright, I'll tell you he was less than thrilled about me taking you out. He didn't care for my timing, given what you're going through, but I can see it's because he feels very protective toward you."

She registered mild surprise. "I think of most of the guys in the squadron like brothers, and Bash is a good friend. But I wondered if he told you more. Since he didn't, I will." She sighed and straightened again, averting her eyes. "I was on Deliverance's wing; he's the weapons officer and one of the best people and finest pilots any of us knows. The crash was my fault, caused by my pride." She coughed softly, and I turned in time to see her emotion playing across her features. "It was an arrogant mistake that's costing a good friend a great deal of pain. That's what Bash meant about me and the difficult time I'm having. I'm…" She looked uncomfortable and clutched her small hands in her lap. "I'm trying to work through what happened and take stock of some things about myself. Unfortunately, they're things that aren't very easy to confront."

Chapter
TWENTY-ONE

"Foggy Mountain Breakdown"

Miles

I'd somehow managed to annihilate a perfectly pleasant first date with a man who could only be described as eatable, and I'd done it efficiently—before we even had time to reach our destination. I came unglued because he was looking at one of my family vacation pictures from Grace Lake, working into the first five minutes of our date the sad information that I'd lost my mother as a child. Now I'd gifted him with the knowledge that I was both at fault in a Class I mishap and currently wrestling with character flaws that might or might not get the better of me. He'd be crazy not to search frantically for an exit.

I glanced surreptitiously at the man seated next to me. Wavy ginger fell across his brow in the unstudied way of a man whose efforts in that department didn't extend beyond barber visits. His build was strong, not overly muscular, and the strength was more of the long and lean variety. A runner's body. He was impossibly tall; he'd have been too tall to pilot a military jet, I realized. Easily six foot four. When we stood side by side, he towered over me, something I liked for reasons unclear to me. His hands were strong, and the long fingers of one hand curled easily around the steering wheel.

When he returned my glance, concerned blue eyes met mine. Flecks of silver and gold warmed the pale blue depths. He was the perfect fucking physical specimen, and every beautiful inch of him pulled me into his orbit. How could I possibly have wrecked my chances with him so thoroughly?

Oh, Bugs. You should have found your A game before you jumped into the deep end.

His delicious accent threaded into my consciousness. "I admire your willingness to be straightforward, Charlotte." He stretched his lanky body in the seat, relaxed and smiling. "Transparency's practically extinct these days. Everyone's so occupied with preening and posturing, especially on a first date." His eyes practically twinkled. Twinkled, for fuck's sake. Who twinkled besides Kris Kringle? I realized I was blatantly staring at his full lower lip and tore my gaze from him.

He refocused on the road. "So then, what's the game plan here? Trying to work through your issues and due diligence with an honest lens…that's a tall order for anyone."

My mouth was still open a bit, so I rectified that before re-centering myself to answer. "Well, if you're actually interested…"

"I am. Lay it on me, Charlotte."

"Deliverance and Coach gave me some ideas. Some direction is in order, I guess. So I'm meeting with this hippie biker therapist friend of Coach's…"

His eyebrows shot into his hairline.

"…and his Uno-playing Tuesday-night therapy group."

The eyebrows maintained their altitude. "Well. I didn't see that coming."

I sighed and closed my eyes, the irony of his understatement not lost on me. "Neither did I."

The restaurant at the base of the ski area served delicious, rustic food throughout the year and specialized in filling the hungry bellies of skiers on the odd occasion when Tucson had enough snow at altitude to support skiing. The air was crisp enough to enjoy the chili and accompanying cornbread recommended by a friendly waitress.

Oliver's eyes crinkled as he smiled across the table, wiping the corner of his mouth with a napkin. "The lunch was tasty, but the pleasure of your company is what's truly brilliant, Charlotte. Thanks for agreeing to come along."

I finished my meal and sat back, patting a full tummy. "I'm all full of warm food and at risk of nodding off on the lift, Oliver."

Hikers and sightseers enjoyed Mt. Lemmon's natural beauty year-round, but occasionally the stars aligned to such a degree that skiing was possible in the unlikely Arizona locale. The lift that shuttled skiers to the modest summit of Mt. Lemmon was pressed into service as a "sky ride" during the rest of the year, inviting leisurely perusal of the landscape during the half hour journey and, eventually, a stunning vista including the Tucson skyline and environs.

Oliver finished taking care of the check and stood, offering his hand. "I solemnly promise to do everything in my power to prevent any lift-related mishaps. Ready to go?"

I nodded and took the hand he offered. The feeling of his strong, warm fingers wrapping mine, however briefly, gave me an unfamiliar but strangely comfortable sensation.

Security. I was unaccustomed to the feeling of protection, no matter how incidental. The walls I'd carefully erected left no place for that. The lanky young lift operator helped us onto the lift and lowered the safety bar into position, and then he sent us off with a friendly wave and singsong, "See ya." The chair lurched forward with a mighty swing, scooping us from the ground, up the hill, and through the trees.

Oliver turned to fix me with a smile and slid one long arm around me. "Is this okay? I don't want to make you uncomfortable."

His hand rested on one shoulder, long fingers skating across my collarbone; and my position in the circle of his arm was more sensed than actually felt. But it was more than okay. My tummy felt light as if it was full of butterflies. It was a sensation I'd read about but never experienced.

"No…I mean, not at all. It's nice, actually." My normal ebullience was somewhat suppressed by mild nervousness. Or maybe it was the effect of the butterflies. I felt almost…what? Girlish? It was a foreign sensation to a woman literally accustomed to playing with the boys. I struggled to be present in the moment with Oliver. The near constant self-examination of the past few weeks was proving a challenge to turn on and off.

"What made you decide to make the jump to a stateside assignment? Obviously, your ties to Bash and Vivvie are a factor." I shifted my position to look up into his face.

"Not *a* factor, really, but *the* factor." The scenery whooshed by, but it faded as I lost myself in the music of his soft, masculine lilt. "Jacob and Vivianne are much more brother and sister to me than cousins, and it's not just because I'm an only child. We've been close since before my Uncle Benji and Aunt Anna brought Vivianne home. Family is terribly important to me, and the bond we share is special. We'd always hoped to be closer geographically, but it took tactical planning to bring it about at last."

His face lit as he spoke of the kinship with Bash and Viv. As pleased as I was for the three of them, it hurt to hear it, reminding me of the sadness that fractured my happy family. I must have sagged visibly, because Oliver's brow snapped together.

"I'm sorry, Charlotte; did I set a foot wrong? We don't have to talk about family; it's bound to be painful for you."

I shook my head, mustering a small smile. "No, no. I want to hear all about it; Bash calls you The Three Musketeers."

He laughed. "I could bore you until sundown with the dubious adventures of Jacob, Oliver, and Vivianne growing up and facing down the perils of middle school and university. I'm not certain it's first date material, though; Jacob's adolescent period wasn't a pretty picture. The knobby knees alone..." He waved a hand. "It's hard to talk about." We both chuckled, although it was objectively impossible to imagine Jacob Travis as anything but sex on a stick.

"I'd be willing to place bets that Vivvie never experienced an awkward phase. She looks like she wakes up in full makeup and designer clothes." Although my encounters with her had been entirely friendly and casual, she was beautiful in an otherworldly way. "She looks like the love child of a Greek god and Priyanka Chopra."

"She does give that impression, but Vivvie's a very down-to-earth woman, believe me." The humor seeped from his tone, and he turned, pulling me infinitesimally closer with the firm hand still on my shoulder. "And what of you, Charlotte Christman—what's your story? I know you must miss your mum; I can't imagine how losing mine would break my heart." He was silent for a beat, studying me. "Is it the only reason your eyes are so sad? Is it all about the beautiful young family in the vacation picture? Or is there more?"

The trees thinned and the earth fell away a bit more as we gained altitude and the skyline of Tucson came into view in the distance. A cool breeze whooshed past, sending shivers through me. It was probably the slight tremble along with my silence that caused Oliver to pull me a bit closer. The wheels in my head spun wildly, and I sorted through the tingles and butterflies inside, trying to make sense of what or how much I'd share. I couldn't just lay myself bare; that wasn't ever in my game plan.

Was it?

I allowed a pause to let the swirling ideas settle. Although I was known as an impulsive risk-taker, acting on emotional instinct was absolutely atypical. I carefully sheltered my feelings, often using humor or bravado to protect myself. It suddenly occurred to me that Charlotte 2.0 might not roll that way. Being more honest with myself might result in the ability to be more transparent with those close to me, and maybe it wouldn't be so bad to allow someone a peek over my carefully constructed walls. Oliver was a stellar choice to test drive my idea; he was kind and steady. I felt reasonably sure I could...

My thoughts were interrupted by warm fingers on my chin, lifting my face to look into his. The voice was low, almost inaudible over the air rushing by. "You don't have to tell me about your family, Charlotte. You don't have to say anything at all. I'm loving every minute next to you; and if your company's all I can enjoy today, it'll be more than enough." The look intensified. "But I'd like to know more about what's inside that head of yours; I can be a vault or a sounding board or a therapist, Charlotte. Or just a friend who's a safe place for you to have a chat. The choice is yours, and I'll be very pleased with whatever you choose to give me." There was a pause. "Even if it's nothing."

Even if it's nothing.

The impact wielded by his words almost moved me physically. People at work rightfully required my time, my expertise, competence, and improvement. But I'd always chafed at the idea of owing everyone else a piece of me. He didn't demand a piece but asked, instead, for a look inside.

Cold air whistled past as I considered my options. The words began to pour out before I'd consciously chosen to share them.

"Losing my mother was as difficult and heartbreaking for me as it would have been for any ten-year-old girl. It's sad how many children have to grow up without a parent—or with no parent at all. But my daddy took it terribly hard too, and our relationship was collateral damage. He reacted to losing Mama by trying to do whatever it took to make sure nothing ever happened to me." I tore my eyes from his and stared, unseeing, toward the skyline.

"But in the end, none of us can control what happens to another person, can we?" His words were quiet.

I shook my head, still avoiding his gaze. "No. We can't. Daddy's grief changed him. He lost perspective and destroyed our relationship, all while trying to keep me safe. I loved him, but I needed room to grow."

Oliver let the silence stretch between us for almost a minute. Finally, he sighed and squeezed my shoulder again.

"And your brother—Robert, is it?"

I let a small smile soften my features, and I turned back to look at him. "I finally learned to say his name, and he was glad to close the door on the 'Bertie' thing." I laughed lightly, remembering how much he disliked the nickname. "I don't see enough of him, and he's important to me. I need to make time to let him know that more often." The little double chairlift dangled us high above the forest floor now, a showy view of Tucson filling the horizon as the sun dipped.

Oliver cleared his throat. "There's hardly anything more important than telling the people…"

His words were abruptly interrupted by a jarring screech above us followed by the sudden arrest of the chair's forward motion. We swung violently in midair, and I gasped. Oliver's muscular arm tightened around me like a vise, and his other hand grasped the safety bar, steadying us both.

The forest was silent beneath us, only the eerie, metallic squeak of the cable above breaking the quiet.

"Are you alright, love?" His voice was solicitous, and I wondered if he could hear the hammering of my heart.

"I'm fine." Considering the events of the past few weeks, which included an aircraft accident and an armed robbery, this shouldn't be more than a blip on the radar. But, in the other two instances, I'd not found myself resting in the unsettling comfort of Oliver's arms.

"Charlotte." Oliver relaxed his grip but squeezed me a bit as the swinging of the chair settled. "Are you well? Look at me."

I shook my head as if to clear it. "Sorry. Lost in my head again; I'm fine." I looked around, taking in the fact that the two lift chairs ahead of and behind us were empty. There wasn't another soul in view. I noted that Oliver did a similar sweep of the landscape, doubtlessly arriving at a similar conclusion.

"Not to worry, Charlotte. The lift keep knows we're here; he'll be along to repair the problem or—at worst—arrange for our rescue." A big grin split his handsome face. "I know you're not worried about heights."

True enough.

He patted my thigh and began to remove his well-worn leather jacket. "I'm sure the cable can be moved along manually. It'll take a bit for the bloke to reach us, but they'll haul us in by hand, if they need to, and Bob's your uncle!"

The absurdity of the British phrase shattered the serious mood, and we both belly-laughed, long and loud, as he wrapped his bomber jacket around my shoulders. Our mirth bounced around the forest before dying off at last; it felt like a release I needed, dismissing the somber discussion of loss and heartbreak. Oliver turned his pale blue eyes on me, his wide smile fading to something darker.

"You're quite stunning, Charlotte." He lifted one hand to my cheek and turned my face slightly. We'd looked into one another's eyes before now, but this time he regarded me leisurely, as if taking in the details of my face. For the first time I could remember, there was no urge to hide myself, to dispel the intensity building between us. I welcomed his perusal. Neither of us made any pretense about looking away, instead wordlessly studying the other, sizing up the attraction and searching for what might lie beyond.

He moved his face into my space, never breaking our gaze, and took a breath as if he might speak. I wished he would say something to bring some clarity to the unfamiliar draw I felt. But he reconsidered and leaned closer, finally brushing my mouth unhurriedly with warm, full lips. The effect was electric. I couldn't remember a kiss over the course of my life that affected me as this one did. His mouth lifted from mine—only a millimeter—our faces so close I felt a tickle as his long lashes brushed my face. My eyes flickered closed, and I didn't breathe, wondering what would come next.

Please, God, let it be more of that mouth.

His deep voice was almost reverent, wholly in harmony with the hush of the mountain. "I feel something for you I can't quite explain, Charlotte. You…you mesmerize me." The palm on my cheek tipped my face up a bit, and my eyes fluttered open. He watched me from beneath a hooded gaze. "I hope you can feel it too."

My throat was too tight to speak, so I just wet my lips and nodded my head, maybe too frantically.

His mouth curved almost imperceptibly on one side. "It's curious, isn't it? I'm doing a poor job of putting words to my thoughts, Charlotte, but you're just…lovely, really. I can't say I'm sorry we're stranded. With any luck, the lift keep will take his time."

Chapter
TWENTY-TWO

"Sky High"

Oliver

It was all happening at once.

Fucking finally.

It was as if circumstances conspired to grant us an opportunity I couldn't have dared wish for. Every occasion I'd had to cross her path resulted in some kind of upheaval or blunder. We could never manage to scale or circumnavigate whatever obstacle kept her from me; so fate intervened and left me suspended in the cool air above Mt. Lemmon, my arms happily full of a willing and pliant Charlotte. The movement of her soft tresses across my face and shoulders brought with it a delicious scent of coconuts. It made me hard, and that was fucking inconvenient.

My face lowered again to hers, the kiss starting tentatively. A request. I explored her soft lips and mouth unhurriedly, stroking her tongue with mine. Tasting. The hand around her shoulders pulled her nearer, and I let the fingers of my other hand slip into her hair, combing through soft curls now ruffled by the breeze. I wanted to inhale her, take everything she'd give and more, but the voice in my head advised restraint. I eased my grasp a bit and pulled back slightly from the sweetness of her kiss. Her eyes fluttered open, and I was unduly pleased to see them unfocused and hazy. She exhaled on a soft moan and relaxed against me. My hard cock beat an insistent appeal, begging for inclusion in the festivities. Her soft breasts pressed into my chest, and I took a breath to steady myself.

"I feel it, too, Oliver." Her small hands reached for me and pulled my face back to hers. She placed little kisses at the corners of my mouth, then along the seam before gently nipping the fullest part of my bottom lip.

I shushed that damned voice of restraint and dove deeply back into her. My mouth fused to hers, giving and taking, the little chair that held us aloft reduced to a whirling vortex separating me from reality. In a bare moment, I was drowning in all of her—the delicious smell, her warm skin and intoxicating touches. Her breathy moans, quietly escaping as I took her mouth, fueled an urgent desire surging through me like wildfire. Words were spare, squeezing into scant moments when we surfaced for gulps of air.

"So good, Charlotte…need you…want more…"

Her small hands smoothed over my torso and belly, petting and stoking the raging inferno higher. I allowed one hand the privilege of the heavy softness of her breast, my thumb stroking upward to encounter a tight nipple through her clothing. Her moans escalated to a whimper, and I dropped my mouth onto the soft skin of her neck to enjoy the sound. We were both running hotter by the second. I fondled her nipple, rolling the tip just a bit between my thumb and finger while she pleaded quietly for more. Somewhere in the fevered recesses of my consciousness, I grappled with the notion that a ski lift chair was among the poorest choices available for a trip around the bases. There were safety considerations this far from the ground, but

I couldn't yet come to grips with the concept of removing my mouth or hands from her body. Her little fists clutched my shirt, pulling me closer with surprising strength. I was utterly fucked.

"Dude…hey, man!" The male voice from somewhere below felt like an ice pick to the head and had the effect of an icy shower on my erection.

"Duuuude." Charlotte and I disentangled ourselves slowly, and I looked below to see the lift operator on a four-wheeler. It must have been thunderously loud as he rode it up the mountain toward us, but I'd not heard a damned thing but the pounding of my heart and Charlotte's moans and whimpers. The lad stood on the footrests of his vehicle, a big grin splitting his face. "Kudos, man…making the best of a bad situation, right?"

I tried and failed to keep irritation from my reply. "None of your concern, now is it? You've come with good news, I hope."

He was nonplussed by my annoyance. "For sure. This happens pretty much on the regular, but don't freak out. I've got this ultimate set of tools; I can fix it."

"Really?" Charlotte muttered under her breath. "This is a good time to quote Ferris Bueller?"

I whispered back conspiratorially with a smile. "Actually, it's *Fast Times at Ridgemont High*." I turned back to address the bloke on the ground who continued to stare up with that shit-eating grin. "Let's be about it, then. It's not getting any warmer up here."

"Give me ten, dude. I've done it a million times." He was off with a casual wave of his hand, his four-wheeler tackling the incline effortlessly.

"You promised me a tedious second date, Oliver." Charlotte's blue eyes danced with laugher as she leveled the accusation. "There were no firearms or martial arts this time around, but I don't think you can make a solid case that you actually delivered on your promise."

We were walking through the parking lot toward my Range Rover, hands casually clasped. "You could be right, love, but we're left with only one option at this point. You're beholden to allow me another chance at a tiresome, prosaic evening together, aren't you?"

She wrinkled her nose. "Prosaic? Are you trying to impress me with your enormous, erm...vocabulary?" She laughed outright at her innuendo, but I assumed an aloof air.

"Not at all, beautiful. I'm just glad to see you."

The drive back to her townhouse was filled with laughter and easy conversation. We continued to share stories about our families and work as one does over the course of early dates, but something already felt as if we'd known one another longer. Something had shifted, and we spoke openly, less self-consciously and guarded than we had on the drive up the mountain. Even at this early juncture, something in me already knew it would be more.

"Don't you dare tell Bashful." Charlotte's lovely blue eyes danced with amusement as I parked the Range Rover in the space near the stairs that led to her front door. "If you tell him I broke the lift on Mt. Lemmon, he'll spread the word that I'm a jinx." She laughed, looking more at ease than I'd seen her before. "If you keep this under your hat, I can still make a case that the Kwik Shopper robbery was just an unfortunate coincidence."

I shrugged as I put the truck in park. "I wouldn't worry too much, lovely. Jacob's a pretty face, to be sure, but he doesn't have too much at work between the ears. I doubt he's bright enough to put the clues together on his own." We both laughed at the notion; the dim bulb persona Vivianne and I used to tease my cousin with was far from the truth of the matter.

The mirth died off gradually, and comfortable silence overtook us. I took one of Charlotte's hands in mine, turning it over and stroking her palm with one of my fingers.

"Would you…Oliver?" She paused. "Would you like to come in for a glass of wine or…" Her words were softly spoken, but I didn't sense hesitation. She was sure of what she was asking.

I looked up to meet her gaze. The blue eyes were quiet, devoid of the restless energy I'd seen there in the past. She was content to be in this moment with me. It was the first time I felt certain her defenses were down, that she was at ease with me, allowing herself to be seen and heard. I wanted her more than I'd ever wanted any single thing in my entire life. I swallowed hard and cupped her face with one hand, enjoying its beauty in the scant light.

"I'd love nothing more than to carry you up the stairs and seal the world out behind a locked door, Charlotte. I'd cherish the chance to spend the entire night and the whole of tomorrow acquainting myself with each exquisite inch of you, worshiping you with my words and body." She didn't blink, blue eyes locked on me as I spoke. "I want nothing more than to make love to you for the first time tonight, and my cock is furious with me for what I'm about to say. This…" I squeezed her cheek gently. "Whatever this is between us…something in me is demanding I treat it with the utmost caution. That I handle your heart carefully. I don't want to hurry anything between us, love; there will be time for that very soon."

I was surprised to see her face soften with a little smile; she touched the hand that rested on her cheek. "Thank you, Oliver. Thank you for watching out for me. For protecting my heart. No one has ever looked out for me this way." She leaned in, kissing me softly before looking down briefly. Long, soft eyelashes brushed my cheek. "But I'm going to hold you to the promise that there will be time for us together soon."

I wound one arm around her, reveling in the magnificent softness, and buried my other hand in the silky auburn curls falling down her back. "Soon, Charlotte. You're worth the wait, but my cock is going to be an impatient bastard."

Chapter
TWENTY-THREE

"There's a Place in the World for a Gambler"

Miles

"I'm feeling fine, Robert, I promise you." I smiled at my brother's concern. It had taken all my powers of persuasion to convince him not to fly to Tucson after the accident, and the intervening three months hadn't assuaged his anxiousness about my condition. The old version of Miles—I'd taken to referring to her as Miles-Dos—would have been eternally annoyed with the worried interrogation Robert was subjecting me to. The fact that the effect was reversed was proof that I was indeed changing, and that brightened my mood this sunny fall afternoon. "I should have let you come after the accident just to prove I was in one piece," I teased my brother. "You're too old to put much stock in newfangled inventions like digital photos and FaceTime, aren't you, old man?"

Robert's big laugh warmed me across the miles. "I'm only thirty-one, Bugs. I don't have a foot in the grave quite yet; I even got some of those fancy electrical lights in my apartment—indoor plumbing, too."

I loved to badger my brother about our age difference, harassing him as if he were a backward geezer who spent his days yelling at kids to get off his lawn. In fact, the opposite was quite obvious in person. Robert was tall and very handsome with lots of dark hair and serious brown eyes. The year I left home for the Air Force Academy, he finally began taking classes again at Iowa State. At first, he continued working at the hardware store and caring for Daddy, shoehorning in classes at night and on the weekend using the distance learning programs. Frustrated at the slow progress, he eventually moved to a small town closer to the university and commuted to classes on campus, working a part-time job to make ends meet. He continued to spend as much time as possible with Daddy, but his concern for our father's depression forced additional solutions. He'd not shared with me all the details during my college years, concerned that my studies would be impacted, but he'd found community resources in Ames to help Daddy. There was group counseling and, eventually, medication. The two of them commuted together two days a week, and Daddy found his own part-time job in the small animal clinic in the College of Veterinary Medicine.

At the end of this past summer, my brother left Iowa State with a master's degree in agricultural economics, graduating summa cum laude. I could not have been prouder of him, especially given the obstacles he'd overcome. The only missing puzzle piece was the void left by Daddy's absence in my life. I wanted to ask Robert why Daddy never called or tried to visit, but the years of separation had taken their toll.

At least I had my big brother.

"Tell me about this man you've met, Bugs. Do I need to come down there and have a look in person? I'm suspicious by nature when it comes to someone who's caught my baby sister's eye."

I smiled. Robert's brand of overprotectiveness warmed my heart. "His name is Oliver, and you'd really like him, Robert. He's kind and good, and he's hot as fuck, but you don't want to hear about that, do you?" I laughed at the gagging sounds and protests.

"No details, Bugs—none! I can't handle it; I'll have to bleach my brain as it is." He paused. "Honestly, though. Is he good to you, Charlotte? Right now, after the accident…you're in no position to get entangled with someone who might not treat you with respect."

Ironic that he brought it up after the way my first date with Oliver ended, but I wouldn't subject him to the details. "He really is a good guy, but it's early. We'll have to see what happens next." I changed the subject quickly before the interrogation got out of hand. "So, what's next for you, Robert? I'm sure the apartment's the cat's snatch, but do you really mean to stay in rural Iowa forever? Manhattan, it ain't."

His laughter always warmed me. "The degree is in agricultural economics, Bugs, not theatre or hospitality management. Did you think I'd be moving to Rome or Paris?" The line was quiet, and I could practically hear him thinking. "One of the silver linings that came out of staying here with Dad was that I discovered I have a real passion for living close to the earth. Improving our abilities to feed ourselves and people around the world."

His words settled me. He'd given up his dreams for Daddy and me, but fate turned that sacrifice into a gift in its own right. "It's good to find your niche, isn't it, Bertie?" For once, he didn't give me grief about the nickname. "I found mine. I just hope it isn't gone for good."

He blew out a breath. "Any idea when the accident investigation board will return findings?" I'd been very honest with Robert from the beginning about every detail surrounding the accident and my journey toward self-discovery.

"Not really. Soon, I hope. I'm ready to know more so I can work on the next chapter in my life, whatever that is." With every passing day, I felt inexplicably more sure the board would recommend taking away my wings. And the more I worked at combating the pride and detachment that had characterized my young life, the more convinced I became that everything would work out as fate intended.

"Speaking of which, it's Tuesday, Bugs. You've got a hot Uno game to get ready for. What are you taking tonight?" Robert was confounded at the idea that I was learning to cook. He'd been sure I was concocting stories when I first told him about the oddities of The Tuesday Game and demanded pictures of the dips and appetizers I'd described taking.

"Actually, I just finished this savory herb cheesecake. It's made with fresh-snipped dill and chives, baked in a water bath, and served with a variety of crackers and fresh veggies. It looks delicious." I sniffed at Robert's incredulous grunt. "It's just science—science and following directions. I have a degree in aerospace engineering; it turns out cooking isn't all that impossible if you put your mind to it."

He sounded dubious, but I knew it was an act. "You know I'm gonna need pictorial proof of this one, Bugs. Send me a picture of the whole group, while you're at it. I want to be able to put faces with the names."

He'd always found time to take a genuine interest in my life; in some ways, I'd realized, he was the parental figure I'd lacked since Mama died. Now that I was an adult, our relationship had settled comfortably into more of a friendship. Fresh from grad school, Robert was enthusiastically looking at new opportunities, and I was thrilled. It felt good to celebrate his successes with him.

"I've got some job prospects and a couple of interviews coming up; I'll keep you in the loop, 'kay?"

His kind voice was like a balm. "I love you, Robert. Say hi to Daddy for me, will you?"

"Sure will, Bugs. Later…"

"Coming…" I shouted at the door as I hurriedly buttoned the cornflower blue silk blouse Grace had insisted I keep from the wardrobe emergency visit the other night. It was nothing I'd ever have selected for myself—too sexy—but Sam said it was the exact shade of my eyes. I thought Oliver might like that, and despite the fact it was Tuesday, tonight was very much about my mouthwatering Brit.

Oliver had business near Ventana Canyon and insisted on coming by to pick me up and deliver me to Keeper and Emmay's house. He wanted to see my latest appetizer masterpiece and use the drop off as an excuse to meet The Tuesday Game cast of characters. He'd also be picking me up once the evening had concluded. He had the next day off. I'd worked Saturday at a fundraiser the flying squadrons held jointly to raise money and awareness for local children's charities. Coach insisted I take a day off this week to make up for the long Saturday I'd volunteered, and I had no difficulty picking Wednesday.

Hello, hump day.

"Hi there, love." When I opened the door, there was Oliver, hot as a fever dream, holding a bouquet of flowers and leaning against my doorframe. His hair was a bit out of regs, curling mischievously and framing the pale blue of his eyes. His button-down shirt was worn with the sleeves rolled to mid-forearm, and the bulge of toned biceps was evident beneath. Most intriguing, however, were the jeans, and I couldn't stop appreciating the way the slim-cut denim hugged him in all the right places. The bulge was unmistakable, and I tried, unsuccessfully, not to stare.

His free arm encircled my waist and pulled me against him.

Now the bulge was hard and impossible to miss. "I'm glad to see you, Charlotte." He paused deliberately. "Very glad, love, but you can feel that, can't you?" He practically growled the words in my ear.

"Y-yes. I can feel it, Oliver." His mouth was on mine, teasing it open and conducting a thorough, unhurried exploration right on my front porch, in full view of anyone who might walk by. When he'd finished, I whispered my thoughts in a shaky tone. "I think I want to abandon The Tuesday Game."

He sent me that devastating smile again. He was wearing glasses; thick black ones with rectangularish frames.

Glasses, for fuck's sake.

There was no hope for concentrating on anything else; I stared openly. "I never saw you wear glasses, Oliver. They're... they're very nice."

"Thanks, love." He held up the bunch of flowers; there were lilies and some roses, and a dozen or so things I didn't recognize, but they were so beautiful. "I have book club tonight."

I smiled as we stepped inside. "Book club? The plot thickens. How could I have missed this juicy tidbit, Oliver?"

He made himself at home on the sofa, stretching his arms wide across the back as I sat on the floor to lace up my Chucks—vintage All Stars in baby blue suede. Who can resist blue suede shoes?

"I found a post about the group on the 'New to D-M' forum online. It's only my fifth or sixth meeting with them, but it's an ideal group for me. A perfect fit." He lowered his voice conspiratorially. "I'm a bit of a raving history nerd, and you've never seen a more jaw-dropping collection of geeky bibliomaniacs in your life. We were made for each other."

He jumped up from his seat when I'd finished, and he offered me a hand. "Have you packed a bag, Charlotte? I don't intend to let you go one moment earlier tomorrow than I absolutely must." His tone was light, but his eyes were very serious.

I was horrified to feel a telltale flush creeping up my chest. When we'd spoken yesterday on the phone, we'd worked out the details of our coinciding days off and his picking me up from the Bond home. He'd asked me to come back to his house for the night; as good fortune would have it, Bash was cross country and wouldn't return until the weekend. That lent the privacy we would obviously need, and there was no practical reason to spell out the fact that he was clearing the decks for our *first time*. We were consenting adults who felt a strong attraction to each other, and I was surely no blushing virgin. But I could feel my face flaming—and see Oliver smiling indulgently at the sight.

"Those pink cheeks are so fetching, love." He gathered me into his arms and whispered in my ear as if we shared a secret. "Don't be shy, lovely. Truth is, I love seeing you like this, looking all skittish and on edge. It's so different from the Miles the rest of the world gets to see, and it feels like a private look into who you really are…something just for me."

I couldn't find any words, and it was just as well because he took advantage of the lull in the conversation to kiss me again, thorough and unhurried. Then he continued whispering. "I've been thinking about seeing you tonight, wondering about all manner of things I know about you. All the parts of you—your confidence and sassy mouth and that bright intellect…the way you've worked so hard to be the best at what you do. The generosity of your heart and the soft spirit you hide from other people." He looked into my eyes steadily, smiling, as he told me all the wonderful things he thought of me. "I love those things about you. I think you're just delightful, Charlotte, inside and out. I want nothing more than to know you even better, love, and tonight I get to take a big step in that direction."

Then his mouth dropped close to my ear once again, and the

pounding of my heart threatened to drown out whatever he'd say. But the words were unmistakable, and I knew I'd never forget them.

"Get ready, Charlotte Christman, because I'm coming for you. And I'm going to win your heart, starting tonight."

Chapter
TWENTY-FOUR

"The Thunder Rolls"

Oliver

The drive back to my house on Tucson's western edge was only slightly over a half hour, but every minute seemed endless. I couldn't help stealing glances at my passenger-seat occupant when she was distracted by the scenery. She was quiet and more thoughtful than usual, but that was usually the case after The Tuesday Game. There had been several since our first date, and I noted Charlotte's demeanor was generally reflective in the immediate aftermath. Had I been unaware of this, I might have worried that she was hesitant about the step we were taking tonight. I'd very deliberately slowed the pace of play after the Mt. Lemmon date. Something powerfully suggested to me I should take every precaution in the progress of our relationship. She was special and required care and mindful treatment. Then again, it could have simply been Jacob's threat to castrate me with a kitchen knife if I hurt her. Either way, I was paying more attention than I'd done with women in the past.

Several quiet minutes had passed, and I wanted to open the

door to conversation. Each week when Charlotte recounted the discussions and the counsel her friends gave, I marveled at the collective wisdom present in this arbitrary group of individuals. When I mentioned my observation a couple of weeks ago, she'd countered with her notion that Keeper was more skilled than he seemed on the surface. She surmised that the gathering was carefully curated, assembled with the goal of equipping people to help one another. If she was right, he was even more extraordinary than I'd originally thought.

"How was tonight, Charlotte?" She smiled and turned toward me, her features lit with the flashes of lightning from a gathering storm.

"It was a good night—a really good night." Her face split open unexpectedly in a huge smile. "Tonight, I got to be the one to help someone. Me, Oliver. I've felt discouraged sometimes over the sensation of being the class project—the one who needs more help than anyone else. I'm grateful for the help—and I'm making strides—but it doesn't feel right to take and take. I wanted to be able to give back, but I haven't had much to offer. At least I didn't until tonight."

My heart felt as if it would leap from my chest; I was so happy for her and this new success she reveled in. I hadn't known it was important to her.

"It was the simplest thing, really. Covington lost his wife to cancer two years ago, and he's had more than his share of obstacles as he's tried to work through the grief. There's a lady he'd like to ask out on a date, but one of his kids caught wind of it and is dealing him all kinds of hell about it. Can you imagine?"

"And what did you tell him?" The light show in the western sky was escalating, I noticed. I hoped we could make it back to the house before the bottom dropped out; Tucson thunderstorms were often remarkably intense.

"I think the first pass was something along the lines of, 'Tell them to mind their own fucking business.'" She chuckled. "But I followed up by talking about the importance of playing the long game as a parent—that his fitness as a father to his children depended, to a degree, on his ability to care for himself. Keeper added that adult children often don't evolve in their ability to see a parent as an adult with physical and emotional needs."

I reached across to rest my hand on her thigh. "I'm so proud of you, Charlotte. It says something important about you when you look outside your own needs to help someone else."

She smiled and turned away again to contemplate the horizon and the incoming storm. "Are you asking about tonight to distract me from what we're going to do when we get to your house?" Her tone was lighthearted, and I was pleased, sensing that most of the tension I'd felt earlier was dissipating. I lifted an eyebrow and smirked at her.

"I've no idea to what you refer, lovely; I've asked you to my home to look at some etchings I display at my residence. I hope you're not thinking of spoiling my virtue, young lady—my mother did warn me about strumpets like you."

She snorted indelicately. "Strumpets? You're so much more British than I feared."

We were both laughing as I pulled the Range Rover into the garage. "Let's go in and open a bottle of wine, Charlotte. It looks like Mother Nature's about to put on a show we don't want to miss."

The patio outside my room was what distinguished my suite in the house Jacob and I'd rented, at least in my opinion. Jacob was very fond of his orgy-sized shower, but I preferred something with a view. There was easy access to the pool alongside the house, but my patio had its privacy as well. I'd taken some effort to furnish it with an outdoor settee and a big oversized chaise lounge that could afford me the possibility of watching the sunset outside my bedroom. Following a brief tour, Charlotte and I settled on the plush settee and awaited the incoming storm.

"Good blend, British. I heartily approve. Reds are tricky… also, I don't know dick about wine."

I smiled and reached for the bottle to top her off. "It's a pity to be unfamiliar; you have access to some of the finest wine in the world here. Arizona isn't too far from Sonoma and Napa."

She acknowledged my refill with a lifted glass. "So, maybe we should plan a road trip to the Wine Country?"

I pulled her closer as the thunder rumbled. "It would be a pleasure to accompany you through the Wine Country. Let's put that on the dance card for the future; but, for now…" She lifted her face to mine, and I allowed my mouth to melt into hers. When the kiss was finally done, her lashes were downcast.

"Does it make you uneasy, love, the thought of us together? Naked. Knowing each other like we didn't yesterday?" She swallowed but didn't say anything as she looked back up into my eyes. I loved how petite she felt held in the curve of my arm. The juxtaposition was pleasing in comparison to my stupidly lanky frame, but I didn't know why.

She cleared her throat, apparently deep in thought. "I wouldn't say uneasy, exactly. This isn't the first time for me, Oliver, but…" There was a long pause and she considered her words. "It's the first time I cared about the outcome. I have skin in the game, and I don't know exactly how invested you are." She hesitated. "I'm in pretty deep."

I turned, sweeping aside the tumble of curls from her shoulder and baring the pale skin of her neck to nuzzle and kiss her there. She hummed softly, deep in her throat, and I noticed that her fingers tightened around the bowl of her wine glass.

My God, she's delectable. Take your time here, Ollie.

"I'm invested, Charlotte," I whispered the words quietly between kisses to the tender spot right between her ear and hairline. "My cock was invested the second I saw you at the picnic; I wanted to stride across the lawn and demand to know why you were sitting with another man." At this, the movement of her face told me she was smiling. "But my head and my heart have been equally smitten, darling girl." I pulled away to meet her eyes. "I've met you at a crossroads in your life where you're confronting truths and questions that would test a saint. And I've watched from the sidelines as you meet each challenge with grace. The honest, humble way you've approached this challenge…it moves me."

Her eyes were shiny with unshed tears, but her gaze never wavered. I took her wine glass and set both on a side table. "One of the ways you've inspired me has been in the desire to wait until the time was absolutely right to take this next step with you. It's been difficult not to leap ahead." She sighed, allowing her head to rest in the crook of my arm, and I took the opportunity to pull her close and let one hand rest under her shirt against the warm skin of her belly.

Her lips curved upward at my touch, and she stroked my face gently with one hand. "I hope your restraint's wearing thin, Oliver. I'm not counting on getting any sleep tonight."

My smile matched hers now, and I leaned closer, allowing my hand to drift up to the softness of her breast. "There's very little restraint left now, love. I think it's time for us both to check our inhibitions at the door." My finger slid into the cup of her bra, finding the velvety softness of her nipple and petting it tenderly. "I've wanted inside you since I first laid eyes on you, and tonight, the only thing I want more is to feel you coming against my fingers." I moved closer until only a hairsbreadth separated us. "And against my lips…and around my cock."

I touched my mouth to hers, allowing the kiss to deepen

gradually and reveling in the tightening of her nipple as I caressed it. We explored each other's mouths languidly, tongues searching and stroking unhurriedly. She deftly unbuttoned my shirt from bottom to top, her hands cool from the wine glass. She brushed her fingers on my chest and along the sensitive skin of my ribcage. I dropped my head again to kiss the line of her jaw down to her neck, one of my hands conducting a brief search for the clasp of her bra. When I was at university, I could unfasten these things skillfully with only one hand, but that was a long time ago.

I felt the hateful garment release her lovely breasts into the care of my hands only a fraction of a second later, and Charlotte responded on a sigh with, "Oh, Oliver..." Both hands now hurried along, divesting her of the silken blouse and pulling her astride me so I could begin learning every delectable inch of her. Our mouths never left one another now, stroking and nipping between long, deep kisses. Her nipples pebbled under the attention of my fingers, and she moaned her approval into my mouth.

The lightning had stayed safely in the distance, but now the light breeze stiffened to a gust, just as large raindrops began to plop into the pool. I wrapped my arms around Charlotte's waist and leaned her back slightly, dipping my mouth to sample the swell of her breasts. She arched her back, thrusting the pink tips toward my mouth. I suckled one, swirling my tongue across the taut peak and teasing her with a gentle bite. She groaned appreciatively, and her bottom rotated against my cock, already suffering mightily.

Patience, big guy. She needs to be wet and begging. Beyond ready.

I could have lived out the remainder of my life teasing and nuzzling her lush breasts and drinking in the sexy little sighs and groans of satisfaction from her lips. She was restless and squirming in my lap, torturing my erection with the softness of her ass cheeks. I contributed to my own burgeoning discomfort by sliding my length in and out of the valley of her plush little bum. The front of my jeans would certainly be wet with the precum my cock was leaking. I would gladly have continued the sweet torment, but Charlotte had different ideas.

She pulled herself upright, breasts bouncing prettily as they fell from my lips. Her hair was damp from the rain, and water droplets ran freely across her shoulders, falling from the nipples I'd left ripe and rosy with my mouth. Her beautiful blue eyes were darker than usual and hooded. "I want more of you, Oliver…" She stood from my lap, backing up a step, and shimmied quickly out of the wet Levi's and little white panties. My cock strained mightily against my zipper, weeping profusely.

She was a fucking goddess, and I told her so. Or I hope I did, deprived of the powers of speech as I was. Her body was flawlessly pale as if carved in ivory but so soft. Her belly was flat and her waist small, decorated only with an adorable little navel. And just below, God help me, was the most perfectly beautiful little pussy I'd ever seen. Only the barest cloud of wispy, dark red hair adorned it, and I could see…holy fuck. I could see how wet she was from where I sat.

"Your thighs are wet, darling." I practically groaned the words. "That precious cunt of yours needs my mouth."

She swallowed so hard, I could see her throat work. Then her gaze swept around the patio and she moved immediately to the oversized chaise lounge, quickly adjusting it until it lay flat—almost the size of a double bed.

Thank you, God, for that pushy salesman at Your Outdoor Heaven.

Charlotte sat at the foot of the chaise, pulling her feet up to rest on the cushion; the rain now ran freely off her arms, breasts, thighs…I reached for the button fly of my jeans.

"Oliver?" She was completely still, staring at the bulging fly where my fingers rested. Her eyes flitted suddenly to my feet, then back to my fingers.

I popped one button free, then a second. "Yes, love?"

Her demeanor shifted like the ground during an earthquake, all in the space of a second. Her eyes darted about nervously. "What, umm…what size shoe do you wear?"

"Charlotte, darling. What kind of question is that?" I flipped the third button, closer every moment to paradise between her thighs.

Oh, wait.

I stopped undressing and closed the distance between us, bending to take her again into my arms. "What's on your mind, love?" She hesitated, although I could tell she wanted to speak.

"What size shoe, British?"

I frowned briefly, sparing a glance at my feet. *Fucking water skis.*

"It's a myth, you know."

"Yeah. A myth. What size, Oliver?"

I hugged her close; the rain was doing a *Flashdance* number on our outdoor sex scene, and I hoped this interlude wouldn't be too intrusive.

"Thirteen, Charlotte, but it's a myth."

I felt her body relax in my arms, and her shoulders shook with laughter. It made me smile.

"Please, British, continue with the Magic Mike routine; I promise not to freak out when I see it."

That seemed a disrespectful tone to use when addressing my trouser snake, so I stood and backed up a few steps, popping open the fourth button with a crooked grin. "I wouldn't want to frighten you, love, but you might want to prepare yourself." The smirk on my face as I opened the final button was meant to let her know I was teasing.

She smiled, arms wrapped around long legs she still had

drawn up to shield her lovely center.

I dropped the jeans, along with my boxer briefs, around my ankles and stepped out of them, naked and hard enough to cut steel. I'd never needed inside someone so much as I did Charlotte.

Her eyes widened, and her mouth opened slightly at the sight of me stepping toward her, stroking the length of my suffering shaft from root to tip. The wide head was almost purple and slick with precum I'd been leaking since we started this dance on the patio. Then she slowly leaned back onto her elbows and wordlessly spread her legs wide.

Chapter
TWENTY-FIVE

"Take My Breath Away"

Miles

*H*oly king-sized disco stick, Batman.

I hoped my face didn't betray the astonishment wracking my entire body at the first sight of a gloriously nude Oliver Bloodworth. The man was fucking beautiful. He was long and sleek, with just enough toned muscle to lend masculine strength to the entire package. And the package, sweet Jesus. He stalked toward me, eyes locked on mine, with the long fingers of one hand fisting his shaft and stroking it slowly. A closely trimmed thatch of ginger surrounded the thick root of his erection, and his balls hugged tight to his body. Most hypnotic of all was the fact he was uncut. I'd not seen an uncircumcised cock before, at least not in person, and I was mesmerized. He stood before me, his body relaxed, and stroked his length rhythmically. I was utterly enthralled to note that the wide mushroom head struggled somewhat to emerge on each stroke as the foreskin stretched across the wide expanse, and I wondered idly what the hell that felt like. He was big all over; it appeared that the "shoe size myth" might have legs.

"Look what you've done, love." His voice snatched me back. "My cock's weeping for the want of you. You're gorgeous there, all spread out for me, Charlotte." He knelt between my legs and placed his hands on my inner thighs, pushing them wider. "Lie back, now. I'm going to feast on this wet little cunt."

I couldn't think of anything intelligent to say, so I simply nodded and allowed myself to sink back onto the pillowed edge of the chaise. Thunder continued to rumble in the distance, and the steady rain caused a haze of steamy mist to envelop the patio, rendering the scene ethereal and almost otherworldly. My forearm draped partially across my face, shielding me from the rain and allowing me to watch Oliver kiss and lick a path across my belly. I buried one hand in his hair, alternately tugging and combing my fingers through the wet curls, grinding my hips toward his mouth all the while.

"Patience, love. I want to enjoy all of you…" His voice sounded like he was in pain, but the groans that punctuated his ministrations told a different story. "I've waited so long to taste you, to love your pussy; I won't be rushed now. Let me feed, darling."

I'd been with other men. I was also very competent at taking care of my own needs and did so regularly. But my body's response as he neared my center was not comparable in any way to anything I'd felt before. The sheer want—the gnawing hunger at my core—didn't compare to anything I'd experienced. If the lounge had suddenly been engulfed in flames, it wouldn't have been a reason sufficient enough for me to move myself from the path his mouth was on. I pulled one of my legs back, abandoning his hair in favor of opening myself further to him. "Please, Oliver. Fuck, please lick me; let me feel your mouth."

His fingers were on me, carefully spreading me open for his examination. His eyes were stormy, and he licked my taste from his lips. One finger dipped into my opening and then spread the wet around my clit, circling gently as he blew out a breath. I shuddered, already so close. "My God, Charlotte. You're beautiful…this is the sweetest, loveliest pussy I've ever had the privilege to see." He rested his cheek on my thigh, still petting my clit steadily, watching his work all the while. "So wet and perfectly tight. Darling, I'm going to love feeling you come on my cock…feeling the clench of you around me while I'm filling you." He glanced up and caught my eyes. "But you're ready to come now, aren't you?"

I nodded, a bit frantic. I was so fucking close and still couldn't form words.

He nodded with me, returning his gaze to his finger working on me. "I can tell you're close. Why don't you let go and let me watch you come for the first time…relax, darling girl, let me help you." And with that, he filled me with two fingers and dropped his face, allowing his tongue to take over the circling motion.

The orgasm was effortless, and I couldn't have controlled or stopped it any more than I could've stopped the rain that steadily pelted our naked, writhing bodies. It grabbed all of me, making my belly ripple in time with the throbbing pleasure that tore through me. I think I cried out, but I couldn't be sure if it was me or the mingled sounds of the rain and thunder. It was as if time had been flung into some alternate dimension; I couldn't tell how long I came on Oliver's gifted tongue, but it seemed much longer than usual. He eased me down gradually, his mouth continuing to suckle and caress, his hands stroking my thighs and belly. When I'd stilled at last, he rested his cheek again on my thigh.

"You're magnificent when you come, Charlotte. Brilliant." His body was above mine, blocking the rain, and his hips settled into the cradle of mine. He held his length and stroked the crown of his shaft slowly through my slickness while he spoke. "I can't wait to watch you and feel you do that again and again."

I finally found my words. "Yes, please, Oliver. I need you inside me." I was pleading in a voice I barely recognized as mine.

He smiled gently, and I reached up to touch his face. "About that. I'm afraid I need to dash inside and grab a condom, darling." He smiled again, still stroking me. "Will you wait here then?"

I clutched his arms. "No, I mean yes, I'll wait. I'm not going anywhere, Oliver, but don't...I have an IUD, and I..."

His face softened further, and he bent forward to kiss me sweetly. "I'm clean, Charlotte, but I don't want you to feel pressured to make a decision like that on the fly. I'm glad to—"

I interrupted him with another kiss, this one slower and searching. "I don't feel pressured. Please, Oliver. I'm clean, and I want you inside me. Nothing between." He tilted his head, studying me.

"If you're certain, Charlotte. There's nothing I want more than that, but..."

"Please." My voice was quiet, threadbare. "Please. I need you." Whatever sparked between Oliver and me all those weeks ago had grown steadily. Despite the timing, the draw between us wasn't diminished by the difficulties I faced. Instead, his gentle encouragement through the valley I was traveling nurtured my desire for him. The seeds of attraction I'd felt back then had evolved into a full-blown hunger for the man I was about to feel inside me.

He rested his weight on his forearms at both sides of my head and settled his hips lower until I felt the hard warmth of him spread me open, but only slightly. I bent my knees and pulled his face down until our foreheads touched. Raindrops rolled off my cheeks and Oliver's beautiful eyes, the flecks of silver and gold glinting, held mine as he pressed himself carefully inside me. So slowly. The combination of unusual length and thickness was more than I'd felt before, but I desperately wanted all of him. He withdrew and then stopped. "Are you alright, Charlotte? Am I hurting you?"

"No. Yes." I was gasping. "Not hurt, please keep going, Oliver. I need to feel you." I wrapped my legs around his waist and pressed my heels into the taut muscles of his bottom. *Oh, God, I need to see that ass.* But not now. "More, please." To my own ears, I sounded like a demanding, begging child.

His eyes crinkled as he smiled, but it dissolved in a pained groan as he sunk back into me. "So tight, love. So fucking tight." This second time our bellies touched, and I could feel the soft skin of his sac nestle into the valley of my ass. My sex tightened around him instinctively, and he groaned again. "I'm going to have to ask you to control that tight little pussy, darling." He allowed a ghost of a smile as he began stroking his length in and out of my slick center. "As it is, I'll be lucky to avoid coming in the next ten seconds like a teenager. You feel like heaven, Charlotte—tight, hot paradise." His voice dropped lower, almost to a whisper. "I've never been inside a woman bare; you're the first, love."

With that, he reached beneath me and cupped my bottom, changing the angle and stroking against the place I needed him most. My hands danced restlessly over his chest, exploring and teasing. Then the broad mushroom shape of his cock began massaging that magic spot, pressing more insistently with each pass, and my belly tightened again.

"Again, darling?" His big hand pressed again, changing the angle only slightly, and he snapped his hips against mine. "Come for me, Charlotte; just once more, love."

Before the words left his lips, the orgasm ripped free. I dug my nails into his shoulders and my heels into the small of his back, chasing his length while he resolutely continued to stroke in and out of me. Through the haze of ecstasy, I heard his voice. "Goddammit, so good…that's it, love; let that beautiful pussy milk my cock." Waves of pleasure continued to roll through me, and he grew impossibly thicker inside me.

I found his eyes and briefly studied the barely restrained lust painting his features. "Let go, Oliver. Come for me and let me feel you filling me…watch me while you come."

One final time, his hips rocked forward, and he pulled me to him, planting his length into the deepest part of me. He throbbed and convulsed hard and long, breathing my name over and over. His expression was almost pained, but he whispered my name reverently, looking into my eyes all the while.

The only sound on the patio was the steady patter of rain interrupted by our breathing. Neither of us moved, holding one another's gaze for perhaps a minute, both reluctant to break the holy moment we held between us. At last, he spoke quietly.

"That was beautiful, Charlotte. Loveliest thing I've ever seen…thank you, darling girl." Without taking himself from me, he rolled us to our sides and tucked my head into his chest. "Thank you, love." He breathed the words several times into my ear as the rain continued to pour over us.

His heart beat a steady rhythm in my ear as I rested my head against him, lulling me into post-coital somnolence. Several additional minutes passed before a chill chased away the drowsiness and a little shiver ran through me. Oliver's arms squeezed me tight once more, and I felt the loss of him. Then he was on his feet, scooping me into his arms, and striding toward his bedroom door. He laughed like a kid as his feet splashed through the puddles, and I grinned up at him, reaching down to slide the big glass door open for us. He tossed me onto the enormous king-sized bed with an admonition, "Stay put, love. Time to warm up." Dashing into the hall, he returned quickly with a colossal, fluffy white blanket and tossed it over me.

The bedroom itself was quite large and very much in keeping with the seventies vintage feel of the entire house. One corner of the room was taken up with a floor-to-ceiling sandstone fireplace. A very naked and still soaking wet Oliver knelt briefly beside it, tinkering with a couple of knobs before the fireplace came alive with dancing flames. He sprung to his feet, affected a comical caveman stance and growled, "Man make fire for woman."

I giggled like a little girl—a sound that even I found very foreign—and he bounded across the room to offer his hand and help me from the bed. There were half a dozen large quilted floor pillows in brightly colored corduroys, stripes and patterns, all stacked in the corner. He tossed them in front of the fire and plopped down unceremoniously, arranging them into a nest around us as I joined him, dragging the blanket along behind me.

"I've only just moved in, so no window coverings yet." He gestured to the double wide patio door showcasing the escalating storm. Thunder rumbled nearby now, and lightning lit the sky with a dramatic display. He arranged two of the pillows facing the fire and pulled me back into his arms, covering us both with the voluminous blanket. The firelight played over his handsome features, highlighting his regal profile and smiling eyes. "Warmer now?"

"So warm. So…overwhelmed, Oliver." I had to look away from his face, staring into the fire as I tried to stitch my thoughts together. "That was…" I gestured toward the patio where the light show continued to intensify. "It was so much more than I expected. More than I've felt before; I'm just a little amazed."

He didn't respond but again tucked my head against his chest. The fire's warmth was hypnotic, and Oliver stroked my hair. Then his low baritone broke the silence with the first few bars of Paul McCartney's "Maybe I'm Amazed." My heart was full, even if my head was overwhelmed, but there was no need to understand everything tonight. Tonight, I had the company and undivided attention of an extraordinary man whose warm body was wound protectively around mine. In those moments, in the wee hours of the morning, we wondered privately at what happened.

And we slept.

Chapter
TWENTY-SIX

"Hell on Heels"

Miles

"Put your back into it, Miles. Sam and Grace are gonna pitch a nuclear hissy fit if we're late. I swear to God I'll yank a knot in you a mile wide if my ass ends up in a sling because of you."

I skidded into my living room, pulling on a long suede jacket over my tee and jeans. Luckie Page stood there, twirling her car keys casually on one finger and giving me the once-over. It should have been intimidating since she looked every inch the runway model she was not, all casual elegance and understated makeup. She shouldered an enormous designer handbag and stared at me.

"What is *this*, Miles—no Chucks? It's blasphemy. I've never seen you without them." She gestured to the short, distressed leather boots I wore with my new not-Levi's.

"Is it too much, Luckie? Does it look weird? It feels weird. I'm the definition of insecure when it comes to dressing myself, but I saw these at DSW and thought they looked nice." It was a foreign idea, feeling unsure about how to dress.

She raised her eyebrows and smiled. "It's possible your taste doesn't all reside in your oral cavity, Miles. They're gorgeous—now let's move." She started toward the door.

I locked the door behind us and followed Luckie to her aged BMW. "Okay, Manhattan girl. What gives with all the country-as-cornbread vocabulary these days?" She stared blankly at me. "Don't give me that, Lucinda Page. 'Pitch a hissy fit?' 'Yank a knot in you?' Is that yokel you're sleeping with rubbing off on you?" I grinned at her.

On the second attempt, the Beemer roared to life. "Well, he's definitely been rubbing on me, if that's what you're getting at. And if he gets tired, I climb on top and take over." She laughed raucously. "I'm crazy about his corn-fed ass."

"Okay, we're picking up Sue at the Starbucks on River Road, and Meg will meet us at Savaya with everyone else." Today's excuse to shop was officially my wardrobe-related incompetence, but I was also looking forward to spending time with two groups of women who were gradually turning me into a girl's girl. There was nothing wrong with being one of the guys, but I was surprised to learn I enjoyed the company of my new friends from The Tuesday Game and the nurses from the TMC emergency department just as much.

"What happened to Lori Beth? I thought she was coming today. We've all been looking forward to meeting the members of the infamous Tuesday Game." Luckie smiled warmly. Our fledgling friendship meant more than she knew, especially given my history with Deliverance. She was clearly in love with the man, and I knew why. He was the finest sort of person. I'd known that before the accident, but his kindness and support of me since that day set the idea in concrete.

"LB couldn't make it, but she promises to clear her calendar next time. Is your whole gang coming along?" I pointed out the Starbucks where we'd pick up Sue, and Luckie maneuvered the BMW into the parking lot. I waved as Sue pushed the door open with her curvy bottom, balancing three large latte cups.

Luckie made a yummy sound in her throat. "I like her already. I think we're all coming, but Camille sounded like shit when I talked to her this morning. I wonder if she's got a touch of something."

Camille had a touch of something alright.

She leaned against the exterior wall of the coffee shop, surrounded by the rest of the group, looking pale and awfully tired. There were dark circles under her eyes, and even her trademark thick blond hair seemed to suffer the ill effects of whatever was going on.

"Don't take this the wrong way, Cam, but you look like turbo-charged ass." Luckie regarded her best friend with sympathy, finger-combing the hair back from her face.

"I'd take offense, but I know you're right." Camille stared down at the untouched coffee in the cup she held, wrinkling her nose at the delicious smell wafting toward her. An impressive cushion-cut engagement ring winked at me from her left hand, but it was the only sparkle to be found on her. "But there's no fever, no body aches. I know there's nothing seriously wrong, and I wanted to have girl fun today. Don't tell Nathan, but his giant cleanup effort is taking it out of me. I think I'm just… tired."

Happy had proposed to Camille a couple of weeks ago, and he was deeply involved in preparations to merge their two households. Evidently, this involved endless packing and unpacking of boxes and meticulous cleaning of closets and drawers. It delighted his compulsively organized soul and exhausted everyone else. I smiled at the thought; this was one of the ways he was taking care of Camille and expressing his love for her. But I wouldn't have recognized it as such only a couple of months ago.

Before anyone else could respond, Samanthe stepped forward; she dialed her phone while she spoke. "I'm sorry you're under the weather, Camille, and I'm no expert…" She stopped and raised her finger in mock surprise. "Oh, wait. I *am* an expert. You don't need to be hauling your ass all over hell's half acre all day. You need to go home, hydrate, and rest." She took the untouched coffee from Camille. "I'd be willing to bet you'd hurl your lungs out if you drank this."

Camille nodded vigorously as Sam continued. "I'm calling Nathan to come get you, and I'll get you off the hook for his household reorganization project." She walked away from the group when Nathan picked up, and Camille slumped against the wall.

We moved to a nearby seating area surrounding a fountain and settled Camille on a bench; she rested her head on Luckie's shoulder while I made introductions. Sam rejoined us as she wound up her phone call.

"…no, stop. Do *not* freak out, Nathan. She is just fine, as I've already told you three hundred times. But she's off your labor camp work detail for the time being, okay? Put her to bed and let her rest until this passes. It's probably just a bug…okay, see you in a few." She hung up. "He'd dropped by to see Davis, so he's five minutes away. He lost his mind when he heard you were ill. I wondered how that escaped his notice, but I'll bet you've been staging a grand cover-up, right?"

Sam raised an eyebrow, and Camille nodded tiredly. "He's a little excitable when it comes to me."

Luckie shot her a wry grin. "The queen of the understatement speaks. But I get it, girl; Tarzan's got the same issues."

Nathan arrived in minutes and was summarily dispatched with a pale but smiling Camille. A quiet disagreement ensued when Happy tried to carry her to the car like a Neanderthal, but Camille won out, walking slowly with his arm protectively around her shoulders. It was a scene I would have scoffed at in the past, but now it warmed me. Only a few days ago, Oliver picked me up and carried me into his lair like a caveman. Of course, it wasn't so much a lair as a mid-century ranch, but still.

"Okay, Miles. You'd better pay attention. This part is important; it's all divide and conquer." Grace's voice was quiet but firm; she and Sam had taken charge of solving my fashion challenges, and that was today's primary objective. We were gathered in the brick courtyard of the shopping mall, lounging on the various benches nearby and a wall that surrounded the fountain. Luckie and Sue were deeply involved in a conversation about southern cooking and the finer points of turning out acceptable grits and fried chicken. Meg and Vivvie were engaged in a lively discussion about remodeling old homes, specifically the advantages of porcelain versus ceramic tile as a bathroom flooring choice.

Samanthe jogged back from the parking lot where she'd retrieved a bag she'd forgotten in her car. She distributed what appeared to be copies of a map, then held up her much larger copy. "Attention, shoppers." She clapped her hands when Luckie and Sue didn't immediately cease their conversation. "Shut it, Lucinda." Luckie stuck her tongue out and slurped her bottled orange juice. "You all hold in your hands the map for today's graduate-level shopping challenge; please make annotations as I give your assignments."

Assignments?

She paced in front of the group like a general preparing troops for battle. "Today's goal is to broaden Miles's wardrobe by adding new options in each of the following categories…" She grabbed another colorful graphic from her bag and pointed as she spoke. "Casual options. Dressier options. Shoes, accessories, and handbags. On your maps, you'll see I've listed all her measurements and sizes. Please note that pure wool makes her itch, and she does not iron. That means linen is out unless it is a blend." She emphasized her words by gesturing with a pen. "You will purchase options in two sizes when there is a question, sizing down at upper-tier shops and up at budget-conscious stores. Color selection should lean toward the warmer choices—autumn tones. Think earthy, fiery, and golden, but keep in mind that Miles has blue eyes and ivory skin, so nothing harsh. We will reassemble at 1600 for happy hour at Blanco's to review purchases. Miles will try everything on at home, and I'll handle returns for her the next day."

I blinked in amazement. Sam told me we were going to have a girls' shopping trip and asked me for a budget, but this looked more like taking the beach at Normandy. "Gosh, Sam, I don't know what to say. Thanks for this—especially for doing the returns. I hate those."

She flashed me a bright smile. "It's gonna be a blast, Miles. Shopping, having fun, making new friends. That's my idea of a productive Saturday." She clapped her hands again. "Luckie and Sue, you're on dressier looks—don't overlook the department stores; there are some sales today. Vivvie and Meg, you've got casual wear. Grace, you take Miles and hit shoes, accessories, and handbags. Make a quick pass through Brighton, but I'd probably avoid silver with her coloring."

Grace rolled her eyes. "Duh. Not my first shopping rodeo, Sammy."

"Right." Sam nodded once. "I will be available for consultations or questions via my cell phone at all times. Call if you need help or want larger bags shuttled back to the car. Let's move, people."

I was clearly out of my depth, but this did have all the hallmarks of a fun day. We took the colorful shopping bags Sam distributed, and the group dispersed in different directions, chatting and laughing.

"I don't think my feet have ever hurt like this before." Grace laughed and patted my hand sympathetically. We were almost to the restaurant where happy hour was scheduled to start in ten minutes. Both of us carried two large bags each, and I wondered why I'd decided to abandon my faithful Chucks, on today of all days. "Shopping with Sam and me does require some stamina, I'll give you that. But you're going to be amazed at the beautiful things everyone found for you. I've done several big wardrobe interventions with Sam at the wheel, and the hard-ass organization pays off every time."

Luckie and Sue waved from a high-top table at the back of the restaurant. We joined them after asking the bartender for a couple of frozen margaritas. "Too bad Camille couldn't join us today; margs are her favorite, and these are the tits." Luckie took a big drink of hers and then motioned the waitress, requesting chips and guacamole for the table.

"Girl, just you wait till you see what we picked up for you." Sue did a little happy dance on her barstool and reached into one of the bags on the floor, pulling out something in a luminous mossy green hue. "Strapless sundress with a high-low hemline. And pockets! That's just the beginning." She indicated Luckie with her thumb. "This girl can squeeze a dollar till it hollers; she found some great deals."

"Well, let's just say I had to develop some skills to survive on a nurse's salary." She grinned at her shopping partner. "Sue and I have had too much fun; she's going to have me over and teach me how to make chicken-fried steak and hummingbird cake."

Sue patted her hand. "That cake will get a ring on this finger, and you can take that to the bank." I'd swear I saw Luckie blush a little—that had to be a first—but before she could reply, Vivvie and Meg joined us, both of them laughing uproariously.

They settled at the table, ordered margaritas, and began to show off a wide assortment of casual clothing they'd selected for me. There were capris in a rainbow of colors, slouchy tops along with skimpier options, some tanks and cute tees—even a pair of loose wrap pants. I never even knew I liked clothes, but the treats they produced from their shopping bags made me anxious to try them on and twirl in front of a mirror. I even wanted to think about what to wear on my next date with Oliver, and that was an entirely alien idea.

"Thanks, everybody. I don't know how to tell you what this means to me; I've never had a day like this." I felt a bit unexpectedly emotional at the friendship these girls had offered me. Sam had joined us; she embraced me from behind and whispered in my ear.

"I told you, Miles. I'm going to be here for you when things suck, but the sun will come up—and it has. I'm here for you when it's time to have fun, and you deserve friends like this group of girls. We can see each other through a world of shit; that's exactly what real friends are for. This group has done it more than once." She spun my barstool around, gyrating her little butt salaciously in a circle between my legs like I'd ordered a lap dance. "We're experienced."

Chapter
TWENTY-SEVEN

"Bridge over Troubled Water"

Miles

It was an unseasonably chilly Monday afternoon in early December, a little over three months since the midair. Three months since I'd climbed into the cockpit and watched the ground fall away. Three months of watching my friend struggle with pain and frustration as he recovered from injuries I was responsible for. Three very long months of waiting to find out what the Air Force's accident investigation board would recommend— and if there was any hope of me keeping my wings. No matter the outcome, I was proud of the strides I'd made. Thanks to Keeper and all my new friends at The Tuesday Game, I'd found the courage to confront my past and begin brainstorming ways to build a relationship again with my father. I'd revisited attitudes about leadership and authority and had been disappointed to discover I hadn't appreciated people who acted consistently with my best interests at heart. Through all the waiting and soul-searching, I was surprised to see a balance developing in my life between self-reliance and a healthy dependence on the network of friends flourishing around me. My world was becoming a bigger, richer place, and nowhere was that more apparent than my relationship with Oliver.

We'd been dating only a month and a half, but it felt like so much longer. I wondered at the timing; I wouldn't have chosen to begin a relationship in the immediate aftermath of one of the worst crises and biggest turning points of my life. I couldn't have faulted Oliver if he'd decided to run fast as soon as he figured out what kind of star he'd hitched his wagon to. I didn't have much experience with romance—and none at all with love—but even I knew the odds didn't favor those cursed with shitty timing. I cared more about him every time we were together. He was calm and steady by nature and everything I wasn't—a perfect counterpoint to my spontaneous, carefree ways. And watching all of Oliver's composure unravel that night on his patio during the storm? Game changer. He'd taken infinite care and attention with me that first time we made love, and the feeling of being cherished in that way defied description. Pondering the details of our first encounter, I saw passion and affection in every detail of how Oliver touched my body and spoke to me. For the first time ever, I could say what I'd experienced was lovemaking. To describe it as sex would've been to sell it grievously short.

I reflected on all these things with a smile as I drove toward the squadron building. I had much to be grateful for, and it seemed fitting to count my blessings during the holiday season. The accident could have had an even more tragic outcome, although I could hardly allow myself to think of it. Even watching Deliverance endure the rehabilitation process paled in comparison to the idea of losing him. With so much change rushing around me, zeroing in on the good in my life paid dividends to my sanity. Davis would be healthy again soon. Today, of all days, I needed to keep a positive attitude. I'd need all the help I could get.

The hot rumor in the squadron was the accident investigation board had returned their findings to General O'Cherry over the weekend. It was not necessary to wait until findings were back for a decision to be rendered regarding my future, but the general had decided to wait in my case. Coach informed me about the general's timeline only a week or so after the original meeting I'd had with them in Happy's office. I tried to ignore the incessant grind of the rumor mill, but it was difficult when I longed for stability and closure. Hope and fear were engaged in a full-blown war inside my head this morning; Coach called last night to let me know I was expected in Colonel Morgan's office this morning for a meeting with the two of them. That could only mean the rumor mill had, this once, been absolutely accurate.

I spent the evening alone, thinking over the ways my life had changed in the past three months and being grateful for the shot at a clean slate. I spoke briefly to Robert who made me promise to call him as soon as I knew something. Then I called Oliver. His kindness and encouraging words lifted my spirits in a way no one else could have done. We spoke of the possible outcomes, good and bad, and he allowed me all the time I needed to mull through the possibilities during our conversation. Then, as we prepared to say goodbye, there was a lengthy pause followed by the rumble of his deep baritone in my ear.

"Charlotte, love. I need you to remember something tomorrow. I need you to remind yourself that you're more than an excellent pilot. You're more than a military officer. You're even more than a sister, a daughter, and a friend. You're a kind, generous woman, a good person with a beautiful soul and mind. You are worthy of happiness, fulfillment, and joy. And no matter what happens tomorrow, I have faith that those things will come to you."

My eyes filled with tears while he spoke, and the lump in my throat made it impossible to speak before he finished his thought.

"And I don't mind telling you, darling girl, that I hope I can be the one to bring some of those things into your life. I'm here for you, love, and my heart will be right beside you tomorrow. Now sleep well."

I rehearsed Oliver's words in my head as I walked down the hall toward the squadron commander's office. It seemed like only yesterday I'd stood in there with Boo and Torch, getting an ass-reaming from Happy. That one was well-deserved, and he'd been well within his rights to wring us out as he'd so thoroughly done. I shook my head ruefully; we'd given Happy a run for his money, that much was sure. I wondered with a wry grin if he'd ever wished he'd ended up commanding a bunch of adults instead of fighter pilots.

I knocked briskly on Happy's door, the feelings entirely different from last time. The anger I'd struggled with had dissipated as I'd found its origin, and I could see Colonel Nathan Morgan for who he was: not a meddling killjoy here to take us down a notch. He was an honorable man who stood firmly on my side, supporting me however he could, despite my terrible mistake. Coach opened the door and welcomed me warmly, as he had before. The entire scene could have been a replay of my visit here the week after the accident with one startling exception.

Davis Foster.

Deliverance sat in a chair at one corner of Happy's desk, his big, ridiculous foot still sporting some sort of surgical shoe. He stood without any noticeable problems and extended his hand. "Hey, Miles. It's great to see you."

I shook his huge hand. "You, too, D. You're looking better every time I see you; how's the leg?"

He settled carefully back into the chair. "It's on the mend, and

I'm feeling damned good." He grinned up at Coach. "I'm down to twice weekly visits with the Queen of Pain, and she's pleased with my progress." He referenced Bibi, of course, Coach's wife and Deliverance's physical therapist. She'd been supervising his rehabilitation since the day after the accident.

Happy stood from where he sat behind his desk. I came to attention and saluted sharply. "Reporting as ordered, sir."

"At ease, Lieutenant." He returned my salute and indicated the chair next to Deliverance. "Go ahead and have a seat so we can get started, Miles."

We were all seated, and Happy leaned forward with his elbows on his desk and his brow knit. He steepled his fingers, seemingly gathering his thoughts. Finally, he cleared his throat and leaned back in his chair, meeting my eyes.

"I know these three plus months have seemed interminable, Miles, especially given that you knew General O'Cherry had opted not to make a decision about how to proceed until after the accident investigation was complete." He sighed. "But I'm sure you heard the results were returned to the general over last weekend, and it's my duty to inform you of the plans going forward." His eyes darted left to Coach's. They both seemed uncharacteristically uneasy, but Happy rapidly regained his composure. "Lieutenant Christman, it's General O'Cherry's decision that you will meet an **FEB** this Friday, December 10, to determine your ongoing fitness to maintain your flying rating based on your lack of judgment in performing rated duties."

An FEB.

His words echoed and clanged in my head like an air raid siren. A Flying Evaluation Board. One of the worst-case scenarios and an eventuality I'd tried not to focus on. I swallowed and tried to sound composed as I responded.

"Yes, sir. I understand. This Friday, sir? That's very soon, if you'll pardon me for saying so."

Happy smiled sadly and nodded. "No need to stand on ceremony here, Miles. It is very soon, and I questioned the general about it. He feels it's in the best interest of the wing that we do our diligence in reviewing your fitness to fly. He further feels it's in your best interest that this matter proceeds without undue delay. I'm sure you have questions, Miles."

I tried to corral my turbulent thoughts. "Yes, sir; I think so. Who will be the voting members of the board?"

Happy looked at Coach, who answered. "I just spoke to the JAG a few minutes ago, and she just finalized it. Major Gambles, the Cobra OpsO—goes by JB?"

Happy acknowledged him with a head nod. "He's a good man."

"The second guy is Captain Clark Evans; call sign's Governor—he's at Wing Safety, and the senior member is Colonel Kane London from the Wing staff."

Deliverance piped up. "Another good man. Call sign Predator."

I looked back to Happy, a sinking feeling in my gut. "So none of the Scorpions will sit on the board?"

Happy shook his head. "No, although you'll note that all the members are rated pilots. That brings me to the reason all three of us are here this morning; I'd assume you wonder why Captain Foster joined us for this meeting."

I'd wondered, but there were too many other things spinning in my head and demanding my attention to ask the question, so I just nodded.

"Coach and I were approached separately by the JAG to ask if we'd sit on the board. We've both done so on several occasions in the past. But both of us, as well as Deliverance, have spoken to the ADC, requesting permission to testify in your defense when the board convenes Friday."

My head whipped around to look over my shoulder to where Davis sat. He leaned forward, resting his elbows on his knees and looking at the floor. When I turned, he looked up and mustered a small smile. "Remember what I said that day in the hospital, Miles? We all make mistakes. We all have lessons to learn from this. I told you that you had to be honest and find the answers to the questions we discussed that morning." He glanced around the room at Coach and Happy. "We all think you've worked hard to look for the truth and start to make changes. We have faith in you."

The multitude of emotions warring inside me must have shown plainly on my face because Happy stood and walked around his desk and then rested his hands on my shoulders. When I looked up, his face was sober and concerned. But his voice was warm, almost reassuring.

"You're a Scorpion, Miles. We're all behind you."

Chapter
TWENTY-EIGHT

"You'll Never Walk Alone"

Miles

The week flew by in a whirlwind of meetings and briefings and endless paperwork. I met with the attorney from the ADC several times and was relieved to find his unflappable temperament soothed my jangled nerves. Coach made sure I had the time necessary to prepare for the FEB, which was no small challenge considering the compressed timeline. I spent little time in the squadron, but almost everyone there went out of their way to ensure I felt their support. I was jogging to my car, having stopped to pick up training records en route to yet another meeting, when I heard a familiar voice call to me from the back door of the squadron building. I turned to see Bashful sprinting in my direction.

"Hey, Miles, wait up." He caught up to me as I reached the car. "I just wanted to say good luck tomorrow morning; I'm not sure which Hallmark greeting card is appropriate in these circumstances." He shot me a wry grin, and I cocked my head, pretending to think.

"How about this…'Good luck at not blowing your only shot, loser.'" I laughed at my own gallows humor. "I never knew until now what that old saying meant—the one about laughing so you won't cry." I leaned against the door of the Mustang and looked affectionately at my friend. "Thanks, Bash. I've been kind of blown away by the way everyone's bent over backward to show their support."

He leaned next to me on the car, eyes fixed on the flight line in the distance. "I know O'Cherry's doing what he thinks is his duty, but it fucking kills me you have to run this gauntlet after everything I've already seen you suffer through. I have every confidence that you're fit to fly and that you're working through your issues. And I want you to know I'd be happy to have you on my wing anytime."

I heaved out a breath. It seemed, lately, that I was forever struggling to keep the fierce storm of emotions in my chest in check. "I can't talk about it too much, Bash; everything's too close to the surface, and it feels like I might come unglued at any moment." I looked up with a smile. "I'll just say thanks and repeat what I told you right before I landed the last time: you've always been one of my favorites."

His arms wrapped around my shoulders for a brief, tight hug, and then he was gone.

The legal office on base, home of both the ADC and JAG was a low, nondescript building with utilitarian furnishings and ominously beige everything. In short, it resembled every military building I'd ever been in. I'd arrived over an hour early, a choice I now realized was a critical error. No one was in the building at that early hour except one of the younger administrative troops who kindly offered me access to the break room coffee pot.

Forty-five minutes later, I'd had far too much caffeine as I tried to fight off the effects of a sleepless night, and I paced the hall restlessly. Like practically every pilot in the Air Force, the fit of my blues was an abomination. They had evidently been tailored to accommodate a version of me with no breasts and a waist five inches larger than I actually was. The second issue was addressed by cinching the uniform belt snug, resulting in the appearance of pleated pants, something I was sure Samanthe would heartily disapprove of.

At last, the ADC attorney, Major Griffin, arrived and invited me to wait in his office. The building gradually came to life and filled with people as the workday began. The FEB would convene at 0900, and I was beyond ready to get things underway.

After what seemed an interminable wait, Major Griffin opened the office door and beckoned for me to join him in the hallway. Once there, he laid one hand on my shoulder and waited for me to turn to him. "Okay, Miles. Try to settle and breathe a little bit." He grinned ruefully. "I thought I'd covered everything, but I see I neglected to mention drinking three pots of coffee on an empty stomach might not be your best move."

I chuckled, relaxing infinitesimally. "Guess it's a little late for that, Major. But I'll try not to embarrass you."

He clapped my shoulder. "Not worried about it, Lieutenant. Let's go kick some ass."

I was surprised to find the proceedings would be conducted in a relatively small conference room with the three board members and the recorder seated at a long table on one end. Behind two additional tables, both attorneys spread out their paperwork. I sat next to Major Griffin, focusing on keeping my hands from fidgeting and twisting in my lap. Only a moment had elapsed when the door opened again to admit General O'Cherry, whose blues, I noted, fit perfectly. Major Gambles called the room to attention, and those assembled rose as one, snapping to attention.

The general saluted. "At ease, everyone." We settled back into our seats, but I was surprised to see General O'Cherry look my direction briefly, catching my eye and nodding in what seemed a friendly gesture. He spoke again, this time to Colonel London. "Colonel Morgan and his party are just arriving; once they're here, you're free to begin."

Only a couple of minutes later, Happy arrived with Coach and Deliverance in tow. I noted that both lieutenant colonels also owned nicely fitted blues, but nothing fit Davis Foster. He was a mountain of a man who looked out of place to me in anything other than his flight suit. Squeezing into his blues today was a testament to our friendship, I thought with a little smile. Happy approached the general for a quiet word and then joined Coach and D in the row of seats behind me. I turned to smile at the three. Conversation didn't seem appropriate. The words might not have come easily anyway, so I simply mouthed, "Thank you for coming."

Colonel London began by introducing General O'Cherry and the voting members of the board. There was also an additional attorney from the JAG office, Major Bentley, who would act as recorder. He explained that the matter would be conducted as a semiformal proceeding, although members would be sworn in before statements and testimony were offered. London was businesslike and precise in his speech, frequently double-checking his remarks with an imposing array of binders and paperwork arranged before him. He turned the floor over to Major Bentley, who would swear in members prior to their testimony. I was unsurprised to learn that, although the recorder had many duties before and during the FEB, recording was not one of them. The military was absolutely predictable in its fondness for the illogical.

The JAG attorney stood and began to speak, distributing large paperwork packets to each of the board members. And just like that, I was Alice down the rabbit hole. The next three hours passed in a swirling haze of testimony, graphs, and large photographs of the accident site near Ajo. Worst of all, there were multiple detailed recountings of the worst day of my life. Of course, I'd tried to prepare myself, but repeatedly living through that agonizing morning was excruciating. I could only imagine what it did to the man who sat right behind me, reliving his own nightmare. Tears wet my cheeks as I recalled the horror of seeing the smoking, black crater in the desert 16,000 feet below me. I longed to turn and tell Davis once more how terribly sorry I was.

Eventually, I was called to the front, sworn in by the recorder, and asked for my recollections of the terrible day. I took care to be accurate in the statements I gave, mindful of my oath to tell the whole truth. While carefully selecting my words, a script played in my subconscious—the story of the first time Coach met Keeper so many years ago. Coach had inadvertently destroyed his treasured motorcycle, but Keeper's words related to the condition of his spirit, not external events. It was indicative of what I'd learned about the man I'd met only a few weeks prior. He'd found the key to what was important..."strengthening my resolve...character development...leading a simple, mindful life."

Resolve. Character. Mindful living.

I don't know how long I'd testified; the time passed in slow motion. But I knew I'd been faithful to what Miles 2.0 had learned: truth, kindness, and generosity were more important than demanding my due. That allowing others into my life, even with the risks it entailed, had paid off in ways I could never have predicted. That once my walls were breached, the possibilities were endless. The war for independence in The Free and

Sovereign State of Charlotte was over, and a victor had emerged.

Love wins.

Then I was back in my seat, not recalling the walk back to the chair next to Major Griffin. He turned to whisper in my ear. "Great job, Lieutenant. You were true to yourself, and you didn't compromise an inch on the truth." I'd dreaded telling my story, and now that hurdle was cleared. But my stomach lurched as I saw Happy approach the recorder and raise his hand, swearing to tell the truth.

The final hour of my FEB was consumed with the testimony and statement of the Scorpion commanding officer, the operations officer, and the weapons officer. It was a sad irony that Deliverance's leadership position would probably have required him to testify today, even if it hadn't been he who suffered most at my hands. I expected their respective testimonies under oath would be additional accounts of the accident, each from their unique perspectives, but I was wrong.

Happy, Coach, and Deliverance were called on to paint a picture of the history and culture within the squadron. A culture that resulted in leniency, bordering on carelessness, with regard to military and flight discipline. Coach cited Rifle's crash, only a few months prior to ours, along with other anecdotal incidents to demonstrate their points. Happy reviewed his challenges upon taking command, and D spoke enthusiastically about the striking shift he'd seen in morale and performance over the past three months.

I was taken by surprise as I heard the content of their testimonies. The blame for what happened was mine alone, and I'd steeled myself mentally to shoulder that blame alone, no matter how serious the consequences. But the board members listened intently and took notes as Major Griffin skillfully questioned the three. When he finally told the board he had no further questions, Deliverance turned to address Colonel London.

"Sir, if I'm permitted, I've prepared a statement for the board, and I'd request a moment to be heard."

The colonel leaned forward, conferring briefly with the other members, then turned back to Deliverance.

"Certainly, Captain Foster. Proceed when you're ready."

Deliverance produced a note card from his pocket, then stood from the chair where he was seated during his testimony. I took in the big man as he composed his thoughts, and I briefly pondered his compassion and concern for me over these past months. There had been so many phone calls and texts on days when guilt and regret weighed heavily on me. He was a genuinely extraordinary person, a giant in more ways than one. Then he began to speak, and my heart, already full and churning with turbulent emotion, threatened to explode.

"Lieutenant Charlotte Christman is my friend as well as my squadron mate. It would be dishonest of me not to characterize our relationship as such right up front. Having been a Scorpion longer than Miles and both the Commander and OpsO, who've just testified before the board, I was present as the cultural shortcomings developed in the 82nd. It's insidious and strangely difficult to recognize when it's happening all around you; I'd surmise it might even be more easily diagnosed by an outsider. But that doesn't keep me from wondering, as a leader in our squadron, how much of the burden I should bear for what happened. During the weeks of recovery, my wings have been clipped, as you can plainly see." He grinned, ever charming and self-deprecating, and indicated the leg he still favored.

"I've had more than my share of downtime, and it's given me a gracious plenty of quiet to explore the question. I've concluded that we all bear a degree of blame when we notice a departure from what's right. In a profession as unforgiving as ours is, it's our duty to demand the very best of ourselves and each other— not only at the range, but in following regulations to the letter and presenting the very best version of ourselves when it's time to fly. I have been negligent in that duty in the past, and I'd venture to say every pilot in this room and in this Air Force might be able to say the same.

"But I've made a promise to myself to do better for my sake, for the ones I love, and for the sake of every Scorpion I work with. We are already making strides in that direction, and that's due in great part to the example of Lieutenant Christman." His eyes wandered from addressing the board and settled on me briefly. "She reappeared in the squadron a week after the accident, grounded and shaken to her core, but she's worked diligently, not only on the tasks assigned to her by Happy and Coach, but on herself. She's made it her objective to find a way to be more than she was, to correct flaws she discovered, and to find any way to contribute to the Scorpions moving toward the goals Happy set in front of us. And in great part because of her, we're getting there.

"In the immediate aftermath of a midair that could easily have claimed her life, Lieutenant Christman was able to summon the composure and skill to land a severely damaged jet in manual reversion, something I've always wondered if I could do. From the moment of impact, Miles made a gut call to change the game and put the Air Force's needs before her own. However broken, she brought the jet home and salvaged the airframe. Our C Flight commander, Captain Jacob Travis, who chased her down final approach and through the landing, said it was the most shit-hot thing he'd ever seen." There was a smattering of laughter from the board, and Deliverance grinned. "His words, not mine, sir.

"I'll close with this, Colonel London. I don't want to lose Miles; I implore the board to keep this excellent pilot on board with the full confidence that she's a better person, a better warrior, and a better Air Force officer than she was that day over Ajo. The Air Force needs her, and the Scorpions need her." He stuffed the note card back into his breast pocket and nodded to the assembly. "Thank you for the opportunity to speak, sir."

Tears ran silently down my cheeks, and I fought to maintain some composure as Colonel London made final remarks and the proceedings were concluded. The general stood; the room came to attention once again and saluted. Following that, the board filed out, and I took several deep breaths. Major Griffin encouraged me to go get lunch; he expected the board to return findings soon, but there was no certainty about exactly when.

I felt a huge hand on my shoulder and reached to grip it as I turned, knowing whose it was. "I don't know what to say, D. I'm overwhelmed." Coach and Happy looked on, smiling, and Deliverance gave my shoulder a playful punch.

"Come on, slugger. Let's get a burger at the Club. And stop crying like a stupid girl, or I'll tell the LPA on you."

Chapter
TWENTY-NINE

"Gonna Fly Now"

Miles

Happy and Coach had wished me well and left to return to work. I thanked them both profusely for their support, and they promised to see both Deliverance and myself the next evening at Bash and Oliver's housewarming shindig. I handled the driving since it was still a bit awkward for Deliverance to squeeze himself behind the wheel. As I approached the curb to pick up my extra-large passenger, I noted he was diligently tapping away at his phone, his tongue peeking slightly from one side of his mouth. Davis was more evolved than his Neanderthal proportions suggested, but his huge thumbs were ungainly. This gave him a reputation as an appalling texter; anyone in receipt of his messages generally required a second opinion to interpret the information. I leaned across the passenger seat and pushed the door open for him. His head snapped up, and he quickly stuffed the phone into a pants pocket.

"Who ya texting with, D?" I shot him a raised eyebrow; he was probably sexting with Luckie. He looked guilty as hell.

"Nobody. Luckie." The rapid-fire words assured me he was lying his ass off. He wasn't sexting after all.

"Liar." I grinned at him. "I don't care. Thanks again, Deliverance. I don't even know what to say about your statement to the board. As if you haven't gone out of your way to watch out for me these past few months…the calls and texts. That huge box of chocolates. I don't deserve a friend as good as you, D." I was sniffling again.

"Dammit, Charlotte Louise. I told you about that boo-hoo-ing. I told you—"

I interrupted him, ice cold. "What the almighty fuck did you just call me, Davis Payne Foster? And how did you know my middle name, assclown?"

He chortled. "Yep. I thought that would do it. There's been an awful pile of paperwork to deal with lately; your official moniker may or may not have been on some of it. I took the opportunity to make a note of it." He looked terribly proud of himself.

"Yeah?" I would've tossed my hair for effect, but it was tightly coiled at the nape of my neck. "Well, you can just forget what you saw, Deliverance. Just forget all about it." I sniffed. He'd done that to distract me, but it worked, and I appreciated it.

"Fine." He leaned back in his seat, muscular arms folded across his chest. "We'll move along. Let's have a word about your love life. What's this I hear about the sexy British flight lieutenant, one Oliver Bloodworth? Rumor has it you two have been canoodling about under the radar and spent a passionate night last Tuesday at One-Eyed Jacks."

"What the fuck are you yammering on about, Deliverance? What went down at One-Eyed Jacks?" Bastard looked so goddamned pleased with himself.

"I'll speak slowly so you can keep up, *Louise*." I shot him a poisonous glare, but he continued. "One-Eyed Jacks is, of course, the fictional brothel from the nineties horror/mystery/drama show, *Twin Peaks*. It was a cult classic. Everybody knows that. It also happens to be the official name of Bash and Oliver's new bachelor hacienda. Said hacienda is where the purported canoodling took place. Confirm or deny?"

Well, fuck me.

My mind careened wildly with panic. We were alone at Oliver's house, weren't we?

"How did you know, D? No bullshit now…I'm freaking out over here." I was practically yelling at him, which was not at all cool, under the circumstances.

He let loose with a belly laugh, only barely containing it enough to speak. "Simmer down, Miles. Total shot in the dark on the One-Eyed Jacks part, but I guess I have my confirmation." The asshole was laughing so hard he had to wipe away a tear before continuing. "I was just trying to distract you, so I guess that part worked. I knew Bash was cross country last week, and one of my neighbors is in that book club with Oliver every third Tuesday. I saw him in the parking lot, and he asked if I knew you. I connected the dots and took a shot." He whooped. "**Shack, two!**"

I sighed. "You're a real piece of work, D. I was peeing my pants over here."

He patted my arm, still wiping his eyes. "Don't worry your pretty little head, Louise. You were all by your lonesome last Tuesday at Oliver's house; nobody saw you taking the F train." He snorted again as I pulled the Mustang into the O'Club parking lot.

I was locking the car when I saw Deliverance wave at someone near the other end of the lot and shout to get their attention. "Over here, man. Come on over."

I looked up to see Oliver, all smiles and beguiling charm, striding in our direction. His long legs ate up the distance quickly, and he offered his hand to Deliverance as he approached.

"Thanks for the heads-up, mate. I really appreciate it." He turned the warmth of his smile on me, and I hoped D couldn't see how smitten I already was. "Hello, love. I needed to see with my own eyes that you're well after this morning's events. Davis here was kind enough to keep me in the loop; he invited me to join you for lunch."

I smiled back at Oliver, heart full just to be near him. It was like a balm on a day like this one. "Thank you for coming, Oliver." I smirked at D. "Did the caveman text you the details, by chance?"

We turned to walk toward the front door. Flanked by two of the tallest men I knew, I felt practically lilliputian. Oliver's hand brushed mine, and I swallowed a gasp.

Simmer down, Bugs. He touched a lot more than that the other night.

"Yes, he texted. I asked if he would, but how did you know?"

I punched D on the shoulder, and he feigned injury. "I know lots of stuff, British. One of the things I know is that this guy is the worst texter in the known universe. I'm surprised you could make out the hieroglyphics."

D tipped an imaginary hat to me. "You're welcome, ma'am. You should be in awe of my sleuthing skills and situational awareness, but whatever."

We'd taken up residence at a corner table in the O'Club's casual bar where Oliver and D ordered big, greasy double burgers and disposed of them like they were canapés. A very nervous stomach prevented me from eating even half of the sad chicken salad still sitting in front of me. Deliverance regaled us with stories of his adventures with Luckie on their recent trip to Savannah. He'd gone as the **ADVON** liaison for an exercise the Scorpions were involved in; spending time with his family in the aftermath of the accident was intended to sweeten the pot. Instead, news of their son's interracial romance had gone over like the proverbial fart in church with his parents. D came from old Savannah money, and his mother decided to combat the issue with passive-aggressive antics meant to send Lucinda running for the border.

"Mama wasn't prepared for a girl from New York to take her to the woodshed." Deliverance grinned and offered Oliver some of the basket of steaming, crispy French fries the waitress had just delivered to our table; I shook my head in amazement. *What kind of place refills fries like they're iced tea?* Oliver chuckled as he continued. "But Mama met her match when she met my girl. They got straight, and now they're thick as thieves." I touched the top of Oliver's hand, admiring his laughing profile as he shoveled more fries onto his plate. He turned, and his eyes darkened as he searched my face. "You've put your hair in that knot, Charlotte. That's how you were wearing it the day we took down the criminal element at the Kwik Shopper." He reached up, gently touching the chignon. I thought he'd say more, but he held my eyes silently, gaze heated.

"Okay." Deliverance slapped the table with both palms, standing. "I gotta hit the head. You two see if you can find a dark corner and get your business handled. I'll be back in a few." I smiled as he left, but Oliver's focus remained steadily on me. He took my hand briefly, caressing my palm with his thumb.

"How are you doing, Charlotte? You're all that's been on my mind since I woke this morning; I got Deliverance's mobile from Jacob so I could stay abreast of how everything was going." His face softened. "He thinks so highly of you; did you know that? He told me about the statement he planned to make to the board."

I nodded, eyes wandering to the wide picture window. In the distance, several Warthogs were tearing up the pattern, the trademark whine of their GE engines a constant soundtrack. "I was stunned…surprised. I don't even know how to tell you how it felt to see the three of them—Happy, Coach, and D—backing me up. By being there and by saying the things they did, especially Davis. I was…" I was rarely at a loss for words.

"Gobsmacked. That's what you were. I understand, love, but they wanted to be there. Davis told me as much."

In my periphery, I noticed the clock above the bar. "Damn. The day's slipped by; I've got to get out to the squadron and finish a couple of things." Deliverance pulled out his chair and sat down as I signaled the waitress for our check. "I completely lost track of time, D; we've got to get back to work before the day's gone. We've been here almost two hours; why didn't you tell me?"

Deliverance just chuckled. "You're my job today, Miles. Happy sent me packing and told me to keep you occupied. I couldn't think of anything better than a long lunch and some eye candy for you." He gestured to Oliver who just laughed.

"A long lunch is an excellent start to the weekend; I'd wrapped everything up out at the range anyway. I have an errand to run here, then I'll be…"

The sound of an incoming text on my phone interrupted him, and I snatched it from my purse to see the message. Throughout the lighthearted lunch banter, the possibility that the board could render a decision this afternoon was never far from my mind. I looked up.

"It's from Major Griffin; the board will reconvene at 1600 and render their decision."

Early again.
The board's findings were to be announced an hour from the time the text had come. Unfortunately, we were only ten minutes away, and thus, early again. I whiled away the endless minutes

with D and Oliver, avoiding coffee like the plague this time, and watching appreciatively as they tried to distract me. It was an impossible chore; my entire future was on the line. With only ten minutes to spare, Major Griffin appeared in the waiting area and introduced himself to Oliver.

"Lieutenant Bloodworth, you and Captain Foster will need to remain here while the decision is announced. It should be a very brief proceeding, but only Lieutenant Christman and I can attend."

I mustered what I hoped was a brave smile and followed Major Griffin into the room we'd occupied previously. The members of the board arrived together, and I was surprised to see General O'Cherry enter the room only moments later. I called the room to attention this time, having noticed the general's arrival first, and we all stood, saluting.

"At ease." The general was seated in the same chair and spoke to the board. "Colonel London, it looks like we're all here; let's get this off the ground."

"Yes, sir." He stood and addressed the small gathering. "The board extends its appreciation to both the ADC and JAG representatives for their excellent work and to General O'Cherry for joining us for this important event." He picked up a sheaf of papers, glancing at it briefly, and looked up to address me more directly. Major Griffin touched my elbow, and we both stood for the reading of the board's findings.

"Lieutenant Christman, this board has heard and reviewed evidence surrounding the Class One mishap that occurred 26 August at approximately 0725 near Ajo, Arizona, involving yourself and Captain Davis Foster, also assigned to the 82nd TFS. Taking into account the accident investigation board's findings, as well as the testimony of the squadron commander, the operations officer, and the weapons officer of your squadron, the 82nd TFS, this Flying Evaluation Board makes the following recommendation…"

I swallowed hard and tried to hear each word he said above the hammering of my heart.

"You will retain your flight rating and your assignment to the 82nd TFS, and you will return immediately to a Mission Qualification Training status. You are directed to re-accomplish the syllabus and requirements of an MQT pilot; all training sorties are to be flown with an instructor pilot. This training will be directly supervised by Colonel Charles Ditka, the squadron operations officer, and monitored by Colonel Nathan Morgan, the squadron commander. These recommendations have been referred to General O'Cherry's office for review and final approval." His eyes met mine and seemed to bore directly into me.

"This board is composed of rated pilots who understand the seriousness of your situation and the gravity of removing a pilot from flight status. While your actions at the time of the mishap are without defense, you've taken impressive measures toward improvement and restitution. We collectively have never heard such an impassioned argument for the preservation of an individual's rating under these circumstances as we did from your supporters. They make a solid case for retaining you on flight status, and we agree. This board wishes you well, Lieutenant Christman."

My voice was small indeed as I answered. "Yes, sir. Thank you, sir."

General O'Cherry stood, and the remainder of the room followed. He turned to me, and his gruff demeanor softened almost imperceptibly. "Lieutenant Christman, your job now is to make us glad the board retained you. Go forth and sin no more." He grinned as he strode toward the door. "Good day, people."

***

Major Griffin shook my hand, and I thanked him for his excellent work on my behalf. I tried to collect myself, but the good news was so fresh and so shocking. I couldn't seem to process it, so I gathered my things and walked up the hall and into the small waiting area where Oliver and Deliverance apparently hadn't settled down enough to be seated.

I didn't know what to say when they turned abruptly from the window where they stood, staring outside. I suppose I must have looked like a deer in the headlights, shocked and mute. Oliver rushed forward, grasping my arms gently.

"Charlotte, are you…" His eyes searched my face. "Oh, darling, you're gutted; I'm so, so sorry."

He was trying to gather me into his arms when I suddenly regained my powers of speech and pushed back. "No. No, Oliver, I'm just—I can't believe it."

D looked cautious and cocked his head. "What are you saying, Miles? What happened in there?"

I couldn't believe the words were about to come out of my mouth. "They're not taking my wings." Emotion overwhelmed me as it had done more times than I could count over the past months, but this time it was laughter—not tears—that burst forth. "They're letting me keep my wings; I'm getting a second chance."

Chapter THIRTY

"House of the Rising Sun"

Oliver

Jacob and I had been living in our new "digs," as he called the sprawling mid-century ranch, for a couple of weeks, and the threat of the impending housewarming party was strong motivation to plow through the hard work of unpacking our belongings. We'd managed to surpass our original goal of clearing a narrow path through the chaos and were instead approaching habitable. As exciting as that was, the reason for my exhilaration this evening was a blue-eyed dream who'd just been handed back her life. Tonight, I'd have the good fortune to enjoy her company without the stress of the unknown weighing on her. The burden of uncertainty that hung over her every moment since I'd laid eyes on her at the summer picnic was gone, and I was chuffed. Now it remained to be seen if what was growing between us could become something more.

Jacob appeared in the door of the kitchen wearing only red boxer briefs. He gestured to his attire with an arched brow. "Too much?"

I rolled my eyes. "Far too little, you tosser. You need to get dressed; we'll have arrivals any time now. And I can't bear to expose Charlotte to," I gestured up and down his nearly naked form, "whatever this is."

Jake struck a dramatic bodybuilder pose. "Dude. I can't turn this off."

I nodded and changed the subject. "Jacob, did you take care of the food? That was your assignment." I knew the answer, of course.

His brow knit, and he appeared to think. "Food? No food; I forgot to hit the deli after the gym. In my defense, it takes a lot of work to look like this." He affected a duck-lip pout and aimed it at me. "I'm hot, cuz."

I shook my head. "You're plug ugly. Useless wanker...doomed to die alone. Good job that I made a stop myself, then." I opened the refrigerator door to check on the two large trays of sub sandwiches I'd picked up at the deli on the way home. They were already conveniently sliced and pleasingly displayed, I noted. Everyone would bring along some sort of snack or another dish to help feed the always-ravenous Scorpion herd, and the random diversity usually worked out just as well as food assignments. I looked around to find my cousin standing on a step ladder in the great room where he'd recently completed a painstaking placement and installation of his Sonos speakers. He'd taken longer to accomplish that task than I had to cut the grass in our half-acre plot. Now he was studying his phone, obviously scrolling through the endless playlists it contained. The overall effect of him doing this mundane task while wearing only his underpants was ridiculous and vaguely obscene.

I waved to get his attention. "When does the beer arrive, Jacob?"

"The LPA's bringing kegs from the Club; they'll be here sometime before six." He climbed down and stashed the ladder in the foyer wardrobe before starting for his room, singing a Bad Company song and swinging his ass as he made his way down the hall.

I consulted my wristwatch and called after him. "I suppose it wouldn't be helpful to point out it's half past, then?" He disappeared, hopefully indicating that he was finally getting dressed. I intended to assure that Charlotte had a wonderful time this evening at the party, as well as afterward, during the wee hours, and first thing in the morning. The idea of settling back in between her milky thighs for a protracted feast made me smile. Seeing Jacob's vulgar beefcake display would be no way to start out her evening.

My internal dialogue was interrupted by a knock at the door followed straightaway by Charlotte's voice calling. "British, are you in there? Come give me a hand." I sprinted to the door and found her balancing two large baking dishes. I smiled at her, took one of the dishes, and bent to press my mouth to hers.

"Hello, love. Welcome back." Jacob's appalling shower song drifted out of the open door to his loo, and Charlotte's eyes widened. "Pay no mind to my roommate; he's a cretin."

"Why is Bashful singing T-Swifty?" She cocked her head, listening as he artlessly warbled the lyrics; it was too grating to ignore.

"He's not. He doesn't even know who Taylor Swift is." Pop music was utterly foreign to Jacob; he favored classic rock. Even as I spoke, he belted several mangled bars about desire and destiny, a prompt and certain rebuke of what I'd just stated. I grinned at Charlotte.

"So it *is* the lovely Miss Swift; I stand corrected." I indicated the way to the kitchen. "Let's get as far away as possible from that atrocious sound."

We placed the two dishes she'd brought on the stove, and I removed one edge of the cling film from the corner of the first one, peeking at the contents. "What have we here, hmmm?" The aroma made my mouth water, but I couldn't identify the dish.

"Sue's been giving me cooking lessons." Charlotte's blue eyes danced, and I realized this was my girl without the burden she'd been carrying. "I always assumed I couldn't cook only because I never had before, but guess what?" She uncovered the second dish, which held dozens of juicy little meatballs studded with caramelized onion and basted in a glossy red sauce. "Swedish meatballs, appetizer-sized, and smoked Gouda and bacon dip with scallions and assorted crackers." She turned the temperature dial on the cooker, removed the remainder of the cling film, and set them both inside. "Sue taught me about 'assorted crackers.' They're classier than potato chips."

When the food was sorted, she turned, and I took her in my arms. "Perhaps classier, but not better tasting. Your American crisps are unparalleled by any I've found at home. Particularly those Ruffles crisps." I kissed her jaw and moved down to taste the skin of her neck while murmuring close to her ear. "Speaking of things that are luscious to taste, darling...I'm looking forward to having you in my bed all night tonight and extending your stay through as much of tomorrow as I'm able." Her hands smoothed a path up and down my ribcage as I nipped and sucked the soft flesh of her neck, and then she moved lower to knead my bum and pull my hips tight to hers. The hard length of my shaft rejoiced at the contact; I couldn't wait to feel her nakedness against me again.

"I've got a long list of things to celebrate this weekend, Oliver." I straightened, reluctantly abandoning my exploration of her neck and meeting hooded eyes, almost navy blue in this shadowy corner of the kitchen. "And I've been looking forward to doing most of my celebrating on that thick cock of yours."

Without wasting another second, I covered her mouth with mine and licked my way inside, settling her more tightly in my embrace for a lengthy quest of her mouth. My tongue stroked and loved hers, drinking in her sweetness. One hand slipped away from her bottom to slide under her blouse and palm the warm, bare skin there, moving further up…"

"Hey, Ollie. What's to eat around here? I never got…" I yanked my hand from Charlotte's softness and broke the kiss to find Jacob rummaging in the refrigerator. Once again clad in his pants alone. He looked up and took us in, Charlotte still in my arms. "Oh, hey, Miles; I didn't hear you come in." He sniffed the air. "What smells so good?" He abandoned his search of the re-frigerator shelves and moved toward the cooker.

Charlotte turned smoothly in my arms, shielding my rapidly deflating hard-on from my cousin's view and blocking his ap-proach to the food warming in the cooker. "Nope. No you don't, Bashful. This is for everyone, and there'll be plenty to eat." She gave him a quick once-over. "Which do you want to explain first, Bash—why you're subjecting me to your nakedity or why you're singing a T-Swizzle song in the shower about love and longing?" She folded her arms and stared at him, waiting for the answer I knew he wouldn't offer.

He broke the stare first, sauntering away. I was glad to see he'd at least changed into a fresh pair of pants after his shower. "I'm gonna get dressed. The LPA will be here any time now with the kegs."

Charlotte shot me a huge grin as he disappeared again down the hall; I bent down to kiss the top of her head. "I didn't need to start tonight by seeing Bash in his drawers, Oliver. It's too much on an empty stomach."

I shrugged. "Maybe he'll put on trousers as a special gesture for you."

Chapter THIRTY-ONE

"Something to Talk About"

Oliver

The party was in full swing. The LPA had eventually arrived with two cold kegs and set them up by the pool. Boo explained they'd been unavoidably detained en route when they passed Torch's favorite Mexican restaurant. Out front, they'd seen a large sign advertising a tableside guacamole and margarita special that was deemed too good to pass up. Fortunately, I had stashed enough Carlsberg and Strongbow in the cooler to bridge the gap and stave off sobriety until their arrival.

The worktop in the kitchen was covered from edge to edge with a variety of savory starters, sandwiches, casseroles, and dip. The table in the adjacent breakfast room was equally laden with sweets—biscuits, cakes, and tarts of every kind. I helped myself to another brownie and studied the room.

The party was ostensibly a housewarming for Jacob and me, but that was clearly only an excuse for music, food, and alcohol. We had no need of any gifts—we hadn't even bought a house.

In truth, the person everyone wanted to see was Charlotte. She told me Happy had specifically reinforced immediately after the accident that she was still very much a Scorpion and had the full faith and support of the squadron. But I'd seen the look in her eyes as we'd talked about her situation and the possible outcomes. I knew the potential loss of her squadron was one of the things that weighed most heavily on her. She'd always enjoyed them individually as friends, but I knew she now saw them more as family. They'd walked through the fire with her, and tonight was her night to come out the other side, shiny and new. Like a beautiful phoenix, rising from the ashes, I thought with a smile.

Each new arrival searched the room as soon as they'd set food dishes down in the kitchen and found Charlotte for a chat and a hug with congratulations. I grabbed my drink and made my way across the crowded family room to where she lounged on one of the long sofas. She was engaged in a lively conversation with Luckie, and Deliverance sat nearby, a look of patient indulgence on his face.

"Able to get a word in here, mate?" I settled in next to Charlotte, resting one hand on her thigh.

He shook his head amiably. "Not in the past fifteen minutes, no. But maybe later." He pulled Luckie to him and kissed the side of her face. "It's freeing, really. Not having to hold up your end of the conversation."

Charlotte looked around, cataloging the room's occupants, then turned back to Luckie. "I see Happy, but where's Camille? I haven't seen her since the shopping trip last week, and she looked like chocolate-covered death that morning."

Luckie narrowed her eyes and shot a meaningful look at D. "See. I told you. Did I not tell you?" She turned to me, punctuating her statement with emphatic gestures. "I told him something was up, but did he believe me? No. *No.* 'You're jumping to conclusions,' he said. 'Seeing something that isn't there,' he said."

Davis turned to me wordlessly and nodded his head toward the two women as if to signify his agreement with her diatribe. "She always takes my calls, answers my texts. And guess what?" Her eyes held mine, but she held her hand out, indicating that Davis should speak.

"She hasn't been taking her calls or answering her texts." Davis spoke to me in a measured tone.

"Precisely." Luckie took up her argument again. "It's entirely obvious. How could she possibly think I wouldn't know? Me?" She brandished her empty glass at Davis. "Screwdriver me, Tarzan."

I raised my eyebrows. "Shall we leave, then? Or would you just like the use of my room?"

Davis stood with a grin. "I think we can keep our clothes on for a little longer. My timid, soft-spoken girl is trying to say she needs more orange juice." He smiled warmly at her. "Evidently, more orange juice and less vodka."

He stood and took her glass before walking toward the kitchen for refills. It was quiet on the sofa for only a moment before Charlotte turned to Luckie with a smile and dawning realization on her face. "She's preggers, isn't she? Happy swung for the fences."

Charlotte looked completely delighted, and Luckie nodded vehemently. "Exactamundo. Bun in the fucking oven, and she hasn't even told her bestie. I'm gonna kick her ass at my earliest convenience." She accepted a glass of what appeared to be straight orange juice from a besotted Davis and turned back to Charlotte, her eyes brimming with tears. "I'm just so happy for her."

Davis pulled her close to him with a laugh as he sat down. "If she's expecting, they'll tell us when they're ready, Peaches."

Charlotte wrinkled her nose. "Expecting? Expecting what?"

Davis rolled his eyes. "Miles. In the Old South, you didn't

mention pregnancy in polite company except in veiled terms."

He'd confused Luckie as well, judging from the look on her face. "Because why? I don't get it."

He shrugged. "Straight-up proof of fucking. An expectant mother is a classic symbol of Madonna-like radiance and virtue. It's jarring to remember that the only reason she got that way was because she was putting out like a Coke machine."

I was still suffering the ill effects of inhaling Strongbow while laughing at his logic when we were joined by two more Scorpions. I extended my hand once I'd caught my breath.

"Good to see you again, Marilyn." I smiled and shook his hand. He was one of the few people in the room as tall as I was, and I wondered how he folded himself into a cockpit. He had a stupidly square jaw, bristled with a day's worth of shadow, and his eyes crinkled as he smiled and shook my hand. He probably had a herd of women at his heels at all times.

"And you as well, Boo. Were you born on Halloween then?" He was a younger bloke, all dark hair and brown eyes that the ladies likely swooned over. He shook my hand warmly in turn.

He grinned in response to my question. "My parents were both big fans of Harper Lee and *To Kill a Mockingbird* in particular." He shrugged. "Coulda been worse, I guess. They might have named me Atticus."

The group immediately descended into a discussion of when Happy and Camille would marry and what parties the union might occasion. Boo held forth on that topic while Charlotte went to refresh her drink. "The central ritual at any wedding has to be the bachelor party. It's the most fun and the part everyone looks forward to the most."

Luckie rolled her eyes. "How do you figure that? By definition, about half of the wedding guests are excluded from the bachelor party because they're primarily friends of the bride, not the groom."

Marilyn chimed in just as Charlotte returned and curled herself into my side. "Don't you mean because they're women? Because that's not always the case." He motioned to Charlotte, now comfortably seated with my arm around her. "There's no way Miles wouldn't be a fixture at any bachelor party we threw for Happy, right Miles?"

"Oh, for sure." She stretched, looking at Boo. "You know, unless I got a better offer from the other side. I think you're making some assumptions about partying with the girls that are mistaken." She motioned toward Luckie, still guzzling orange juice. "This girl knows about having a good time."

"So, I've gotta ask. Why One-Eyed Jacks?" Marilyn leaned back, spreading his arm over the back of the cushion, easily taking up half of the large settee. "I'm familiar with the *Twin Peaks* reference, of course, but why that name?" His grin was easy.

"I think the main purpose is to annoy Vivianne; any other positive outcomes are just a windfall. Jacob seemed sure naming the place after a house of ill repute would get her hackles up, but she doesn't seem bothered so far."

"Probably because she doesn't know about it, but that will be short-lived." He indicated Boo with his cup. "The LPA put a sign on the door welcoming everyone to your den of iniquity. Vivvie isn't here yet, is she?"

Luckie shook her head. "Not yet; she had to work today. She texted to let me know she's on her way, and she's bringing Grace along."

The name caught my attention. That would make my cousin happy; she was the one he'd mentioned several weeks ago when I was trying to tell the wanker I was asking out Charlotte.

"I'll assume Grace is unwittingly playing the part of Vivvie's matchmaking victim?" I addressed the question to Luckie, certain that she was the only one who'd know the answer.

"Correct." Luckie gave a decisive nod. "The good news is that

Viv plays Cupid better than she cooks. But she does everything better than she cooks."

Our laughter was interrupted by a screech emanating from the vicinity of the front door. "Jacob Archibald Travis! What in the holy hell are you thinking naming this house after a whorehouse like common trash?" Vivianne stood in the open front door, green eyes flashing. There was a stunning woman with long, dark hair just behind Viv barely suppressing a smile at her outburst. On the front door, I saw for the first time the sign gifted to us by the LPA. It was a large poster board welcoming all and sundry to "One-Eyed Jacks—Best Bang for Your Buck (We'll Tickle Your Pickle for Only a Nickel)."

Charlotte and Marilyn turned to each other, snickering, and mouthed, "Archibald?"

"My father's name," I supplied, "but no less offensive when given to a newborn. At least he's not called by it."

Jacob was on his feet, laughing as he strode to the door and kissed his sister's cheek. "I just knew you'd love it, sis. Come on in and take a load off." He straightened and I swore I saw him affect an extra bit of the signature Jake Travis swagger as he took in the lovely young woman behind his sister.

"Well, Grace, to what do we owe the honor of your beauty this evening? Whatever I did, I want to do it again."

I couldn't hear her response, but she blushed bright pink from the roots of her hair to the tips of her ears and then hurried to catch up to Vivianne. Jacob looked perplexed. His trademark charm rarely failed him. Now it seemed he might have a challenge on his hands.

Charlotte leaned in. "You don't often see Bashful strike out, do you?"

"No, I'm kind of enjoying the show."

Happy had materialized during the kerfuffle at the front door and now stood in front of us, arms folded in front of him. "Mind if I park it here for a few minutes, Miles?"

We rearranged the growing assembly of bodies lounging on the settees to make room, and Happy settled in. "It's a great house, Oliver. Great house for parties, too; you'll be in heavy rotation out here once the weather warms up. The pool will be a nice draw when it's hot."

"Not sure it's this warm in England in August, Happy. I'm ill-equipped to handle what Tucson dishes out in the summer; the pool was a matter of self-preservation. Now I just have to work out how to refrigerate it." Everyone laughed, but the effects of the alcohol caused a brief but semi-serious discussion about having mammoth blocks of ice airlifted in for the pool on a daily basis during the summer.

Charlotte reached across me, touching the colonel's arm to gain his attention. When he turned, she leaned across me to speak more privately to him alone. "Happy, I wanted to say thanks one more time. Actually, I may never stop saying thank you for not giving up on me. I don't deserve all that you did, but I'll spend all the time I have left in the Hawg—hell, in any cockpit—trying to make sure you're proud of me. And that you never doubt that the extra effort you expended was worth it."

It was easy to see that Happy was touched by her gratitude; he reached over me and patted her hand. "You will prove yourself many times over the course of a career, Miles, whether it's military or civilian, but you have nothing to prove to me. I'm already a believer; you were worth it from the start."

Charlotte looked a bit overcome; all the well-wishers this evening had reinforced what I already knew. Charlotte was a valued member of the team, and they were grateful that she'd remain a part. But the outpouring of emotion was hard for her, so I tried to think of a way to lighten the mood. Unnecessary, as it turned out, since the LPA was in attendance.

"Ladies and gentlemen—welcome to the housewarming

of One-Eyed Jacks, the finest brothel in west Tucson." A quick glance around the room revealed Rock standing on the coffee table with a large and obviously fake microphone. Vivianne pelted him with popcorn from a small sack she held, making a few choice comments about her opinions of the house's name, but Rock only chuckled. "Tonight's a special night, and the LPA felt it called for some very special entertainment, but first I'd like to introduce my backup singers." From the hallway, a lumbering trio of cross-dressing nightmares sashayed toward Rock. Torch, Boo, and Bashful were attired in a stunningly unattractive array of floral housedresses, scarves, gaudy jewelry, and high heels. As they positioned themselves in front of the coffee table, Rock swept his hand dramatically. "Scorpions, these are The Bitchez, and I am Herb. This one's for you, Miles." The music started, subjecting everyone to a very poorly lip-synced version of the seventies ballad "Reunited," by Peaches and Herb. The lyrics were accompanied by some truly marginal choreography led by Jacob, and the song finished with Rock singing from his knees, consumed with feigned emotion, in front of Charlotte.

She laughed until her face was pink, then jumped up to hug the entertainment as their tribute came to a close. Happy stood and said a few words, congratulating Jacob and me on the new house and adding a few lighthearted words to welcome Charlotte back to flying. He seemed to recognize the way all the emotion weighed on her.

The party continued, powered by good food, conversation, and alcohol as midnight approached. A constantly changing array of Scorpions and their spouses or dates perched on or around the settees, laughing and telling stories. They were an entertaining lot, to be certain, but I was focused on Charlotte. The cautiousness I'd sensed in her demeanor when we first met seemed to have dissipated. She seemed more comfortable in my space, occasionally touching my arm or knee and settling the warmth of her body close to mine. Her scent was intoxicating, and I leaned in idly to enjoy the coconut scent of her loose red tresses. There was a brief lull in the conversation, and I took the occasion to lean down and whisper in her ear.

"Go down the hall, into my bathroom, and close the doors. No lights. Clothes off."

With only the smallest smile, she stood immediately and left the room.

Chapter
THIRTY-TWO

"Burning Down the House"

Oliver

The steady drone of animated conversation and laughter, underscored with Jacob's lively music playlist, allowed me to slip from the room unnoticed only a few minutes after Charlotte disappeared. I walked the length of the rambling ranch house, double-checking as the corridor turned sharply right to make certain no one was nearby. My suite lay in the back corner of the house, far removed from the hub of activity. I slipped into the darkness of my room, clicking the lock as the door closed, and undressed silently. The low thump of a rhythmic bass from a song I didn't recognize reverberated along the hard length of my shaft. I strode across the room, anxious for the woman who waited for me, opened the bathroom door soundlessly, and stepped inside.

I'd asked her to wait in the bathroom rather than on the bed for this very reason. The room was dark, so dark it was impossible to tell whether your eyes were open or closed. This would be furtive, blistering, and very fast; the softness of my bed was for later. There, I'd spend the remainder of tonight and tomorrow worshiping all of Charlotte's softness and drinking in her wet heat.

Right now, I'd fuck her lights out.

I could smell her, coconut and sweet, hot Charlotte. The only sound was her shallow breathing.

"Oliver?" She sounded uncharacteristically tentative and breathy. My cock pounded its need in time to the music's beat. "Is that you?"

Her voice told me she was leaning against the door to the water closet, and two long strides brought my body against hers. Her breathing hitched as we touched, and her arms wound around my neck.

"It is me, Charlotte. Be very quiet, now; I'm going to fuck you fast and hard. Turn around and put your hands flat against the door." My voice was low and quiet. I bent my knees, allowing the length of my shaft to settle in the valley of her smooth ass cheeks. I slid it slowly up and down, torturing my cock with the softness, then reached around to cup her breasts. "I'll bet that sweet little pussy is wet for me, isn't it, darling?" She mewled and arched her back, meeting my dick on the upstroke. I plucked one tight nipple with a sound pinch, and her needy whine disintegrated into a groan.

"Oh, Oliver, yes. More, please, I…"

I smacked her bottom sharply and then used both hands to pull her hips hard against mine. My balls felt as if they might empty themselves straight away between the warm curves of her bottom, and I fought momentarily for control. "Very quiet, darling girl. I need to fuck you and come inside your tight little cunt, but you will be perfectly silent for me. Do you understand, Charlotte?"

She nodded her head, breathing picking up the pace. I smiled to myself; it had been a bit of calculated risk.

Excellent. She liked the smack to her bottom. But probably not as much as I liked giving it to her.

I dipped my mouth to her, breathing in the coconut fragrance and blowing hot breath on her neck. She groaned again and wiggled her little bottom on my cock. I allowed one hand to trail down her tummy, brushing her clit lightly for only a moment. Then, as I sank two fingers inside her, I bit her neck, just a touch beyond what I knew would be comfortable. She was warm and so wet inside; I'd have been surprised to find her otherwise after sending her ahead to undress and anticipate. My blood heated further as I felt the tremble and flutter of her escalating around my fingers. She was close to coming already; the thought set me on edge, and my cock became nearly unmanageable. Precum slicked the head of my shaft as it continued to stroke between the cheeks of her ass.

I bent my legs a bit further and growled low in her ear before biting the lobe. "Are you ready for me, love? I'm going to fuck you now." She only moaned, arching her back and giving me easy access to what I needed more than air. My broad head probed her slick entrance briefly; then I snapped my hips up without warning, burying myself deep and eliciting a groan from both of us. My head fell forward onto her shoulder as I began long, slow strokes and one hand found her clit. "I want you to come, Charlotte…want to feel you let go around my dick." I picked up speed and slid two fingers over the swollen knot, one on each side, in time with my thrusts. Her hands scrabbled for leverage against the door, and she pressed her clit against my fingers, seeking relief. I swelled inside her, nearing a tipping point, but solely focusing on the sleek, wet woman who needed me.

"Does it feel good, darling girl? My cock stretching you?" I drove in harder now, gentling the force with kisses on the damp skin of her neck and sweet words whispered in between. The silky heat tightened, and she cried out as her perfection rippled around me.

"Come inside me, Oliver; do it now..." Her voice pleaded, and her walls suckled my length, milking the cum from me as I buried myself deep. "Yes, Oliver...give me everything." Her breathing was harsh, and her hands eventually reached behind to curl around my neck while I pulsed inside her. The rush of blood pounded in my ears, and the darkness compounded the hazy delirium I felt in the moment. It was only meant to be a quick, hot shag—a bit of fun to take the edge off for both of us until we could finally settle in for the main course after the festivities concluded.

But I was startled at how deeply affected I was by this hasty coupling. I placed one hand flat on the door in front of us as we returned to Earth, breathing finally slowing. With the other hand, I palmed Charlotte's flat tummy and pulled her close. "You're a magnificent woman, Charlotte Christman." I kissed the side of her neck and her cheek gently, over and over. "I've never known anyone like you, darling girl."

She turned and lifted her face to mine for a proper kiss, and I could feel her smile beneath my lips.

We'd managed to clean up, dress, and sneak separately back into the party, escaping the notice of the crowd. The festivities showed no signs of slowing down, at least as far as I could tell, so I returned to the kitchen to round up snacks and hydration for Charlotte. I'd stacked a small plate with a variety of cookies and brownies, and I was pouring a tall glass of cold milk for her when a beautiful woman with piercing blue eyes and a long champagne-colored braid that reached the middle of her back approached, studying me. She offered her hand and sized me up while she waited. I set the carton of milk aside and took her hand, shaking it. "How do you do?"

"And you must be Oliver." Her tone wasn't unfriendly, but she studied me carefully. "I'm Samanthe Barber, a good friend of Miles's, but I don't believe I've had the pleasure of meeting you," she looked me up and down once more, "Oliver."

So this is the Sam I've heard so much about.

"A pleasure, Samanthe. I've actually heard quite a lot about you; Charlotte thinks the world of you. I'm glad we finally have the opportunity to meet." Perhaps a dollop of British charm could dispel the suspicion. She helped herself to a macadamia nut cookie from the plate on the worktop, continuing to regard me wordlessly, so I hurried on. "She told me you were the one who came to care for her after the accident. That you were a virtual stranger who went well beyond what most people would have done." My expression softened as I remembered the emotion tingeing Charlotte's voice when she told me the story. "I care for her deeply, and I thank you for what you did."

Her cool expression thawed noticeably, but she still seemed a bit distant. "It was my privilege to be there for Miles; I was glad to help. And I gained a great friend that day." As she spoke, Charlotte approached from behind her, wrapping her arms around Samanthe's waist and kissing her neck loudly.

Sam whirled and flung her arms around Charlotte. "Hi there, pretty girl—I've just been interrogating your boy toy." She threw a mischievous look over her shoulder at me. "He doesn't scare easily; what fun is that?"

I handed the glass of milk to Charlotte, who promptly drained half of it and reached for the brownie I offered. Sam lifted a brow and cut her eyes back and forth between the two of us. "Thirsty, Miles? Hungry too, hmm? Could that have anything to do with the stand-up booty call you were knocking off when I arrived?"

I felt my face and throat heat to what was doubtlessly bright red, but Charlotte only laughed. "And what if it is, Sam? Nothing wrong with a little 'How's your father' between consenting adults, is there?"

I laughed at her use of the thoroughly British expression. "Brilliant, Charlotte. Nicely done." I turned to Sam. "My apologies for being otherwise engaged when you arrived, Samanthe. If I'd known your arrival was imminent…"

Charlotte interrupted. "It wouldn't have made a damned bit of difference. No offense intended." She smiled widely at her friend.

"And none taken." Sam lifted a glass she'd set aside previously. "I'm late, but it looks like the celebration continues." Her face softened, and she took Charlotte's hand. "Vivvie invited me, and when I heard your good news…well, I just had to come congratulate you in person." The two of them embraced, and I saw tears in Sam's eyes as she hugged my girl. "I'm just so happy for you, Miles; you've worked hard, and you deserved this break." She broke the embrace and held Charlotte at arm's length, looking into her eyes. "I just know you're going to do great things, and I'm proud to be your friend."

Just as their conversation ended, Rock approached the kitchen, his eyes fixed on Samanthe. He stared a beat too long, but she was still involved in her conversation with Charlotte, so Rock shifted his attention to me, offering his hand. "Hey again, Oliver. Congrats on the house; this is some great party palace. And it'll only get better once it's warmer, and we can press the pool into service." He turned to Charlotte as she turned at the sound of his voice.

"Hiya, Miles. Hope you enjoyed our musical tribute." He shot her a crooked grin and snagged a cookie. The pile was dwindling.

"It was just so…" Charlotte feigned the search for an appropriate word, "…disturbing. I'm glad at least you were wearing pants. I've seen more of Bashful today than anyone should in an entire lifetime. I really didn't need to be subjected to the drag version of Jake Travis."

Everyone laughed, and I doubted anyone besides me noticed that Rock was working overtime not to stare at Samanthe. It was a chore, I was sure; she was absolutely lovely, especially when she laughed. Charlotte finally seemed to catch up to the unspoken request Rock was shouting in her direction. She touched Rock's arm.

"Say, Rock, have you met my friend? This is Samanthe Barber; she's one of the emergency room nurses who works with Luckie and Viv and Camille...you know, everybody. Sam, this is one of my very best friends, Hayes Hudson. Everyone calls him Rock."

Rock, always smoothly unflappable and oozing charm, seemed at a loss for words, at least momentarily. Sam extended her hand.

"Well hello, Hayes. Everyone calls me Sam. But you can call me Samanthe."

It was half past one when Jacob and I said our goodnights to Rock and Torch. I'd washed up most of the dishes while Jacob gathered the rubbish in bags and deposited them in the bin outside. Charlotte saw our last guests to the door, then sent me a sleepy smile as she curled up on the settee with a book, happy but completely knackered. I was sure she wouldn't make it through the first page, so I dimmed the lights and turned on a lamp nearby before kissing the top of her head.

Jacob and I had enjoyed a scotch together after the final departure, tidying all the while. It would be worth the effort not to awake to a pigsty in the morning. Once he'd disposed of the last bag of rubbish, he settled in at the breakfast table, feet propped on top.

"Grace seems lovely." Jacob didn't take the bait, instead

furrowing his brow and sipping his scotch. So I tried again.

"I saw you chatting her up, mate; how'd that go?" I snagged a tea towel and began drying a sink full of glasses.

He sighed. "Yeah, it's not the first time. I've approached her before, but she's so quiet." He shook his head.

"Do you think she's shy? Or what's the American saying?" I thought for a moment. "She's just not that into you?" I chuckled at the thought; Jacob's universal appeal to the gentler sex was a running joke in our family and a widely accepted truth. I would never have taken the piss out of him if there was a serious possibility she wasn't attracted to him.

He shook his head. "I don't think she's shy. But I'm not making any headway, and I don't know why."

We finished our drinks mostly in silence, and he put his tumbler in the sink, yawning. "I'm hitting the sack, cousin; great party." With that, he meandered toward his room.

I turned off the remaining lights and went to check on Charlotte. She was fast asleep, as I predicted, and I allowed myself a moment to take in her beauty, soft and almost childlike in sleep. I eased the paperback from her fingers and turned off the lights. She barely stirred as I lifted her, carried her to my room, and deposited her gently on the bed.

It was already past two, and I thanked my lucky stars the one set of window coverings I'd had the foresight to install right after we'd moved in were room darkening blinds. It would eventually help stave off the summer heat, but it would also allow me a long, luxurious sleep tonight wound around my Charlotte's soft body. I undressed her carefully so as not to wake her, and I settled both of us under the cotton quilts. The last memory of the evening was the sweetest—wrapping her in my arms and pulling her close enough to nod off to the soft rhythm of her quiet breathing. Something in the center of me stilled, anchored and comforted. She felt like home.

Chapter THIRTY-THREE

"I Was Made to Love Her"

Oliver

W hen I awoke, it was so dark as to be disorienting, but the faint aroma of coconuts from the mass of curly hair on my pillow reminded me of where I was. Charlotte was still cocooned in a deep sleep, her endearing, faint snuffle of a snore the only sound in the room. I pulled her warm nakedness close and settled her into the crook of my arm. Her presence was like a drug. I longed for her in a way that was curiously intense, given that I had no designs on meeting a woman when I relocated to the States.

I didn't come halfway around the world for any reason other than to be close to the family I love. The climate here was anathema to my constitution, which was accustomed to cool, damp English days. I was now living farther from Mum and Dad than I ever had, but this was a change I'd embraced for a specific reason, sure it would be the only occasion where Jacob, Vivvie, and I could live near one another as adults. It was only a matter of time until one of us had the joy of additional family obligations. If not that, either the United States or Royal Air Force would throw a spanner in the works by sending Jacob or me to live out the next chapter of our adventure in the service of our respective country somewhere else.

Any number of stories about love, family, and fortune are built around the truth that life doesn't often go as one imagines it will. I don't know what arrogance caused me to assume I was exempt from that truth. But now I was finding myself in the center of that very reality, I suddenly couldn't imagine the story of my life any other way. Each event and every fragment of my existence until this minute had been preparing me to love the sleeping woman I held in my arms. An epiphany landed squarely as I sat in the darkness, pondering these things, and it was as tangible as a physical blow. And as surely as my life had been preparing me for this moment, Charlotte's path had been leading her to me.

She stirred, and I knew she was waking because her breathing changed. I pressed my lips to her forehead and inhaled the scent of her wild, coconut-perfumed hair, loathe to disturb the hushed perfection of the room. Finally, I whispered, "Good morning, darling."

She snuggled closer. "Is it morning? Or afternoon?" She almost giggled, and it was delightfully uncharacteristic.

"I suppose it doesn't matter too much, does it? Did you sleep well, Charlotte?" She nodded, yawning, and her hands swept across my naked chest, coming to rest on the lower part of my belly. She petted the soft hair there affectionately. My cock stretched in response, morning wood well underway already.

I found one lush breast and allowed my fingers to toy with her nipple until I felt her begin to shift restlessly under the attention. She turned her face into my chest and nudged a nipple with her nose. "Are these…" She administered a little attention of her own, rubbing with her cheek and the tip of her nose until I responded.

"Are they sensitive?" I tweaked her gently. "Yes, they are; just like yours, darling. Marvelously sensitive." My restraint was running dangerously thin, so I flipped her onto her back, catching her unaware. Then I buried my face in her neck, licking and suckling, as I worked my way back down between the valley of her breasts. "Morning is my favorite time, Charlotte. Nothing compares to leisurely lovemaking on a lazy morning." I lifted one breast to my mouth, lapping at the nipple before suckling at it.

She groaned. "Leisurely lovemaking, lazy morning…is this what it's like getting naked with a book nerd—foreplay with a side of alliteration?" I smiled while licking the side of her breast. "You're making a believer out of me, British." Her fingers coiled in my hair as I continued to lavish her with attention. I freed one hand to smooth across her mound, toying with the wisp of hair there and she heated noticeably, becoming more vocal.

"Need your pussy, darling." I pushed her legs open, lifting them one at a time over my shoulders as I kissed my way across the smooth skin of her tummy and further down. "Are you ready for my mouth? Ready to come the first time this morning for me, sweet girl?" I didn't wait for an answer, but her hands in my hair urged me closer to her center. She lifted her hips to me, encouraging my mouth nearer to what I craved, but I settled one hand flat on her stomach and rubbed gently. "Relax now, Charlotte. There's no hurry; let me enjoy you."

She reluctantly relaxed her hips and allowed the weight of her legs to rest on my back. In the dark, I was mostly unable to see the pussy I was about to feast upon, and it was startlingly arousing. I allowed myself to revel in the heat and heady scent of her before moving close for one long, leisurely taste from the tiny, pleated opening of her bum, up and through her warm, wet slit. Upon reaching the apex, I circled the point of my tongue slowly about the bud of her clit, noticing how swollen it was already, and was rewarded with an uncensored moan. My cock bucked against the bedclothing; it was so enticing to lure Charlotte away from her usual controlled state. It was quite like seeing a majestic animal in the wild and reveling in its savage nature. I allowed myself to continue bathing the knot of nerves with lazy circles and enjoying her as she abandoned control. It required real effort to hold her hips on the bed as I picked up the pace and ate her luscious pussy in earnest, lapping away occasionally at the sweetness that trickled from her slit. In time, her heels dug into my back, and she ground herself against my face, thrashing a bit and calling out to me over and over.

"Oliver, please…please. Let me come; please let me…"

I only continued feeding, allowing her essence to bathe my face and awaiting the first orgasm and what I knew would be a long morning of pleasure. "Come for me, darling…let me taste you."

With that, she groaned low and began to pulse against my mouth, hard and slow. The sounds she made harassed my tormented cock; the quilt would be wet with precum when we moved. She clutched at my hair, and I delighted in the sensation of being wrapped in her glorious legs. She gripped me with them so tightly that it was occasionally difficult to catch a breath, but her shredded control only goaded me forward, more determined than ever to inundate her with bliss. Gradually, the pulsing against my lips subsided, and Charlotte's limbs loosened their hold on me. Her muscles relaxed and uncoiled. She was sated and sleepy once again, and we had that most singular of luxuries this morning—unfettered time. Rather than burying myself in her creamy heat, I slid back up her body and settled myself next to her once again. She was unbearably pliant and acquiescent in this state, seemingly entrusting the safekeeping of her unprotected heart to me in these moments. She curled against me, and I caressed and soothed her in the darkness. After several minutes, I finally spoke softly, smoothing my fingers through her hair.

"I thought I knew what the events and relationships of my life were preparing me for—the love of my family, the education, the military training. I saw the path laid in front of me, and it was easy enough to connect the dots. To see my work, my personal strengths and passions and how they would eventually weave together and make a meaningful life." I cupped her jaw and lifted her face toward mine, an errant beam of sunlight having cast minimal illumination over our bare skin. She watched me speak with quiet wonder showing on her face. My random collection of thought must have seemed particularly curious in these circumstances.

"I was thinking only a few minutes ago, while you slept, about why I've lived the life I have, walking along this path with the family and friends and events that have touched and shaped me. It occurred to me that fate's efforts are not wasted on us—that she was preparing me for a sacred trust. And that it was something more precious and significant than anything I'd ever done." I paused, taking her in and consciously studying, then memorizing the details of her face. Her fathomless blue eyes. I hoped to enjoy reliving this moment in years to come.

"I love you, Charlotte. My whole life and everything I've done has been readying me to fall in love with you, to care for you. I want to be the guardian of your heart for as long as you'll have me." I couldn't wait another second to press my lips to hers, sealing my words with a taste of her mouth. When we parted, her eyes were wet, and the look she gave me telegraphed incredulous awe. Her mouth moved, but no words emerged, so I put one finger to her lips. "You don't have to say anything, darling." I laughed lightly. "I can see that I've caught you by surprise. Believe me, love, no one is more surprised than I am at falling in love." I rearranged us slightly to enjoy a view of the dawn's light that was beginning to chase a few of the room's shadows; I wanted her to have some emotional space to take in what I'd given her.

"It makes sense when I see it in retrospect. I had the most wonderful family to teach me what love looks like, how unselfish and patient it is. But I never gave much serious consideration to romance; the prospect didn't draw me like it did so many of my friends. I assumed it would come if it was meant to, but I see now that the timing wasn't right. My heart was waiting." At that, I allowed the silence to stretch while I stroked her skin and let her process my words.

"You think you surprised me." Her tone held a touch of irony, but she laughed a bit after she spoke. Then it was quiet again, so I turned to see her face. She smiled and lifted one hand to touch my cheek. "I'm sure I looked shocked, and I suppose I am. But not for the reasons you think, Oliver."

I loved that neither of us seemed to feel in any hurry to rush through the treasure trove of thoughts and words and feelings heaped on this bed with us. This conversation was like a rare wine; it deserved to be savored. I had waited my whole life to share myself with someone in this way. Now I wanted to relish each word that fell from Charlotte's lips.

"I've come to realize over the past couple of months that I never enjoyed anything serious with a man because of the defenses I'd put in place to shelter myself. I valued my freedom above every other thing, so it stands to reason that loving someone—or allowing myself to be loved—wouldn't be in the cards for someone like me. Or so I thought."

I gave her a little smile of encouragement but said nothing.

Keep going, love. You're going to get there.

"My view of independence was twisted. That desire for freedom had warped into a near obsession with absolute self-sufficiency." She stared toward the window, and a new thought seemed to cross her mind. "Deliverance told me once, there is a silver lining to everything, no matter how bad things look on the surface. That there could even be a silver lining to something as stupid and tragic as our midair. Maybe this is one of those." She turned back and looked into my eyes, still deep in thought.

"After the accident, it was as if karma let loose with a flood of new people in my life. People who surrounded me with support and undeserved kindness, advising and encouraging me. Holding me accountable and letting me lean on them. Even new girlfriends, Oliver." She shook her head as if she couldn't believe what she was saying. "Girlfriends. I've *never* had those as an adult. All these people sent to help me see what could be. Helping me move into uncharted territory."

It was so much to take in, watching Charlotte piece together the changes in herself since the accident. It was like watching someone weaving together threads of every kind, the dark and light ones, the flawless and expensive threads alongside the torn and knotted ones. In the end, I was witness to the creation of a beautiful tapestry that wasn't diminished because of the imperfection of the poorer threads. They were necessary to create the beauty of the finished work. I took her hand and turned it over, kissing the palm gently.

"I'm sure you have the 'High Flight' sonnet framed and hanging on the wall of your townhouse somewhere, don't you, love?" She grinned and rolled her eyes. Every pilot the world over had a copy of that poem and could likely quote it from memory. "I recall the bit about the 'untrespassed sanctity of space,' and it makes me think of where you are. It's uncharted and undiscovered. Untrespassed."

She nodded as she listened thoughtfully. "There have been so many people who've loved me through this, Oliver. But no one has given me what you have." Her eyes were bright as she looked into me. "You were kind and steadfast. You showed me a side of myself I didn't know existed, and now you've given me your heart. I knew everything would be different with you, almost from the moment we met." She smiled even though one tear wet her cheek. "And I didn't know I would fall deeply in love with you too, but that's exactly what happened." She stretched up, touching her lips to mine. "I love you too, Oliver."

Her words were like a match to gasoline, heating my blood to incendiary levels, but I reined in the instinct to thrust inside her and claim her as mine. The love I felt was priceless to me, and Charlotte was irreplaceable; the way I was about to make love to her needed to communicate everything about how I cherished her.

"Beautiful, darling girl…" I took her in my arms, freeing one hand to stroke wild curls away from her face. "My life has been blessed and full, but today you've given me a gift I could never have imagined." I bent and took her mouth, all the time in the world to love and know all of her.

We explored every part of one another, unhurried and untethered from time and the outside world. I drank deeply from her mouth for minutes at a time, swallowing the cries and moans she gave me while my fingers stroked between her creamy folds and at the pearly swelling of her clit. I clutched the bedclothes and battled every instinct in my body as she swallowed the length of my shaft and stroked it reverently with her tongue. My hips rose to meet her until I couldn't take another moment; then I pulled myself reluctantly from the tightest part of her throat. I rolled her onto her back and pushed myself slowly inside her sweet pussy, stroking every inch of myself in and out of the fragrant heat she offered between widely parted thighs. I met her eyes, hot and full of longing, and searched for words to tell her what my heart felt for her. Her snug walls tugged at me as I thrust steadily, giving her everything with every stroke of my cock and urging both of us closer to sealing the bond between us.

Several moments later, as the pounding of our hearts began to slow, the words finally surfaced. Holding Charlotte's soft, sated body and her gaze, I smiled and whispered the timeless words of the Bard, "'My bounty is as boundless as the sea, my love as deep; the more I give to thee, the more I have...'" She lifted her lips once again to mine, murmuring the final words with me.

"'...for both are infinite.'"

Chapter
THIRTY-FOUR

"Eagle When She Flies"

Miles

It was the Monday before Christmas, and it had been four long months since I'd flown. Every day of my Air Force career since leaving the Air Force Academy had been concentrated on flying—preparing, studying, training, briefing, debriefing—it was part of the fabric of my life. I spent each day in my country's service honing my skills and becoming the best warrior I could be. I was paid to shape myself into a formidable weapon, ready to obstruct any force that stood in the path of freedom's objectives.

All of that was unceremoniously interrupted because of my own stubborn recklessness. Before the accident, even I didn't understand how integral flying was to how I saw myself. In the past few years, it had insidiously become not only my profession but my joy. Like so many pilots, I loved the peaceful buoyancy I felt high above the earth. Worry and preoccupation had a tendency to fall away as the ground did. Flying brought my life into sharp focus.

The past four months had been difficult on several fronts. As I grappled with guilt, anger, and disappointment, I did so while grieving the potential loss of something that gave me a great deal of fulfillment. It had been challenging to confront the possibility that my temporary grounding might morph into a permanent end to being a rated military pilot. Had the FEB ruled in favor of taking my wings, I would have been required to complete the years of my military commitment in a non-flying capacity.

Instead, this morning I'd dressed for work in my flight suit for the first time in months, filling the half dozen pockets with pens, my dog tags, foam earplugs, and sunglasses. I'd laced my boots and locked the front door before walking across the parking lot to the Mustang. There was a spring in my step that had been absent for some time. Today was finally the day.

Keeper and all my friends in The Tuesday Game had been invaluable in guiding me, more or less gently, through a thorny maze of self-discovery. They'd helped me see parts of myself I didn't care to examine carefully and to pinpoint unhealthy behaviors, which I began, with their encouragement, to address. My tendencies to be emotionally aloof and to resist anything I saw as a threat to my independence had begun to diminish. My initial tentative efforts, mostly socializing within The Tuesday Game group and with a few of the nurses, had been unexpectedly enjoyable. The result, as I'd mentioned to Oliver, was an unexpected abundance of friendship and support, often in the quarters where I least expected it. The singular dark cloud tainting my exuberance today was the fact that it would still be a few months before Deliverance would make it back into the cockpit. His healing was progressing ahead of schedule, and everyone seemed confident of his return to flying status, but I knew it wasn't right that I'd be flying again before he would.

I wasn't too surprised at the sight that greeted me as I maneuvered into a space in the squadron's parking lot. D's grin was as wide as his face as he walked toward my car; he opened my door before I could collect my things.

"Get the lead out, Miles. Let's get you back in the air." Deliverance's disposition was always relentlessly sunny, but it was especially remarkable to me this morning. His tone held not an iota of bitterness. He was genuinely glad for me.

We walked together to the door of the building, which he opened and held for me. "It was important to me to be here for you today, Miles." He turned to look at my face as we walked down the hall, nearing the briefing room. "I need to tell you something before you go in there." He indicated the open door where Hung sat at a table, scribbling notes on a pad of paper in preparation for our flight together. I stopped and leaned against the cinder block wall.

"You didn't have to come in early just to talk to me, D. But since you did, I just want to say how badly I feel that I'm going back up before you are. I'm so sorry, Deliverance, I really—"

He interrupted me with an indulgent smile and a wave of the hand. "And that's exactly why I *had* to be here in person, to look into your eyes and say this, Miles. I need you to know, before you take off again, that what happened in August is in the past. We can't change it, and we're not going to let it dictate what happens from today on. I don't hold anything against you, and there's no blame for you to shoulder going forward. The board says you're ready; the Big Blue Team needs you. And I couldn't agree more."

I'd had a respite of almost a week since the troublesome lump of emotion had appeared and lodged in my throat. But it was back with a fucking vengeance. I swallowed hard and nodded because it was all I could do. Deliverance guffawed.

"Don't try to talk, kiddo. It won't be long for me; you go have a great flight." The big oaf socked me playfully on the shoulder, almost knocking me over. "I'm right behind you."

He waved at Hung who called a greeting to D before smiling

a big, brilliant smile at me and waving me in. "Get in here, Miles. Let's knock out the briefing and get this show on the road." The board had stipulated that all of my requalification flights would be accomplished with an instructor pilot. The flight commanders were instructors as well as Coach and Happy. Having Hung on my wing was an especially good choice for me; his easy-going manner was a perfect match for me today. He would chase me as number two and put me through my paces. There was a prescribed set of maneuvers in the syllabus for each ride, and I was glad to benefit from Hung's experience and relaxed demeanor.

The Warthog was unique in so many ways, but one was of particular interest on a training mission like this one. Almost all single-seat fighters joined the Air Force's inventory alongside several copies with two seats, comically known as "family models." These versions were useful for training, allowing an instructor to assure safety and offer instruction by riding in the same jet with the trainee. There were no such two-seat versions of the A-10. Even throughout initial training in the Hawg, each flight was flown solo. The instructor chased the trainee, keeping in contact over the radio.

It was a cold morning for Tucson, but still pleasant at forty degrees, as I climbed the ladder and settled myself into the cockpit. I scanned the clear sky appreciatively; even the weather seemed to be in my corner. It was very much the beginning of a new day for me as I taxied the behemoth onto the end of the runway. All the possibilities I'd longed for as a young girl and later as a new Air Force pilot looked new and untested as I surveyed some odd 13,000 feet of runway stretched out in front of me. The last time I sat on this runway, I'd just limped my jet home from a horrific accident that changed my life.

This time I made the final preparations for takeoff, my booted feet holding the brakes on the floor and big General Electric engines roaring on either side of my cockpit. I couldn't suppress a grin as I recalled Deliverance's words: "Have a great flight…I'm right behind you." I was confident he was right, and that chased away the singular regret that cast a shadow on today. I released the brakes, and the jet began its takeoff roll. I briefly scanned the gauges again before beginning to laugh as the runway disappeared behind me.

It was a paradox, the seeming awkwardness of the heavy aircraft taxiing along on the rangy landing gear and the smooth, masterful way it broke from terra firma and rotated effortlessly before taking me flying. Hung dropped his brakes ten seconds behind me and began his own trip down the runway.

The controller's voice came through the radio as I surveyed the sky, and the months of stress and worry magically melted away. "Hung flight, contact departure channel three. Welcome back, ma'am."

Chapter
THIRTY-FIVE

"Anything Could Happen"

Oliver
About Four Months Later

I t was quite unlike me to feel the least bit apprehensive when meeting new people or encountering unfamiliar situations, but today was very different, I reasoned to myself. The 737 taxied a short distance to the gate, and the usual crowding ensued when the seat belt light chimed off, everyone clamoring for their bag in the overhead bin and jockeying for position in the aisle. I stayed put, taking the final opportunity for solitude and asking myself the question I'd already turned over and over in my head.

How will today play out?

I had little doubt that moving ahead with Charlotte was the right thing to do; hell, it was almost as if I had no choice. The love I had for my little red-haired ball of fire grew exponentially as the days passed, and I could no more see my future without her than I could have spread my arms and flown here from Arizona. So I'd made the necessary arrangements and flown out over a weekend when Jacob and Charlotte were cross country. They'd left this morning and wouldn't return until Monday, giving me plenty of time to accomplish what I came to do before flying home on Sunday. With the airplane mostly empty, I grabbed my duffel and made my way toward the front. I smiled at the friendly flight attendant and strode along the corridor, following signs to the ground transportation meeting area. Along the way, I tapped out a quick text with an estimate of when I'd arrive at the curb near baggage claim.

The pickup truck was bright red and easily recognizable, just as he'd said it would be. It moved to the curb when I waved my hand, and I took a deep breath as the occupant parked, opened the door, and jogged around the front, hand extended.

"Hey there, man. You must be Oliver." Robert's face was open and friendly. The wide smile said he really was glad to meet me, and I relaxed incrementally.

"I am. It's great to meet you at last, mate." I shook his hand warmly, and he took my duffel, tossing it into the truck bed. We both settled into the seats, and Robert pulled skillfully into the melee of traffic, turning down the country music that played on the radio.

"Now, I know Bugs still calls me Robert, but I'm RJ to everyone else. Our daddy's Robert Senior. He goes by Bob, but it still got pretty overwrought, what with all the Robert/Bob business. So go ahead and call me RJ; it'll be less confusing. It's about an hour drive out to the farm; we'll have supper with Dad tonight. He's making chicken-fried steak and mashed potatoes, so we'd better save room. It took him a while after Mama, but he's turned into quite the cook. Do you need to make a quick stop for a bite before we head back?" He laughed easily. "I know they don't feed you a damn thing on the airplanes anymore. I just took a five-hour flight to a job interview, wondering the whole time how a guy my size is supposed to make five little shrunk-up pretzels last for the whole trip without eating the in-flight magazine."

I already liked RJ. He was friendly and easy to talk to, just like his sister; I knew this from our conversations on the phone. But today I got the impression he was going out of his way to be sure I was comfortable; he must have sensed how far I'd strayed from my comfort zone. I'd called only last month to inquire about meeting RJ and his father. Charlotte talked with great affection about her brother and how much she wished to spend more time with him; she'd brought him up in conversation frequently since we'd met.

But I'd noticed recently she also spoke more often about her father and her desire to mend their fractured relationship. Privately, I supposed this evolution was due to her involvement with Keeper and the other members of The Tuesday Game. As we lay in the dark a couple of months ago, whispering pillow talk after making love, she became tearful as she spoke of her relationship with her father. She was beginning to suffer from real regret as she considered the lost opportunities during the years they'd been estranged. She confessed that she wanted to rebuild their relationship but struggled with the first step.

She'd grown more important to me over the past few months than I ever thought any woman outside my family could. We'd known for some time that the love between us was real, and I'd watched with interest as our relationship grew and intensified. We'd grown increasingly adept with communication and meeting each other's emotional needs. And now I had begun to think about the way I wanted to spend every day with her, perhaps forever. I was completely gone for this girl, and she was suffering because of the severed bond with her father. I knew all too well the feeling of indecision over how to sort a thorny problem. It always seemed too easy to put a foot wrong, and that uncertainty could easily paralyze a person. As I considered how to lend Charlotte the support she needed to move forward, I'd received a call from a most unlikely person.

Samanthe rang me to discuss the possibility of celebrating Charlotte's upcoming twenty-fifth birthday with a surprise party. She lived in a spacious home in the foothills of Tucson and wanted to host "the birthday party to end all parties." I was enthusiastic about the idea, and we set about planning and inviting a diverse group that included the Scorpion clan, the emergency department nurses, and members of The Tuesday Game. Sam assured me she'd handle the food and decorations; I was placed in charge of music and entertainment. It was during the planning process that I conjured the idea of the best birthday gift I could give my girl.

Immediately, I engaged Jacob to be my partner in crime, assigning him the duty of finding her brother's contact information. He asked Happy for assistance, and the phone number was easily procured since RJ was her emergency contact. The phone conversations between us were cordial from the beginning; he was an agreeable bloke, having obviously passed all the fireball genes to his younger sister. He extended the invitation for us to visit, and I countered by asking if I could make a clandestine trip to Iowa and meet him as well as his father. After explaining about the upcoming birthday celebration, he readily agreed.

I was fascinated with the contour of the Midwestern landscape, having never visited this area of the States. The short drive passed far too quickly, and RJ told me the story of how he'd eventually returned to university and received a master's degree in agricultural economics after Charlotte left for the Air Force Academy. He was direct and candid as he spoke of the struggles within the Christman family, and I was able to see a man who loved his dad and sister so deeply that he'd placed their needs ahead of his own throughout his life. It was impossible not to feel an easy kinship with someone who hadn't hesitated to sacrifice for the woman I loved.

"Dad just couldn't overcome the heartbreak that came with losing Mama." He shook his head, sorrow still apparent in his eyes. "It's easy to understand; that woman was his whole world. But as much as it hurts, the world just keeps spinning when tragedy hits your family. You can either sink or find a way to swim— but Daddy couldn't do it alone. He was sinking the whole time Charlotte was growing up. I saw and remember more because I was already eighteen when Mama passed; Charlotte was only ten. He reacted to losing Mama by panicking and overreacting about something happening to Bugs."

I smiled at the affection in his voice and the pet name.

He turned to me with a big smile. "Say, we're too early for supper; could you go in for a cold beverage to pass the time?"

That sounded like just the thing after a five-hour flight, and I told him so.

He thought for a minute before engaging the turn indicator. "What do you say we stop in at the Mucky Duck for a pint or two? I'll bet we can find something that tastes like home to you, and we can continue this discussion." He chuckled. "Hell, maybe I can even learn a little about you, Oliver. It sounds like you may be around for a while."

The Mucky Duck was a no-nonsense roadhouse with great beer and space at the bar when we arrived around four p.m. There was a plethora of beer choices, so I picked a local Scotch ale, and RJ had a pint of a favorite IPA. I regaled him with the story of meeting Charlotte at an armed robbery, a tale she'd told him but without me specifically in the picture. She'd also conveniently neglected to mention our crime-fighting antics, which made for terrific comic relief. I also recounted our first proper date and the malfunctioning lift chair incident as well as Charlotte's first well-intentioned culinary efforts as she brought her cooking skills up to Tuesday Game standards.

We passed a pleasant hour, laughing all the while before RJ

consulted his watch and called for our check. "We'd better get a move on; Daddy will have supper on the table at six. Don't want to be late."

I insisted on picking up the small tab before walking to the truck with RJ. I felt as if I'd made a new friend and silently scolded myself for the hesitancy I'd felt earlier. Surely anyone who shared DNA with my sweet Charlotte couldn't be anything other than...what was that term Jacob used? It took only a moment to remember.

RJ Christman was good people.

Chapter
THIRTY-SIX

"What I Did for Love"

Oliver

The farmhouse was more or less as I'd envisioned it, but my imagination had been augmented by the many detailed descriptions and stories Charlotte had related over the past months. The property was expansive, and we wound along a gravel road for several hundred yards before the house came into view. It was two stories, constructed of clapboard, and freshly painted the pale yellow color of clotted cream. The details were modest, but a wide front porch beckoned, just as she'd described. I studied the building as RJ found my duffel in the truck's bed before joining me.

"It feels almost as if I've been here before." He raised a quizzical eyebrow before I continued. "She's told me so many stories, and they often include details about the rooms and the furniture. The porch here on the front looks like a wonderful place to pass the evening, but I know the back porch is her favorite, as it is your father's."

He smiled and nodded. "Mama and Daddy had a ritual that

dates to the time before either of us were born. She'd sit in a glider on the back porch overlooking the farm in the late afternoon and do her mending or work on a quilt. When Daddy finished his work in the fields, he'd come up on the porch to wash up and help her get the sewing inside. They almost never wavered from the routine, and her glider still sits on the back porch."

No wonder it was her favorite place; she felt close to her mother there, even after she was gone. My heart hurt for the motherless child; I loved my mum and still depended on her kindness and wisdom. The door opened as we climbed the porch steps, revealing a man who could have been no one other than RJ's father; the resemblance was uncanny. Both men were tall, only a few inches shorter than I, but Charlotte's father's frame was more slender, his shoulders rounded from a lifetime of hard work. His hair was wavy and perfectly white—prematurely so, I thought—where RJ's was dark. It took only a split second to catalog the details of Charlotte's father's appearance and less time than that for my pulse to pick up speed.

Showtime.

Then his face broke into a big, warm smile, the same one he'd absolutely passed on to his daughter and the same one that drew me the moment I saw it gracing her lovely face at the picnic last fall. He walked quickly toward me, hand outstretched. "Evenin', son. You must be Oliver; I'm Bob Christman—welcome to the farm." He pumped my hand energetically. "RJ and I sure are glad you're here." He gestured to the open door. "Come on in and take a load off; supper's almost ready."

I followed him inside and took in the house's comfortably furnished interior. It was just as I'd imagined, and I envisioned Charlotte here as a child, then a teenage girl. "Thank you for having me, sir. I was telling RJ I feel as if I've already visited; your daughter speaks so often of her childhood and growing up here." As soon as the words left my mouth, I regretted having said them and wondered if they'd be distressing to Bob. He looked a bit wistful as RJ and I settled into ladder-back chairs at the big pine kitchen table, but he rallied right away.

"Yes, it's been too long since Charlotte's been home…too long since many things happened, but that's only one of the reasons I'm glad you're here to visit, Oliver. You boys have some tea with your supper?" He reached into the refrigerator and produced a tall glass pitcher, immediately dispelling my hopes of a proper cuppa with the meal.

"Yes, sir. Iced tea would be brilliant. I should learn to make that so I can keep it handy for Charlotte; she'd enjoy that on a hot day." I smiled and accepted the glass from Bob. "We have quite a few of those in Tucson."

"I'd reckon so." Bob's smile crinkled his weathered face as he stirred a pot of beans on the stove. "Sounds like you know a good little bit about RJ and me from Bugs, so why don't you tell us about yourself, Oliver? How'd a limey like yourself wind up in the desert Southwest? You must be as out of place as a fish on a bicycle." He chuckled at his joke as he slid a tin of scones into the cooker.

Bob poured himself a glass of tea and settled in as I related the story of my family and upbringing and how my closeness with Jacob and Vivianne had brought me to the States. They both listened attentively, chiming in here and there as I eventually brought the story around to the picnic where I'd first seen Charlotte.

"She is a very special woman; I could tell that even before I'd been properly introduced, because of the way she was loved and protected by her friends. My very own cousin Jacob didn't want me to date her—and he's my best mate." I joined in as they laughed good-naturedly at my plight. "I'm a decent bloke, I swear, but he knew it was a difficult time for Charlotte; the accident had happened only the month before."

RJ stood and began to set the table with plates and flatware, stopping briefly to peek into the cooker. "Now go on and tell Dad about when you and Bugs finally met at the convenience store." He guffawed. "Dad, you're not gonna believe this one."

Bob laughed as hard as his son had at his daughter's antics, and RJ enjoyed the story a second time as he set the table and pulled food from the cooker and refrigerator. "Mr. Christman, your daughter's one of a kind, and I'm not the only one who thinks so." I finished my story and stood to refill the iced tea glasses.

"Now, Oliver, I don't disagree with you on that point for a minute. She's always had her mother's red-haired temperament and the stubborn streak to go with it. By the way, it's Bob—please call me Bob. And let's eat; I'm starving."

We dined on a country feast fit for the Queen herself of chicken-fried steak, homemade mashed potatoes, something RJ called pole beans that grew in his garden, and tall, fluffy scones with real butter. Bob explained that they were biscuits, which prompted an in-depth discussion about the differences in British and American English as it regarded biscuits, cookies, scones, chips, fries, and the like. When I thought I could eat not one more morsel, Bob produced a colorful, cooled pudding from the refrigerator.

"It's Dad's famous strawberry shortcake, Oliver. You have to try it—it's made him a household name around here." RJ clapped his dad on the back, obviously proud. "After Mama passed on, I figured everybody under this roof would starve or die from scurvy while I was doing all the cooking." He shook his head as he prepared three small bowls of the delightful pudding for us. "I get by in the kitchen, but it's nothing to write home about. After Dad started feeling better and finally got the help he needed, his counselor suggested he take a class of some sort to get out of the house and meet folks. I always said he showed a great interest in self-preservation when he took that cooking class at the college. He knew getting me out of the kitchen was a wise move." The shortcake was unbelievably delicious; I wondered if Charlotte knew how to make it.

"Then he shocked both of us by becoming a great cook, probably better than Mama, if I'm honest." He looked heavenward with a grin. "Sorry, Mama."

I was struck with the parallels between Bob and his daughter. "You might be interested in learning that your Charlotte has recently become keen on learning to cook and bake, as well. One of her new friends, Sue, is an excellent Southern chef and has taken her on as an informal student, or as Charlotte says, her pet project. It sounds as if you've both found your way around the kitchen during adulthood."

Bob looked thoughtful. "Something in common with my daughter; I wonder if she'd like to help me make supper one day. I'd sure like that chance." His eyes filled with tears momentarily, but he quickly refocused. "Let's put off the dishes and sit out on the porch for a short spell. I'll bring the tea pitcher along."

I picked up my empty glass, following Bob and RJ through the family room and out the back door. It was easy enough to see why Charlotte's mother loved it here, and it was clear her husband and son enjoyed it still. Rolling land stretched out as far as I could see, neatly tilled in rows where crops were beginning to sprout. Nearer the house, a generous green swath of grass would've made a fine yard for young children. It was neat and well-tended and even boasted a small flower bed. The porch itself was double the depth of the front porch and covered; two swings hung from sprung chains in the ceiling joist, and one double-wide glider with a fresh coat of shiny red paint sat at an angle in the corner. Bob settled himself there.

"This was Louise's favorite spot. We scraped together enough for a down payment on this place right after we got married, about two years before RJ came along." He chortled, shaking his head. "Lord, money was tight, I'm telling you. We didn't have a pot to pee in or a window to throw it out of, but we were awful happy." His eyes met mine. "I couldn't hope for anything greater for my children, as I often tell RJ, than to find someone to love like I did their Mama." He glanced away briefly before continuing. "I want the chance to say those things to my Bugs again. I was a fool, even if I was a brokenhearted fool. But I loved her with my whole heart—I still do—and I hope you'll be able to tell me if I might have a second chance with my girl again."

This was the heart of the reason I'd traveled to Iowa, so I took care to choose my words. "Charlotte has shared with me about the loss of her mother and how brokenhearted you all were. How your lives and relationships changed because of it. It sounds as if Louise was an amazing woman; I wish I'd had the chance to meet her." Both Bob and RJ smiled sadly but allowed me to continue.

"Raising a teenage girl must have presented a challenge for a widowed father, especially one as strong-willed as Charlotte must have been." We all grinned at that. "It probably wouldn't surprise anyone that the two of you had a relatively contentious relationship. But it's been—what—about seven years now since she left for university? You seem such a good-hearted bloke. So why the reluctance to reach out to her on your own, Bob? I can see that you miss her."

The older man leaned forward, studying his clasped hands. A lifetime of pain played out on his face in a matter of moments as he seemed to consider what he wanted to say. Finally, he began to speak in a shaky voice. "I loved that little girl with every fiber of my being from the moment I laid eyes on her, but I made her life impossible after her mama left us. I can see it now, but I was blinded by grief then—convinced I could control what God meant to be as free and unfettered as the wind. She was a wild spirit, and I wanted to tie her down." He shook his head slowly.

"It's as I said; I was a brokenhearted fool, and I don't deserve the second chance I'm asking for. I decided when I started to get better, during my counseling, that I would give Charlotte back the thing I took from her when she was here. I'd give her freedom, this time the freedom to reach out to me, if and when she ever decided she wanted me in her life."

I sighed and smiled at him, resting my elbow on my knees before looking out over the fields. The sun was beginning to set, and the Rockwellian beauty was unlike anything I'd ever seen. "Bob, you know I can't speak for Charlotte; I don't think I've ever met a woman surer of herself. You can always count on Charlotte to know exactly what she wants, and that's been doubly true with the changes I've seen in her in the aftermath of the aircraft accident last fall. I believe she wants to be part of your life again. It's hard to be the first one to reach out—to take the risk of hurt or rejection. And that's why I wanted to come here and meet you and RJ in person."

The older man allowed a small smile, and I saw hope on his face for the first time since we sat down. Laying all my cards on the table seemed risky considering I'd only just met Bob and RJ, but something told me they would be part of my life for a very long time. I'd already taken a huge leap of faith in flying across the country to meet them without Charlotte's knowledge.

In for a penny...

I swallowed hard. "You obviously know Charlotte's birthday is around the corner. I knew if there was a gift I could give her that could somehow demonstrate the way I feel for her, it wouldn't be anything I could purchase in a store or wrap in paper and a bow." I cleared my throat once before continuing. "I love your daughter, sir, and I needed to take a risk for her. Coming here to meet you both and try to smooth the way for you to be part of her life again, it's a gamble. But she's important to me and worthy of the chance. I needed to give her something so good and so pure...I needed to show her what my heart feels."

His eyes shone with tears, and he stared for a long minute at his work boots before responding. "You love my Bugs?"

I nodded. "Yes, sir. I do. I've never felt the way I did about that girl I saw in the Kwik Shopper holding the odious blue ice drink, but she's it for me. She's my first love, and I believe with my whole heart she'll be my last." It felt as if a weight had been lifted as my ears heard those words aloud, and I grinned like a fool at the feeling of freedom the words brought. When I met Bob's eyes, he was smiling too, so I finished my thought.

"And she doesn't know it yet, Bob, but I intend to make her my wife."

Chapter THIRTY-SEVEN

"Runnin' Down a Dream"

Oliver

I volunteered for driving duty since my Range Rover was far better suited to chauffeuring the three of us to the Morgan-Sullivan wedding extravaganza than Jacob's pickup truck. Traveling with Vivianne at the wheel was obviously out of the question; riding with her was almost as dangerous as eating her cooking. Jacob was entertaining us with a hilarious recounting of the ill-fated stag weekend in Las Vegas a couple of weeks ago. We were laughing so hard by the time he finished the story of Boo and the transgendered hooker, I was wiping my eyes.

"I don't think I've ever been so bevvied that I'd have taken a bloke for a bird." I shook my head, still laughing at poor Boo.

But Jacob shook his head. "You might be surprised, cousin. He was damned good-looking; everybody thought so." He snorted. "But nobody liked him as much as Boo. He was a sad son of a bitch after Deliverance cut his date loose."

"Who elected Deliverance? That had to be an assignment nobody wanted." Vivianne rummaged in the cooler she'd packed full of drinks and snacks for the three of us to share over the weekend.

"Best man for the job. You want your biggest guy if you're letting a six-foot-tall hustler down easy—that was his whole night's work gone tits up. So to speak." Jacob guffawed. "I'm a funny guy."

"He was a six-foot-tall male in drag, and Boo couldn't do the math?" Viv shook her head, marveling. "You guys must've been packing away the alcohol. Who was minding the store?"

Jacob thought for a moment. "Well, Rock handled the driving chores all the way to Vegas, but then we parked the bus and walked or cabbed or took the monorail everywhere else we went. I'd probably say Miles was the adult in charge for the remainder of the weekend."

Now he was the one with a look of amazement on his face. "I can't believe those words just came out of my mouth. It really goes to show how far she's come." He was quiet for a minute before continuing the thought. "I know you didn't even know her yet, Ollie, but your Charlotte was a very different person before. It's hard to believe it hasn't even been a year. I always liked Miles, even considered her one of my best friends. But everything that happened has taught her to give back the friendship people had been showing her for years."

Vivvie leaned forward from her place in the back seat and thrust a big cellophane bag into our line of sight. It was filled to overflowing with an unappealing concoction of what appeared to be greasy oatmeal and seeds with multi-colored miniature marshmallows and peanut M&M'S. "Hey, you guys. You gotta try this; I made homemade granola with my own signature twist. Rainbow marshmallows—genius, right?"

She shook the bag menacingly, and Jacob shot me a look telegraphing unadulterated terror. "No need to fight over it." Vivianne smiled sweetly. "I have a bag for each of you."

The drive was a short forty-five minutes from Vivvie's home on Craycroft where we'd picked her up after work. It was no time at all until we pulled onto the sprawling Tanque Verde Ranch. We checked in quickly and made arrangements to meet at the casita I would be sharing with Charlotte in the Roadrunner Ridge area of the ranch. The casitas were warm and romantic with kiva fireplaces. Pity we wouldn't be needing those, but the May weather was already warm enough to rule out an evening fire. On a very positive note, however, there were cozy patios with brilliant, unrestricted views of the Saguaro National Park. I looked forward to enjoying at least one sunset there with Charlotte; we'd already proven adept at enjoying ourselves outdoors, I thought with a smirk.

It was a quick jaunt down the hill from my casita to the Doghouse Saloon where we'd been instructed to meet with the other wedding guests. Various people would be arriving throughout the afternoon and evening as their work schedules permitted. Charlotte was on the schedule today to fly with Colonel Ditka, so she'd made arrangements to carpool with other members of the LPA. I was told Bibi would be joining their group. Coach was tasked with any details that required attention at the end of the flying day before buttoning up the squadron building for the long weekend. Practically every member of the squadron would be celebrating Happy and Camille's wedding with them.

Our little family group walked along the path toward the saloon, sipping beers Jacob supplied from the small refrigerator in his casita. "I wonder who will drive the LPA's group to the ranch after work." Vivvie was so captivated by the scenery that she tripped over a tree root in the path; she almost fell, but I caught her arm.

"Careful there, grace," I teased, setting her right again. "Don't want to spoil that beautiful face before the party starts; what will Captain Jackson think if he finds you looking less than your usual stunning self?"

Vivianne wouldn't answer, and I would've sworn I saw a bit of a blush on her cheeks. Vivvie never blushed; I didn't think I'd seen her embarrassed or even so much as mildly chagrined before, not even for a moment. I didn't push further but cataloged that information for investigation at a later time. Just then Jacob piped up, shooting me a suspicious glare.

"What did you just say about Grace? You did say she'd be here, didn't you, Viv?"

"Of course, Jake. It's Camille's wedding, for God's sake, pay attention. You're distracted." She cocked her head and looked appraisingly at her brother. "Have you got pretty little Grace Marshall on the brain?" She poked a finger his direction, stabbing the air to emphasize her point. "If you do, Jacob Archibald Travis, you'd better bring your A game. I will *not* have you dicking around with that lovely girl."

Jacob mumbled under his breath.

That remark earned him a poisonous look before the tirade continued. "She is not like me, Jake. She is kind and sweet and *quiet.*" That word was shouted for extra emphasis. "And don't you dare mistake what I'm saying; she is a grown woman who can take care of herself with no problem at all, but she is special. She is certainly not another one of those hoochie mamas from the Bashful Travis Taco Circus." She huffed and finger-quoted the last bit for emphasis.

Jake and I held our breath. The diatribe seemed to have come to its end, but we knew to wait. Just to make certain.

"So you'd better be nice to her."

Jacob rubbed Vivianne's back, trying his best to relax her. "Yes, ma'am. I promise." Her eyes shot over to study him. "No kidding, Viv. I promise."

Anxious to soothe the beautiful, savage beast, I seized the opportunity to change the subject as we approached the saloon.

"I wonder who has a vehicle that can accommodate the entire LPA with Bibi along for the ride as well. Jacob, perhaps Rock still has his uncle's bus?" We all burst into laughter at the thought of the luckless little bus from the Las Vegas trip being pressed into service again. Jacob told me that Marilyn and Coach kissed the ground upon their return; I wasn't sure if they were more grateful because the bus had delivered them safely home or because they'd successfully navigated the LPA-planned stag weekend. Either way, that group made me laugh. I gave Viv a hug as I opened the door for the three of us.

The bar was already filling with wedding guests, which meant there was friendly conversation, laughter, and lots of familiar faces in evidence. I didn't see Charlotte yet, but that wasn't surprising. She'd be along soon. Also missing were the prospective bridegroom and his intended. Deliverance waved at Viv from his seat across the room with Luckie, so we made our way to their table and re-accomplished introductions. It had been quite some time since I'd seen them. The bartender came from the other side of the bar to take our orders, and we settled into pleasant conversation while awaiting the arrival of the others.

The noise level in the room spiked dramatically with the arrival of Bibi and the LPA—Rock, Boo, Torch, and the stunning redhead I'd been waiting impatiently to see. I excused myself and met her at the bar, touching her hand lightly before lifting it to my lips for a brief kiss.

"At last, my evening is looking up." I grinned at her. "I've been trapped in the bosom of my beloved kin, and they're in rare form tonight. How was your day, lovely?"

Charlotte was mouthwatering and entirely fuckable in some slim little jeans that only reached the top of her ankle and a dark green shirt made of some mysteriously silky material. The scooped front almost showed the tops of her beautiful breasts, causing my mouth to water at the prospect of spending some time with her succulent nipples in my mouth.

Charlotte recounted a few pertinent details about her flight earlier as I paid for her drink and retook her hand, this time tugging her out a side door onto a small porch behind a large planter containing a hedge for privacy. I pulled her against me with one hand splayed on her waist and sunk the other hand into the silkiness of her curls. My voice sounded more animal than human as I spoke to her.

"Sorry to steal you away, darling, but I'm afraid I couldn't wait one more second for a taste of my woman." I took her mouth with an urgency that, once again, took me aback. She felt around frantically for a ledge to hold her drink before winding her arms around my neck. I was already deep in the warmth of her mouth, exploring and relearning its depths after only a few days apart. My cock had hardened at the sight of her in the doorway of the bar; the situation now threatened to become unmanageable without the benefit of a couple of hours and a bed full of naked Charlotte.

She rubbed the length of her body along my hard-on, moaning into my mouth before breaking the kiss. Her eyes remained closed, and I sensed she was trying to stop the agonizing movement along my steely erection. "Sorry, British. I'm trying here, but you feel so damned good." At length, she looked up with a guilty little smile. "Guess I missed you, too."

It took a moment to compose myself, and Charlotte powdered her nose before we slipped back in the side door. The party was rocking. Vivianne approached on Hung's arm, laughing and holding out a drink for Charlotte that looked identical to the pinkish-raspberry concoction she sipped. "There you two are. Miles, I got this for you—you have to try it. It's a prickly pear margarita, and it's the dog's balls." She handed the glass to Charlotte, toasting, and tossed back a healthy slurp. Walker gazed at her as if the sun rose and set on her.

Charlotte smiled and took a big sip, eyes widening as she did. "Wow, okay. That's really good, but I guess it's been a while since I've had anything that strong." She toasted Viv and Walker. "So here's to you two and to everyone else here; I'd rather be with the people in this room than with the finest people I know." She made us all laugh, and we raised our glasses.

"Hear! Hear!" Hung sipped his beer and then kissed my cousin thoroughly. She looked a bit dazed when he allowed her to come up for air and motioned to Charlotte, her eyes still glued to Walker. "Let's go powder our noses, Miles."

Charlotte looked a bit confused. "Actually, I just did. I think I'm—"

"Shiny," Vivianne interrupted. "You're very shiny. Come on." She grabbed Charlotte, who shot me a questioning look while extending her drink for me to hold.

Vivvie's brow knit. "Bring your drink, Miles. We don't know how much powdering needs to be done." She looked at us over her shoulder as they walked away. "We might be a minute, fellas."

Walker and I watched them walk into the bathroom, Viv whispering into Charlotte's ear as they disappeared behind the door. He turned to me and nodded wordlessly, sipping his beer. We stood together silently, contemplating our next move for perhaps half a beer; then I spoke. "I've known Vivianne Serafina Travis for twenty-eight years; she's my cousin and my best female friend. But I need to ask you, mate…how long do you suppose it is before we know what's going on inside those beautiful heads?"

Walker's tone was unflappable as he put an arm around my

shoulders and directed me to a seat at the bar. "Longer than either of us know, my friend." He signaled the bartender. "Another round for the British gentleman and me. Johnnie Walker Double Black, if you have it."

He shot a look at the closed door of the ladies' room. "Looks like it could be a minute."

There was plenty of time to enjoy my Johnnie Walker with Hung, and Marilyn joined us as well. At one point, the bartender picked up a phone call on the landline, wrinkling his brow, and mumbled a few words before hanging up. He then expertly mixed two prickly pear margaritas, placed them on a tray, and delivered them to the door of the ladies' washroom. Vivianne's manicured hand appeared through the slightly opened door, depositing a twenty on his tray before retrieving both drinks and closing the door. I ordered a round of beer for the three of us, and the conversation proceeded as before.

Twenty minutes or so elapsed before the two women emerged from their conference room, laughing and rosy-cheeked. Viv approached and wrapped her arms around an indulgently smiling Hung who patted her hands and listened as she whispered in his ear.

"Did you enjoy your girl time, darling?" Charlotte looked relaxed and perhaps a bit buzzed, but she still had a nearly full drink in her hand.

"Oh, yes. Your cousin is quite a character, but I guess I don't have to tell you that." She laughed and shot a loaded look to Viv. "She just needed a sounding board. Hung's a pretty reserved guy, known for being easy-going on the surface. That's why he and Marilyn are so tight. Brothers from different mothers or something. But it's always the quiet ones, isn't it?" She seemed thoughtful as she watched the two of them, and she murmured under her breath. "Boy, you just really never know about people, do you?"

I considered asking more about what she meant, but the musical volume suddenly picked up when the acoustic guitar player, who'd been covering a variety of western ballads, was joined by an additional guitar and an acoustic stand-up bass. They swung into the opening bars of "Dixieland Delight." The crowd rumbled their approval, and a few men appeared to move tables around, clearing a small dance floor. Several couples got up to dance, and Hung wandered over to chat with Deliverance and Luckie.

Before I could make my move, Vivianne swept by and caught Charlotte by the hand, leading her to the dance floor. What followed could only be described as some fervid male fantasy. Viv and Charlotte took to the middle of the recently cleared dance floor, shimmying and laughing uproariously while dancing suggestively. The crowd was highly entertained, judging by the catcalls and whistling that ensued, and no one more so than Boo and Rock, who joined in, showcasing their best moves. It was only another moment before Vivianne, forever the bad influence had coaxed my gorgeous red-haired girlfriend onto a chair to perform some sort of perverse version of an all-girl lap dance. It would've indeed been the perfect male fantasy had the two beautiful participants not been my cousin and my girlfriend.

Nevertheless, my eyes didn't stray for an instant from the enticing vision that was Charlotte's heart-shaped ass, shaking in time to the rhythm of the music. My cock was in extraordinary straits, and I made hasty plans for an exit, quickly settling our bar tab and moving nearer the dance floor. The song ended and the band segued into a slower song, dispersing the crowd somewhat. I approached as Charlotte studied her options for climbing off the chair and offered her my hand. She stepped down, and I leaned down to whisper in her ear.

"That was quite a performance, darling. I could barely keep my cock from tearing through my fly; that's exactly how keen I am to get you away from anyone's eyes but my own. And I need to fuck you right now." I brought her hand to my lips and brushed it with a quick kiss. She allowed her lashes to sweep down with a demure smile and then whispered back into my ear.

"Let's see what we can do about making that happen, British. I'm ready if you are."

Chapter THIRTY-EIGHT

"You Belong to Me"

Miles

I was a little breathless, and I didn't think it was from the quick walk back to Oliver's casita. He'd been so very gentle with me since we'd met, even during sex—hell, especially during sex. He was generally tender and attentive. I'd not had too many long, hard looks at the alpha male side of Oliver Bloodworth. But the look in his eyes was fierce as he helped me off the dance floor where Vivvie and I had been clowning around; there was the definite feel of a snorting, pawing bull, and I'd inadvertently waved the red cape.

Well, hot damn and game on.

The cowboy loitering in the lobby when I'd checked in with Rock, Boo, et al had offered to drop my bags in Oliver's casita, and I'd gladly agreed. That allowed us to join the party earlier, the five-dollar tip a small price to pay. But that meant I hadn't yet been subjected to the panty-dropping view from the porch's vantage point. Stars twinkled as far as the eye could see, lending magical light to a sky that was so much darker than we ever saw living in the city. Oliver led me to the front door, stopping briefly in the dark to press me against the door and palm my bottom before pulling me against what felt like a steel pipe in his jeans. His mouth searched mine thoroughly before he released it, still holding me against him, and unlocked the door.

The room was darkened, but enough light filtered throughout to make out the firm line of Oliver's jaw. The air practically fizzed and popped with unvoiced tension as he unbuttoned his shirt and the top button of his jeans while kicking his loafers under a nearby chair. His eyes never left mine. The resolute stare was difficult to read. He wasn't angry, I decided. He was hungry. I must've said it aloud because his expression changed. His eyes were dark, hooded, and he walked a few steps closer to where I stood, still right by the closed front door. His long fingers wrapped around the length of his denim-clad erection. When he spoke, his voice was a low rumble, so soft in the room's stillness, I had to strain to hear him.

"Yes, Charlotte, I'm ravenous, but you probably know that, don't you? You're a thirst I can't quench. A meal I never finish because the more I feast, the more I need. The more I learn about you, the more I want to consume."

I swallowed hard because the need he radiated and the greedy lust heating his gaze made my knees weak. A pulse pounded insistently between my legs as I stole glances at his right hand, now stroking the length of his cock. He still hadn't removed the jeans, but that just made me want to hurry the process along. My mouth watered unexpectedly to taste the clear, salty precum I knew leaked from the slit of that beautiful, uncut cock right this minute. I stepped toward him, reaching for his fly, but he caught my wrists in both hands. His grip was tight, and he pulled me roughly against his body. Then he bent his knees, pushed his hips hard against me, and dragged the steely length of his dick up until it lodged between my legs.

His mouth was against my ear. His breathing was uneven, and when he spoke, the sound of his voice grated like broken glass. "Charlotte, you have become not only my love, but my greatest desire. And tonight, you're my obsession."

He held both my wrists as he backed up and sat on the armless chair near the fireplace; then he pulled me onto his lap facing him with my legs on either side of his. He squeezed my wrists, reminding me that I was restrained until he decided otherwise, then looked right into my eyes as he spoke. "When I saw you dancing on that chair, something primal let loose in my gut. I wanted to bend you over that table and make you take my dick until you couldn't remember anything but the name of the man who was pleasuring your sweet, wet pussy. I needed to drive myself inside you and own every tight inch of your creamy cunt, give you my cum, then pound it so deep inside your hot little body that your panties wouldn't even be wet when we were done."

I'd never wanted to be full of him more than I did at this moment. All of the blood that should have been in my head was rushing to my clit and making my pussy so slippery I could feel it on my thighs. I couldn't think, so I said something stupid. "But I…I'm not wearing any panties, Oliver."

"Unbutton your shirt, Charlotte." His voice was a low growl and brooked no discussion. He released my wrists, and I nodded, fumbling with the buttons. Once the front of the blouse gaped open, he flicked open the front clasp of my bra and sucked one hard nipple into his mouth. He drew hard at the tender tip, using his hand at the small of my back to pull me closer to his mouth. The fingers of his other hand toyed with my other breast, stroking gently before pinching the nipple hard enough to make me cry out. He nursed at me with the single-minded focus of the starving man he professed to be, pulling me close when I tried to move. My bottom wiggled restlessly against his hardness—still hidden under those fucking jeans, desperately chasing relief.

I watched from my elevated vantage point, as Oliver's delicious mouth fed and suckled me into mindless oblivion. He hadn't touched a sliver of skin, bare or otherwise, below my waist, but I was already a reckless puddle of want. Without pausing, he switched his attention to the other breast and deftly divested me of the blouse and bra. I was begging, more or less irrationally, for him to touch me the whole time. My efforts at finding relief through our clothing weren't getting me anywhere, but he was enjoying himself either despite or because of my frustration.

He took a quick detour from teasing my nipple and nibbled on the skin of my neck while whispering encouragement with a gravelly voice. "Yes, darling. There's a good girl; take care of that needy little pussy of yours. Rub yourself on my cock, sweetheart; my mouth's busy right now tasting all this warm skin." He growled and nipped at me, eliciting another cry of pain and pleasure. "But you can be sure I'll be moving down between your thighs as the hours go by. This is just the beginning of a very long night, Charlotte." He looked up briefly, his stare searing right through me. "A very long night when I'll make certain you know you're mine. I don't ever want you to doubt you belong to me."

Did he say hours?

With that, he stood with me in his arms and carried me to the bed, depositing me there gently. I had a brief flash of the first night we'd shared on the patio at his house and prayed fervently for a repeat performance. My prayers were answered when he unzipped and dropped his jeans.

Commando this time. Thank God.

That gorgeous shaft was back in his right hand in a flash, stroking as slowly as if he was going to make good on his promise to take all night with me. The thick, mushroom-shaped head pushed insistently through his foreskin as he stroked, the tip leaking as I knew it would. I was mesmerized and studied his motions unconsciously, maybe hoping to replicate them later for his enjoyment. The only noise interrupting the quiet was a low groan slipping from Oliver's lips when he allowed his thumb to roll over the broad head of his cock every fourth or fifth stroke, spreading slick wetness across its breadth.

His eyes swept lazily across the length of my body as he stroked, taking more time to stare at my breasts, still pink and wet from his mouth. "You can take off your trousers now." He frowned briefly. "But you said you've no knickers, didn't you?" I shook my head and wiggled out of my slacks, my gaze never wavering from the hand on his cock. "Just as well, then. Spread your legs wide, love. I want to enjoy the view of your beautiful cunt while I stroke myself."

Once I was undressed, I arranged myself just as he'd asked with my legs spread very wide and my feet flat on the bed. It felt like something beyond naked. I felt exposed. Vulnerable. What's more, I could tell from his expression of satisfaction that the effect was precisely what he wanted. He was orchestrating this night for my pleasure, but also for his. That gave me a jolt of unexpected satisfaction. His open voyeurism and obvious enjoyment of my body was a source of excitement all by itself. His stare was frankly lascivious, and the pace of his strokes picked up speed as I bared my center to his eyes. He walked forward and knelt on the bed, lowering his head without losing a beat. Then he put his face between my thighs, only a few hair's breadths from my pussy. He inhaled slowly and groaned, surprising me by lapping me leisurely from bottom to top with the flat of his tongue.

"Oh, Charlotte...fuck. You have the sweetest, most delectable little pussy. I live for a taste of you." His breath was hot on my center, but his tongue didn't touch me again, despite my ardent wishes to the contrary.

"Please, Oliver..."

He straightened back onto his knees right away, between my

splayed legs. "What is it, sweetheart?" He arched one brow and gave me a crooked half grin. The bastard was enjoying my misery. The stroking continued unabated, and I stared at his cock, hypnotized.

"Please touch me, Oliver." I was begging, and it was very unbecoming.

"My face is up here, Charlotte." I jerked my gaze from his crotch to his face. He was smiling in earnest now. "Sorry, but you were speaking to John Thomas instead of me. And I apologize for relishing your distress." His eyes darkened, and the light-hearted moment ended abruptly. "I have an idea of how to repay my transgression." With that, he turned his body perpendicular to mine and positioned one of my legs across his belly. He turned onto his side and dipped his face to study my soaked, desperate core. "I love to tease you, darling. But I love to eat you more."

He favored me with a brief smile before settling his face between my legs again. He'd taken time to make himself comfortable, his head resting on my thigh, and one hand positioned my leg as he wished. In a split second, I recognized what his efforts meant—he truly intended to make this a long night I'd remember forever. The wet heat of his tongue licked along one thigh, then he nibbled and suckled my lips. I pressed my hips upward, asking wordlessly for more; but his hand flattened across my tummy and stroked soothingly. "Relax now, love. Let me make you feel good," he murmured against me. He licked idly, carefully attending every fold between my legs but studiously avoiding the suffering bundle of nerves I tried to thrust into the path of his tongue. "Does my sweet girl need to come...hmmm?"

I groaned my assent; my entire body felt ready to catch fire. I was teetering on the precipice, but he slowed his roll maddeningly while using the hand splayed on my belly to coax me into relaxing. "I'll take care of you, Charlotte. All of you." He murmured the words between my legs, licking and suckling until I sighed my resignation. It seemed almost impossible to cede control, but I had a momentary flash that the evolution of Charlotte 2.0 encompassed every part of my life. So I took a risk, making another conscious effort to be the girl I'd never been before—this time in bed.

I whispered the words under my breath to the universe. "I'll gratefully take what you give." But judging from the smile I felt bloom on his lips as he lapped at my center, Oliver heard me and decided my acquiescence was directed at him.

"Now it's time, love." His fingers speared my wet opening, stretching me and reaching deep. He plunged right past my G spot, tucking two fingers into the small space right in front of my cervix and gently stroking there while his tongue lashed my clit mercilessly. I had no idea what black magic he was inflicting on me, but my body detonated with an explosive orgasm. The sudden and powerful nature of it surprised me, and my body convulsed around him. Quite some time passed before the throbbing began to diminish and I could run my hands through his hair.

"Oliver…what did you…" I was still gasping, trying to still my mind and reach for the right words. "What did you do to me?"

He ignored me, kindly tending my sex as I continued to ache in the aftermath. His hand withdrew slowly, and his tongue gradually slowed. Only then did he rest his cheek on my thigh and point his blindingly magnetic smile at me. "Did you like that, darling?"

"In the name of all that's holy, British. I'm insisting you come clean. What the everlasting fuck did you do to me? I've never…"

The smile didn't waver, but he studied the two wet fingers of his right hand before plunging them into his mouth and making a show of sucking them clean. He growled. "Delectable, lovely Charlotte. You're a delicious fucking treat." He cocked an eyebrow with a wicked grin. "That was just a bit of something I picked up during my gap year, love. Not to worry, though." He chuckled as he lowered his face back between my thighs. "There's more where that came from."

Oliver's handsome face disappeared once again between my thighs, and time slowed to a crawl in the darkened room. Despite my slightly fuck-drunk state, a couple of things were crystal clear. Oliver genuinely loved pleasuring me, and his intuitive knowledge of what I needed was uncanny. What amazed me further was how obviously aroused he became in the process, even when I hadn't yet touched him.

His position reclining between my legs at an angle afforded me a front row seat to enjoy his magnificent erection. The fat mushroom head strained against the constraint of his foreskin, a sight I was beginning to crave. I reached out to touch him as he fed on my pussy, well on the way to my second orgasm. His uninhibited groan reverberated against me, and his hips thrust upward into my hand. I managed only a few cursory strokes before becoming impatient, twisting my body to reach his. I bent at the waist—careful not to move out of his mouth's reach—and slid my lips over the swollen, angry head of his cock.

His salty taste and masculine scent drove my desire ever higher, and I struggled to position myself to take more of him. This dance continued with both of us chasing our orgasms while teasing and sucking the other until Oliver's mouth pulled away from me on a broken gasp.

His hips bucked once, then a second time, and he growled like a feral animal. "God, Charlotte, if you don't stop right now..." He tried halfheartedly to retreat from my mouth, but I pulled him closer with one palm firmly grasping his tight ass cheek. This time, I consciously relaxed and groaned my approval as he sunk deeper, already pulsing.

I slid one finger along the crease of his ass, searching, then pressed a finger firmly against the tight pucker there. He chanted my name in a fractured sob, and then his thick length began to throb, hard and slow, from my lips to the back of my throat. I swallowed several times, taking each drop of his offering. He cried out a little and shuddered every time my throat constricted around him, and I held him inside me until I no longer could.

He rolled away, and our eyes met. "Thank you, lovely." His breath still came in pants, and he reached for my face, wiping away the cum spilling from my mouth. He leaned in and pressed his lips to mine reverently, kissing me thoroughly as his fingers again found my center. He massaged the creamy warmth of my clit, kissing me deeply until I pulled him closer and broke the kiss.

"Coming, Oliver..." Now I was the one breathing hard. "Now..."

His whisper was gentle, and I closed my eyes as the first wave hit hard. "Yes, darling...come for me. I've got you, love."

Chapter
THIRTY-NINE

"The Heart of the Matter"

Oliver

I t had been one short week since Happy and Camille tied the knot at Tanque Verde Ranch, an event that did nothing but solidify my resolve to convince Charlotte Christman that she needed to be mine. Permanently. Thoughts on that subject ran on a continuous loop in my subconscious, but celebrating her birthday was the first order of business.

I'd rung RJ and spoken with him at length regarding the best course of action for their visit. We determined that Bob would fly in with him on the Wednesday before Charlotte's surprise birthday party that following Saturday. The single hitch in timing the party was that Happy and Camille would still be on their honeymoon in Cabo San Lucas. Otherwise, the guest list had responded enthusiastically; Sam would have a full house.

Sam was brilliant with coordinating the details and had announced in the invitation that the theme would be "Girl Power." Everyone was instructed to dress as a famous, influential, or otherwise well-known woman. Even the men. *Especially* the men,

Sam told me with a straight face. Never ones to shy away from a challenge, Scorpion costume planning was underway with everyone scrupulously guarding their ideas with secrecy customarily reserved for planning nuclear attacks. With Bob and RJ in attendance and all the fun that was planned, the celebration promised to be a memorable evening for my girl.

I knew beyond a doubt that Charlotte longed to reestablish a relationship with her father, but that didn't mean the path would be an easy one. And she remained in the dark about my communications with RJ and my covert trip to Iowa. If I were honest with myself, I'd have admitted some second-guessing on my decision to meet with Bob and RJ without Charlotte's knowledge, but it was done now. I had to hope everything I'd done would bring her happiness because the moment was at hand.

Just past lunchtime, I waited in the arrivals lobby, scanning the area impatiently and allowing myself to enjoy thoughts of Charlotte reuniting with her father. I knew it was one of her heart's fondest desires, intensified by a new awareness of the importance of relationships. I marveled how short the time had been since she'd been awakened to her need for connection—and how fortunate I'd been in that regard. It was likely the blessings of love and support my family had poured into me that gave me the courage to take this chance. I wanted the most important person in my life to enjoy for herself what I had.

My reflections were interrupted by RJ's smiling face and shouted greeting. "Oliver! Great to see you, man." He approached with his father, and I stretched out my hand to the older man. He bypassed my hand and wrapped his arms around me in a hug.

"I have a good feeling we're gonna be family, son, so I'm not aimin' to stand on ceremony." He thumped my back enthusiastically. "I've been counting the days ever since RJ told me we were flying out." He grinned at me as he sorted his grip and rolled it along beside me. "I'm not gonna lie, now; I've been as nervous as a pig in a bacon factory ever since I woke up this morning."

I laughed along with them as we walked out of the airport's front door and toward the short-term parking lot. "I understand the feeling, Bob; I was the one in the hot seat two months ago when I went to Iowa. But I'd say things have turned out well."

We loaded the luggage into the Range Rover, and I settled into the driver's seat next to Bob. We chatted for a few minutes about their flight and the already oppressive heat Tucson was serving up in May, and then I laid out the plan for their visit. "We'll be on our way to my house out on the city's west side; I share the house with my cousin Jacob, as I mentioned. The house is rather expansive, so we have plenty of room for guests, and the two of you will fit right into the bachelor lifestyle."

Bob chortled. "I know that one well, all right. Let me guess." He ticked off the items on one hand. "No curtains at the windows. A general lack of throw pillows, lamps, and knick-knacks. A stereo as big and expensive as your car." He smiled triumphantly. "And a refrigerator full of red meat, frozen meals, and beer."

I barked a laugh, everlastingly surprised at how comfortable the repartee had already grown. "You almost pegged it, Bob. But you didn't take into account Jacob's audiophile tendencies. The stereo definitely cost more than his beat-up pickup truck…"

"Hey, watch it there," RJ growled with mock ferocity from the back seat.

I turned the Rover down our street. "I'm looking forward to introducing the two of you to my cousin; he's a close friend of Charlotte's. In fact, he's the one who flew home on her wing after the accident and helped her land the jet safely."

Having arrived at our house, I parked the Rover and helped them unload their belongings from the boot. "Charlotte's been threatening to cook a meal for me to show off a new recipe Sue taught her, so I asked if I could bring a couple of friends to dinner at her condominium this evening." I grinned at RJ. "Obviously, you'll be playing the part of the two friends."

I showed them to the guest room, which currently held two beds. There was a queen-sized one Jacob had abandoned in favor of his current bed: an oversized king-sized behemoth that was hard as a rock—he called it The Workbench. There was also a more manageable double-sized one I'd brought along from my parents' endless furniture stash. Mum had insisted. "You should always have at least one room equipped to welcome guests, Oliver." Mum was right once again.

I made sandwiches and poured crisps into a large bowl for lunch before encouraging my guests to rest and wash up. Their day had already been a long one, and the best of it was still to come. At least I hoped so.

"I don't think I've been this nervous since I took Louise out on our first date when I was seventeen." Bob was visibly on edge, perspiring a bit and shifting his weight from side to side while adjusting the belt on his slacks. "I don't know why in tarnation I thought wool slacks were a good idea for Tucson; it's still chilly on the farm during the evenings." He picked at a daisy petal in the oversized bouquet he'd bought on the way to Charlotte's condo.

I took the two bottles of wine I'd selected for dinner, along with a chilled bottle of 2009 Dom Perignon, from the box in the rear seat and locked the Rover. I'd parked out of the condo's line of sight in hopes of keeping my secret until the last minute. I put a friendly hand on Bob's shoulder and patted it encouragingly.

"Try not to be nervous, Bob; I have a good feeling about to-night." I laughed, trying to keep the mood light. "Otherwise, I'm out a couple hundred bucks on champagne."

We walked together to Charlotte's front door, and I gave Bob one last encouraging smile as I rapped firmly on the door. I heard my girl's voice calling from the kitchen and opened the door, allowing RJ and Bob in ahead of me. Charlotte's back was to us, and I briefly admired her curvy little bum, currently framed by the ties of the apron wrapped neatly about her waist.

"Give me just a minute here, British. I'm trying to french trim this rack of lamb, and there's a good chance I could cut my hand off in the process…so I'm trying to pay attention." Although she hadn't looked as we entered, she obviously knew it was me. I debated possibilities for divesting her of the knife in her hand before she turned around. But there was no time to act on my thoughts because Bob stepped toward the kitchen and answered her in a quiet voice.

"Maybe I can give you a hand with that, Bugs. I've gotten pretty handy in the kitchen lately."

Charlotte's eyes were as wide and round as saucers as she turned slowly, carefully placing the knife on the worktop. She grabbed a kitchen towel and wiped her hands. Silence cloaked the room as her gaze flitted from Bob to RJ to me. Her mouth was a perfect O, and I could all but see the gears spinning with blinding speed in her head.

Despite his apprehension, Bob soldiered on, taking a couple of tentative steps toward his daughter as he spoke. "I can't even find the words, Bugs." His voice was soft and heavily tinged with emotion. "You're so beautiful—look at you, all grown. I've missed you more than I can say, loving you every day and praying that this day would come. I've hoped you could find it in your—"

His words were interrupted as Charlotte broke from where she'd stood anchored to the floor and rapidly closed the distance between them, falling into the arms he stretched out to catch her. She didn't weep but instead buried her face in his neck and whispered. I held my breath and strained to hear what she said.

"Daddy…I can't believe you're here, Daddy." She pulled back and looked up at him with her eyes brimming and a big smile spread across her face.

"Charlotte, honey, I'm just so damned sorry, baby. I was so brokenhearted, so foolish. I've missed you every day. Hoped for another chance. I just couldn't bear to...I didn't want to be the one who..." He reached for the words, brow knit, as Charlotte continued to smile brilliantly, undisguised joy lighting her face.

"No, Daddy. That's enough; it's over." She interrupted him and leaned back to take him in, running one hand through his curly, white hair. "It's all over now. I didn't know how to take the first step, so you did it for me, didn't you?"

Bob pulled her close again, his face the very picture of contentment. "Well, actually, Bugs, your young man took the first step for both of us. We've had a little time to visit, and I don't mind telling you—he's pretty good people. He may have just given me the best gift anyone has since your mama gave me you and RJ." He stroked her hair before kissing her forehead and letting her go.

She smiled through the tears that now ran down her cheeks and then looked over at me and RJ. "I have quite a few questions, British. Is that wine you have in your hand?"

I stepped forward and brushed her mouth with a soft kiss. "Champagne, actually. I think we're celebrating, don't you?"

"So was this with the mustard glaze or the dry mustard rub?" Bob speared the final morsel of lamb from his plate, pointing his fork at Charlotte as they discussed dinner. "I haven't ever used a rub, but we have an herb garden that might produce some tasty additions to a dry rub." He popped the bite into his mouth, obviously enjoying the flavor. RJ had been reserved during dinner, watching the interaction between his sister and Bob, but he looked my direction, raising his wine glass.

"Thank you, Oliver. You took a big risk, and it's paid off." He toasted me and drank deeply, settling his big frame back into the chair and grinning at Charlotte.

Dinner had been a delight, Charlotte's excellent food unexpectedly enhanced by the dawn of a new day with her father. They chatted in fits and starts, swapping stories and details missed over the past few years and bonding easily over the shared new love of cooking.

"We should try a prime rib, Bugs." Bob stood as the meal came to its conclusion and began to load plates into the dishwasher. "Your birthday's only a couple of days away; I'll find a butcher and pick one up so we can cook together. Which is better—your house or Oliver's?" He laughed at Charlotte's expression. "No offense, Bugs, but we're bunking at One-Eyed Jacks; I've been told it's the ideal lodging for a couple of single guys in town for the weekend."

Charlotte rolled her eyes. "Good God, British. I can't bear to think of my father in a whorehouse."

Chapter FORTY

"Trip Around the Sun"

Oliver

The past couple of days had been a whirlwind of shopping and sightseeing for the reunited Christman family. In the meantime, I tried to keep the plates spinning at work while organizing last-minute party details with Sam and wracking my brain in search of the perfect costume. Sam had let it be known that she expected wholehearted enthusiasm and one hundred percent participation in the dress-up portion of the celebration. I didn't question her assertion that it was in the best interest of each person attending to play along or prepare to suffer dire consequences. Like Charlotte, she didn't seem like a woman to be trifled with.

The ruse concealing the surprise was easily concocted using the excuse of Bob and RJ's visit. I told Miles we would pick her up at her house for dinner around seven p.m. on the Saturday of her birthday. She believed we were on our way out for a special dinner where I had booked a chef's table, an easily believable fib considering her newfound affinity for cooking. The hitch was how we would make an unscheduled stop at Samanthe's house, only a few miles from Charlotte's condo in the foothills. But Sam had that covered too.

Right on cue, Charlotte's phone rang. Her voice was bright, and she answered. "Oh, hi there, Samanthe—great to hear your voice." There was a pause, and she smiled. "Oh, gosh thanks. That's so nice of you. Yes, it is today, and I've had the most amazing surprise this week—I was going to text you and tell you all about it. My daddy and brother are here celebrating with me. Oliver is taking us all to dinner tonight."

There was another brief pause while Sam spoke, and I turned to give her what I hoped was a questioning look. Then she spoke again. "You didn't have to do that. No, we're out right now—I'm not sure if we have time. Let me check with Oliver."

She turned to me with her hand over the phone speaker. "Samanthe wanted to drop my birthday gift by the condo. She was calling to see if we were home, but we're only about a half mile from her house now. Do we have time to stop by and have a glass of wine so that she can meet Daddy and RJ?"

Perfect timing, Sam. As if there was ever a doubt. I smiled. "Let's make it happen—she's been such a good friend to you. I'll call the restaurant and move the reservation a bit."

Charlotte and Samanthe rang off, and I made a mental note that my initial impression about trifling with Samanthe was spot on. RJ grinned at me in the rearview mirror.

A short couple of moments later, we were assembled at Samanthe's front door. Her home was every bit as interesting as the faux whorehouse Jacob and I rented, but in an entirely different way. Samanthe had inherited a time capsule—there was no other way to describe it—from her great aunt. It was a rather large home with only two bedrooms. And it was round. It looked as if a spaceship had settled on top of one of the most picturesque hilltops in Tucson. Along with the house, Sam had inherited its contents, a singular collection of sixties and seventies vintage furniture, kitchen appliances, and fascinating details—everything was a perfect match for the unique home it furnished. I'd been especially delighted to see how much it would add to Charlotte's birthday celebration when I'd dropped by to discuss the menu with Sam a couple of weeks ago.

"It doesn't even look like she's home." Charlotte surveyed the darkened exterior of Samanthe's groovy abode. The porch light was on, but there were no other signs of life, I noted with admiration. Sam had really covered our tracks—I wondered where all the bodies were buried and where the cars were parked.

"Go ahead and ring the bell, she's got to be here somewhere." I smiled encouragingly at Charlotte and winked at Bob behind her back.

Samanthe's voice shouted to us from the interior of the house. "Hey there, Miles—come on in. I've got my hands full, but the door is unlocked." Charlotte turned to me, shrugging, and tried the door, pushing it open and walking into the darkened interior of the house. I braced myself for the onslaught and was not disappointed.

The voices shouting "Surprise!" and "Happy birthday!" sounded right before all the lights in the house came on and the Beatles' "Birthday" sounded at deafening levels from the stereo speakers. Charlotte's scream of delight at the surprise was unusually girly. The surprise lay not only in the shouts of the crowd and so many people springing from their hiding places in closets and from behind the furniture, but also in the shocking variety of costumes. Sam's living room was filled with Scorpions dressed in drag, complete with cheap wigs and Goodwill clothing.

Samanthe sprang from the crowd to embrace Charlotte. She wore a flight suit and boots as well as a long, curly red wig. Her name tag was made of construction paper and read "Badass."

Most interestingly, however, the flight suit was cut off high on her thigh, making it a perverse romper of some kind. At the cuff of her romper was a sign that read, "Here are the Miles of legs." There was an arrow pointing down to indicate the aforementioned attraction.

"Happy birthday, you extraordinary girl." Samanthe flung her arms around Charlotte, hugging her tight while Charlotte continued to survey the room, mouth agape.

"In case you didn't guess, tonight's theme is 'Girl Power' and everyone is dressed as a famous or influential woman." Samanthe beamed at Charlotte while she talked. "I gave them a lot of latitude, but you have to at least try to guess." She spread her arms, posing. "First off, you have to guess who I am. I'll give you a hint—she's a very strong woman whom I admire deeply. And she has a shit-hot body and legs that'll give a dead man a hard-on." She pointed a dazzling smile at Bob and RJ. "I'm so sorry, gentlemen, I certainly don't mean to offend."

Everyone laughed, and I lifted the birthday girl's hand to my lips, brushing a soft kiss there. "With that hair and those legs, someone who's widely known as 'Badass' could only be one person. Happy birthday, Charlotte." I looked into her eyes, both of us still for just a moment in the middle of the melee. "I hope this is a wonderful day for you, for a variety of reasons; I love you so much, my Charlotte."

I turned to begin introducing Bob and RJ to Samanthe just as Rock, Torch, and Boo approached in long gowns and feather boas. They all wore false eyelashes, although I noted they might have benefited from some assistance in the application. They also wore bouffant platinum wigs and sported plenty of décolletage, courtesy of several ill-concealed rolls of tube socks. Torch had neglected to shave, so his ginger beard added to the gender-confused vibe. Boo fiddled with the unlit cigarette between his scarlet-painted lips in a ridiculously long cigarette holder. He experimented with various poses as if trying to channel Audrey Hepburn.

"Where the hell did he find a cigarette holder?" Sam whispered to no one in particular. Rock sauntered to the front and planted sloppy kisses on both of Charlotte's cheeks, leaving sizeable red lip prints there.

"Hello, daaahling. My sisters and I wanted to extend our fondest happy birthday wishes to you. I am Eva Gabor, and zeeese are my sisters, Zsa Zsa and Magda."

Charlotte laughed and hugged her friends while scanning the group. The music was already loud, and the room was full of lively conversation and groups of people introducing themselves to one another. Sam put her arm around Charlotte. "There's a ton of food and a full bar, so why don't you and your dad and brother grab something to eat and drink? Then you can begin making your way around the room with introductions. I know everyone is going to want to meet your father." She flashed a brilliant smile at both of them. "I need to check on something in the kitchen now, but please make yourselves at home."

She was gone, and I began to herd the group toward the generous buffet just as Luckie, Grace, and Vivianne approached us. Viv put her hand out in the universal sign for "stop."

"Don't embarrass yourself, cousin. We decided to bring a little class to this costume thing, so the three of us are dressed as historically prominent nurses. But before you guess, the priority is to meet these handsome gentlemen you brought along."

Following introductions, I guessed two of the three accurately; Vivianne's Florence Nightingale was almost a given, and Grace's Clara Barton wore a prominent Red Cross symbol on her smock that was a dead giveaway. But I missed Luckie's Sojourner Truth, a nineteenth-century African-American women's rights activist and abolitionist. Luckie declared me exempt from the lecture she planned for anyone else who didn't know her identity due to my status as a British subject.

Several of The Tuesday Game crowd were in attendance, allowing the men in the group to become acquainted. Charlotte informed me that many of the women already knew one another, having participated in Sam and Grace's shopping trip late last year. Sue, a tall, stunning woman with a charming southern accent was dressed as Julia Child, complete with an oversized glass of wine and a copy of *Mastering the Art of French Cooking*. She hugged Miles enthusiastically, and then held her at arm's length, admiring her strapless, mossy green dress.

"I remember this one from the shopping trip at La Encantada—I picked it out for you." She put her arm around Luckie and hugged her. "I met this gal that day, and we've spent a couple of great afternoons in the kitchen since then, haven't we?" Luckie returned her hug.

"Sure have. And this week, we used you as an excuse to drink two bottles of Chardonnay and bake you a red velvet birthday cake." She gestured as Davis approached our group, wrapping Luckie in his arms from behind and kissing her neck. "It's Tarzan's favorite."

It was hard to describe the discomfiture one experienced seeing the mountainous man—in a beaded dress and towering blond bouffant wig as Dolly Parton—embracing the striking Luckie in the unadorned gray dress and white turban of the slave-turned-activist. Charlotte must have agreed because she shook her head, as if to clear the image, and turned to speak to me.

"I don't think my brain can process what it's seeing." We all laughed, and I motioned for Bob to come around for introductions.

Just then, Colonel Ditka, resplendent in a leather jacket and old-fashioned flying helmet with goggles, stepped onto a chair near the magnificently retro suspended fireplace. He pushed his goggles up and whistled to gain the room's attention.

"Good evening, Christman family, members of The Tuesday Game, sundry TMC staff members, and Scorpions." He raised his beer in salute. "On behalf of the lovely Samanthe Barber, I welcome you to her amazing home." There were toasts in Sam's direction and murmurs of agreement. The place was a genuine marvel. "Tonight is such an important occasion that I, Amelia Earhart, have returned from my self-imposed exile in the South Pacific—at the ripe old age of about 115—to wish a very happy birthday to the only aviator I know who is more skilled than yours truly." There were more ripples of laughter, and Coach smiled at Charlotte.

"In all seriousness, Miles, I speak for all the Scorpions tonight when I say that we are very grateful to have the gift of your friendship. The events of the past year have driven home—for all of us—how important we are to one another. In particular, the military often makes more than coworkers out of those who work together day to day. The relationships can become akin to family, especially since most of us are far from our families during the course of our careers. Sometimes, we need to be reminded not to take one another for granted, and I'd say that lesson was well learned for many of us. Through the entire ordeal, Miles, you have been an example to each of us of how to face challenges with integrity and honesty, and how to come out the other side a better, brighter version of ourselves. Thank you for that.

"Happy and Camille are sorry not to be with us this evening, but I did get a phone call this afternoon from them asking that I extend their wishes for a happy birthday, as well. Camille said something as we were hanging up that I thought was particularly telling. She said, 'I don't think Miles even understands how much of a linchpin of the squadron she has become.' I would echo that, Miles, and add that we are all better for knowing you. Here's to the first twenty-five years and all those still to come. Everyone raise a glass to the woman of the hour—to Miles."

The toasting proceeded, and several people nearby hugged Charlotte, who was looking a bit the worse for the wear and emotional, but very happy. Coach whistled once again to gain the room's attention and continue his speech.

"Without further ado, I'd like to introduce four very famous musicians—one of them deceased—who are present tonight to congratulate the birthday girl with a musical tribute that will be unforgettable no matter how hard we try. Please welcome Yoko Ono, Mama Cass Elliot, Cher, and Lady Gaga!"

The stereo blared "Born this Way" as Emmay, Keeper, Jacob, and Bibi paraded into the living room. The party was so well attended that it was easy to overlook the fact that several key players were missing up to this point. They had sequestered themselves somewhere to enhance the surprise, and the effect worked well. Keeper's majestic beard combined with Cass's signature caftan for a truly unique effect, and Emmay nailed Yoko Ono—they were a dashing pair. Bibi riffed on Gaga's look with yet another long blond wig; I reflected briefly that the costume party-goers must have used every available blond wig in the city. She'd also used a strangely striated red and pink fabric to assemble Gaga's infamous meat dress. The effect was surprisingly accurate.

Despite the superlative efforts of the first three, Jacob as Cher was the standout. He rocked striped bell-bottom pants held up with the widest belt I'd ever seen, as well as a wig that closely resembled Cher's signature sleek, dark mane. He whipped it from side to side, expertly pursing his lips before bursting forth with a very passable Cher-like imitation of "Happy Birthday." The other "stars" joined in straight away, each in his own particular idiom, resulting in a mind-boggling chorus. The room resounded with laughter, the merriment continuing long after the last note faded.

I turned to watch Charlotte, her eyes twinkling with laughter as she surveyed the scene. It was difficult to picture a moment more perfect than this one, a fit gift for the woman who had turned her twenty-fifth year into a fresh beginning.

Chapter
FORTY-ONE

"Baby, What a Big Surprise"

Miles

The party had been underway for a couple of hours now. I withdrew to a corner to savor the scene, loving what I saw. People from different parts of my life gathered and the groups mixed, everyone laughing. There was a relaxed feeling in the room, the conversations comfortable. Oliver informed me that the delicious food and free-flowing beverages were due to Sam's gift for organization and party planning. The costumes had added so much levity to the proceedings; I was amazed and amused by the level of creativity.

Daddy was holding court on the sofa between Oliver and Bashful, beers in their hands and smiles on their faces. They leaned in to hear the details of whatever yarn Daddy was spinning—an embarrassing tale from my childhood, no doubt. I grinned at the thought. A year ago I could never have guessed my relationship with my father would be healing, and it was due, in great part, to the man seated next to him.

I never tired of looking at Oliver. His long fingers circled the bottle he held, and his eyes danced as he listened to the story Daddy told. Bash's wig from earlier was now discarded, and he'd shed the mod pants as well. He relaxed with his arms stretched across the sofa's back cushions, laughing loudly at something Daddy said.

Toward the rear of the room, something far more interesting caught my eye. Robert sat in one of two small chairs in the corner of the room. He was leaning forward, resting his elbows on his knees and listening intently to the person who spoke to him, a half-smile dancing around his lips. He was so terribly handsome. I'd thought so since I was a little girl, and now I realized he was the very image of a younger version of our father.

The person who commanded his attention was Meg; she laughed and gestured animatedly as she spoke to my brother. At some point, he leaned into her space and placed a hand on her knee, speaking to her with a more serious expression. Then as he began to remove his hand, she covered it with her own.

Well, now. What a fascinating development. I'd been intermittently concerned for years now that Robert had postponed his happiness in favor of mine and my father's. He told me that he dated from time to time, but I didn't have any confidence that he was telling the unrevised truth. Watching the scene playing out before me gave me greater confidence that Robert would someday find the love and companionship he deserved. Meg was a kindhearted and complex woman—not to mention beautiful. I loved the idea of the two of them enjoying the attention of one another this evening.

It was unusual to have the opportunity to privately observe the events around me—especially at my own birthday party—and I was reveling in the occasion, wondering how long it would last when I saw something from the corner of my eye that almost made me laugh aloud.

Deliverance, like many others, had divested himself of the

more uncomfortable bits of his "influential woman" costume; in his case, this meant he'd lost the spangled dress and accompanying breasts as well as the big, blond wig. He was left in a Scorpion tee shirt and basketball shorts and was now sneaking—as covertly as a six-foot-three-inch man could—down the hallway in bare feet. To make himself even more conspicuous, he had Luckie in tow, and she looked for all the world like a glamorous refugee from the Underground Railroad.

They could hardly have been more obvious, but Deliverance seemed confident that they were invisible as he checked six before opening the door to the closet in the hall. He urged a giggling Luckie inside and then disappeared into the closet behind her, closing the door quietly. It was a step-by-step replay of one of the worst-kept secrets in Scorpion history. Last summer, on the night of the flight suit party, pheromones and passion had overcome the pair, resulting in a closet rendezvous in the O'Club. Deliverance denied the whole rumor for a while, but Luckie had confirmed at least some details to the girl posse.

I felt a hand at the small of my back and warm breath on my ear. "Hello, love. I neglected to mention it earlier, but you're looking quite eatable this evening. I'd love nothing more than to bend you over, slip that pretty dress over your lovely bottom, and slide inside you."

Oh, my.

He pulled my back to his front with one hand splayed on my belly and sighed. "That's what I'd like to do, but I'll try to control myself so your brother doesn't kick my ass." Oliver's voice was low, and its growly quality did things to my lady bits. He chuckled under his breath. "Did you just see what I saw in the hall?"

I turned and flashed a big smile. "They have a history of getting busy in closets, believe it or not. D doesn't look like the guy who could pull that off, but the rumor mill doesn't lie."

He kissed my neck with a groan. "Actually, darling, that's

pretty much all the rumor mill does, but I believe you. I can't wait to get you out of here. Once I get everyone delivered home and tucked into bed, I have a plan to get you moaning and wet and full of my cock."

I saw Daddy smiling at Oliver's antics, so I reluctantly swatted him away from my neck. He groaned his displeasure. "Alright, alright. I'll rein it in for a few more minutes." He wrapped my waist with his arms and turned us to face the room where the party continued. "Now what's going on over in the corner? Is Jacob chatting up Grace?"

I zeroed in on the action in a shadowy corner of the expansive living room; apparently the darkness was obscuring all sorts of clandestine activity. Bashful leaned on one arm with his big, muscular frame, almost completely concealing Grace. She stood against the wall under his arm, hands clasped behind her. She looked toward the floor, but I could see a smile playing over her lips. Between the shy posture and her wholly fetching expression, she was absolutely adorable. No wonder Bash was toast.

"So." I turned to look at Oliver suspiciously. "You're his cousin. I assume you've known about Bashful's bad case of Grace Marshall for some time."

He shrugged. "Maybe. I'm not sure what's going on exactly. What I do know is that Jacob doesn't normally need to put forth any effort at all in the quest for female companionship. It's been that way so long it's become a bit of a running family joke." As we continued to spy on Bash and Grace, it suddenly seemed as if his fortunes had changed. Grace looked up at him—the height difference was surely almost a foot—and nodded almost imperceptibly with a little smile. Bash's face lit up, and he lifted her hand to his lips, brushing her knuckles with a kiss. Then the pair slipped silently through a nearby door that I knew led to Sam's guest bedroom, still holding hands.

Oliver grinned at me. "Well. It looks as if my cousin's patented charm is finally making headway with the timid Miss Marshall."

I barked out a laugh. "Color me unsurprised. You do realize he earned his call sign specifically because bashful is one thing he is definitely not."

There was no area in the room carved out to be a dance floor, but that didn't prevent Oliver from taking me back into his arms when Norah Jones's sensuous voice drifted through the room with the opening words to "Come Away with Me." We swayed silently for a few bars, and then he lifted my face with a finger under my chin. His voice was low.

"If I could have one wish, Charlotte, this would be it." I raised my eyebrows in an unspoken question; his eyes held mine for a beat before he answered. "That I could have you to myself, that we could disappear together for a time...no distractions, no work or friends or family. Just my body learning and loving and worshiping yours. And my heart falling even more deeply in love with yours."

I was speechless, and he was right. Nine months had passed since I first laid eyes on the devastatingly handsome ginger Brit at the squadron picnic. Nine months that had been an uninterrupted whirlwind of near-tragedy, stress, and life-altering changes. There was so much good in my life, but Oliver and I had fallen in love during scraps of time stolen from the vortex of my existence. I had been gifted with a love so startling and unexpected that I may not have treated it—and Oliver—with the reverence it deserved. That had to change right away. I stood on tiptoes to press my lips to his.

"You're absolutely right, Oliver. Let's do it. You say where and when...I'm so ready to leave the world behind."

Still surrounded by the noise of the party and the company of our friends, Oliver's soft mouth was on mine, and I melted against his long, powerful frame. His tongue stroked me—tasting, then taking—until I moaned in frustrated need. Just as my fevered brain registered how far things had gone, there was a mild hubbub behind us from the vicinity of the hallway.

Oliver and I hastily broke free from our embrace and turned, confounded by the curious scene that met our eyes.

Deliverance, still barefoot and now wearing only shorts, blocked the hallway entrance with his oversized frame. His expression was one of awestruck delight, but tears streamed freely down his cheeks. In his arms, he held Luckie, who now wore only the plain gray dress from her costume. Between bouts of plastering his face with kisses, she laughed aloud, swinging her feet with carefree abandon. They both appeared to have lost their powers of speech temporarily.

I waved my hand in his line of sight, just a little concerned. "Deliverance…hey, Davis…are you okay?"

He squeezed Luckie tighter to his bare chest and looked at me, finally answering in an unsteady voice.

"She said 'yes,' Miles…she said 'yes.'" Luckie freed her left hand, flashing a dazzling rock the size of Gibraltar. Then D looked around, smiling so wide I thought his face would break in two, and shouted it to the room at large.

"She said 'yes,' y'all—we're gettin' married!"

Epilogue

"Forever and Ever, Amen"

Miles
About Three Months Later

"Shut up, Sam. I mean it." I glared at my friend, tears staining the perfection of her face. She snuffled and produced a hankie from her tiny Tory Burch clutch. She blew loudly and grimaced.

"I can't help it—not my fault." She gave me a thorough look, up and down. "This would be too much emotional torture for anyone, Miles. You can't blame me. And, by the way," she stepped forward, gingerly touching the ivory lace adorning the bodice of my dress, "I think Miss Louise would love the way you look in her dress. I have a feeling she's watching you right now."

I hugged Sam and sighed. She was right. It was going to be emotional torture, which was exactly what I thought I could avoid with a quick courthouse wedding.

I was wrong. So *very* wrong.

One Tuesday evening a month or so after my birthday, Oliver surprised me by pulling into the parking lot of the Kwik Shopper on our way to Tucson Tamale Company for a casual dinner. In the muddy, pothole-ridden parking lot, he dropped to one knee, pulled a beautiful, dark blue sapphire ring from one pocket, and slid it onto my finger. His voice wavered, but only slightly, and I thought my heart would explode as he spoke. "I don't even think I can ask, lovely one. You've become my entire life—my heart— and I can't live without you." His crooked smile warmed me, and he lifted my left hand, now adorned with what I learned was six carats of blue brilliance, kissing it reverently. "If you're inclined to make me beg, darling, I'll do it without hesitation—just tell me you'll be my wife, Charlotte. Spend every day until forever with me."

I couldn't wait to join my life to Oliver's, so we set out along the shortest path to matrimony I could conjure. Once he proposed, a quick internet search revealed that the most romantic courthouse in all the land was located in downtown Tucson, so I paid a visit and made our appointment. Piece of cake.

Or not.

Sam got wind of my idea and told Vivvie, who, according to Bash, "didn't fucking think so." When I further confessed that our plan consisted of a lunchtime ceremony with strangers acting as witnesses, a scene ensued. Sam interrupted Vivianne's tirade to gently remind me that friends and family would be disappointed if they were denied the chance to share the day. I recognized her instincts were on target, but my idea of a low-maintenance event suffered a mortal blow.

Alternate plans were concocted, but Sam and Vivvie graciously handled every detail. They intuitively understood that I'd rather rip my toenails out with pliers than plan a wedding.

And so it came to pass that I stood in the spare bedroom of Keeper and Emmay's little adobe cottage, staring out a picture window that overlooked their expansive backyard and the edge of Catalina Foothills. No one involved in the planning process was surprised to find that Keeper was an ordained minister and had performed dozens of ceremonies over the years. Though not formally religious, he was one of the most spiritual people I'd ever known. When Emmay learned of our plans, she offered their home's lovingly tended backyard for the ceremony. Now the spacious lawn was welcoming Oliver's family and mine, as well as a very small group of our dearest friends. They gathered at the edge of the flower beds, chatting in small groups and admiring the vistas as Sam put the finishing touches on what she called my "wedding look."

I wore my grandmother's meticulously altered wedding gown, also worn by my mother on her own wedding day, some thirty-five years ago. Once Daddy offered it for my use, Robert made a special trip to visit, couriering the dress to me personally. He flew to Tucson with the box containing the gown in his lap, carefully swathed in the same muslin that had protected it in the years since Mama's death. It was a tea-length ivory confection with lace adorning the half-sleeves and hem, all of it hand-tatted by my grandmother. Double crinolines made the skirt stand out like a fifties vintage prom dress.

I had vivid childhood memories of sitting in Mama's lap as she turned the pages of her wedding photo album and told me the stories from that day. Now it was my turn to wear the dress when I met Oliver to make our promises to one another.

Sam asked me to leave my wedding day footwear to her. I recognized the large bag she searched now as the one she'd brought when we met at the hospital on the day of the accident. I craned my neck for a look, but she yanked the bag away with a grin. "Close your eyes, pretty girl." I obliged and held out grabby hands. "I had so much fun helping expand your fashion horizons, Miles, and it was special because that was one of the things that brought us closer." She sighed, but I heard a smile in her voice as she placed something in my hands. "But you should be every inch Charlotte Louise Christman today, and I think this is exactly what the Miles I met a year ago would wear to get married."

I opened my eyes. In my hands I held a pair of pristine white Chuck Taylor high-tops; tiny, ivory seed pearls covered every millimeter of the cloth, and the standard laces had been replaced with a soft satin ribbon.

I lifted my eyes back to meet Sam's. "They're the most perfect pair of shoes I've ever seen, Samanthe...thank you. I love them."

We chatted excitedly as I laced up my wedding Chucks and admired the effect in the mirror Sam brought from home and leaned against one wall. The sun dipped low in the sky, I noted through the window, and the butterflies fluttering in my tummy tuned up in earnest.

"It's almost time, honey. Are you ready?" Sam rested a hand on my shoulder, and we watched the guests forming a loose circle at what appeared to be instruction from Keeper. "I need to go..."

Her goodbye was interrupted by a soft rap at the door. When it opened, Daddy's face appeared. He was every bit as handsome as I had ever seen him look, silvery white hair wet and slicked back just as he used to wear it when we went to church. He wore a tan linen jacket and matching slacks, completely atypical of anything I could visualize him having in his closet. As it turned out, I was right; Bash had taken him shopping once he'd arrived in Arizona a week before the ceremony. Daddy's closet was almost completely devoid of dress clothes, and linen wasn't terribly serviceable in the Midwest. Daddy grinned as he faced my general direction, but his eyes were squeezed closed.

"You decent, Bugs? I don't know if I'm allowed to see the bride before the wedding. Your mother told me it was bad luck, but the rules might be different since I'm playing a different role this time." He smirked a bit, and the resemblance between him and my brother went from strong to uncanny. I smoothed the front of my dress and stood up straight.

"Open your eyes, Daddy. I'm ready." He stepped fully into the room and opened his eyes, his regard sweeping me from top to bottom. His jaw slackened a bit, and I saw tears threaten as his composure crumbled slightly.

"You're the image of your mama, Bugs; it's just about the nicest gift anyone could have given me today." He held his arms open wide, and I walked into his embrace, swallowing hard. "She'd be so proud of you, Charlotte; I hope you know that. And having a second chance with you is more than I could ever have asked."

"Thank you, Daddy." I whispered the words in a voice rough with emotion. "It means everything that you're here." Sam had slipped away quietly, leaving the two of us alone. Daddy turned back toward the door and offered me the crook of his arm with a big smile.

"Should we go, Bugs? There's a very anxious young Brit waiting for you; and from the look on his face, I'd wager it'd be cruel to keep him waiting."

An old upright piano that normally resided in one corner of Keeper and Emmay's family room had been moved—presumably with great difficulty, considering its size—onto the small patio overlooking the backyard. The strains of Debussy's achingly beautiful "Clair de lune" drifted through the empty house as Daddy and I walked to the open double doors leading to the backyard. Rounding the corner, I saw Emmay seated at the piano, a floral chiffon dress fluttering about her ankles in the gentle breeze. Her eyes were closed, and an expression of pure joy painted her features as she played.

Just beyond, Keeper stood in the middle of a large circle formed by the clasped hands of our friends and family. Looking around, I noticed for the first time that there were no chairs in evidence anywhere in the yard. Keeper wore a long, embroidered tunic and something that looked like a clergyman's stole around his neck. His face broke into a smile that crinkled his eyes as he saw Daddy and me appear in the doorway.

A makeshift aisle was marked with flower petals, beginning at the patio and leading to the circle's edge. At the group's center, in front of Keeper, stood the man I loved. He was flanked by his parents, Serafina and Archie, all three faces lit with happiness. Oliver wore a pair of pale blue linen slacks and a matching vest. His ivory dress shirt was open at the neck, and the sleeves were rolled to just below his elbow, revealing strong forearms. His demeanor was calm, but I noticed with some amusement that he held a small shiny ring in his hand, turning it over and over with long fingers. As our eyes met, he deposited the ring in his pocket and stepped away from his parents, walking my direction.

The company parted as Daddy and I approached. Oliver met us near the circle's edge, shaking the hand that Daddy offered and leaning forward briefly to whisper something I couldn't hear into his ear. Daddy's arms reached around both of us, hugging us tightly for a moment; then he kissed my cheek gently and moved to take his place next to Robert in the circle.

Oliver took my hand, pressing it to his lips. "My love. Today is the best day of my life, because it brings with it the biggest privilege I've ever been offered. Are you ready to become my wife, Charlotte?"

The tears gathering in the corners of my eyes threatened to spill down my cheeks, but that didn't dim an ounce of the joy my heart felt. "I'm so ready, Oliver." I whispered my next words; these were for him alone. "I didn't know it, but I've been waiting all my life for you."

He shot me a dazzling smile before tucking my hand into the bend of his elbow, and we turned to face Keeper. As we walked toward where he stood, the circle behind us drew back together, the guests joining hands once again.

Keeper reached out, laying his hands on the place where ours were clasped, and spoke in a deep voice, tinged with emotion. "Friends, the days are brighter, the good in our lives richer and more complete, and the heartbreak more bearable when we walk life's path with the one the universe intended for us.

"One perfect day, only a short year ago, destiny placed Charlotte Christman on a journey with Oliver Bloodworth. The blessed collision of their spirits has borne the fruit of constancy, trust, and devoted love. Today they stand surrounded, literally and figuratively, by those who love them most—ready to give themselves to one another."

Oliver's beautiful blue eyes shone with the promise of everything he'd already pledged to me. The way he sheltered my heart didn't confine me or limit me. It didn't hobble my liberty—it gave me wings to fly. To explore "the high untrespassed sanctity of space."

English is pleased to request the pleasure of your company for the continuation of Davis and Lucinda's forever in the novella, *The Night the Lights Went Out in Georgia.*
Coming in 2019.

Visit my website anytime for updates: englishmichaels.com

The Hard Broke Series chronicles the adventures of the Scorpion squadron and the emergency room nurses who cross their paths and change their lives.
Follow along as their fortunes unfold and they encounter life and love along the way.

Surly Bonds (Book One) Nathan and Camille
Buy on Amazon/other Retailers

A Hundred Things You Haven't Dreamed Of (Book Two) Davis and Lucinda
Buy on Amazon/other Retailers

Untrespassed (Book Three) Oliver and Charlotte

For an author, an honest review of their work is a precious commodity. If you would kindly consider leaving a review, however brief, at the vendor where you purchased my book, I'd be very grateful.

About the
AUTHOR

English Michaels is a wife, mom, and recovering registered nurse. Several lifetimes ago, in a galaxy that seems very far away, she was a wide-eyed newlywed, just married to a freshly minted U.S. Air Force pilot. The first years of married life afforded her a look behind the curtain into the realm of one of the most elite—and least understood—communities in the military: the intriguing world of the fighter pilot.

English is an inveterate Pinterest junkie who has spent a king's ransom on paint and craft supplies. She's mostly disillusioned with television and is waging a low-energy battle with a Diet Coke addiction. She isn't going to mention that she enjoys travel, because who doesn't? She makes her home in the southern U.S. with Mister English and a whole lot of leftover paint. Her first book, Surly Bonds, marked the beginning of a long-awaited evolution from real person to writer.